UNFORGETTABLE SPANISH TYCOON

BY
CHRISTY MCKELLEN

First Published in Great Britain 2017
By Mills & Boon, an imprint of HarperCollins*Publishers*
1 London Bridge Street, London, SE1 9GF

© 2017 Christy McKellen

ISBN: 978-0-263-93081-8

23-0217

Our policy is to use papers that are natural, renewable and recyclable products and made from wood grown in sustainable forests. The logging and manufacturing processes conform to the legal environmental regulations of the country of origin.

Printed and bound in Spain
by CPI, Barcelona

Romantic Getaways
Escape to Paradise!

This Valentine's Day escape to four of
the world's most romantic destinations
with these sparkling books from
Mills & Boon Romance!

From the awe-inspiring desert to
vibrant Barcelona, and from the stunning
coral reefs of Australia to heart-stoppingly
romantic Venice—get swept away
by these wonderful romances!

The Sheikh's Convenient Princess
by Liz Fielding

The Unforgettable Spanish Tycoon
by Christy McKellen

The Billionaire of Coral Bay
by Nikki Logan

Her First-Date Honeymoon
by Katrina Cudmore

Formerly a video and radio producer, **Christy McKellen** now spends her time writing fun, impassioned and emotive romance with an undercurrent of sensual tension. When she's not writing she can be found enjoying life with her husband and three children, walking for pleasure, and researching other people's deepest secrets and desires.

Christy loves to hear from readers. You can get hold of her at www.christymckellen.com.

This story is dedicated to my super-smart friend Erica,
who talked me through the different types of amnesia
and their symptoms, then patiently listened to my
rambling and slightly bonkers story idea and
still pronounced it something she'd love to read.

I really appreciate the time you took
to help me shape it into something workable.

And thanks for always being such a good friend.

CHAPTER ONE

IT WAS UNSEASONABLY hot in Barcelona for February and, what with the adrenaline-spiked blood rushing through her veins and the brilliant sunshine that beat in waves at her back as she alighted from the cab outside Araya Industries' ultra-modern offices, Elena Jones was just about ready to combust in her made-for-English-weather woollen suit.

After giving her name in the wonderfully cool air-conditioned reception area, she was shown into a meeting room by a rather anxious-looking PA, acutely aware of the sound of her heels clicking loudly on the highly patterned ceramic tile flooring.

Swallowing down a twinge of nerves, Elena accepted the offer of a drink of water from the young woman, who for some reason didn't seem to be able to look her in the eye, then chose a chair at the head of the imposing twenty-seater frosted glass-topped table, carefully hanging her suit jacket over the back of the sharply stylish but rather uncomfortable-looking chair so it didn't get crumpled. She wanted to look her absolute best today in the hope it would provide her with the boost of confidence she needed to get a positive result from this meeting.

What was making her most nervous was not knowing how Caleb Araya was going to react to seeing her again after all this time. She was actually annoyed by just how anxious she felt about being out of her comfort zone. After running her own company for the last five years she'd become far better at taking risks and getting a grip on her fear of the unknown, and it took something rather exceptional to faze her now.

Apparently the thought of coming face-to-face with Caleb again was to be one of those things.

Would he have forgiven her by now?

Her heart gave an extra hard thump in her chest.

He had to have done, surely? What happened between them had been fifteen years ago; he couldn't still be holding a grudge. He was a businessman after all, a hugely successful one by all accounts, who wouldn't pass up the opportunity to get in on a profitable deal just because they had a bit of a rocky past.

Would he?

Staring out of the floor-to-ceiling windows at the busy street below, she remembered how she'd felt the very first time she'd met him during her second year at the University of Cambridge. At the tender age of twenty she'd thought Caleb Araya was the most arresting, ambitious and charismatic man she'd ever met.

They'd been good friends once, able to talk for hours about their passion for engineering and their hopes of making a mark on the world after they'd gained their degrees.

They'd made a strange pair, the two of them, so much so that their classmates had found their friendship a great source of amusement: she a petite, middle class, inner-city-living bookworm and he a hulking bad boy from the wrong side of a small Spanish town.

But away from other people the formerly laconic, gruff Caleb had been playful, gentle and animated. He'd fascinated her with his passion and drive, not to mention his dangerous sex appeal, and had excited her in ways she'd never experienced before.

What she'd most loved about him was that despite having a tough start in life Caleb hadn't let it beat him down. He'd been determined to better his situation through sheer hard work and making intelligent decisions.

Looking around her now, she could see he'd certainly achieved his goal, and then some. According to the articles she'd read on the Web, his was now the most successful technology and engineering company ever to come out of Spain.

The door in the remarkably fingerprint-free wall of glass that divided the room from the large, plush reception area swung open, letting in the sound of Spanish chatter, and she stood up, taking a deep breath and preparing herself to face Caleb with a cool head and a warm smile.

She was determined not to let her shame about the heartless way she'd treated him in the past get in the way of her objective here today.

Hopefully, he wouldn't let any residual antipathy towards her get in the way of a promising business partnership either.

A wave of nervous tension made her skin prickle as the man himself strode into the room with his PA hot on his heels.

Caleb was just as captivating as she remembered, probably even more so now that he'd grown into his darkly arresting looks and six foot five, broad-shouldered frame. It seemed he'd only built on the animal magnetism she remembered so keenly too. With his dark, hooded eyes and jet-black hair slicked away from his strong-boned face he looked fierce, indomitable and rather dangerous.

No wonder his PA seemed so afraid of him.

The scowl currently marring his craggy features as he approached was so intimidating it made Elena's heart leap about in her chest.

'Elena Jones,' he drawled in that same beautiful gravelly Spanish accent she remembered so well, his voice sounding not so much friendly as vaguely amused.

Her stomach jumped with nerves as he came to a halt in front of where she stood.

Instead of holding out a hand in greeting, he folded his enormous arms, making his shirt sleeves tighten over his bulging muscles, and looked down at her with one dark eyebrow raised, as if waiting for her to explain how she could possibly have the nerve to show her face here.

He hadn't forgiven her then.

She swallowed hard, wishing she could take a quick sip of water to loosen her suddenly dry throat, but she didn't want to weaken her position by breaking eye contact with him so she ignored the impulse.

'It's good to see you again, Caleb. Thank you for agreeing to this meeting.'

His mouth twitched at the corner as if he were suppressing a smile. 'My former PA made it without my knowledge,' he said, glancing quickly towards his current PA, who seemed to shrink into herself a little, as if afraid she was about to take the fall for her predecessor's mistake. 'But when I saw your name in my diary I couldn't help but be curious about what you could possibly want from me after all this time.'

His presence seemed to grow, crowding out the light in the room as he dropped his arms and drew his shoulders back, pulling himself up to his full height. 'I'm guessing you're only here because you need something from me—rather desperately, judging by the power suit and heels.'

Damn, his dispassionate attitude was going to make her job here so much harder. But there was no way she was giving up that easily. Just because he wasn't prepared to be friendly it didn't mean she couldn't persuade him to agree to give her what she needed. She was going to have to play this meeting carefully though. Apologise—again—if that was what it took.

Just not yet.

It was probably best to keep things on a purely business tack for now.

'I'm here to put a proposition to you,' she said, forcing herself to keep her gaze firmly fixed to his. 'Although to say I'm "desperate" isn't at all accurate,' she lied.

If she knew Caleb at all, and she thought that she did, showing any kind of weakness at this point would be a huge mistake.

'A proposition?' he said, a hint of incredulity colouring his voice.

Elena nodded jerkily, cursing her churning stomach. 'Yes. I'm sure it's something you're going to be very interested in.'

There was a heavy pause while Caleb ran his piercing gaze over her face—perhaps looking for signs of a set-up, or even a joke—before appearing to decide that she was absolutely serious.

'Then I suppose we'd better sit down,' he said, gesturing towards the chair she'd vacated and taking another one two places away, which he turned around so it was facing her.

'You won't need to take any notes,' he said to his PA, waving his hand dismissively. 'This won't be a long meeting.'

Trying not to show how much his glib assumption riled her, Elena took her own seat and smiled encouragingly at the PA, who gave her a nervous nod in return before scuttling out of the room.

Poor woman.

Biting her lip to refrain from saying something to Caleb about his ogre-like behaviour, Elena sat up straighter in her chair and fixed him with a serious stare.

He looked back at her with one eyebrow raised in

apparent curiosity, though the look in his eyes was still hard enough to cut diamonds.

'I don't know whether you know, but I'm the Managing Director and owner of a company in England called Zipabout,' she began, leaning forward a little in her chair.

His expression gave no hint as to whether he'd known that or not so she decided to just forge ahead with the pitch.

'We've designed an electric car specifically suited for a single person to make short trips around towns and cities. It's safer than riding a bike and easy to park in small spaces, but the overarching benefits are that it'll help cut down on air pollution and unnecessary fuel usage.' She took a breath. 'Right now we're looking to source a large rechargeable battery to run it. The one that your company makes would be a perfect fit for our design.'

The smile he gave her made her think of a wild animal about to pounce.

'You're asking me to partner with you?' he asked with dry amusement in his voice.

She cleared her throat to try and defuse the tension that was building there.

'That's exactly what I'm proposing.'

He nodded slowly, his intense gaze never leaving her face.

'Why did you choose my battery?'

'It's the best one on the market.' She held back on revealing that it was the *only* one that would work with the design now that their previous choice was no longer viable.

When their former supplier had called a meeting at the eleventh hour to let her know there was an unfixable fault with the battery they'd planned to use in the car, Elena had done some frantic research, only to come to the uncomfortable conclusion that Caleb's company was the only other manufacturer of a battery compatible with the design. If she didn't get him to agree to supply her company today it was quite likely the car's product launch would be perilously held up and they'd lose all the pre-orders they'd worked so hard to accrue.

'And I think a partnership would be highly beneficial for both our companies,' she went on, hoping to goodness that her nerves weren't beginning to show. Her whole body was rigid with tension because, most crucially, if he didn't agree to supply the battery Zipabout could go under and her entire workforce, who had become like family to her over the last five years, would all lose their jobs.

Tamping down on the dread that sank through her at the thought of it, she widened her smile. 'I sent some information over to your PA this morning in case you had a chance to look at it before the meeting, but I'm guessing from your reaction that you haven't. I have a short presentation on my laptop with me though; perhaps you'd like to see it?'

He regarded her without speaking for what felt like minutes, his dark eyes narrowed in thought. There was something else there in his expression that she didn't like the look of. Something cold and hard.

'No, I don't think I would,' he said finally.

She stared at him, wondering whether she'd mis-heard. Surely he couldn't be dismissing the idea with-out at least looking at her proposal?

'What—?' she whispered, giving herself a little shake, then leaning in closer to him. 'Caleb, at least look at the sales projections—'

But he cut her off with a wave of his hand. 'I'm not interested in partnering with you, Elena.' He stood up. 'Now, if you'll excuse me, I have a busy day—'

'Wait!' She raised her hand with all but her point-ing finger clenched into a fist so he wouldn't see how sweaty her palm was. 'I haven't given you all the salient details yet,' she said desperately.

'I don't need to hear them; I've already made my decision.'

'But—' She could feel panic rising from her gut. 'Why, Caleb?'

He took a step towards her, his face completely de-void of emotion. 'Because, Elena, I don't do business with people whose word I don't trust.'

She shook her head in disbelief. 'That was a long time ago, Caleb. I can't believe you're still angry with me for that.' Getting shakily to her feet, she took a step towards him. 'Please know I still feel bad about the way I handled it all, but we were both so young and naïve—'

'You were naïve,' he cut in angrily. 'I wasn't. I'd ex-perienced far too much ignorance and cruelty in my life for that to be the case.'

'And you're really still harbouring bad feelings about it? It was fifteen years ago! Surely you've experienced enough happiness in your life now to get over it?' She swallowed down her regret. 'I read that you got engaged last year.'

He batted away her questioning look, his gaze finally slipping from hers. 'It didn't work out.'

Something twisted and tightened in her chest, making it harder for her to breathe. 'I'm sorry to hear that.'

His expression darkened. 'Are you? Since when do you care about my love life?'

'I—' She didn't know how to answer that. The truth was she'd kept tabs on what he'd been up to over the intervening years because, despite the fact their friendship had ended badly, she still cared about him. Not that she thought telling him that right now would do anything to strengthen her case. He'd probably just see it as more weakness.

Caleb used her hesitation to push the knife in deeper.

'How *is*—what was his name?—Johnny, was it? Are the two of you still living your safe, comfortable life together?'

Heat raced to her cheeks. 'His name was Jimmy and, no, we're not together any more. We split up a number of years ago.' Which was yet another painful regret. She still felt guilty about backing away from her and Jimmy's wedding, even though she'd known it was the right thing to do at the time.

The main problem had been that the memories of Caleb had never left her, even though she'd tried her hardest to forget him. He'd stayed with her, buried deep in her heart.

There wasn't a flicker of reaction on Caleb's face at

this news though, not even a twitch of an eye. Clearly he didn't care a jot about her any more. But then, if that was true, why was he being so pig-headed about not listening to her?

Because he was punishing her for hurting him *fifteen* years ago.

Frustration surged through her. 'I can't believe you're still holding a grudge, Caleb. Surely someone of your standing and success has no need to be so small-minded.' She could hear the anger vibrating in her voice and it seemed Caleb did too because he widened his eyes a little before replacing his flash of surprise with an amused smirk.

'Is this the controlled, cautious Elena I knew all those years ago? My, how you've changed.'

'For the better, Caleb. I'm not the naïve young girl you used to know.' She refrained from saying *and love*, knowing that would be taking things a step too far. He'd never said such a thing to her, he'd been too proud for that, though it had been implied in his every action.

Unless she'd read him wrongly.

Which was quite possible.

She'd been wrong about a lot of things.

There was a quiet knock on the glass door and Caleb's PA crept, hunch-shouldered, into the room.

Before she could speak, Caleb let out a growl of frustration and snapped, 'I thought I told you I didn't want to be interrupted!'

Because Caleb had spoken to her in English, and perhaps in deference to Elena's presence there too, his PA replied in English. 'I'm so sorry, but I thought you'd want to know about this straight away. Apparently there's a problem with the meeting with the Americans on Monday. Señor Carter's PA is saying he's having second thoughts—'

Caleb held up a hand to stop her speaking, his gaze flicking momentarily to Elena before returning to his PA, his expression thunderous, as if furious that Elena had been a party to hearing about the setback.

This time he replied in Spanish and, even though Elena didn't understand a word of it, not being a Spanish speaker, she could see that his words had cut his PA deeply when she backed out of the room with tears glinting in her eyes.

'How can you be so cold? So *mean*!' she blurted when he turned back to look at her. 'That poor woman was just doing her job.'

Mouth dry, she reached for the glass of water but when she saw how much her hand was trembling she quickly dropped it to her side again.

'How could you treat her like that, Caleb?'

'Like what?' he growled.

'Like nothing. Less than nothing. I would have thought you'd have made every effort to make sure your subordinates were treated with kindness and respect after what you went through when you were young.'

Anger flickered in his eyes. 'I'm respectful to people when they work hard and make good choices.'

'But people won't learn from their mistakes if you don't nurture them. They become afraid to take necessary risks and everything grinds to a halt.'

'Is that what's happened to your business, Elena?'

he asked quietly. 'Did you drive it into the ground with your inept handling of your staff so you were forced to come here, begging for my help? What a fall from grace that must be for you.'

Hot rage rushed through her body. How could the smart, compassionate man she remembered have become so hard and mean? 'I knew you could be a bit on the curt side, Caleb, but the man I knew was never cruel. Or a bully!'

Shock flashed momentarily across his face before it was replaced with a stony scowl. 'Enough! This meeting is over. I don't need you coming in here, telling me how to treat my staff. Go home and run your own business—' he leant in closer to her so she saw the conviction plainly in his eyes '—without my battery.'

With that closing shot, he turned his back on her and strode out of the room, leaving the glass door swinging in his wake.

Caleb Araya paced the floor of his corner office, his blood pumping frantically through his veins.

Who did Elena Jones think she was, turning up after fifteen years of silence and presuming to tell him how to run his business and treat his staff?

The woman certainly had some nerve.

And a skewed sense of priorities.

Not that he didn't already know that from experience.

To his utter frustration, and despite the fact they hadn't seen each other in a very long time, as soon as he'd seen her standing there in his meeting room he'd been hit hard by that same immediate connection they'd always shared.

It had put him on the back foot.

It had always been like that with her—she affected him like no other woman ever had. The moment he'd met her at the beginning of his Erasmus exchange year to the University of Cambridge he'd found himself drawn to her.

Her cool integrity and assertive sense of self had set her apart from the other immature, entitled female students that had swarmed around him, believing him to be an ideal candidate for the bad boy fling they were so keen to tick off their list before settling down with their rich, boring husbands.

They hadn't bothered to get to know *him* at all.

Elena, on the other hand, had made him feel as if he didn't need to pretend to be somebody he wasn't when he was with her. She'd liked him for his erudite conversation and refreshing views on the world. Or so she'd said.

After growing up as the poor, pitied son of a woman who was infamous in the small town where he lived for being the mistress of a married man and a woman of loose morals, he'd promised himself he'd make sure his adulthood would be very different.

Because of the disgrace that surrounded his family, his early life had been pretty tough by all accounts: friendless, violent and isolated. But after he'd been threatened with expulsion from the elite school that he'd later found, to his chagrin, that his mother's sugar daddy had funded, he'd pulled up his socks and eschewed everything and everyone for a life dedicated to study so he could get away from the small town and its even smaller mentality.

He was going to be someone that people looked up to and respected, and Elena had made him feel as though he'd achieved that—for a short time anyway.

To his shame and regret, it had turned out he'd been very wrong about how much she'd actually cared about him and she'd been the first and last person he'd ever trusted.

The memory of her betrayal had stayed with him over the years, tarnishing every relationship he'd had, as if she were a devil on his shoulder, judging his choices, prodding at his conscience, reminding him he could never truly trust anyone with his heart.

When he'd seen her name in his diary this morning it had sent a shock of such intense regret-fuelled nostalgia through him he'd had to sit down and take a few deep breaths to regain his composure. He'd been on the cusp of telling his PA to cancel the meeting, but curiosity and a deep-seated urge to regain some sort of equilibrium over past hurts had stopped him at the last minute.

He wanted to feel as though he finally had a handle on his feelings about Elena Jones.

It had been going well, with him feeling in control of the meeting until she'd caught him out by accusing him of being a bully.

It had shocked him to his core.

Was that really what she thought he'd become?

It had been such a long time since someone had stood up to him like that, he had no idea whether his behaviour was out of line or not. The thought that it might have been had rattled him. *She'd* rattled him, despite his determination not to let her get to him.

He stabbed at the buzzer on the phone to summon his PA.

Benita hurried into the room, her hands tightly clasped in front of her and her gaze lowered as if she was afraid she'd get another dressing-down for what had just happened.

He'd been furious when she'd let it slip in front of Elena that things weren't exactly going to plan with the Americans. He'd not wanted her to know that things weren't running as smoothly as he'd wanted to project, for the sake of his professional pride, but he was aware, now that he'd calmed down a little, that he'd perhaps been a bit too harsh on the woman. She'd not been working for him for long, having stepped into the role after his usual PA had gone on maternity leave, and they hadn't found the right rhythm for working together yet.

But he wasn't a complete monster, as Elena had so brazenly suggested. He was firm and expected total professionalism at all times, but he made sure to reward those who did a good job for him.

'Benita, I wanted to say good work on putting that file together for me yesterday. It was very helpful in my meeting.'

His PA stared at him, as if in shock.

Surely it wasn't that surprising that he'd offered her a compliment.

Was it?

No. He was letting Elena Jones get into his head and

that was the last place he wanted her to be. He was over his feelings for her. It had taken him years to get rid of the ache he'd carried around after she'd rejected him, but he'd finally managed it.

'Thank you.' Benita paused, a worried frown now pinching her brow. 'Are you okay? Is there anything I can get you?' she asked with hesitation in her voice.

He opened his mouth to dismiss her misplaced concern, annoyed that she'd noticed his agitation, but pulled himself back at the last second, now hyper-aware of Elena's comments.

Damn the woman!

'I'm fine,' he muttered, forcing his mouth into a smile.

But, instead of seeming reassured by this, his PA took a hurried step away from him as if suspicious about his sudden change in attitude.

He sighed and ran a hand through his hair, pacing to the window to look down at the street below and collect himself.

What was happening to him today? His head was a mess.

At least he was free of Elena now though. His outright rejection of her proposal would surely mean she'd never darken his door again.

The street was busy with people milling about between office blocks and cafés and he watched them scurrying around for a moment, his thoughts jumping between relief and dissatisfaction. He knew he'd been petty, not even agreeing to look at the proposal she'd brought all the way from England, but she'd humiliated and hurt him once and he wasn't prepared to let her get anywhere near him again.

A partnership between them—their *companies*, he corrected himself—could never work.

For a second he wondered whether his mind was playing tricks on him as a familiar lone figure on the street opposite his building caught his eye. His stomach lurched as he watched her pace back and forth, then throw her gaze up towards Araya Industries and frown, as if hatching a plan to get back in here and torment him again.

Apparently he couldn't have been more wrong about having chased Elena Jones away for good.

Well, he wasn't having it.

'Hold my calls for a while longer,' he said to his PA as he swept out of the room past her and headed towards the lift that would take him down to street level.

Apparently he hadn't made it clear enough to Elena that there would be no further opportunities to meet with him, so he was going to rectify that right here and now. He was going to tell her to go home and that he wanted nothing more to do with her.

Storming onto the street, blood pulsing feverishly through his veins, he called out her name and she turned to meet his eye, her expression registering first surprise then hope.

Hope away, cariño—*you're not getting a thing from me except a wave goodbye.*

The street was quiet as he drew level with where she stood on the pavement opposite and he glanced quickly left, not seeing anything coming his way, anger at her audacity buzzing in his head.

Elena's eyes were fixed firmly on him as he began to cross the street towards her but, as he stepped into the middle of the road, something made her glance away then quickly back to him again.

This time there was an altogether different expression on her face.

Panic.

Blood thumping in his ears, he swivelled to look at what had spooked her and time seemed to slow down. There was a motorbike coming towards him at speed and he knew in that moment, with absolute certainty, that there was no way he could get out of its path in time.

Memories flashed before his eyes: of him and Elena laughing together after one of their classes at university, of her sitting in his room telling him she was thinking about splitting up with her childhood sweetheart, and all the blood rushing from his head as he realised he finally had a chance to have what he'd wanted for so long, of the look of abject hurt and distress on her face just now when he'd told her he wouldn't partner with her.

Lights and colours danced before his eyes and a strange kind of euphoria lifted his senses, making his surroundings hyper-loud and vividly real.

And then the bike hit him, the impact throwing his body into the air, knocking all the breath from his lungs. In a panic he flailed his limbs wildly as he tried to grab hold of something, anything, to anchor him as he spun through the void. A moment later his body made rough, painful impact with the ground, quickly followed by his head.

And everything went black.

CHAPTER TWO

ELENA STOOD IN SHOCK, her arms still outstretched as if she'd thought she could do something, some kind of magic perhaps, to stop Caleb from being hit by the motorbike that had sped round the corner just as he'd stepped into its path.

She felt light-headed and displaced from reality, as if this was all some horrible dream—though the heavy thump of her heart in her throat and the adrenaline that roared through her body told her otherwise.

The rider was picking himself up from the ground after coming off his bike and miraculously seemed not to be injured in any way, but Caleb's slumped body, which had been flung at least ten feet, was still lying half on the pavement and half on the road. And he wasn't moving.

A cacophony of noise suddenly rushed in on her as people began running towards where Caleb lay, finally shocking Elena out of her dazed state. She stumbled towards him, falling to her knees by his side, barely registering the rough ground biting into her skin, and put her shaking hand onto his torso. His eyes were closed, but she could feel his chest rising and falling with his breathing.

So he was still alive. *Thank God.*

She could feel tears pressing at the back of her eyes but she blinked them away, determined to keep it together for his sake.

'Caleb? Can you hear me?' she whispered, leaning in closer to him and breathing in the distinctive scent of him that had haunted her throughout the years, usually at the most inopportune moments.

Somebody—a woman—asked her a question in Spanish and Elena shook her head, mouthing back ineffectually, totally unable to summon even the basic Spanish phrase for *I don't understand.*

The woman frowned, then asked, 'Are you English?'

Was it that obvious?

Judging by the fact she was wearing a highly inappropriate woollen suit for the weather and had skin so light it was almost translucent, she guessed it must be.

'Yes!' Elena said, relief flooding through her that the woman would be able to help her. 'I don't speak Spanish.' She swallowed hard. 'I need to call an ambulance. Can you help me?'

'Don't worry,' the woman said, gesturing behind her. 'My husband has already called them.'

Caleb let out a low groan and Elena swivelled back to look at him, her heart leaping with relief. 'Caleb? Are you okay? I'm so sorry—this is all my fault.'

At least it felt like it was her fault, even though rationally she knew it had been an accident. But it was also another thing for him to hold against her.

She should have left this area and gone to regroup somewhere else—to give Caleb a chance to calm down—then come back again once her head was clear and her plan fully formed, instead of pacing about in front of his building like a lunatic. He must have seen her prowling around out here and decided to come out to ask her what the hell she thought she was doing.

When she'd heard him call her name from across the street her first thought had been that he'd changed his mind and decided to listen to her after all and her heart had leapt with excitement and relief. But as he'd crossed the street and she'd seen the look of frustrated fury in his eyes it had become powerfully obvious that she'd been very wrong to suppose that.

He hadn't wanted to turn back the clock. He'd wanted her gone.

The woman laid a hand gently onto her back, dragging her out of her distraught reflection. 'He'll be okay, don't worry. The ambulance is on its way.'

Elena nodded gratefully, this time unable to stop tears from welling in her eyes. 'He was crossing the road to meet me and didn't see the bike.'

'It's okay. Not your fault,' the woman said in a soothing tone, rubbing Elena's arm in sympathy.

If only that were true. She already felt guilty enough about the anguish she'd caused Caleb in the past and now she'd hurt him again, only physically this time. He never would have been out here if it wasn't for her.

A moment later the sound of a siren broke through the low murmurs of the crowd that had gathered around them and an ambulance sped round the corner and parked up nearby, its flashing lights bouncing off the windows of the buildings opposite.

The paramedics jumped out of the cab and ran towards where Caleb lay, pushing their way through the large group of bystanders that had gathered to ogle the drama playing out in front of them.

The helpful woman disappeared from Elena's side as the paramedics came to kneel next to Caleb and check his vital signs. The female paramedic turned to ask Elena a question in Spanish, indicating towards Caleb, and Elena guessed she must be asking whether she knew him.

Novia meant friend, didn't it? It sounded like a friendly kind of word.

'*Sí, sí!*' she said, her voice sounding shaky and weak from shock. The woman nodded and gave her a reassuring smile, then turned back to help her colleague tend to the now silent and deathly still Caleb.

A short while later he was lifted onto a stretcher wearing a neck brace, then into the back of the ambulance.

Elena stood there stupidly, watching as they secured the straps to keep the makeshift bed from rolling around in the back of the vehicle, her chest tight with worry.

What if he died?

No. She couldn't think like that. He'd be fine. The paramedics weren't rushing around shouting and wielding scary-looking equipment as if they were worried that he was in grave danger. Mercifully, there was hardly any blood on the ground where he'd lain, just a little from where he'd cut his temple.

Perhaps he'd just been knocked out and not badly hurt. Just a bit bruised and battered.

Please.

Please.

Elena didn't realise the female paramedic had said something to her until the woman waved a hand in front of her face and spoke again, her expression registering sympathy. 'You come. To hospital.'

Elena nodded dumbly, not entirely sure it was appropriate that she should be the one to go with Caleb, but no one from his company had rushed out to be here with him. It looked as though the paramedics wanted to get him straight to hospital now so there wasn't time to go into his building and find someone.

She should just go with him and call his office from there to let them know what was going on. Then she'd leave him be and go back to the hotel to get her head together.

One thing was for sure, going to pieces was not going to help anyone right now.

Mind made up, she gave the paramedic a wobbly smile and climbed into the back of the ambulance.

There was something wrong with the light in his bedroom, Caleb thought fuzzily as he woke up from a deep, dreamless sleep. And his cleaning lady seemed to have used a different kind of product than usual because he didn't recognise the smell in here either.

'Ah, you're awake,' came a voice from somewhere to his left and he wondered wildly who he'd gone to bed with the night before.

He couldn't remember.

In fact, now he thought about it, he found his mind was strangely blank, as if it had been wiped of details. How much had he drunk last night to wake up in this state? It must have been a lot because he had the unsettling feeling that he wasn't at home at all. In fact, he realised with a lurch as his vision cleared, he had no idea where he was or how he'd got here. The walls were painted an institutional green colour and were disturbingly free of any kind of decoration. Turning his head, he saw with a shock that he was lying next to some kind of flashing, beeping, monitoring machine with wires and drips hanging from it.

Which were attached to him.

He tried to sit up and felt his whole body complain, pain shooting through his abdomen.

'No, no, don't try and get up. You had an accident and you've cracked a rib and banged your head so you may feel dizzy and disorientated for a while.'

'An accident?' he asked, shocked by how rough and raspy his voice sounded. His throat was so dry it felt as if he hadn't had a drink in days.

'Here,' the voice said and he turned towards where it came from to see a middle-aged woman in a crisp white uniform standing next to the bed where he lay, pushing a straw towards his mouth.

He sipped gratefully from the drink, feeling the cool liquid soothe his throat and begin to refresh him.

'Your girlfriend's very worried about you,' the nurse said, taking the cup away once he'd finished and putting it on the nightstand next to his bed. 'She saw you get hit by the motorbike and is blaming herself for the accident because you were crossing the road to see her when it happened, so be nice to her when she comes in to see you.'

'My girlfriend?' He didn't remember having a girl-friend.

His heart began to race as panic swept through him, nausea welling in his stomach as the room started to slowly spin. He shook his head, trying to clear the feeling, determined not to give in to it.

He didn't do panic, dammit.

Not appearing to notice his disorientation, the nurse helped him sit up a little so she could fluff up his pillow and he gripped the rail at the side of the bed hard, racking his brain for the memory of how he came to be here in an attempt to centre himself. The nurse had said a motorbike had hit him but he had absolutely no recollection of it.

How could he not remember something so serious?

'I think she needs a hug and some reassurance that you don't hate her,' she said, smiling at him. 'Judging by the way she's been pacing the halls and badgering us every ten minutes for updates on your condition, she obviously cares about you very much. You're a lucky man to have someone who loves you like that.'

He just nodded, not wanting to let on that he had no idea who she was talking about, or that he was becoming more and more aware of other rather worrying gaps in his memory. He knew his name and that he owned a company called Araya Industries, which he'd built up from scratch, and that he lived in the L'Eixample district of Barcelona. He even knew what the inside of his penthouse looked like, but things like where he grew up and who his friends were seemed to have escaped him. And he definitely didn't remember being hit by the motorbike. The last thing he did remember was getting into work this morning and turning on his computer, but after that it was all a blank.

This disjoin in his memory made him feel sick if he thought about it too much, so he decided to put it out of his head for now. It would all come back after he'd been awake for a while and had got his bearings again. And he didn't want any fuss; he just wanted to get out of here, back to his home. Maybe once in familiar surroundings his mind would catch up with everything else.

'I'll let her know you're awake so she can come in and see you,' the nurse said, coming over to him and smoothing down the sheet that was covering him up to his armpits. It seemed they'd stripped him of the rest of his clothes, perhaps to check him over for injuries.

'Who?' he asked distractedly, still trying to get a handle on the anxiety that stubbornly surged through his body.

'Your girlfriend, Elena.' The nurse frowned, as if beginning to suspect that all was not entirely well with him.

He shot her a quick smile and said, 'Okay, good, I'd like to see her.'

Perhaps as soon as he saw this Elena he'd recognise her right away and the rest of his memory would come flooding back with it.

The nurse nodded curtly, clearly still a little suspicious about his well-being, but then turned and left the room.

A moment later there was a tentative knock at the door. He sat up a little straighter in bed and called, 'Come in.'

A woman with ice-blue eyes and long blonde hair hanging loosely around her slim shoulders entered the room and walked towards him, coming to a stop a couple of feet away from the bed. Her movements appeared graceful and controlled, but he could see from her strained smile that she was tense and worried.

Something about her shot a bolt of intense sensation through him, almost like déjà vu, though he could have sworn he'd never set eyes on her before in his life. He had vague memories of relationships with other women, beautiful, smart women, but there was something about Elena, something almost untouchable, that unnerved him. Or was that just his addled brain playing tricks on him? He'd obviously banged his head pretty hard if he'd forgotten he was having a relationship with a woman as attractive as this.

'How are you feeling?' she asked in English, which for some reason seemed absolutely right and totally expected.

'I'm okay—a bit banged up, but I'll live,' he said, patting a space on the bed next to him, wanting her to come nearer so he could study her closer. He had the strangest feeling that if he touched her he'd feel more grounded.

She looked at him warily for a moment then visibly

swallowed before stepping up to perch on the edge of the mattress, as if worried about getting too close and knocking him and causing him pain.

Desire shot through him as the scent of her perfume hit his senses and he closed his eyes for a moment, feeling another wave of déjà vu sweep through him.

Come on brain, catch up.

'It's good to see you awake. I was really worried about you,' she said, her voice sounding a little croaky.

'You're trembling,' he murmured, reaching out to touch her arm, feeling her practically vibrating under his fingertips.

'I wasn't sure what to expect when I came in here,' she said, her gaze darting away from his face to look down at where his tanned hand rested on her pale skin.

'Well, you don't need to worry. I'm fine,' he stated vehemently, hoping to reassure her—and perhaps himself a little too—though, judging by the tremble in her bottom lip, it didn't appear to have worked.

He *was* fine though, he told himself hazily, just a bit disorientated…that was all. Just because the sight of her hadn't brought his memory back, it didn't mean it was gone for good.

Perhaps if he kissed her, it would spark something in his brain.

She certainly looked as though she could do with some proof that he was still the man she knew and cared about. What was it the nurse had said? That she blamed herself for the accident because he'd been crossing the road to see her at the time? Was that the problem here—was she worried he was angry with her?

'Come closer,' he said, moving his hand up to slide his fingers under her jaw, feeling a strong urge to wipe the concern from her beautiful face now.

She stilled under his touch and her eyes widened as if she was surprised by what he was doing.

'Stop worrying,' he murmured, then drew her towards him and pressed his mouth firmly to hers.

She sucked in a startled-sounding breath but he paid it no mind, pulling her closer to him, ignoring the twinge of pain this caused in his damaged rib and hoping against hope that this would make everything right again.

Her mouth felt wonderful against his but he was blurrily aware that the kiss wasn't having the effect he'd hoped for. Determined not to give up that easily, he opened his lips and slipped his tongue into the heat of her mouth. As he'd suspected, she tasted incredible, like honey and harmony and sex…

And then his brain seemed to switch gear and suddenly he couldn't get enough of her. It was like having that first drink of water all over again, his body reacting with a forceful relief that shook him to his very soul. Her full mouth was soft but not as pliant as he would have liked, so he kissed her harder, feeling the pulse in her neck racing against the heel of his hand where he cupped her jaw.

A deep growl rumbled in the back of his throat as he began to lose control of his restraint and she let out a breathy moan in reply and dug her nails into the flesh of his upper arms.

He sank into the possessiveness of her grip, lost in

the sensual taste of her, feeling the strangest mixture of comfort and desire and relief—until he suddenly became aware that she was trying to pull away from him.

Reluctantly, he slid his hands away from her jaw and let her go.

'What's wrong?' he ground out, frustrated that she'd cut the kiss short when he'd been enjoying it so much.

It had been the first time he'd felt anything like himself since he'd woken up here.

Her eyes were wide and her expression a little wild. 'Why did you kiss me?' Almost absent-mindedly, she brushed her fingers against her lips and his body reacted with such erotic force he very nearly dragged her back to him again for another round.

But the look in her eyes stopped him.

He could see now that she was shaken by the kiss and not because she'd enjoyed it as much as he had.

'Why shouldn't I kiss you?' he demanded, feeling panic begin to work its way back under his skin again.

She blinked at him, looking utterly bewildered, her cheeks flushed with colour and her brow creased. 'Because of what happened this morning. We had a row.'

He frowned, his mind spinning with confusion. 'You mean before the accident? Look, I'm sure that wasn't your fault; I can't have been looking where I was going.'

Getting up from the bed, she took a step away from him, crossing her arms and frowning hard as if she didn't understand what she was hearing. 'Caleb, don't you remember what happened?'

He wanted to say yes, that he remembered everything, but he knew, with a slow sinking feeling of dread, that there was actually something very, very wrong here.

Throwing up his hands in frustration, he said, 'No! Okay! I don't remember!'

She flinched in surprise, then stared at him in horror, her mouth forming a perfect O shape.

Closing his eyes, he attempted to pull his focus back and took a long, deep breath. Fighting to keep his voice steady this time, he said, 'The truth is my memory's been a little fuzzy since I woke up.' He ran a hand over his face then looked up at her. 'I don't remember anything between getting to work this morning and waking up in the hospital and anything before my life here in Barcelona is a little difficult to pin down—'

She was still staring at him in dismay. 'Oh, no, Caleb. That's not good.'

He flapped a hand dismissively, hating the idea of her pitying him. 'It's fine; it'll come back to me soon. It's probably just the drugs messing with my head.'

Taking a step closer to him, she said with a shake in her voice, 'Caleb, do you remember who I am?'

'Yes, you're Elena, my girlfriend,' he said airily, hoping it sounded more convincing to her than it did to him.

Her eyes grew comically wide. 'What makes you think I'm your girlfriend?'

Confusion swirled through his head again. 'Because… I thought…' He paused and frowned. 'The nurse told me you were, and I *know* I know you. You're very familiar to me.'

Elena shifted on the spot, looking uncomfortable now. 'I don't speak Spanish so I must have misinterpreted the paramedic's question when she asked me about my relationship to you,' she muttered to herself, staring down at the floor. 'Or perhaps the nurse got the wrong end of the stick or something.' She looked up at him again, her brow pinched into a frown. 'Anyway, however it happened, I'm not your girlfriend.'

He looked at her for a moment and got the distinct impression there was more to this than she was telling him.

'So we're what?' he asked slowly, one eyebrow raised. 'Just friends?'

Elena knew that lying to Caleb was the last thing she should do right now but she didn't want to add any unnecessary stress to the situation, not when he'd only just woken up from an accident with a head injury and seemed to be rather confused.

And the thing was, they *had* been friends once, very good friends, and if she had any say in the matter she'd make sure they got past their differences to become friends again.

But that would be all. Just friends.

Even though the kiss they'd just shared had rocked her world. Her whole body still buzzed from the after-effects of the feel of his firm mouth on hers—her pulse jumping in her throat and her nerves on fire with a wild, almost frightening demand for more that she'd not felt the like of in years.

Not since the last time he'd kissed her.

'Uh-huh. We haven't seen each other for a long time though. We knew each other at university.' She waited for him to recall the fact that they weren't exactly friends any more but his expression remained blank. It seemed he really didn't remember her.

'I'm just visiting from England for a few days and dropped in to see you,' she added, wondering if that would help jog his memory, but it didn't appear to. He was looking at her with such an intense expression in his eyes now, as if he was thinking about kissing her again, that she had to drag her gaze away and look down instead at the sheet that was tucked up against his rather impressive bare chest. She tried not to stare too hard at it, or at the dark bruises marking his skin. Apart from those, he was in really good shape, his limbs strong and muscled, his torso toned and hard.

Stop gawping, you fool!

'I'm sorry if I've made you feel awkward,' Caleb said, frowning and shaking his head, then closing one eye and squinting as if the movement had caused him great pain.

She went to put out a hand to touch him, then withdrew it. 'Is your head hurting?'

'Like crazy.'

'I'll get the doctor.'

She started to walk away, then paused and turned back to face him. 'Is there someone else you want me to call to be here with you?'

He looked at her in surprise, before frowning. 'No, I don't think so. To be honest, I can't think of who I would call.' He looked so uncomfortable she couldn't help but feel a rush of sympathy for him.

She was just about to offer to stay until they were

able to contact a friend in Barcelona for him when his expression cleared and he said, 'Could you ring my office and ask my PA to come here?'

'I've already called her,' she told him. 'She's on her way over. I asked her who your emergency contact is but she wasn't sure. Apparently she hasn't been working for you for long.'

'No. My regular PA has just had a baby.'

'It's not yours, is it?' she quipped, then regretted it when she saw a look of panic flash across his face.

'I'm just joking, Caleb. Sorry, that was tasteless of me considering your state of mind at the moment.' She squeezed her eyes shut and wrinkled her nose. 'I'm still a little shaken up after what just happened.'

But, instead of giving her a piece of his mind, he gave her a slow, wry smile instead, like the ones he used to give her back when they were friends. It was such an incredible sight and something she'd not seen for such a long time it stopped her in her tracks.

'I'll…er…go and find a doctor,' she said hurriedly, swallowing down the lump that had formed in her throat.

Turning away, she strode out of the room on rather shaky legs, relieved to be able to get away from his befuddling presence for a moment so she could figure out how the heck she was going to handle this situation from this point on.

Just as she reached the nurses' station Caleb's PA hurried around the corner and, spotting her, gave a little wave of recognition.

'Benita, thank you for coming,' Elena said as the

woman came to a breathless halt in front of her. 'Caleb's okay, but he's banged his head and is having trouble re-membering which friend to call to come and look after him. Has he mentioned anyone to you that he's close to?' she asked.

Benita shook her head, biting her lip and looking a little anxious. 'I've only been working for him for a few days and he never talks about anything of a personal nature. I checked his computer and his work mobile—which he'd left on his desk,' she added a little defen-sively, as if Elena might accuse her of snooping, 'but there was no one obvious I should call.' Turning away, she began rifling through her bag, her movements be-coming increasingly desperate as she failed to locate what she was looking for. '*Caramba!* I forgot to put his phone in here.'

Elena put a steadying hand onto the woman's arm. 'It's okay. He's in no state to be using his phone right now anyway. In fact, it's probably better if he doesn't have it right away. Less stress.'

She nodded, though the expression in her eyes re-flected her worry. 'I'll drop it round to his apartment later.'

'I'm sure that would be fine,' Elena said in an at-tempt to soothe the poor woman.

Sighing, Benita shook her head. 'Carla would never have forgotten it.'

That gave Elena an idea. 'Hey, would Carla know of a friend of his to contact?' she asked hopefully.

Benita shook her head again. 'I called her but she said the same thing. He never gave away much personal information about himself. He had a few girlfriends over the time she worked for him but she never met any of them and he's not seeing anyone now, as far as she knows. He doesn't have any family left either, now his mother's passed away.'

Elena experienced a pang of sorrow on his behalf. She knew from their time at university that he'd always been a bit of a loner and that his mother had been his only family, not that they'd been particularly close. He'd been angry with her for continuing to have a long-term relationship with a married man. He didn't know who his father was either; his mother had refused to tell him, saying he was just a man she'd met in a bar one night. Unfortunately for Caleb, that had been a well chewed over piece of gossip in the town where he'd grown up, which had followed him round like a bad smell.

It was really no wonder he was so keen to keep his private life private these days.

'When did his mother pass away?' she asked.

'About six months ago, I think. Carla mentioned something about it because he'd actually taken some time off work for once to be with her in the hospice. It was cancer, apparently, that took her.'

The two women stood quietly for a moment, reflecting on this.

'Well, I'd better get back to the office now I know he's okay,' Benita said suddenly, smiling, as if Elena's presence there had released her from her own duties to Caleb. 'I'll let the other managers know what's happened and that he won't be in work for the rest of the week. Please tell him everything's under control. I know he'll worry otherwise.'

'Don't you want to go in and see him?' Elena asked, a little shocked by the woman's intention to withdraw without even saying hello to Caleb.

Benita shook her head, taking a step backwards. 'No, no. Just tell him I hope he feels better soon.'

'Well, perhaps someone else from work could come over and sort out who can look after him—' Elena said rather desperately, but Benita was backing away now, clearly keen to get out of there and return to the sanctuary of a Caleb-free office.

'I doubt anyone there will know any more than me,' she said, giving one last tight smile, then turning and rushing away.

Sighing, Elena rubbed a hand over her face, her insides sinking with a mixture of sadness for Caleb at his apparent lack of close friendships and nerves about exactly what she'd got herself into here.

The sad fact was, it looked as though the only person available to take care of him right now was her.

As she thought about this a crazy idea began to form in her head and her stomach gave a nervous little flip. Maybe if she could show him she was happy to be here for him, and prepared to help in any way she could, it might go some way towards rebuilding their friendship— without the prejudice and anger he seemed to be holding on to from the past getting in the way—and help her reconnect with the man she knew was in there, hiding behind that hard shell she'd seen earlier. Otherwise, once his memory came back she might never have the opportunity to speak to him again, especially when he remembered why he'd been crossing that road, but if she could be a good friend to him now and prove how much she cared about him, perhaps he'd think twice before pushing her away again.

It was worth a try.

Anything was worth a try at this point.

But if she did stay to look after him there would be no more kissing, she told herself firmly, setting back her shoulders and heading towards the desk to ask the staff there to contact his doctor.

Definitely not.

CHAPTER THREE

THE MEMORY OF Elena's captivating ice-blue eyes and her long slender legs with their dirty, scuffed up knees remained stubbornly imprinted in Caleb's mind as he lay back in bed and waited impatiently for her to return.

Just friends, huh? What on earth had stopped him from pursuing more than friendship with her? He'd very much like to know that. He found her intensely attractive and she was clearly a smart, compassionate person—qualities he valued highly.

An English rose.

The phrase floated into his mind. Yes, that summed her up perfectly.

A moment later the door opened and she strode back into the room with a tall dark-haired woman following closely behind her.

'Sorry I was away for so long; I bumped into your PA out there—she said to tell you she hopes you feel better soon and that she's got everything under control at work so you can rest without worrying—and then it took me a while to locate your doctor.' She gestured towards the woman she'd entered with.

'Señor Araya,' the doctor said, walking over to his bed and picking up the clipboard that hung at the end of it, 'how are you feeling?' She scanned the paperwork quickly before replacing the clipboard.

'I feel fine,' he said confidently. He didn't want to give her any reason to keep him here unnecessarily. He was uncomfortable with being in hospital; it made him feel vulnerable and edgy for some reason. He'd be much better off in his own home with his things around him. Maybe then his memory would come back.

The doctor pressed her lips together. 'So it seems you have a cracked rib and a bump on your head, but apart from that you got off pretty lightly, considering you were hit by a motorbike travelling at speed.'

'Can you speak English so Elena can understand?' he snapped, riled by the doctor's officious manner and not wanting Elena to feel ignored when she'd been good enough to stay and check on him. Unlike his PA.

'Yes, of course,' the doctor said, switching easily to English and giving Elena an indulgent smile before turning back to fix her scrutinising gaze on him again.

'I'd like you to stay here tonight. Head injuries can be serious and I'd like to keep you under observation for a while longer to make sure you're okay.'

The thought of staying here any longer filled him with a sinking dread. 'No,' he stated firmly. 'I want to go home. Now.'

'I don't think that's advisable—' the doctor began, a concerned frown pinching her brow.

'I feel fine. I don't want to take up a bed unnecessarily when someone who's really sick could use it. I'll be okay at home,' Caleb said gruffly. He wasn't used to people telling him what he could and couldn't do and it rankled.

'I really don't think—'

'I don't care what you think. I'm going home,' he said, levering himself up and readying himself to swing his legs out of bed.

The only way he was staying here was if they called Security and tied him down.

The doctor sighed as if she'd seen this scenario before and knew there was no way to stop someone like this once they'd made up their mind.

'I can't prevent you from leaving, Señor Araya, but I must insist you don't go home on your own,' she said sternly. 'You'll need someone responsible there to keep an eye on you in case there are any after-effects from the head injury. The CAT scan we gave you didn't show up anything worrying, but it's better to be safe.'

Frustration rattled through him. He just wanted to be at home now, without people fussing over him any more.

'I'll be fine. I can call my GP if I start to feel ill,' he bit out.

The doctor shook her head. 'That's not good enough. You need someone there with you full-time for the next forty-eight hours at least.'

Elena must have sensed his unease because she stepped forwards and said, 'I can stay with him, at his home.'

The doctor studied her for a moment. 'Are you his partner?'

There was an infinitesimal pause before Elena said, 'Yes.'

He glanced at her in surprise but she didn't turn to catch his eye, just kept her steady, confident gaze trained on the doctor.

The doctor nodded, seeming to decide that Elena was a sensible and trustworthy sort of person.

He could see why. She certainly gave that impression. Caleb really liked that about her. She was no-nonsense, just the kind of person he liked to have around. He couldn't do with women who simpered and flapped about ineffectually. Having her at home with him for a short while would be fine by him. It might even give him more time to try and figure out the real state of their relationship. He was positive there had to be more to it than 'just friends', as she'd claimed.

Turning back to Caleb now and fixing him with a steely stare, the doctor asked, 'Have you been sick since you woke up or had any dizziness? Any memory loss?'

Out of the corner of his eye he saw Elena stiffen and waited for her to tell the doctor about his elusive memory, preparing himself for a fight, but when he turned to look directly at her she just gazed back at him with those bright, intelligent eyes of hers, her mouth firmly shut. A strange kind of unspoken agreement seemed to pass between them and he realised she was letting him know that she was on his side.

She wasn't going to give him up.

Well, that proved something at least; she must care about him if she was willing to twist the truth to help him get out of here. The thought warmed him.

'No, I feel fine,' he said, tearing his gaze away from her to look at the doctor again, feeling the weight of anxiety begin to lift from his chest.

The doctor nodded, apparently convinced that he was telling the truth. 'Okay then, I'll go and fill out the paperwork. You'll need to come in next week for further tests though, Señor Araya, to make sure we haven't missed anything.'

Caleb nodded but didn't say anything. He'd deal with all that later. He just wanted to get out of here now.

'I'll let you get dressed then. Your clothes and personal effects will be in the cupboard at the side of your bed,' the doctor said, moving towards the door. 'You might need a bit of help getting dressed because of the pain in your rib. I can call a nurse if you like,' she said, turning back with an expectant look on her face.

'I don't need a nurse,' he said dismissively.

'I can help him if he needs me to,' Elena chimed in, throwing him a chiding look.

The doctor just nodded briskly.

'Thank you, Doctor,' Elena added, giving the woman a warm smile.

Once the doctor had left the room, Elena busied herself by pulling all his things out of the bedside cabinet and laying them out on the bed. Picking up his shirt, she looked at it with her nose wrinkled. 'I'm afraid there's some blood on this from where you cut your head.'

'I don't care about that. Pass it to me, will you,' he said, reaching out for the clothing and wincing as his cracked rib made itself known.

She batted his hand away, frowning. 'I'll do it. If you can just sit up a bit more—'

Ignoring his huff of frustration, she put one hand carefully behind each shoulder and pulled gently, forcing him to sit up enough so she could slip the shirt around his back and hold it out for him to slide his arms into the sleeves.

Her hands had been cool and the sensation of her skin on his hot flesh lingered there while she leant in to do the buttons up for him.

Her nearness made him want to pull her in for another kiss but, despite his still rather woolly-headed state, he was aware that it would be a highly inappropriate thing to do.

He growled with irritation, hating how weak and vulnerable he must appear to her right now. 'This is ridiculous. I'm not a child. I can do my own buttons up!'

A small smile lifted the corners of her mouth and she raised an eyebrow at him. 'Stop being so proud and let me help. If you won't let me take care of you I'm going to have to tell the doctor that I can't go home with you after all and you'll have to stay in the hospital with the nurses fussing around you instead.'

He let out a harrumphing noise, but let her do the rest of the buttons up. Despite feeling annoyed that she was using his injuries against him, he was impressed that she hadn't been upset by his shortness and obviously wasn't about to let it put her off coming home with him.

Most women would have let him have his way and backed off, but it seemed that Elena wasn't most women.

He drew the line though when she tried to help him

get out of bed and firmly batted her outstretched hand away as he swung his legs out. He pulled on his suit trousers over the boxers he was mercifully still wearing, managing after a moment or two of pained fumbling to pull the zip up and hook the fastener, then sat for a moment to catch his breath.

'Is this your address?' Elena asked as he slowly levered himself up off the bed, fighting back a wave of nausea as he stood up and felt a heavy weight of darkness pressing down on his head.

He must have moved too quickly.

Blinking hard to clear his vision, he stared at the driving licence she was holding up, which was sandwiched behind a clear plastic window in his wallet.

'That's it,' he said, taking a long breath to steady himself.

'Okay, I'll go and arrange for a taxi to take us home,' she said, giving him a pointed glance that said, *Take it easy until I get back.*

He got the distinct feeling that this was only the beginning of his time being ordered around by this woman.

To his surprise, he found he didn't entirely hate the idea.

The cab drew up in front of the building where Caleb lived and Elena swallowed hard, her stomach doing a slow somersault now they'd reached their destination.

It had been fine in the hospital while she was distracted by the practical aspects of getting Caleb home, but now they were finally here, and were going to be totally alone for the first time since the disastrous meet-ing this morning—where she'd had a worrying amount of trouble keeping her emotions under wraps—she was beginning to regret her rash promise to look after him for the next couple of days.

She was determined to follow it through though—because she owed him. If it hadn't been for her he never would have had the accident in the first place.

The moment she'd sensed how determined he was to get out of hospital she'd made a snap decision. Not calling out his lie to the doctor about his memory being sound had almost been a step too far for her, but she'd told herself that if she stuck with him around the clock she'd be able to alert the doctors the moment he seemed to be even vaguely struggling. In the busy hospital he could have been left alone for long periods of time, but here in his house she'd be there to keep an eye on him every second of the day.

Unless he suddenly remembered that he hated her and sent her away, of course.

Her stomach did another sickening flip.

If that happened he'd be left alone in his apartment without anyone there to look out for him. And what if he passed out or fell and hurt himself once she'd gone?

She took a steadying breath then blew it out towards the sky, imagining it was her fears she was expelling as they exploded into a million pieces in her mind.

No. She wasn't going to worry about that right now. Hopefully, if he did remember what had happened be-tween them, the fact that she'd helped bail him out of hospital and offered to stick around to take care of him would at least make him pause before chucking her out. If she was really lucky, her presence here might even prove to him that she was genuinely sorry for what had happened in the past and that she was serious about wanting to make amends for hurting him.

That she still cared about him.

Not that she'd ever really stopped, even when she'd pushed him away.

'Elena?' Caleb said beside her and she could tell from the tone of his voice that he was wondering what the heck she was doing, still sitting here like a lemon when they'd reached their destination.

'Are you sure you want to come in with me?' he asked brusquely. 'You don't have to, you know. I can take care of myself from here.'

She turned to fix him with a stern glare. 'No, you can't, Caleb; you heard what the doctor said. You need someone around, especially if you're still feeling a bit confused.'

He shrugged as if it was neither here nor there to him whether she stayed or not, but she could have sworn she saw a flash of a smile in his eyes.

'Okay, let's go,' she said, opening the cab door and telling herself that the best thing all round was just to take one step at a time and deal with any consequences as and when they came.

Caleb's penthouse apartment was breathtaking, and exactly the sort of place she would have expected him to choose to live. Light poured in through the large warehouse-style windows, bathing the stylish but comfortable-looking furniture in soft spring sunlight.

The colours he'd chosen to furnish the place were earthy and muted in a warm and comforting way, with terra-cotta tiles on the floor and dark tan leather and stained wood sofas and tables gathered in the middle of the vast space. It was a really restful room to be in and Elena let out a breath as she felt herself relax a little.

She was still acutely aware that she was here under false pretences, but she reassured herself that this was about making sure Caleb was safe and cared for; it had nothing whatsoever to do with her trying to persuade him to listen to her business proposal. She'd deal with all that once he was fully well again. There was no way she'd take advantage of his lapse in memory.

She was here as his friend, nothing more.

His only friend, by the sounds of it.

Judging by the fact he didn't have anyone obvious to call upon when he was in the hospital, she guessed she wasn't the only one he'd kept at arm's length.

The thought of how alone he was made sorrow well heavily in her gut.

She knew she should have sought him out before now. She'd wanted to, had for years, but she'd never quite plucked up the courage to face him again—until it had been absolutely essential. That made her a coward, she knew that, but she'd always been afraid of how out of control Caleb made her feel and she'd needed every ounce of strength over the intervening years to build a successful career for herself. It wasn't easy being a woman in a male-dominated arena.

At least that was what she was telling herself.

The passion of his kiss earlier came back to haunt

her as he walked past her into the living area and she caught the unique scent of him in the air.

Moving quickly away from him, she marched into the kitchen diner at the other end of the large room, aware that her heart was racing, and pretended to be admiring the high-tech gadgets he had in there to give herself a moment to pull herself together.

'Can I make you something to eat? Or drink?' she asked, turning back to look at him. He was standing by the largest sofa, watching her with a perplexed sort of frown.

'You don't need to mollycoddle me, Elena—I can fix my own food. In fact, I should be cooking for you to say thanks for bailing me out at the hospital.'

She held up a hand. 'Not a chance. Unless your cooking skills have improved since university?' she said with a slow grin.

He threw her a look of mock offence. 'Was it that bad?' He frowned. 'I don't remember.'

'It was passable,' she said, her mouth still twitching with mirth at the memory of it.

In truth, it had been terrible. The one time he'd cooked for her, when she'd gone over to his place to study for an exam, she'd pulled such a face after the first mouthful that Caleb had scraped the lot into the bin and called for takeout pizza instead.

'Well, like I said earlier, you don't have to stay here with me; I'll be fine,' he said, sitting down carefully on the sofa and wincing a little as his rib appeared to give him trouble.

She folded her arms. 'Like *I* said, there's no way I'm leaving you alone.'

She'd always stood up to him like this, refusing to be intimidated by his gruff demeanour, but deep down his dominating personality had twisted her into knots, threatening her carefully constructed cool.

Fifteen years ago he'd made her question everything she'd thought she wanted in a man. He was bold and charismatic, but he also seemed exactly the sort to smash her heart to pieces should things go wrong between them. At the time she wasn't prepared to put herself in danger of that happening, not after working so hard to get into her first choice of university and make her first move towards the kind of life she'd always dreamed of building for herself.

But she hadn't been able to stay away from him.

Struggling to keep her feelings under control, she'd found the safest thing had been to pretend that they didn't exist. It had been the only way to protect herself.

Except that somewhere along the line that had stopped working.

Caleb could sense that Elena wasn't altogether comfortable being here in his apartment with him and he wondered again what it was she wasn't telling him.

'If you're worried about where you're going to sleep, you're welcome to take one of the guest rooms.' He pointed towards a door that led to the corridor of four bedrooms.

'Okay, thank you,' she said a little distractedly.

'Is there somewhere else you need to be today?' he

asked, concerned now that he was keeping her from something important. The last thing he wanted was to be a burden to her.

'No, nowhere,' she answered, coming to sit down on an armchair opposite where he sat, finally giving him her full attention.

A sense of relief took him by surprise. He was still feeling pretty woozy and disorientated and it was soothing to know she'd be staying there with him for a while. Even if she did feel like a total stranger to him at the moment.

'So, *friend*, I guess I need to get to know you all over again. Do you have a partner? Husband? Boyfriend in England?' he asked.

She recoiled a little, as if the question had caught her by surprise. 'Not at the moment. I've been too busy recently with work to hold down a serious relationship.'

'When you say recently—?'

She flashed him a self-conscious smile. 'For the last few years.'

'You haven't had a serious relationship for a *few years*?'

She shrugged as she smoothed her hands down the sides of her skirt. 'I've dated, but I've not clicked with anyone.'

'I find that hard to believe.'

The air between them seemed to throb with tension and she gave him a strained smile, then glanced away.

He was making her uncomfortable. But why?

'Elena?'

She looked back at him, her expression now impassive, as if she'd pulled a mask back into place. 'Do you mind if I make myself a drink?' she said suddenly, slapping her hands onto her knees. 'I'm dying for a cup of tea.'

He frowned at the sudden change of subject but didn't press her on the reason for it. Perhaps she was just tired after the stress and strain of the day. He was pretty tired himself now, even though he'd slept for a lot of it. 'Sure, help yourself,' he said.

She got up and walked over to the kitchen. 'Would you like one?' she asked, reaching for the kettle on the work surface.

'No, thanks.' He sat forward in his seat. 'I should take a shower.' He sniffed at his shirt, inhaling the institutional smell of stringent cleaning fluid and decay and, just like that, a memory flew to the front of his mind and he knew why he'd wanted to get out of that hospital so quickly.

His anguish must have shown on his face because Elena said, 'Caleb? Is everything okay? Did you remember something?' her voice sounding breathy with concern.

'Just why I wanted to leave the hospital. My mother died about six months ago and I spent an awful lot of time visiting her in one.'

The expression on her face changed from worry to one of sympathy. 'Your PA told me. I'm so sorry for your loss,' she said, her bright blue eyes soft with compassion.

He nodded, accepting her condolences, and ran a hand over his face, feeling stubble rasp at his palm.

There was something more to the memory of losing his mother but he couldn't put his finger on what it was. Some kind of underlying emotion bubbling under the surface, not quite clear enough for him to fully grasp.

'I don't seem to be able to remember a lot about her at the moment. I know the time I spent with her at the end of her life was…difficult…but I'm not entirely sure why.'

Elena folded her arms and leant against the counter top. 'From what you've told me about her, I don't think you were particularly close, at least not when you were younger. You were keen to move away from the place where you grew up and she didn't want you to.'

She looked at him, as if expecting this to jog his memory, but nothing new came to him.

Sadness swelled in his chest.

What was wrong with him? Why was he getting maudlin all of a sudden? Perhaps the trauma to his head was somehow affecting his emotional state. That had to be it. He knew it wasn't his usual way to discuss how he was feeling with anyone, particularly not a woman. It was one of the things that had contributed to destroying his relationship with his ex-fiancée. Her constant need to try and get into his head and fix him had caused him to feel both hounded and suffocated.

There was something about Elena that invited confidences though.

But what was it?

A half-formed answer flitted around the edges of his mind, just out of reach, and he pushed an unnerving resurgence of panic away, telling himself there was no point in trying to force his memory to come back; it would reappear in its own good time. Perhaps after he'd had a good night's sleep in his own bed.

He stood up carefully, relieved to find his dizziness had subsided, and started to make his way towards the door to the corridor that led through to his bedroom and en suite bathroom.

'Where are you going?' Elena asked, dashing out of the kitchen to intercept him.

He bristled at her bossy tone. 'I told you, I need a shower.'

'Not on your own. What if you get dizzy and fall?'

'Are you offering to join me?' he asked with a teasing smile, feeling his pulse pick up at the thought of it.

She visibly tensed, then shot him a cool, reproving smile. 'I'll wait in your bedroom, just in case you need me,' she said, turning on the spot and striding away from him, her body language looking a little stiff and awkward now.

He wanted to call after her that he wouldn't need her, that he didn't need anybody, that he was fine on his own. But he had the oddest feeling that that wasn't the case at all.

CHAPTER FOUR

CALEB MANAGED FINE by himself in the shower, despite the sharp pain that shot through his chest every time he moved his left arm. Checking over his body now that he was naked, he was shocked to see how much of it was covered in angry-looking bruises. It made him realise just how lightly he'd got off considering he'd been hit by a motorbike.

Or so he'd been told.

He still couldn't remember a thing about it.

Tamping down on the now familiar swell of unease, he wrapped a towel tightly around his waist and stared at himself in the mirror, tentatively touching the raised bump in his hairline where he'd hit his head. Perhaps all his errant memories were trapped in the bump and when it went down they'd be released back into his brain.

He shook his head at himself, wondering where his normally sane self had disappeared to. He really didn't feel like himself at the moment. There was a strange sense of having lost something heavy from deep within him, as if a weight he'd been carrying around had lifted from his body and was hovering somewhere over his head.

Or perhaps the accident had just knocked all the sense out of him.

Whatever it was, the best thing he could do right now was carry on as normal. There was no way he was letting a slight blip in memory and a small fracture stop him from functioning properly.

Giving his reflection a firm nod, he turned away from the mirror and left the en suite.

He expected to find Elena waiting there for him and was preparing to bat away any help she tried to offer and prove to her he wasn't as frail and vulnerable as she clearly suspected he was, so was surprised—and, if he was honest, a little disappointed—to find the room empty.

The sound of voices floated in through the open bedroom door and he heard the swish and click of the front door closing, then the gentle pad of feet on the hallway tiles as someone walked towards the bedroom.

'Oh, you're out,' Elena said as she emerged in the doorway, her cheeks flushing with colour as she eyed him standing there with just a towel slung around his hips.

He suppressed a smile as she averted her gaze and pretended to be studying a picture on the wall next to her, as if making a point of not staring at his half-naked body.

'Who was at the door?' he asked.

'Benita.'

'What did she want?'

'She brought your mobile phone over, which you'd left on your desk. She thought you'd want it, but I told her you wouldn't be dealing with anything work-related today because you need to rest.' She turned to look at him now, her expression serious. 'I also said that you wouldn't be back in the office for a while.'

'You did, huh? Well, unfortunately, I don't have time to be off work right now.' He held out his hand. 'I'll take the phone.'

When she flashed him an I-don't-think-so expression he added a determined, 'Thank you.'

'Caleb, I really don't think you should—'

'I'm not interested in what you think,' he said, feeling irritation prick at the back of his neck.

But, instead of handing the phone over like most people would have done when he used that tone of voice, she crossed her arms and fixed him with a hard stare.

'There is no way I'm giving you this phone tonight. You need to rest and get a good night's sleep and you're not going to do that if you're worrying about what's going on at work without you. I'm sure you've hired an exceptional team of staff and they're more than capable of handling things there without you for a couple of days.'

He glared at her in disbelief. No one ever talked to him like that and it was rather shocking to have her facing off with him, especially here in his own home. In his own bedroom.

'How do you intend to stop me from taking it from you?' he asked, putting on an amused smile to cover his incredulity.

She didn't even blink. 'By doing this,' she said, lifting open the front of her blouse and sliding the phone down inside the neck, so that it nestled in between her breasts.

He swallowed hard. There was no way he could physically try to take it from her now. Even though he ached to. Very much.

'Cute,' he growled, his frustration coming over loud and clear.

She smiled serenely. 'Someone has to save you from yourself.'

'I don't need saving,' he ground out, folding his arms.

'I beg to differ. I know you, Caleb; you'll work all night tonight to make up for the time you lost in the hospital.'

He frowned. 'How would you know that?'

'Because you regularly worked through the night when we were at university to make up for any time you lost.'

'That sounds like me,' he said slowly, as the unsettling feeling of not remembering his university days bit at his nerves again.

'So I'm staging an intervention. Again.'

'Again? What else have you kept so close to your chest from me?' he asked, raising a suggestive eyebrow.

Her jaw appeared to tighten and she frowned. 'I mean it's not the only time I've had to point out that you work too hard, that's all,' she said, looking a little uncomfortable now.

Despite the fact he could probably have held both of her wrists in one hand and easily retrieved his phone, he could tell from the steely look in her eyes that she wouldn't tolerate such behaviour.

Frustration pinched at him. He was going to have to let her win this one.

'Right, well, now that's settled I'll leave you to get dressed,' Elena said, her mouth twitching at the corner with what looked like suppressed amusement.

She was enjoying ordering him around. Damn her.

As soon as she'd walked away he strode to the door and swung it shut with a little more force than was entirely necessary.

Okay, so he was grateful to her for helping him get out of the hospital, but he had the unsettling feeling he would have been better off staying there if this was the kind of treatment he was going to have to put up with for the next couple of days.

Elena walked out of the room with blood rushing loudly in her ears. She couldn't quite believe she'd just hidden his phone down her top, but it had been obvious he wasn't going to allow himself to rest if she didn't force him to. After an accident like this he needed time to recover and heal. Especially as it appeared his memory still hadn't fully returned—even though he was clearly trying to brush that tiny detail under the carpet.

She was painfully aware that she'd know the moment it all came back to him because she'd probably find herself out on her ear.

Though hopefully that wouldn't happen any time soon.

The phone pressed uncomfortably against her breastbone as she walked away from him and as soon as she reached one of the spare bedrooms she removed it and stuffed it under the mattress at the side of the bed she always slept on. If he came into the room to look for it while she was asleep—just the thought of *that* gave her the jitters—he'd have to lift both her and the mattress up in order to get to it.

Not that she believed for a second he'd actually do that. He was too proud. She had wondered for one panicked moment earlier though whether he'd ignore her insistence that he took the evening off work and stuff his hand down her blouse to grab his phone, but luckily decorum had prevailed. She gave a little shiver. That would have been altogether too much to handle. She'd already been struggling to hold it together in his half-dressed, badly bruised presence, and his touching her like that would have tipped her right over the edge. Into what, she wasn't quite sure. But it was definitely better not to find out.

Flopping back onto the bed, she ran her hand over her eyes, which felt gritty and sore with tiredness. She was exhausted now after all the stress of the day, not to mention the tension she was carrying around with her, worrying about her staff and the fate of her business.

There was a loud rap at the door and she sat up quickly, smoothing her hair away from her face, not wanting Caleb to see any kind of chink in her armour.

He strode into the room, thankfully dressed now in a pair of faded jeans and a casual shirt, which fitted him so well she suspected they must have cost a fortune, despite their lived-in appearance.

'Will you be okay sleeping in here?' he asked, his

eyes scanning the room as if checking for anything that might be wrong with it.

'Yes, thanks, I'll be fine.'

'Okay, well, if you're not going to give me my phone back I'm going to watch TV in the living room for a few minutes, then go to bed. You're welcome to join me—' he shot her a wicked grin '—watching television, I mean.'

'Er...no, thank you. I have a bit of work to catch up on, so I'll stay in here so I don't disturb you,' she said, giving him a strained smile back and trying to ignore the warmth blooming between her thighs at the mere suggestion of sharing his bed. The most disconcerting thing was that she wasn't entirely sure whether he was genuinely flirting with her, or just teasing her to get his own back for her phone-hiding stunt.

She guessed the latter, knowing from experience how much he struggled with not being fully in control of every situation.

'How's your head now?' she asked, keeping her hands folded in her lap so he wouldn't see how nervous she was having him loom over her while she sat on the bed.

'It's fine. I have a low-level headache but pieces of my memory seem to be coming back now.' He looked away from her as a strained expression flitted over his face, proving to her that she'd been right about him trying to hide how unsettled he really felt about it.

She wanted to reach out to him, to somehow soothe away his worry with her touch, but she was acutely aware that it would be entirely inappropriate considering their former relationship.

'I'm sure it'll all come back soon, perhaps after a good rest.'

He nodded, his expression now coolly nonchalant. 'I hope you'll be comfortable in here,' he said brusquely. 'There are some T-shirts in there if you want something to sleep in,' he added, waving towards a wardrobe on the other side of the room.

'Thank you,' she said, touched that he was concerned about her comfort. 'Is there anything I can do for you?' she blurted as he began to turn away from her.

His slow, loaded grin made her insides swoop but she ignored the feeling, continuing to look at him steadily until he shook his head.

'Nothing, Elena. I'm fine. I'll see you in the morning.' And, with that, he turned on the spot and exited the room, leaving his tantalising, clean scent hanging in the air behind him.

Flopping back onto the bed again, she took a deep calming breath, willing her heartbeat to slow down. It was so unnerving, being here in Caleb's house as a guest. She almost didn't want to go to sleep in case she woke up to find him back to the beast of a man she'd encountered this morning in his meeting room.

She'd enjoyed seeing the small flashes of his personality coming through since they'd left the hospital though and part of her ached to join him in the living room and push him to show her some more of them.

But she knew, deep down, that that could be a dangerous game to play.

No, she'd leave her door open to keep an ear out for him in case he needed her, but it was probably best to give him a bit of space now.

After getting washed in the en suite in her room and changing into one of the large, soft cotton T-shirts Caleb had loaned her she slid beneath the sheets and lay listening to the low murmur of the television in the other room, feeling exhaustion dragging at her eyelids until she could no longer keep them open.

She slept fitfully, her dreams punctuated with disturbing images from the accident.

Waking up in the early hours with her heart racing, she had a sudden panic that Caleb might have had a turn for the worse in his sleep and she slipped out of bed to tiptoe silently to his room to check on him. Pushing the door open quietly, she was confused to find his bed empty and looking as though it hadn't been slept in all night.

Where was he? Had he left the apartment without her knowing?

Blood pulsed hard in her head as she moved quickly down the corridor, checking the other rooms, which all appeared to be empty, then ran into the living area, her heartbeat erratic now.

Relief rushed through her as she spotted him lying on the sofa nearest the windows with a laptop perched precariously on his lap, breathing gently, his face smoothed of its usual fierceness in repose.

She stood and watched him sleeping for a while, letting the still and silent darkness envelop her as she tried to get a handle on the intense rush of feelings that cascaded through her.

She'd cared so deeply for him once, had thought at one point that her future would be with him by her side, but then she'd blown it, naïvely choosing the safe—boring, as Caleb had called it—option instead.

Looking at him now, she realised with a surge of emotion that she missed him. So intensely it hurt. Over the intervening years she'd been able to quash the waves of regret she'd experienced in her weaker moments, but she knew now that she still craved the elated, excited way he'd made her feel, like a habit she couldn't kick.

She wasn't here to get him back though, she told herself sternly, forcing herself to unclench her fists as she walked quietly over to where he lay to lift the laptop off his lap so she could take it back to the bedroom with her—just in case he woke up and decided to keep working. It was highly unlikely he'd ever trust her again, not after the way she'd let him down.

He was altogether too proud for that.

But she was determined to make it up to him somehow. Perhaps, if she was lucky, once he was better he'd remember this time they'd spent together and decide it was worth giving their friendship another chance.

Tiptoeing out of the room, she glanced back briefly to where he lay sleeping, his chest rising and falling in a steady rhythm.

All she could do now was hope for the best.

Caleb woke bleary-eyed from such a heavy sleep it took him a few moments to figure out where he was.

As the room came into focus he realised he was lying on the sofa in his living room.

Huh, strange.

Levering himself up to a sitting position, he felt a twinge of pain in his chest and the memory of waking up in the hospital yesterday after an accident came flooding back. As did the baffling appearance of the beautiful woman who had turned up to take care of him. A woman he couldn't remember ever seeing before in his life.

Though he knew her. He *knew* her.

And why did he feel as though there was something more to their friendship?

Feeling his heart rate begin to rise, he forced the perturbing question out of his head for now and turned his attention to what he usually thought about upon waking instead.

His business.

He hadn't intended to work for long last night—just wanting to make sure he hadn't missed anything important whilst he'd been at the hospital—and had brought out the laptop he'd had stashed under the coffee table, feeling a sense of relief that Elena hadn't noticed and confiscated that too. After skimming a number of things that didn't require his urgent attention, the words beginning to blur together in front of his tired eyes, he'd come across a message from Benita that had made him start with worry, causing him to wince with pain as his cracked rib complained.

He'd turned the problem over and over in his mind for a while, desperately trying to keep his attention focused on solving this hiccup, but his tired brain had had other ideas, insistently pulling him into a deep, overpowering sleep.

He was awake now though.

Reaching down onto his lap where he'd left his laptop, he was confused to find it wasn't there. He sat up carefully, mindful of his damaged rib, and felt along the floor next to the sofa, guessing it must have slipped off his knee whilst he was asleep.

'Looking for this?' came a softly chastising voice from the other side of the room and he turned his head to see a woman—Elena—standing there with his computer held between her hands. Her brow was creased and her expression guarded.

'I thought you were going to give your poor brain a rest last night so it had a chance to recover.'

He shrugged and swung his legs off the sofa, then stood up carefully, turning to face her. Twisting his body was not at all comfortable at the moment.

'Like I said, I don't have time to take a break right now.'

She huffed out a sigh. 'Why not?'

He threw up his hands in frustration, wincing at the twinge of pain this caused. 'Because there are things going on that need my immediate attention.'

'Like what?'

Clearly she wasn't going to give up her questioning. He wasn't entirely sure he could trust her with details about his business, but something in him, something he couldn't identify, told him it would be okay to talk to her.

He sighed. 'I need to convince a potential American supplier of my small appliance-sized battery that I'm an easy and reliable person to partner with,' he muttered, folding his arms and rocking back on his heels as he thought about the problem again.

'Apparently he has concerns and is considering backing out of a meeting I've taken great pains to set up while he's over here in Spain. He's supposed to be coming to Araya Industries on the last day of his visit and I'd hoped to persuade him to include one of my rechargeable batteries in their product range.'

Walking over to the kitchen, he opened the fridge and extracted a carton of orange juice, which he held up towards her to ask if she'd like some. When she nodded, he grabbed two glasses and poured them both a good measure of it.

'According to Benita, his PA let slip he'd heard a rumour about me being a difficult man to work with and is considering taking a meeting with one of my competitors instead—who is apparently the stable, patriarchal type that Carter prefers to work with.' He put the carton back into the fridge and slammed the door shut, noticing her jump a little at the forcefulness with which he did this.

Taking a calming breath, he picked up one of the glasses and handed it to her, then grabbed his own and took a long drink from it.

He really needed to keep his cool here if he was going to get on top of this problem. Especially as he was still having a bit of trouble thinking straight after the accident.

'The fact that I don't have a partner, let alone a wife, is troubling to him,' he said, running a hand over his face, trying to wake himself up a bit. 'But if I can convince him I'm a good bet it could be a hugely lucrative deal that would give us a strong foothold in the American market.'

'How are you going to do that? Convince him, I mean,' Elena asked, looking at him from over the rim of her glass.

'I'm going to offer to take him and his wife out for dinner tonight and show them I'm not the ogre they seem to think I am,' he said decisively.

'You're going to meet them on your own?'

He hesitated, thinking about this. 'It's better if I don't make it too business-formal, so I don't think I should take anyone else from the office,' he said slowly. 'It needs to be a more laid-back affair.'

'But you're concerned it might confirm his suspicions about you if you turn up on your own.'

His gaze snapped to hers. How did she seem to know what he was thinking? It was as if she could read his addled mind.

She shrugged a shoulder. 'I know you don't remember, but I run my own manufacturing engineering company in England and I've been in a similar situation before. In my experience it's better to have someone else to make up a four, especially if he's bringing his wife.'

He ran a hand across his jaw, frustration needling him. 'I don't have a girlfriend at the moment and I haven't worked with Benita long enough to build up a convincing rapport with her.'

'No,' Elena said, making it sound as if taking Benita would be the last thing she'd suggest.

'And it would be helpful to have someone who knows something about the industry and how to behave in business meetings already,' he said as an idea began to form in his head.

'That's true, especially as your memory isn't exactly at its best right now.'

'So that only leaves one person,' he said, folding his arms and giving her a pointed stare.

'Who?' she asked, frowning at first, then widening her eyes as she caught on to just what he was suggesting.

'That's right, Elena. *You.*'

CHAPTER FIVE

'*ME?*' ELENA'S HEART leapt into her throat.

Caleb gave her a firm smile, as if the matter had already been decided.

Though, to be fair, she guessed it had.

There was no way she could refuse to help him, of course. For one thing, she couldn't let him go out on his own when his head injury was still an issue, and for another she was keenly aware that this could be the perfect opportunity to atone for the way she'd treated him in their younger years. She could really help him here—do something of substance.

'It's the ideal solution,' he said, nodding sagely.

'How are we going to convince them we're a couple when you don't remember a thing about me though?' she asked, her nerves biting a little.

He waved a hand, dismissing her concern. 'We'll do a cramming session before the meeting.'

She swallowed, feeling tension building in her throat. She was going to have to be careful what she told him if she was going to avoid the small matter of her being his number one enemy.

'Okay, well, I'll need to dash over to the hotel where I'm staying first and fetch my bag so I can change. I'll need something more appropriate to wear to dinner,' she said, gesturing to her now rather crumpled suit.

And she could do with a few minutes on her own to get her head together.

'Which hotel are you staying in?' he asked.

'The Barcelona Gran Mar, near the beach.'

He looked at her long and hard for a moment. 'Okay, I'll come with you. We can walk from here; it's not far.'

Her stomach sank. 'No, you should stay here and rest.'

'I'm fine,' he said in that no-nonsense manner she knew so well. 'Anyway, how are you going to keep your beady eye on me otherwise?'

She sighed and shook her head at his droll expression. The man had an answer for everything. It had been the same when they were younger too.

'Okay, fine, come with me then. Perhaps you can point out some of the famous landmarks on the way. I've not had a chance to see any of them since I arrived.'

She waited while Caleb put in a call to Benita, asking her to get hold of Carter's PA and arrange a dinner meeting for that evening. Once he'd hung up, they shrugged on their jackets and left the apartment, Elena's heart beating at twice its usual speed as she contemplated the idea of spending the whole day with Caleb by her side.

Gaudi's mesmerising art nouveau Casa Milà building was only a couple of streets away from Caleb's apartment, fortuitously in the right direction for her hotel near the Nova Icaria beach, so they strolled past it, Elena admiring the strange, cave-like curves and outlandish quirks of the architecture. The whole building looked as though it had been hand-carved out of an enormous piece of rock by prehistoric man, looking truly anachronistic next to its more modern neighbours.

'He really was a genius,' she said in wonder, gazing up at the breathtaking façade. 'Such a visionary.'

'Unparalleled,' Caleb agreed, using his hand to shield his eyes against the bright glare of the sun as he squinted up at it. 'You know, I'm a little embarrassed to admit this, but I barely notice it's there any more. It's become part of the street furniture to me after all my years living here.'

'That's terrible,' Elena said, frowning up at the building.

'I'm so busy getting from one place to another I forget to look up,' he murmured.

She glanced at him. 'I do the same thing in London,' she said, feeling a little rush of poignancy that their lives had followed such a parallel path, despite the distance between them. 'It's very easy to take beauty for granted,' she added.

'Yes.' He paused then said, 'It's funny, but losing big chunks of my past seems to have brought the present into sharper focus.'

When she looked round at him she experienced a little frisson at the intense way he was looking at her.

'Are you happy with your life?' she blurted, her nerves getting the better of her.

His brow furrowed as he thought about this. 'I'm satisfied with the way my business is growing and I enjoy living in Barcelona.'

There was a heavy pause while she waited for him to continue. 'And, for the purposes of our dinner this evening, I'm very happy with my love life.' He flashed her a wolfish grin, making her tummy flip over.

He gestured for them to start walking again and she fell into step with him as they made their way along the pavement, feeling even more jumpy now than when they'd first started out.

'Speaking of which, I guess we ought to decide how long we've been an item, for the purpose of tonight's charade,' Caleb said, a wry grin turning up the corner of his mouth.

Elena took a breath, feeling her pulse jitter. 'Yes, I guess we should get our story straight. How about we tell them that we met at university but were just friends then, and bumped into each other again a year ago at a business conference and things progressed from there.'

'Dull, but believable, I suppose,' Caleb said with a thoughtful nod.

A coach had parked a little way down the street and as they approached it the pavement suddenly became overrun by a large tour group that filed off to look at the famous building they'd just left.

She felt Caleb slip his arm protectively around her as they began to be jostled by the crowd moving past them and she allowed herself to sink against his strong body for a moment, her heart beginning to race as she breathed in his zesty, familiar scent.

Once they were clear of the crowd he let her go and

she dazedly rubbed at her arm where his hand had gripped her, her skin feeling tingly and sensitive where their bodies had connected.

'You're going to have to get used to me touching you,' Caleb said in a low voice, looking at her arm where she was rubbing it. 'Or they're not going to believe we're a couple.'

Elena swallowed hard, balling her fists. 'Yes, of course. You just took me by surprise then, that's all.'

He looked at her with one eyebrow raised. 'Were you always this jumpy around me?'

'No, no! I'm just a little off balance today. This is all a bit strange, to be honest.' She flashed him a strained smile. 'You have to admit, we've got ourselves into a rather odd situation here.'

She tried not to notice the puzzled look he gave her and strode on confidently, looking deliberately around her, at anything but him, to give her some time to pull herself together.

Good grief, if she couldn't even act normally around him when they were on their own how was she going to manage it when they had an audience tonight?

She needed to get herself into a more relaxed and *friendly* mindset.

A little further on they walked past Gaudi's Sagrada Família, which rose majestically into the sky like a discarded giant elf king's crown.

'It makes me think of something from the *Lord of the Rings*,' Elena said in wonder as she took in the arresting quirkiness of it. 'We spent a whole weekend at university once, working our way through the trilogy of films. I could barely keep my eyes open at the end of it and I dreamt about it intensively for the next few nights.' She glanced at him speculatively. 'Do you remember?'

He shook his head, agitation flashing in his eyes. 'I have no recollection of ever seeing those films.'

Her heart went out to him. It must be so distressing for him to lose so many of his memories—though, now she thought about it, the hard shell she'd witnessed at their initial meeting had definitely softened a little since they'd been gone. Perhaps the absence of deep-seated anger that had driven him for most of his life was finally allowing his true nature to emerge from the dark place where it had been hiding.

'Well, perhaps you should think of it as a good thing,' she said with forced jollity, in an attempt to lighten the sombre atmosphere that seemed to have fallen between them now. 'You get to experience the excitement of watching them afresh. I wish I could do that.'

His eyebrow shot up. 'Losing the first twenty-five years of your life is a high price to pay though, don't you think?'

She shrugged. 'I think it's worth taking every positive you can out of an experience. Even if it is a testing one.'

'You're quite the optimist,' Caleb drawled, raising a derisive eyebrow.

Her skin prickled with annoyance. 'And you're a cynic! Life's too short to dwell on the negative.'

Although perhaps she should learn to take her own advice, she thought wryly, considering how much anxiety she seemed to be carrying around with her at the moment.

Caleb looked taken aback at her outburst, but after a moment his features softened and he let out a low laugh. 'Maybe you're right,' he said. 'I have little enough "life" outside of the business as it is; I guess I should spend it enjoying what I work so hard to have.'

They walked on again in silence for a minute, their arms swinging at their sides.

'To be fair, I'm just as bad about spending too much time working and not enjoying all life has to offer,' Elena said after a while. 'I can regularly spend up to ten hours a day at work and sometimes carry on into the evenings if I need to. I've lost count of the number of parties and get-togethers I've cried off recently. My friends despair of me.'

'You don't go out much?' he asked.

'Not as much as I should. There's no wonder I'm single; my personal life could definitely do with some TLC.'

'Why have you *really* been on your own for so long?' he asked in such a casual tone she felt sure he'd been waiting for the right opportunity to broach that question.

So this was it then—time to be totally honest with him.

'Well, the thing is, I nearly got married some years ago, to a guy called Jimmy,' she said, bracing herself in case the mention of his name jogged Caleb's memory, but he didn't react, just looked at her with interest. 'And I needed some time on my own after the relationship finished to get my head straight and then I got so busy at work I let things drift,' she said.

'Why did you split up with him?' he asked brusquely.

She sighed, feeling the old familiar tug of guilt in her chest. 'I changed my mind about whether he was the right guy for me and called the wedding off at the last minute.'

He blinked, but his expression remained impassive. 'Do you regret it now?'

'No. It was the right decision. It wouldn't have worked out. He was a really nice guy, but being married to Jimmy would have stifled me in the end, killed my spirit.'

Caleb nodded as if he understood exactly what she was talking about.

'I think I felt the same about my ex-fiancée,' he said, surprising her with his direct honesty.

'She was a beautiful woman, incredibly smart and very driven, but there was something missing for me. I thought for a long while that it wouldn't matter, but as soon as we started to talk seriously about arranging the wedding it became apparent it wasn't going to work for me. There was something else wrong too, but I can't remember what it was.' He squeezed his eyes shut as if trying to bring the memory to the fore.

Don't let this be the moment when he remembers everything, she prayed silently—not when they were just starting to get on so well.

'I think my problem's always been that I was brought up by two parents who argued all the time and I found my life growing up incredibly stressful,' she jumped in, hoping to divert his attention back to her story in order to impart the whole sorry tale, just in case she found herself suddenly talking to the pre-accident Caleb—who she was sure wouldn't be quite so interested in her reasons for letting him down so badly in the past.

'They seemed to be on the verge of divorce all the time and I hated it. It made me so anxious I used to lock myself in my bedroom and turn my music up really loud so I didn't have to hear the constant bickering. It made me crave stability, so when I met Jimmy a year before I left for university I thought he was the perfect person to give me what I needed.'

Caleb just looked at her as if to tell her to carry on, so she continued.

'He was such a calm and well-balanced person—the embodiment of a safe, solid future in my mind. Exactly the sort of man I wanted to settle down with. The complete opposite of my dad.'

And you, *Caleb.*

She cleared her throat nervously. 'Somehow the relationship survived through our time at separate universities—with a small blip—' She glanced at him then hurried on, 'And he proposed to me a couple of years after we graduated.'

It was nearing midday now and the sun was out in full force. Elena was beginning to feel increasingly stifled in her suit so she slipped her jacket off, looping it over her arm to carry it instead.

'I thought I wanted a relationship like that at the time, but as it got closer to our wedding day this strange kind of panic engulfed me. I was terrified I was heading for a life of middling satisfaction and settling for someone I didn't feel any true passion for. I loved him, but I realised it was only as a friend.'

And she knew this because she knew what real passion felt like. After meeting Caleb at university her feelings for him had crept up on her, day by day, until she could barely see straight with confusion. She'd wanted him, so much, but the sensible side of her brain had told her that Jimmy was a much better bet for a future partner. Caleb was fierce and impulsive and somewhat wild: the kind of man who scared her with his dominating intensity and passion, not to mention his overwhelming sex appeal.

Something that was still powerfully evident today.

'I hurt Jimmy really badly and I still feel awful about it, but it was for the best. He's fine now. He met someone else and they've just had a little girl. I hear they're getting married next year.'

When she finally turned to look at him again, Caleb was nodding thoughtfully as if he understood where she was coming from.

They'd reached her hotel now, which had views from the city's beach across the sparkling blue of the Balearic Sea.

'It won't take me long to grab my bag; I'm on the first floor.'

To her surprise, he followed her to the lift.

Shrugging off a twist of nerves, she pressed the button and waited for the lift to arrive.

She guessed he was following her mandate to keep him in her sights at all times to the absolute letter.

Typical Caleb.

Once up on her corridor it took her three attempts to make her key card work in her door and she finally stumbled into the room, flushed in the face and her skin prickling with awareness as Caleb followed her inside.

'Okay, I'll just be a minute. I need to grab my things from the bathroom and wardrobe then we can go.'

He just nodded, watching her as she shoved her meagre possessions into her suitcase then strugged to zip it up.

'Here, let me do that,' he said, putting his hands on her shoulders and gently but firmly guiding her out of the way so he could get to the case.

She saw him wince with pain as his cracked rib protested when he bent down and started tugging at the zip.

'Caleb, stop! I can do it.'

Without thinking, she pressed her hand against his chest, feeling the dips and peaks of his muscles shift under her touch as he tensed with surprise.

It suddenly felt too seductive in that small room— the two of them standing so close together, only inches away from the bed. She could feel the heat from his body throbbing against the palm of her hand and his enticing scent flooded her nose, making her senses reel.

When she looked up into his face he was gazing at her with such intensity in his eyes she thought she might melt under the heat of it.

Little shivers of excitement raced over her skin and she drew in a shaky breath, feeling her blood pulse thickly through her veins.

No, no, no, this shouldn't be happening. She shouldn't

be looking at the full firmness of his mouth and thinking how wonderful it would be to feel it on hers again,
or about how much she wanted the comforting strength
of his arms around her, or how she longed for him to
guide her over to the bed and lay her down, trapping
her underneath him so she could experience the feeling
of their bodies pressed closely together.

She shouldn't be wanting all that.

But she was. She was.

Denying herself was almost too much to bear.

But she *had* to.

Withdrawing her hand from where it still lay over
his heart, she forced her mouth into a wobbly smile.

'I don't want you in pain because of me,' she muttered, the tormenting subtext of the words not lost on
her.

He frowned, his eyes dark with confusion.

'Let's get out of here,' she mumbled, turning away
and hurriedly zipping up the final side of the case, not
daring to look at him again in case he saw how much
she ached for him to touch her reflected in her expression.

They didn't say a word to each other as they left
the room and walked side by side down the corridor
and into the lift, the air around them throbbing with a
strange new tension.

Once back on the street, Elena stood blinking in the
bright afternoon sunlight feeling as if they'd moved
into some kind of parallel universe up there in the hotel
room.

'Let's grab a bite to eat from that café on the beach,'

Caleb said, pointing to the place in question, his voice sounding a little rough.

'Okay, sure. I could eat,' Elena said, deciding the best thing to do was just pretend the incident in the hotel had never happened. That was the only way she was possibly going to get through the next twenty-four hours.

After locating a suitable table, she watched him stroll over to the counter and place their order for food and coffee. The woman serving him gave him a coquettish grin and leant forward in a seductive manner to ask him a question and Elena experienced a pinch of jealousy as she saw him return her smile.

She put her hand over her heart where it hurt the most and gave a gentle rub there.

Oh, no.

She was in such trouble.

He returned a minute later, balancing a couple of plates of food in one hand and grasping the handles of two mugs of coffee in the other.

'Here, let me help you,' Elena said, rising to take the plates from him so he could put the mugs down on the table without spilling the hot liquid everywhere.

She was horrified to find her hands were shaking and sat down quickly, placing them in her lap before he noticed.

When she looked up to say thanks for the drink he'd put in front of her she saw he was frowning, as if something was bothering him.

'Did we spend a lot of time together at university?' he asked.

The memory of her and Caleb sharing a bottle of

wine in his room after a study session flitted across her vision, stealing her breath away. It had been on that night that everything had changed between them.

That fateful night, in a drunken haze, when she'd admitted her true feelings for him and he'd dragged her into his arms and kissed her, making her insides melt and her blood fizz with excitement.

Forcing herself to unclench her now sweaty hands, she gave him as composed a smile as she could muster.

'Yes, we were pretty close back then. We were doing the same course so we had a lot in common. Our tutor put us together as partners on a project at the beginning of the first term and found we worked well together.'

The memory of her broken promise to Caleb that she'd return to university after the Christmas holidays a free woman after breaking up with Jimmy, ready to commit her newly unchained heart to him, pressed heavily on her.

Picking up her drink to give her restless hands something to do, she took a tentative sip of the hot liquid.

'So why haven't we seen each other for so long?' Caleb asked, the look in his eyes so searching she choked on her drink.

'Are you okay?' he asked with amusement in his voice as he reached over to pat her gently on the back.

'I'm fine,' she gasped, taking the opportunity to wipe her eyes with the napkin that had come with the sandwich so she didn't need to look at him while she answered.

'I guess life just got in the way. We've both been so focused on our careers.'

When she finally looked up at him again he nodded slowly. 'Tell me more about our time together at university,' he said, giving her the impression that he needed to hear about it to help him understand something.

So she did. She told him about the way they'd met on the first day of term and how grumpy he'd been with her when their tutor had paired them up.

'I was so annoyed with you I gave you a real dressing-down at the end of that lesson. I think I said something about how just because I was a woman it didn't mean I couldn't beat your arrogant arse at engineering.' She smiled at the memory, remembering how it had taken a lot of guts to say that to him, and how proud she was of herself afterwards that she hadn't let him just walk all over her.

He'd been taken aback by her defensiveness at first, but once he realised she meant every word he'd challenged her to a quiz on engineering terms.

'And I won,' she told him, smiling at his raised eyebrow. 'But you were a good loser. You just gave me this respectful kind of nod and then offered to take me to the nearest pub to toast my win. We ended up staying there all night and by the end of it we were firm friends.'

He snorted with laughter, clearly amused by this, though the expression on his face told her he was impressed by what she was telling him.

'We spent a lot of time together after that,' she continued, warming to her theme now, 'and talked about a lot of personal stuff too, especially the things we found tough growing up. Like you being brought up in a single-parent household and being bullied at school, and me living with parents that constantly rowed or sniped at each other. I think we felt a certain kind of affinity with each other after that.'

He continued to look at her with a frown pinching his brow now, but didn't comment. Clearly he had no memory of any of that.

'We liked the same kind of movies too—sci-fi and fantasy,' she said, to fill the silence that had fallen between them.

He nodded in agreement, a relieved sort of smile playing about his mouth as if this made total sense to him.

'Most of our other friends weren't interested in them so we often went to the cinema together to see them and stay up late dissecting them afterwards.' She smiled, trying to hide how sad those memories made her feel now. 'Good times.'

'It sounds like we had fun together,' he murmured, his eyes never leaving hers.

She gazed back at him, remembering how happy they'd both been then, how full of vigour and positivity and excitement for the future—a future she'd hoped would have him in it in some way—and felt her spirits plummet. Would he have been a happier, less angry man today if they'd stayed together then?

'We did,' she said quietly, swallowing past the lump in her throat.

He opened his mouth to ask her something else but, before he could get the words out, his mobile began to ring, mercifully diverting his attention away from her rapidly heating face.

'That was Benita,' he said once he'd concluded the call and put his mobile down on the table. 'She managed to get hold of Carter. He's agreed to meet for dinner tonight and, as we anticipated, he's bringing his wife with him.'

He raised both eyebrows. 'Looks like we're on, girlfriend.'

She covered a resurgence of nerves with a smile. 'Great.'

Once they'd polished off their food, at Elena's request they spent the walk back to his apartment going over any relevant points about Araya Industries that might come up in conversation with the Americans, making sure she was fully briefed—or at least as much as a girlfriend working in the same industry might be.

It was fascinating to hear how he'd chosen to run his business, but Elena experienced a twinge of guilt at being trusted with detailed strategies and projections when Caleb had been so keen not to allow her anywhere near his business operation only the day before.

This was all to help him though, she reminded herself firmly. She wasn't going to take advantage of it at any point.

'So tell me about your business,' he said once they'd covered all the salient points about his.

His question caught her off guard and she stumbled a little, feeling him grab her elbow to right her, and gave him a strained smile.

'Er…well, I run a company in England called Zipabout. We make single-person electric vehicles to be used for short trips around towns and cities.'

He raised his eyebrows with interest. 'And what sort of battery are you using to power them?'

She thought about telling him the truth, somehow bringing the conversation round to the fact she was hoping his company would be the one to supply it, but her conscience wouldn't let her. It would be totally inappropriate to mention it when he didn't remember the row they'd already had about it.

With a sinking heart she said, 'We're looking into that at the moment. I have a few leads.'

Darn, darn, darn! And it could have been such a good opportunity to find out whether he'd be interested in supplying his battery to her without the angst and anger from their past getting in the way. But it was too much of a morally ambiguous move for her to do that.

Caleb was nodding slowly, looking as though he was going to ask something else, and she held her breath, poised to fudge an answer, but, as luck would have it, at that moment his attention was diverted as he looked round to fully take in their surroundings and said, 'We need to take this turn for my apartment.'

It was just the distraction she needed in order to redirect the topic of conversation without it seeming strange.

'So how long have you lived on this street?' she asked, waving her hands around expansively. 'It's a lovely area.'

As they walked out onto his street, with him telling her he'd been here for the last four years and how he came to find it, it suddenly struck her how businesslike the area was. The apartments were large and expensive-looking, but didn't give the impression of being held together by a cohesive community. It was a district for people who liked to live alone within a bustling major city.

It made her spirits sink to think of Caleb like that. But then he'd always been fiercely independent and protective of his personal space and she guessed this was just a grown-up extension of that, she reminded herself.

As soon as they walked into his apartment she excused herself, saying she needed a rest before they went out for dinner, in desperate need of some space away from him in order to regroup before their meeting tonight.

Shutting her bedroom door firmly behind her, she took the opportunity to check her email. Her stomach lurched as she saw a message from her Sales Director asking her how it was going with Caleb and checking whether there was any news about being able to use his battery in their car yet.

Closing the laptop with a snap, she resolved not to look at her messages again until after the meal this evening. She was going to need her wits about her tonight, not only for the sake of Caleb's business but also in order to keep her cool whilst looking as though she was intimately acquainted with the man. He already turned her insides to goo every time he so much as looked at her and if he was going to be touching her all night too she was going to need every ounce of strength she had to remain unflustered and in control. The last thing she wanted was for Caleb to suspect she was enjoying his company as more than a friend.

That was a complication neither of them needed at the moment.

CHAPTER SIX

CALEB TOOK A long shower, feeling energised by the time he'd spent getting to know a bit more about Elena today.

The intense moment they'd shared in the hotel room, where the air had positively crackled between them, had convinced him that there had to have been more between them than just friendship during their time at university.

Judging by her jumpiness around him afterwards, she'd definitely felt the same weight of possibility that had hummed between them as they stood gazing at each other with her hand pressed against his heart.

Having the space to think about it now, he realised he'd been aware of an odd kind of tension between them all day, as if she was trying to suppress something—or hide something, maybe. Had they not taken their relationship further because she'd been seeing that Jimmy guy? Had he, Caleb, been the blip she'd mentioned?

Perhaps this connection he felt had always been there, but even though they were both single now Elena didn't think it appropriate to act on it when he was just out of hospital after the accident.

Well, to hell with that. Why should a bang on the head stop them from exploring this thing between them? He wasn't an invalid. He knew his own mind.

Pulling on a smart shirt and trousers for dinner with a determination to find out whether he was right later, he walked out into the living area to discover Elena was also dressed for their meeting and was waiting for him.

The pale pink dress she had on was beautifully understated but entirely beguiling at the same time. It had a halter top, which tied behind her long, elegant neck and showcased her pale, slender shoulders. He couldn't help but notice how the bodice of the dress dipped in under her full breasts then gently curved against her slender waist, perfectly emphasising her hourglass figure.

Feeling her watching him, he dropped his gaze to look at the skirt instead, which was slim-fitting and narrowed at the knee, making her legs look as if they went on for miles.

Forcing himself to snap his mouth shut and pull his gaze up to her face, he gave her a nod of hello and went into the kitchen to get himself a very cold drink of water.

Right now wasn't the time to explore his theory. He had more immediate things to deal with, in the shape of persuading Jonathan Carter to take his business.

'Will you be ready to go in five minutes?' he asked, placing the glass carefully into the sink with an unsteady hand.

'I'm ready when you are,' she replied, but he could have sworn he saw a flash of concern on her face. Perhaps she was nervous about the charade they were about to embark on. It suddenly occurred to him that every time Elena saw him after a break she seemed a little more tense, as if she was expecting him to do or say something she was afraid of. But why?

He remembered with a jolt that she'd mentioned at the hospital that they'd had a row right before his accident, but in his befuddled state he'd not asked her what it had been about.

'Elena?'

She looked round at him as she went to grab her handbag from the table by the door.

'What did we argue about before my accident?'

Her face seemed to blanch a little.

'Er…' Wrapping her arms around her body, she fixed him with an awkward smile. 'It was an old argument from when we were at university. I don't think it's a good idea for us to talk about it now though. We need to be totally focused on the meeting.' She looked so stricken he decided not to push it any further. Especially when she was doing him such a favour by attending this meeting with him.

But why was she so tense? Perhaps she was still feeling responsible for him being hit by that bike. He wished, not for the first time, that he could remember it.

'Fair enough,' he said, 'but, whatever it was, stop worrying that I'm going to bite your head off every time I see you. We're friends after all.'

'Uh-huh,' she mumbled, not looking at him now.

Walking slowly over to where she stood, he put his hand on her bare arm and felt her quiver under his touch.

She took a quick step away, breaking their contact and folding her arms across her chest.

'We should go. We don't want to be late.'

'Of course,' he said, forcing himself to remain where he was and not touch her again, just to see what she'd do. The urge to provoke more of a reaction was intoxicating.

Grabbing his warm weather overcoat, he slid his arms carefully into the sleeves. He was going to have to be careful not to let Carter see he'd been in an accident or it might serve as another mark against him, especially if the man thought he was in any way mentally incapacitated as well at the moment.

It was funny but refusing to show any physical weakness felt like something he was well acquainted with, but he couldn't quite put his finger on why. It eluded him, like something flittering on the edge of his vision. He knew something important was there, but he couldn't fully grasp what he was looking at.

Damn memory—it was playing havoc with his self-assurance.

But it would all be okay; he'd make sure it was.

As for Elena, he'd get the full story from her eventually, but for now she was right—he needed to keep his head in the game.

The restaurant that Benita had booked them into was on a small, winding side street off the famous grand La Rambla, a tree-lined pedestrian mall in the oldest part of the city.

On Elena's request, the car that Caleb had ordered dropped them in the Plaça de Catalunya, next to the magnificent fountain and the looming Francesc Macià monument—that looked to Elena a bit like an upside-down staircase—so they could soak up the buzzy atmosphere on their way to the restaurant.

They walked together, close but not touching, along the busy street bustling with tourists and locals alike, then detoured down one of the small side streets and through a labyrinth of roads crowded on both sides with a mixture of brightly lit pavement cafés, designer clothes shops and trinket stalls, until they reached the Gothic Quarter, where their final destination was located.

According to Caleb, El Gótico had served its famous fusion of Spanish and Mediterranean fare for the past ten years and was a favourite with Barcelonans, as well as the handful of tourists that occasionally stumbled across it.

The décor was a mixture of warm, earthy colours with rustic wooden furniture and a tiled terracotta floor which contrasted sharply with the angular metal and glass of the staircase and bar. Bright splashes of primary colours were picked out on the back wall, which were also reflected in the small lamps and glass water carafes on each table, giving the place the impression of chic modernism. The whole effect was both comforting and uplifting.

The delicious smell of the place wrapped around Elena's senses, making her mouth water as they made their way to the bar, where the greeter stood waiting to welcome them.

Caleb spoke to the woman in rapid Spanish and a

moment later they were whisked towards the staircase leading to the upper mezzanine of the restaurant, which had a long glass balcony affording diners views of the lamplit tables below.

Just as he was about to mount the stairs, Elena put her hand on Caleb's arm to stop him. She wanted to make sure they made the most of this opportunity to charm the Americans and for that to happen Caleb was going to have to rein in his more dominating side for a while.

'I'm sure I don't need to say this, but go easy on the man tonight, okay? Just until everyone's had a chance to find their feet here.'

Caleb's eyebrow shot up. 'You think I'm going to dangle him from the balcony if he doesn't agree to a partnership?'

She batted a hand at him, suppressing a smile. 'No, of course not. But I know you; you'll want to go in all guns blazing. I recommend a lighter touch. If he's here with his wife he's not going to take too kindly to being bullied and harangued.'

'I wouldn't—'

She put up a hand to pre-empt his angry rebuttal. 'Not intentionally, I know, but you can come across as a little bit abrasive and intimidating until someone gets to know you. Show him a bit of your soft side too, that's my advice.'

Caleb blinked at her, his brows drawn into a tight frown as he appeared to consider what she'd said. After a moment he nodded slowly, his frustrated expression clearing and being replaced with a wolfish grin. There was something else in his eyes too that made her tummy flip and her blood begin to race. She stared at his mouth, wondering erratically how she would react if he leant forwards and kissed her right now.

'Okay, I'll be nice,' he murmured.

Shoving away her lustful urges, she nodded. 'Good.' She let out a gasp of surprise as he suddenly slipped his hand around her back and drew her closer to him.

'Just relax, *cariño*. You seem tense and that's going to look strange to our guests.'

Swallowing hard, she gave him a jerky nod, her heart banging hard against her chest and her nerves jangling due to their intimate proximity.

'Perhaps I should practice my soft side on you before they get here,' he murmured, his dark eyes boring into hers.

'How are you going to do that?' she asked, but before she could draw breath he leant in towards her and brushed his mouth against hers.

Fireworks seemed to go off deep inside her body and she wondered wildly for a second how the other diners would react if she suddenly burst into flames in front of them.

Caleb's lips were warm and firm, his mouth fitting perfectly with hers. She stood frozen to the spot, too befuddled to react, as a crazy surge of desire unfolded deep inside her, spiralling out to the very ends of her fingers and toes.

His hands slid into her hair and instinctively she sank against him, her body craving the hard press of his against it.

A moment later she was left gasping for air when he drew away from her, giving her a strange knowing kind of smile and nodding towards the upper mezzanine, his arm pressing into her back as he encouraged her to mount the staircase with him.

'Let's go and find our seats, ready for the show,' he murmured into her ear, his breath tickling the sensitive skin on her exposed neck and making her shiver with longing.

Oh, goodness, it was going to be impossible to keep her cool if he was going to be this physically attentive all evening.

Somehow she managed to make it up the stairs on rather wobbly legs and had just settled herself into a chair that Caleb held out for her when Carter and his wife arrived and she had to stand up again to greet them.

In a fit of continued nerves at Caleb's proximity, Elena managed to knock her knife onto the floor, which then skidded under the table, causing a flurry of amused response as they all tried to locate it so she could retrieve it, apologising profusely as she did so, which fortuitously broke what could have been an icy start to the meeting.

There was something so healthy and vibrant about the couple, Elena thought dazedly as she smiled a more composed hello to them once she'd straightened up after her little mishap. She guessed that was what people who had incredible wealth and an inclination to take care of themselves looked like—polished and dauntingly self-assured. They put Elena in mind of a high-powered couple from the eighties' American soap operas she used to watch for guilty pleasure late at night during her university days.

Mrs Carter, who must have been in her early fifties, wore a flattering shift dress with wide shoulders and her hair was so coiffed it looked as though every strand had been sprayed separately into place. Mr Carter, who looked to be of a similar age, was just as polished in a dark grey double-breasted suit and blindingly white shirt to match his blindingly white teeth.

Caleb took the lead by holding out his hand for them to shake and introducing Elena as his girlfriend—which only added to the fluttering sensation in the pit of her stomach—then gesturing for them all to take a seat.

The atmosphere was a little awkward at first; Mr Carter appeared to be on the defensive, as if waiting for Caleb to become angry about the fact he was considering walking away from the partnership they'd been discussing, but after a few minutes of attentive questions from Caleb about how he and his wife liked Barcelona and being given a few pointers on the places they must visit whilst here, he appeared to relax a little.

The waiter came over and they ordered a bottle of local wine and a selection of food for the table on Caleb's recommendation and the conversation turned to business.

At first Elena sat back, drinking her wine a little too fast and watching Caleb lead the discussion with something close to awe. She found his clear handle on the market and technical, as well as fiscal, knowledge truly breathtaking and he seemed to be impressing Carter too, because the man was actually sitting back in his seat now and had taken his hand off his wife's lap, where they'd been holding hands.

Putting down her glass, Elena gave the woman a smile and was rewarded with a genuinely warm grin back.

'So how long have you two been together?' Brie Carter asked her with an inquisitive glint in her eye as the two men expounded on the state of the recharge-able battery market in the States.

Elena's stomach lurched. 'Er…well, we've known each other since we met at Cambridge. Caleb was doing an Erasmus exchange year and we became good friends.'

'And that turned into more, I see,' Brie said with a hint of a plea for some juicy gossip to break up the work talk.

Elena glanced at Caleb to check whether he was lis-tening, but he seemed to be deep in conversation with Jonathan Carter. Taking another large gulp of her wine and feeling its warming effect steady her nerves, she leant forward in her chair and said, 'To be honest, it was a love-hate relationship for a long while, but we met again recently and worked things out and we're a strong couple now.'

'I guess that's what makes powerful men so exciting to be with,' Brie said with a glimmer of recognition in her eyes. 'The unpredictability of them.'

Elena smiled. 'Yes, I've always had trouble working Caleb out. He keeps his emotions close to his chest and can come across as a bit of a prickly character, but he's actually an intensely kind, passionate and caring man.'

It wasn't just the alcohol warming her veins now, but also the recognition of the truth in her words. She'd never met anyone else like Caleb and she suspected she never would again. He was one of a kind.

'That's good to hear,' Brie said with a thoughtful nod.

Sensing an advantage in convincing Carter's wife about Caleb's suitability for a working relationship with her husband, she took the opportunity to endorse him some more.

'He's the most brilliant, focused and hard-working person I've ever met and he'll be the best business partner your husband's ever had,' she said, throwing the older woman a conspiratorial smile. 'He never fails to excite and inspire me, both in a business sense and on a personal level. Always has.'

She felt Caleb shift next to her as he slid his arm across her back to rest gently on her shoulders. She nearly jumped out of her seat as she felt his fingers brush against the exposed skin of her upper arm, sending little electric currents rushing across her nerve endings. Turning her head, she saw he was looking at her with that dark intensity in his gaze again and her cheeks flooded with heat as panic rose in her chest. Had he heard what she'd just said about him?

If so, did he realise she was telling the truth and not just putting on an act for the Americans?

But his expression gave nothing away, his attention seemingly focused on the complex business discussion he was involved in as he asked her to qualify an answer to something about the market for rechargeable batteries in the UK. She forced herself to relax her rigid posture and answer as clearly and succinctly as possible while her pulse raced and her palms grew hot with worry that he'd overheard her gushing admiration of him.

But when she'd finished he nodded his thanks, removed his arm and turned back to Carter, as if he'd not noticed a thing.

It seemed he hadn't heard what she'd said about him and he was just playing the part of attentive boyfriend.

Thank goodness.

It could put them both in a really difficult position if he knew how she really felt about him, especially as their relationship was such a tangled mess. Her stomach lurched as she allowed herself to consider how it might feel to pursue a real relationship with him. It was a disconcerting yet also unnervingly exciting idea, but she'd be a fool to even entertain it. She'd come to Barcelona in the hopes of being his partner in business only—which, of course, she'd thoroughly messed up—and to hope, even for a second, that anything of a romantic nature might develop with Caleb now, when he couldn't remember what had happened between them, was completely reprehensible.

Pushing the notion to the back of her mind, she made sure to keep the conversation focused on Brie after that and they spent the rest of the meal chatting happily about her daughters and the wedding that she was helping to plan, which was taking place in Boston that August.

Elena tried her best to concentrate on what Brie was

saying but she couldn't help but tune in to what Caleb and Jonathan were discussing, especially when their voices became more animated. Thankfully, it seemed it was just friendly rivalry, and the two men became more and more relaxed with each other as more wine was consumed and the evening wore on.

Despite her worry about Caleb struggling due to his head injury, he'd coped admirably with the questions that Carter fired at him. It seemed he'd done it; he'd kept his cool and turned the American's opinion of him around. In fact, to Elena's delight and relief, he appeared to have returned to the man she remembered knowing all those years ago at university.

The idea of it made her heart flutter.

She'd become increasingly aware of him sitting only inches away from her throughout the end of the meal, his heady, clean scent in her nose and the heat from his body warming her side, so it was something of a relief to her addled senses when Jonathan pronounced it time for them to go back to their hotel.

The four of them stood and the two men shook hands firmly, Carter's initial wariness nowhere to be seen now as he clapped Caleb jovially on the back.

'Good to meet you, Caleb. I'll get my team to contact you about moving forward with this partnership as soon as we get back to the States.'

Brie leaned in to give Elena an elegant air-kiss near each cheek, then drew her close on the pretext of giving her a hug to whisper in her ear. 'It's wonderful to see how Caleb inspires such genuine loyalty in you. I can tell by the way you look at him how much you care about him.'

She drew back to look Elena in the eye. 'It's heartening to see, especially after the rumours we've heard about what a hard character he is to get on with,' she murmured. 'But, after meeting the two of you tonight, I sincerely think my husband's going to find working with him a positive experience.'

Jonathan Carter turned from listening to Caleb's assurances he'd be primed for the next point of contact to give Elena a dazzling smile. 'It was wonderful to meet you too, Elena. Caleb here's a lucky man.' He slapped Caleb on the back again and Elena had to hide her frown of concern when she noticed him wincing in pain from his injured rib.

'Thank you for preventing my wife from dying of boredom with all our business talk,' Carter went on, not seeming to notice Caleb's physical discomfort. 'It looked like the two of you had a lot in common, no doubt swapping tales about the two of us!' he boomed, gesturing between himself and Caleb, then sliding his arm around his wife's waist and giving her a hard squeeze which made her gasp and slap him gently on the chest in retaliation.

Elena's breath caught in her throat as she felt Caleb slide his arm around her waist and pull her closer to him, as if wanting to mirror the American's loving behaviour.

As part of the act, Elena reminded herself fuzzily.

Heart thumping in her throat, she watched the couple as they weaved away through the tables towards the stairs leading to the ground floor, then carefully extricated herself from Caleb's hold on the pretence of grabbing her jacket from the back of her chair.

'Well, that went well, I think,' she said, looking up into Caleb's face to find him frowning, as if perplexed about something.

Because she'd moved away from him so deliberately? Probably.

She felt pretty sure he wasn't used to women rejecting his touch.

It made her wonder again whether he'd heard her gushing praise of him.

'You did a great job, Caleb; it sounds like a partnership is in the bag,' she said, shrugging her jacket on awkwardly. She couldn't quite look him in the eye now. Not after she'd seen the way he was looking at her a moment ago.

As much as she wanted him to know she was sorry for the way she'd treated him in the past and wanted to make amends, she also didn't want to give him the wrong impression here tonight.

She needed to be more careful.

'Yes, he seemed to be on board,' Caleb said, his voice a low, seductive rumble that sent a shiver of unwelcome longing down her spine.

'Shall we go?' she asked, her voice sounding prim and strained as she overcompensated for her body's inappropriate reaction.

'Sure. Lead the way,' he said, gesturing for her to leave first, with a somewhat unnerving glint in his eyes.

* * *

As they walked away from the Gothic quarter, Caleb finally allowed himself to think about what he'd overheard Elena saying to Carter's wife about him.

She could have just been playing the game of being his lover, of course, but there had been something in the way she'd said it that had made his breath catch in his throat. Clearly she'd thought he wasn't listening because when he'd turned to catch her eye she'd looked almost—shifty.

So there *was* something more than friendship between them, just as he'd suspected. But if that was the case, why was she pretending that there wasn't?

He had no idea.

What he did know was that he was going to make sure to find out before she left for England and do everything in his power to smooth things over with her.

The kiss they'd shared before Carter and his wife had arrived had made his body hum with tension all evening. When he'd seen the look of concern on her face he'd wanted to do something to reassure her he was going to do whatever it took to win the Americans over, but as soon as his mouth had met hers he'd been lost in a great surge of hunger for her. The sounds and sights of the restaurant had faded away until all he was aware of was the gentle sway and press of Elena's body against his and the sweet, exotic fragrance of her. Her mouth had felt so good against his it had taken a monumental effort to drag himself away from her and not grab her hand and run with her out of the restaurant and jump into the next cab to take them home.

After that, watching her charming Carter's wife and dazzling the couple with her wit, intelligence and profound beauty—he'd found it almost impossible to keep his mind solely on the business conversation.

Throughout the entire evening he'd been intensely aware of the connection between them, taut and alive, as if it was a tangible thing drawing them ever closer together.

He wanted to know more about what was going on between them—*had* to know, for the sake of his sanity.

Yes, he assured himself, he wasn't going to let her go until he'd got the full measure of Elena Jones.

CHAPTER SEVEN

THE CAR PICKED them up a couple of streets away from the restaurant and took them straight home to Caleb's apartment, the two of them sitting in a buzzing, tension-filled silence as they looked out at the wide city streets flashing by.

'You were great tonight,' Caleb said after his driver had pulled up outside his building and he'd helped Elena out of the car, feeling her cool, small hand in his and marvelling at how good it felt to have it there. 'Carter's wife really seemed to like you.'

She flashed him an equable smile as she straightened up. 'I liked her; she was a really lovely woman, very focused on her family.'

'Well, I owe you big for what you did for me tonight.'

There was a loaded moment where they stood and looked at each other, the gentle, far-off sounds of the city at night making him feel as though they were trapped in a bubble together. Caleb broke the strange energy by smiling and saying, 'Anyway, thanks, Elena. I really appreciate your help.'

She shuffled a little on the spot and nodded, her

bright eyes gleaming in the light thrown out from the streetlight above them.

'It was my pleasure. Anything for a friend.'

The emphasis she put on the word 'friend' made him bristle.

It suddenly struck him that by tomorrow her forty-eight hours of observation of him would be up and she might well leave and return to England.

And he found he really didn't want her to go.

He wondered where this intense need to keep her here longer had sprung from. Okay, he found her really attractive and was impressed with her business acumen and how smart and savvy she was, but he never normally felt this sort of draw to a woman.

There was something different about her, something *compulsive*.

He had to explore what this thing was between them, or it would haunt him for ever.

Turning back to look into her hooded eyes, he was intrigued to see she seemed to be having her own non-verbal debate with herself. Was she only holding back because she thought he was still incapacitated? *Weak?* Frustration surged through him. Well, he wasn't. He was completely in his right mind and he knew damn well what he wanted—her, and now.

Pulling his key card out of his pocket, he let them into his building and they stepped into the lift that would take them up to his apartment, Elena swaying gently in her heels beside him.

Being around her felt *right*, dammit—as if she were a missing link in his life.

And he was going to do whatever it took to have her back in it.

'Elena?' he said, turning to face her once the lift had begun its smooth ascent.

'I know what happened between us at university. I know we were more than just friends. And I know we didn't act on it because of Jimmy.'

Elena swallowed hard as blood rushed to her head and her stomach did a backflip.

His memory had finally returned.

'You remember?' she whispered through lips that would barely form the words.

He nodded, his beautiful mouth curving into another of its wolfish, dangerous smiles.

The lift came to an abrupt stop, making her stomach do an extra flip for good measure. She could barely breathe with worry about what he was going to say now he remembered what had happened all those years ago. Would he be angry with her? Shout and swear at her, or just be coldly dismissive again?

Her pulse throbbed in her head. She really hoped he wouldn't go ballistic and chuck her out on the street now, not after what they'd just been through together. Not now she'd finally met the real Caleb again. She couldn't bear it.

The door of the lift swished open and he strode out and straight over to his door without another word, slipping the key into the lock then holding the door open for her to walk through it.

She strode into his apartment with her head held resolutely high, determined to keep her cool, to restate her case and hopefully prove to him once and for all that she was sorry about how their relationship had ended.

Her heart hammered in her chest as she watched him shrug off his jacket and hang it up before finally turning back to face her.

His expression was impassive as his dark gaze bored into hers.

'We've wasted a lot of time leading our separate lives and I think it's time to remedy that.'

She stared at him in shock. Had she misheard? It sounded as though he was talking about pursuing more than friendship with her. 'I'm sorry?' she stuttered, aware that her hands had begun to shake at her sides.

'What happened was a long time ago, and we're both free and single now,' he continued, apparently oblivious to her befuddlement. 'Without anything standing in our way. No partners, no memory loss—'

'Do you remember everything that happened between us?' she asked, her voice sounding shaky with anticipation and hope.

There was a flash of something in his eyes, remembered pain perhaps, but it quickly disappeared. 'Yes.'

'And you forgive me for it?'

He took a deliberate pace towards her and raised his hand to touch her face, smoothing the backs of his long fingers gently over her cheek.

'I'm not going to let some stupid argument from the past get in the way of what we have here—right now. We're good together, you and I. We fit.'

'Caleb—are you sure?' Her voice came out as a low

breath of air as sensation rushed over her skin at his touch. Had she really done it? Made up for the hurt she'd caused him in the past? Her spirits soared as the heavy weight of guilt began to lift and she finally felt as though she could breathe properly again.

'Yes, I'm sure,' he said with a conviction she felt deep in her chest.

Letting out a breathy laugh, she said, 'This is all happening so quickly. I don't know what to think—'

'I understand why you might be unsure about restarting something between us,' he murmured, cutting her off. 'We live in different cities, live different lives, but we can work around that.'

She swallowed hard, her thoughts spinning wildly. Could she finally be about to get her Caleb back?

'This would make me happy and I think it would make you happy too—you and me, here together, tonight.' His mouth curved into a seductive smile, making her insides quiver and her heart leap about in her chest.

Heat rose to her face as a strange sort of panic settled in her stomach. Was she ready for this? After all this time, regretting what had happened between them and hoping, wishing she could do something to make it better—that she could go back in time and do it all differently—now that she was actually here in the moment, a moment where her whole life could change, she was afraid. Terrified.

What if it all went wrong again?

'It seems too soon to be jumping into something, especially after your accident—' she hedged.

He shrugged away her concern. 'I'm fine now. You

don't need to worry about me any more.' He moved even closer, making the air crackle around her. 'And I thought you were the one who liked to take every positive out of a situation.'

There was no comeback for that.

'I *know* you, Elena.'

'You do?' she asked breathlessly.

'Yes. And I know we still want the same thing.'

The look of desire in his eyes made her whole body shiver with longing.

'And what's that?' she said, knowing exactly what he was going to say, but hoping he wouldn't because then she'd have to make a really difficult decision.

'That you still want me as much as I want you.'

He was so close now, the feel of his soft breath on her skin making her lips tingle with the craving to feel his mouth on hers again. Somewhere in the back of her mind she was aware that she should stop this, draw away and be the sensible one, insist they talk about all that had happened between them first, point out that it was too soon for them to fall into bed together. That she didn't think it was a good idea.

But that would have been a lie. And she wasn't going to lie to him any more.

So instead she said, 'Yes, I want you.'

Before she could qualify that with 'but I still don't know if it's a good idea *right now*' he'd closed the tiny gap between them and pressed his mouth hard to hers.

Her body responded without conscious thought, her lips opening against his to allow his tongue to dip into her mouth, tasting her, possessing her.

Being careful not to crush his broken rib, she pressed herself against him and felt his arms slip tightly around her back, holding her close to him. His strength enveloped her, making her senses reel with pleasure, and she stumbled backwards as he moved forwards, guiding her gently but purposefully towards the corridor where his empty bedroom waited for them.

They reached the bed in a tangle of limbs, with her grabbing at his clothes with a frenzy and a need that took her by surprise.

Elena had never felt so wanted, so worshipped, as Caleb tugged his shirt over his head, not seeming to care that he was ripping buttons off in his haste. She almost stopped when she heard him grunt as his broken rib must have twanged with pain but, before she could say a word, he shook his head and said, 'I'm fine,' grasping the straps tied behind her head to release the halter neck of her dress then tug at the zip so the silky material fell open and glided down to pool at her feet.

'So beautiful,' he muttered as he bent to kiss her again, sliding his hands down her back, tracing the lines of her body with his fingertips and sending her into raptures of ecstasy. Just the feel of his hands on her was enough to make her shudder with joy.

'There's nothing like making up for lost time,' he murmured against her mouth and all she could do was smile and nod in agreement, her brain too fuzzy with lust to help her form anything like intelligible words.

He guided her gently backwards until her legs hit the side of the bed, but she knew she'd have to be the one to lead this because of his injury, so she wrapped her hands around his arms and steered him round so the bed was behind him instead and used the momentum of him being slightly off balance to make him first sit, then lie down.

Then she climbed carefully on top of him, kissing him hard and covetously, the sense of finally being allowed to have him back after all these years of yearning for it making her frantic and greedy.

And some time shortly after that her brain shut down completely and all that was left was the feel of their two bodies moving together and sweet, sweet fulfilment.

The next morning Elena woke to find sun pouring in through the large warehouse-sized windows of Caleb's bedroom.

Blinking blearily, it took her a moment for the events of the night before to rush back to her—and remember exactly what had happened between them.

She'd slept with Caleb.

And it had been amazing.

In the heat of the moment, with his mouth on hers and his body pressed so close they'd almost become one, she'd completely lost herself in him, hazily justifying her easy capitulation by telling herself she owed him some happiness, though in truth she knew deep down she'd done it for her own purely selfish reasons. She'd wanted him so much it had caused her physical pain to imagine tearing herself away from him and stopping it.

And it had been such an incredible night, so full of passion and pleasure.

But it all felt like a surreal dream now.

Turning to look at Caleb lying next to her, she felt her insides flutter and heat with pleasure.

In truth, she was still confused about his sudden change in attitude towards her, especially after he'd been so vociferous at their first meeting about not wanting to have anything to do with her again, but she guessed that after helping him turn Carter's opinion of him around he must have felt she'd paid her dues.

Not that she'd done it for that reason alone. She'd wanted him to be successful with the meeting; she could sense how much it meant to him to win the partnership deal and keep his business thriving—the company he'd worked so hard to build from nothing, just like she had with hers. She wanted him to be happy. To be the man she remembered again.

Trying not to think about how precarious the future of her own company still was, she watched him for a while, his eyelids flickering gently in REM sleep and his wide brow smooth now without his regulation frown creasing it.

She'd been happy too last night, happier than she could remember being in a very long time. Because of him. The guilt and regret that had followed her around for so long that it had felt like an intrinsic part of her seemed to have vanished, leaving a strange, yearning ache in its wake. One she hoped to satisfy with something new and positive and exciting.

A relationship with Caleb, perhaps.

Pushing away a strange nervous sensation in her chest, she slid out of bed and went into his en suite bathroom to take a quick shower, lathering herself all over with his zesty-smelling body wash.

The way he'd looked at her last night when they'd arrived back in his apartment had shaken her to her core. There had been such heat in his eyes, a little like the carnal ferocity she'd seen during their first meeting, although this time it had been driven by desire rather than anger.

He'd looked at her like that before—the night she'd told him how she really felt about him at university—and the impression it had left on her had stayed with her for the rest of her life.

That feeling of being so coveted, so *wanted* was a hard one to forget. She'd craved it over the years, desperately trying to find a way to feel like that again, but she'd not been successful.

Until now.

She knew she was being reckless here, jumping into something so intense with him so quickly, but she was sick and tired of being sensible. It had brought her nothing but pain and stress in the past and it was high time she started being brave and taking some risks with her heart. Otherwise her life would only ever be half lived and what a waste that would be.

After drying herself, she pulled on an oversized towelling robe that she found on the back of the door and padded quietly back over to the bed.

He was lying on his side facing away from her, towards the wall, apparently still asleep if his regular breathing pattern was anything to go by. Moving to stand by his side of the bed, she looked down at him, at his strong, arresting face, with his usually neatly swept back dark hair mussed and falling over his forehead, making him look younger and less fierce.

She jumped in shock as his eyes sprang open and he grabbed for her, wrapping his arm around her legs and pulling her roughly towards him so she lost her balance and toppled onto him with a squeal of surprise. He kissed her hard before rolling her over, so he was on top now, his brow momentarily pinched as he remembered his damaged rib.

'What are you doing, you maniac?' she spluttered, laughing at his self-reproachful grimace.

'Just saying good morning,' he replied, flashing her a grin before he kissed her again so thoroughly it made her toes curl.

'Well, okay then,' she purred, cupping his jaw in her hands, her whole body buzzing with the joy of finding herself in his arms again. 'I'm so glad we're friends again.'

He frowned, looking a little perplexed. 'Friends? Do you do this with all of your friends?' he asked, nuzzling her neck and placing soft, sensuous kisses against her hyper-sensitised skin.

She laughed, then sighed, running her hands into his bedhead hair. 'No, just you.'

Pulling back, he looked straight into her eyes, his gaze unflinching and determined.

'I know you don't need to be here with me any more, but I want you to stay for a bit longer. We should go to Gaudi's Park Güell today. It's an amazing place. I'd like to show it to you.'

'I don't know, Caleb; perhaps you should rest today—'

He held up a hand to cut her off. 'You can't come all the way to Barcelona and not visit all the places of interest.'

'Places of interest? You sound like a tour guide,' she said with a tease in her tone.

'There's no one better than a resident to show you all the best bits of a city,' he said with a seductive lift of his eyebrow. 'I know all its secrets,' he murmured, lifting his hand to trace the line of her jaw and sending little currents of sensation down her throat, which joined with the ones already humming deep inside her body.

She gave him a dazed sort of smile, barely able to concentrate as he slid the backs of his fingers down her throat, then lower to skim over the swell of her breasts.

'Well, that would be…really…amazing…' she murmured, her voice coming out broken and husky as she struggled to concentrate on forming the words.

Lust twisted her insides as he leant forwards and kissed her hard again. She responded instinctively to his touch, sliding her arms around his back and wriggling closer to him.

Pulling her underneath his strong, hard body, he murmured, 'Okay, but we'll go later. Much, much later.'

They spent the rest of the morning in bed, only getting out of it for a minute to fetch some food from his fridge for lunch, which they ate right there, sitting naked on top of the covers.

'This reminds me of all those meals we ate sitting on

my bed whilst working on our project at uni—though of course we were fully clothed for those,' Elena said, grinning at him with one eyebrow raised. 'I found breadcrumbs in my sheets for days after that. Who knows where we'll find them after this.'

She laughed and he smiled back at her, wishing he could remember the time she was reminiscing about. It was getting harder and harder to pretend he knew the stories she relayed without it seeming suspicious that he didn't bring up some of his own recollections.

He felt a little guilty about lying to her last night, but he'd been so sick of her holding back and wasting time when it had been so clear they were destined to end up like this anyway.

Anyway, she seemed much happier now, and if she was happy then so was he.

After they'd finished eating she left the room and returned a few minutes later in a pair of jeans and a loose-fitting, soft pink T-shirt with her hair scraped back into a ponytail, her lips shiny with some kind of clear lipstick that he wanted to kiss off immediately. She didn't need make-up; she was just as beautiful without it.

'Come on, lazybones, get your carcass out of bed. I thought you were going to show me some of your secrets,' she said, giving him a wide grin.

He rolled out of bed with a grunt and stood up. Pulling her towards him, he kissed her until she squealed with pleasure, but she pushed him away when he began to drag her back towards the bed.

'No, no, you said we should go out and I think you're right; we can't spend all day in bed.'

'Why not?' he murmured, thinking it would be more than okay with him. He couldn't get enough of her—the scent of her soft skin, the feel of her strong legs wrapped around him, the little breathy moans she made in his ear as they moved together...

'Caleb, seriously, get dressed so we can go out.'

He shot her a grimace of annoyance. 'Okay, okay, but it won't be as much fun as staying here,' he ground out. 'I have plenty more secrets I could show you right here in the bedroom.'

'Later,' she said with laughter in her voice.

He loved it when she smiled like that—like she couldn't have stopped herself even if she'd wanted to.

He took her to Palo Alto, an enclosed old manufacturing complex situated a few roads back from the beach, which was like a hidden island of industrial-style buildings festooned with brightly coloured creepers and greenery that had turned it into a wonderful garden oasis. The buildings had all been converted over the years into light, open workshops for businesses focused on regeneration and rehabilitation of the city and beyond.

'No tourists know about it, only the residents of the city,' Caleb told her as they walked through the alleyways between the buildings, soaking up the effervescent but peaceful air of the place. 'I love wandering around here; I find it a really inspiring place to be. You know, Araya Industries started out in one of these workshops so it'll always be a special place for me. It's where I realised my dreams.'

'It's wonderful. Thank you for trusting me—an outsider—' she winked at him '—to see it. I'm honoured,' she said, turning to kiss him next to a cascade of fuchsia flowers and russet-coloured leaves.

Then afterwards, at Elena's request, they took a cab out to the spectacular multicoloured Park Güell, which had been designed by Gaudi. He watched her run her hand along the top of the wave-shaped benches that had been decorated with millions of pieces of brightly patterned broken tiles, enjoying her delight at the eccentricity of the design.

After sitting for a while, looking out over the picturesque views of the city and the fairy tale–style gatehouses that looked as if they could be made from gingerbread and icing, they went down the steps to see the forest of Greek Doric columns underneath, which had been designed to house an old marketplace beneath the plateau of the park.

He watched her as she wound her way through the pillars, tracing her fingers over the smooth stone and gazing up at the colourful cornices on the ceiling, and it hit him that for the first time since he'd seen her in that hospital room she looked truly relaxed.

The idea that he could be responsible for that made him feel heady with pleasure, as if he could deal with anything life threw at him right now, as long as Elena was here with him. She made him feel light and positive, buzzed and excited…and what was that other sensation…?

Happy.

His breath caught in his throat as the word pierced through him.

It was a feeling that had been missing from his life for far too long now. And Elena was the catalyst—because he knew without a doubt that she was his ideal woman—smart, sexy and so beautiful it made his chest ache to look at her.

And then, out of nowhere, something strange happened.

A memory flashed through his mind: of Elena's face, cold and hard with indifference, just before she slammed a door in his face.

It left him winded, gasping to drag air into his lungs again, his head swimming and thick, as though too heavy for his body to hold up. A slow trickle of horror-tinged despair slid sickeningly through him and he had to lean against the nearest pillar to stop himself from sliding to the floor.

A moment later the real Elena was there next to him, her hands on his shoulders and a look of deep concern on her beautiful face.

'Caleb! Are you okay?'

The face that looked into his now was so different from the one his mind had conjured up a moment ago he felt relief flood through him. Had it just been his subconscious warning him not to get too carried away with what was developing between them? Not to get too close in case it went wrong like all his other relationships had over the last few years?

Well, to hell with that. He wasn't going to let her get

away because he was afraid of this thing between them failing. He wouldn't let it.

'I'm fine,' he said, forcing his mouth into a reassuring smile. 'My rib's just giving me a bit of pain, that's all.'

She nodded, still frowning. 'Okay, then let's get out of here. You're probably pushing yourself too hard.'

'I'm fine, Elena,' he growled, annoyed at her fussing around him, not wanting this one small blip to ruin the wonderful day they'd been having.

She seemed to sense the agitation with himself behind his snappiness because she gave him a knowing smile and said, 'Okay, then let's go and get something to eat. I don't know about you but I could eat a horse right now.'

He nodded his agreement, grateful to her for not making a big scene. He didn't want the remainder of their time together marred by his minor ailments.

Pulling her towards him, he placed a firm kiss on her mouth, wanting to prove to her how happy he was to have her here with him and that he hoped there would be much more of it to come.

She kissed him back with a fervour that rocked him to his soul, proving to him the connection he felt to her wasn't one-sided.

They were going to need to have a serious conversation soon about how to make a relationship work when they were living so far away from each other. Because he knew now that was what he wanted.

He so wished he could remember the relationship they'd had when they were younger. Perhaps it would give him more insight into how to solidify their connection now.

That damn accident had been such bad timing—though it had at least prompted her to stay in Spain a bit longer, and in his apartment too, for which he knew he should be very grateful. It had brought them together after all.

It was disconcerting though, not having all that information about her available to him. Still, more things seemed to be coming back to him in dribs and drabs now so perhaps his brain was beginning to heal.

Pushing away his lingering unease, he kissed her once more before taking her hand to lead her out of the park.

It would all be fine once the rest of his memory came back.

CHAPTER EIGHT

THE NEXT MORNING Caleb rolled reluctantly out of bed, leaving a sexily rumpled and tantalisingly warm Elena in it.

'Do you want me to come to the hospital with you?' she murmured sleepily as he strode towards the en suite bathroom for a shower.

He stopped in his tracks and looked back at her. She was smiling at him in that earnest, intent way that always made his heart turn over.

In truth, he loved the idea of spending the whole of the day with her by his side, but he definitely didn't want her coming to the hospital with him just in case something happened there that made it obvious his memory hadn't fully returned yet.

'No, it'll be boring for you. You stay here, or go shopping or sightseeing or something. I need to go into the office to make sure everything is running smoothly without me but I'll be back here to spend the afternoon with you.'

She gave him a pained look. 'Okay, but don't get

caught up in the office and forget the time. You should really be resting at home still.'

He walked back to the bed and sat down on the side of it, brushing a rogue strand of hair away from her forehead. 'I tell you what, why don't you just spend all day naked in my bed—that'll give me all the incentive I need to come home as soon as possible.'

Laughing, she pulled him down for a kiss and he gave in to her demand and kissed her back, pulling the sheet that separated them away and rolling on top of her, telling himself he still had plenty of time to make his appointment.

He was late for his appointment.

Luckily, the doctor was also running late with his last patient so Caleb didn't need to apologise for his tardiness as he strode into the consulting room. The extra time he'd got to spend with Elena would have been totally worth missing the appointment for anyway. He was fine, still a bit blurry about the events in his past, but, as he told the doctor, who looked at him with a mixture of concern and perplexity at his attitude, he didn't care—he was alive and he had a beautiful, compassionate woman waiting for him back at home and that was what mattered.

Life was good.

After being put through some rather over-the-top extensive tests by the consultant and agreeing reluctantly to come back later in the week for additional testing, he finally managed to escape the hospital, intent on dropping in at Araya Industries for the barest of moments to satisfy himself that everything was running well there before heading straight back to Elena's warm smile and comforting embrace.

Striding through Reception, he greeted a couple of the PAs who worked for his colleagues with a smile, both of them blinking at him in surprise before hurriedly returning his cheery salutation.

Up on his floor he found a rather bemused Benita sitting at her desk outside his office, and he flashed her a smile in greeting then asked her if she could please come in once she'd finished the email she was typing. She stared at him in surprise, also seemingly unnerved by his new jovial attitude, before nodding jerkily, the expression on her face remaining wary as if worried he was just lulling her into a false sense of security before putting the boot in.

Clearly he had a lot of work to do on his people skills.

He'd always been aware that he came across as intense and forthright, but he'd never considered it to be a failing before, too caught up in the running of his business to pay it much mind. Elena's appearance in his life and her bravery in challenging him about it had opened his eyes to it though. It was as if she'd drawn out something that had been buried for far too long within him. With this in mind he made a firm resolution to review the way he dealt with his colleagues in the future.

Sitting down at his desk, he turned on his computer and was just about to look over his email when there was a tentative knock on his door. He called, 'Come in,' and a moment later Benita's head appeared around the door, her face set in a circumspect smile as if she was a little afraid to enter the room in case he was waiting in there to bite her head off.

'Benita, come in,' he said kindly, giving her an encouraging nod.

She shuffled into the room, keeping a good four feet back from the desk where he was sitting.

'How are you feeling?' she asked with trepidation in her voice.

'I'm fine,' he said, wincing inside as he caught the brusqueness in his tone. 'Thanks for asking,' he added and almost laughed at the look of incredulity on her face.

'So, did Carter's people get in contact?' he asked.

She nodded, moving closer to the desk now as if she was beginning to trust his new upbeat attitude. 'I've put the minutes of the Skype meeting onto the DRM and the relevant account managers have been briefed.'

'Good, good,' he said, nodding. 'Thanks.'

She cleared her throat. 'It's good to see you back, Señor Araya. We were worried when we heard about your accident. It looks like your friend took good care of you though.'

'Yes, she did,' he said, the thought of Elena lying naked in his bed waiting for him distracting him for a moment.

'Did you work out your differences about partnering with her business?' Benita asked.

He stared at her like an idiot for a moment, wondering whether his wandering thoughts had somehow made him mix up the words Benita had said to him.

'What did you say?'

She looked a little taken aback, as if she might have put her foot in it. 'I just meant—it seemed as though you were getting on well again—after your meeting didn't go as smoothly as you'd hoped.'

'Our meeting?'

'With Señorita Jones. On the morning before your accident.'

She was looking at him as if she was worried that he'd gone insane.

He batted a hand at her, his thoughts swirling and confused as a strange sinking feeling appeared out of nowhere and slid through his chest. 'Yes, yes, I remember.' He thought hard for a moment. 'Benita, did you forward me the supporting documents for that meeting?'

'Er…no, you asked me not to. I got the impression you weren't very keen to partner with her company.'

That was strange. Why would he have thought that?

'Well, send them over to me now, will you? I need to take a look at them.'

'Yes, of course.' She paused. 'Is there anything else I can do for you?'

He shook his head, his confusion about what was going on making his brain hurt. 'No, no, that'll be all. Thanks.'

She gave him a nod, then slipped out of the room.

Caleb booted up the DRM programme and clicked on the links that Benita sent through, which connected to a presentation Elena had apparently sent over before a meeting they were meant to be having on Friday.

A meeting he had no memory of.

He read through her proposal with interest, wondering why the hell he'd not jumped at the opportunity she'd put to him. She needed his battery for her cars and it looked to be a very lucrative deal for both of them.

What was wrong with him? Had he really been so blind or so busy with the American deal that he'd not recognised such a good prospect when she brought it directly to him?

When she'd helped him clinch Carter's business at the meeting the other day he'd been hugely impressed with her knowledge of the industry and her insight into what he did, so much so, he'd made a mental note to look up the company she ran in England, so why had he said no?

He remembered with a sting of conscience that she'd not wanted to discuss the row they'd apparently had right before they'd left for their meeting with the Carters. Had the argument been about him turning the possible partnership between their companies down?

And what had made him do it.

Now he thought about it, whenever he'd pressed her for more information about her business she'd changed the subject. This had surprised him at the time, but he'd written it off as her not wanting to discuss work during her time off.

Or perhaps she'd not wanted to discuss it while she thought he was mentally challenged.

Shutting off his screen, he decided it was time to go home and ask Elena some direct questions before she walked away and went to find someone else to partner with—an idea that filled him with anxiety. After all she'd done for him over the last few days he felt he owed her a debt of gratitude and perhaps this would be the perfect way to repay it.

Walking past Benita's desk, an idea occurred to him.

'Benita, could you book a table at Restaurant Hora for tomorrow night for two people? I know it's Valentine's night,' he said before she could say the words of warning that were clearly on her lips, 'but I know the owner. Just tell him it's for me and he'll find a way to fit us in.'

'Okay, consider it done,' Benita said with a reverential smile, something he'd not seen on her face before. 'Your friend's a lucky lady,' she called as he walked away.

'She is,' he threw back over his shoulder with a wry grin.

Though I think we've moved well past the friends stage now, he thought determinedly to himself as he made to set off home.

His apartment was quiet when he arrived back and he wondered whether she'd decided to go out and sightsee on her own after all, but as he strolled to his bedroom his spirits lifted when he saw she was sitting up naked in his bed with just a pair of glasses perched on her nose, tapping away on her laptop.

She was so absorbed in what she was doing she gave a little start when she finally noticed him standing in the doorway watching her and quickly snapped her laptop shut.

'Did you miss me?' he asked, shedding his clothes and dropping them on the floor as he moved towards her.

The expression in her eyes softened as he climbed onto the bed next to her and she twisted away for a second to put the laptop carefully by the side of the bed before turning back to face him.

He kissed her hard, feeling her sink against his body as he dragged her closer, the heat and softness of her skin soothing away his tension from being away from her.

'You were only gone a couple of hours,' she chided, but couldn't seem to help herself from smiling and saying, 'but yes, I missed you.'

'Good,' he said, sliding his hands down her body so she made a soft little sighing noise in the back of her throat.

It felt so right having her there in his arms, like nothing he'd ever experienced before. And it wasn't just lust driving that feeling, it was a sense of belonging too. She *belonged* here in his bed. He just needed to find a way to keep her there indefinitely now.

'So, Elena, tell me more about why you need my battery for your car?' he murmured into her hair as she kissed the spot at the back of his jaw that always sent him wild.

Whipping her head back, she looked at him, startled.

'What…er…what do you want to know?' she asked, her expression suddenly guarded.

The wariness in her eyes gave him pause.

'Why are you so jumpy? What aren't you telling me? Every time I've asked questions about your business you've changed the subject.'

Closing her eyes, she let out a long, frustrated sigh,

then seemed to give herself a little shake and pull herself together.

'It seemed wrong to discuss business when you weren't well.' She looked down at her fingers, which were plucking nervously at the sheet. 'And the truth is, I didn't give you the full story then about what's going on with it. I was afraid you might see it as a weakness.'

Ah, so, as he'd suspected, there was more to it than she'd initially let on.

'Okay, I'm listening and I promise not to judge.'

She nodded and he saw her swallow hard. 'The truth is, we used to have a supplier who had designed a battery specifically to fit in the car. Initially we wanted to use an English company so we could say the car was fully manufactured in the UK, but very recently they've let us know that there's a fatal flaw with the design of it and they can't figure out how to fix it. So we're in a precarious position now. We have a lot of pre-orders and the shell of the car ready to go, but no battery to power it.'

He frowned, comprehending now why she'd be so panicked. It could be catastrophic for her business if she didn't find a replacement battery.

He nodded, thinking hard. 'Well, from what you've told me, and the documents I looked at today, it seems to me like it could be a mutually beneficial partnership. I don't see why it would be a problem to let you have the battery for your car.'

She stared at him, her eyes wide with surprise. 'What?'

He smiled at her bemusement. 'I'm saying I'd be happy to let your company use my battery in the car.'

To his consternation, instead of flinging herself into his arms with joy she continued to stare at him with a mixture of confusion and reticence. 'I don't know if that's a great idea now, Caleb.'

'Why not?'

Folding her arms, she fixed him with a hard stare. 'Because of what's happened here, with us. To be honest, I'd be a little nervous about mixing a business partnership with a personal one. What if things went wrong between us? It's a risk.'

He shook his head. 'You can't worry about that. We're adults. We can keep the two things separate. I can't imagine anything that could tear us apart now.'

Moving closer to her, he put his finger under her chin and tipped it up so she had to look right into his eyes. 'I think I've got a pretty good measure of you, Elena Jones, and I want us to move forward—together. What happened in the past doesn't matter any more. I want you to believe that.'

'I do believe that,' she murmured, tears welling in her eyes.

'Then trust me. Trust us.'

After a small pause filled with almost painful expectancy, she smiled and said, 'Yes, okay. I trust us.'

He nodded, feeling his heart turn over with relief. 'I'll talk to the team tomorrow about working out a partnership agreement.' He held up a finger. 'On one condition.'

Blinking away the tears, she raised her eyebrows in anticipation.

'That you agree to stay here for the rest of the week and go out with me tomorrow evening for Valentine's night. I've booked a table at Hora; it's the best Michelin-starred restaurant in town.'

Elena gazed at Caleb, her heart hammering hard in her chest, barely able to believe that her fortunes could have changed so significantly in the space of a few days. Blessed relief at the thought that she might now have a way to save her business and the livelihoods of her workforce cascaded through her.

Pulling him roughly to her, she dropped kisses all over his face until he started to laugh. 'I'd love to go to dinner with you. I've never been out on Valentine's Day before. Jimmy thought it was just a big marketing ploy to pressure men into spending ridiculous amounts of money on their girlfriends just to boost the big businesses' coffers.'

'Hmm, no wonder you left him—what a loser,' he said, running his fingers into her hair and looking deeply into her eyes. 'You deserve to be worshipped in every way possible, Elena Jones.'

The last of the worry she'd been carrying on her shoulders finally lifted, leaving her euphoric and light-headed.

Could this really be happening? Was it possible she'd not only found a way to save her business and quite likely propel it into a hugely successful venture with

Araya Industries' help, but that she'd also got Caleb back into the bargain?

A small voice in her head told her not to get too excited about that last part just yet. It was still early days, and it had all moved so fast. While he seemed intent on rebuilding their fractured relationship right now, she was aware that he might change his mind once the first flush of excitement had worn off.

Although, perhaps the accident really had made him reconsider his whole outlook on life. Maybe he was tired of carrying around the anger and resentment that had broken their connection in the first place and was genuinely taking her advice about being more positive.

But she still couldn't help but worry that it could all change again in the blink of an eye.

She'd just have to be careful.

Though she knew deep down that she was probably far too late to rein back her feelings now.

She knew exactly what this feeling was that warmed her heart and lifted her soul.

She was in love with him.

And always had been.

When she zoned back in she realised he was looking at her with a mixture of concern and amusement.

'Are you okay? Have I blown your mind?' he asked with laughter in his voice.

A shiver of delight ran through her. It was so wonderful to see him happy again.

'Yes,' she said, returning his smile, 'but in the very best way.'

'Good.'

She took a breath and clapped her hands onto her knees. 'Well, if I'm going to stay here for a bit longer and go out for a fancy meal to celebrate with you tomorrow I'm going to need to buy more clothes. I only brought enough for a couple of days.'

'Okay. I can recommend a few places in the city to look for some,' he said, shifting closer to her. 'There are some great independent boutiques in the Gothic Quarter. But for now,' he murmured, reaching out a hand to trace the dips and hollows of her throat and shoulder blades with his fingertips, sending waves of pleasure rushing through her body, 'I think we should celebrate our partnership in a very different, but just as appropriate, way.'

'Sounds like a wonderful idea to me,' she said with a smile, then pressed her mouth hard to his, sinking into the heady reassurance of his embrace.

CHAPTER NINE

THE BOUTIQUE CLOTHES shops that Caleb had recommended were exactly what Elena was looking for and she spent a happy couple of hours browsing through rails of perfectly tailored dresses in a range of delicate, lush materials, heartened by the knowledge that he was so tuned in to her taste. There was something rather wonderful about being so well understood.

It had been a long time since she'd felt this excited about picking out new clothes for a date; in fact, it had been a long time since she'd even gone shopping like this, preferring to buy her clothes over the Internet for speed and efficiency.

Her friend Hannah had often tried to get her to join her at the weekends to browse through the stores and go for long, lazy lunches, but Elena had always been up to her eyeballs in work and had felt that going shopping would be a waste of her time.

How could she have allowed herself to become so practical? So insular. So narrow-minded? It was such a waste of her younger years, spending all her time focused on work instead of enjoying the friendships and opportunities for fun that she had at her fingertips. This time she'd spent with Caleb had really brought that to the fore for her and she challenged herself to make more of her time outside of work from now on.

Hopefully with Caleb there to enjoy it alongside her.

She didn't like to think about how they were going to make a long distance relationship work when they were both so busy with their businesses, but she guessed if they were both fully invested in it they'd make it happen somehow. In fact she rather liked the idea of moving to Barcelona to be near him. Once the Zipabout car had its battery and had been released onto the market she'd be looking for a new project to start on anyway. The rest of her team could handle the day-to-day running of the sales and marketing side so she could work on new ideas remotely, at least to begin with.

But she was getting ahead of herself here. Caleb hadn't talked about continuing their relationship past the end of this week and she'd be a fool to start planning her whole future around him.

Even if she wanted to. Very, very much.

She'd never felt more alive and excited about life than when she was with him. He had a way of bringing out the very best in her.

After choosing some new outfits and underwear to last her for the rest of the week she popped into a perfumery, which she'd spotted on one of the small side streets on her way there, sniffing at each of the bottles with delight and trying to identify the main ingredients in them.

Something shifted strangely inside her as she picked

up a small, dark bottle in the shape of a swan. There was something incredibly familiar about it. Lifting it to her nose, she realised with a shock that she recognised the fragrance. It was one that Caleb had bought for her for a Christmas present, before they'd fallen out with each other. It had been the most exquisite thing she'd ever smelt and the revealing gesture of him taking the time to pick out and give her such a personal and intimate present had been the thing that had pushed her to finally admit how she really felt about him. She'd worn it on her skin for the whole week leading up to the last day of term, after they'd had their heart-to-heart about how they were perfect for each other and she'd promised him she'd finish her relationship with Jimmy as soon as she got home.

After she'd failed to come through on that promise and Caleb had made it clear he wanted nothing more to do with her she'd felt sick with shame and sadness every time she smelled that scent and had thrown it away.

She'd regretted that rashness for a long time afterwards though. In the end it was the only thing she'd had left to remind her of him. Despite repeated attempts to contact him and apologise, once he'd gone back to Spain she'd never heard from him again. It had been as if he'd never existed.

Smelling the scent again now brought back her intensely confused feelings of desperation to be with him, despite her fears that they just weren't practically suited. A memory of him drawing her close, leaning in on the pretext of smelling the perfume on her neck and instead brushing his lips against her skin, flashed across her mind. It had been one of the happiest, most intimate, most electrifying moments of her life.

She'd often wished she could have bottled that feeling to remind her of happier times.

And now she had it, right here in her hand.

Striding over to the counter, she handed the perfume to the sales assistant and drew her purse out of her bag.

'I've been searching for this for years,' she said, giving the woman a delighted grin. 'I'm so happy I've finally found it again.'

Caleb spent the day at work after calling his colleagues into a meeting to discuss how they'd move forward with both the partnership with the Americans and also with Elena's company.

He'd set the tone at the very beginning by being more friendly and relaxed than usual and had smiled to himself as he'd caught the looks of bemusement and surprise that had passed between his colleagues.

There had been a real buzz of excitement in the room as he laid out what had happened in the last few days. He'd made a point of taking a step back so that the project managers had a chance to take the lead, even though he itched to stay fully in control, and it had yielded great results. They were all smiling and buoyed up by the time the meeting concluded, which, he realised with a shock of sudden insight, was an unusual occurrence. Before he would have left the roomful of people a little subdued after he'd demanded their best from them. Today he'd let *them* decide to do the best job they could, and it seemed to have paid off.

He'd learnt an important lesson recently about taking a less aggressive attitude towards business and he knew he had Elena to thank for that.

She was good for him—helped balance him somehow.

He showered and changed at work, putting on his best casual suit for dinner, aware of a low level of excitement about seeing Elena again this evening that had buzzed through his veins all day.

The traffic was bad and he tapped his fingers impatiently against the armrest of the car as his driver wound slowly through the early evening traffic.

'It looks like everyone's out for Valentine's night, clogging up the roads,' the driver muttered.

Caleb smiled at his grumpiness, thinking how great it was to be one of the people looking forward to an evening of romance for once.

Striding through the entrance of the restaurant, he bumped into a couple of people he knew socially who were also there for a romantic meal and they exchanged pleasantries, Caleb's pulse jumping with impatience to see Elena again after spending the day away from her.

He appeared to have turned into a teenager again. Not that he could remember those years clearly. Bits and pieces had come back to him over the last couple of days, mostly feelings of not having fitted in to a small, close-knit community in the small town where he'd been raised, a few miles west of Barcelona.

It was strange, but he was aware that this bothered him much less now—now he knew he'd made something of himself and proved all those naysayers wrong about him. Now that he had Elena.

Finally finding an out in the conversation so he could say a polite farewell to his acquaintances, he made his way towards the maître d's desk, where he was greeted with a smile of reverence and a warm welcome before being shown towards his table where, he was told, Elena was already waiting for him.

He'd chosen this restaurant because he liked its clean lines and no fuss décor, with its wall of glass which looked out onto a courtyard of flowers and olive trees, which were lit up tonight like some magical grotto. The simple wooden spoke-back chairs juxtaposed sharply with the pristine white tablecloths and blank walls, giving it all an understated but refined air. It was classy without being showy and he knew from experience that the food here was out of this world.

The perfect place to celebrate with Elena.

The table where she'd been seated was right next to the glass wall and the candle that flickered in front of her threw shadows onto the reflective surface, making it look as though she was sitting next to her ghostly double.

When she spotted him she stood up and smiled and his pulse skittered then began to jump in his throat. Gazing at her now brought home to him just how truly beautiful she was. Tonight she was wearing a fitted cocktail dress in a deep turquoise colour that made her iridescent eyes glow with warmth. Her pale golden hair flowed around her shoulders in waves, looking so lustrous in the soft light he ached to run his fingers through it.

In fact his overriding instinct right that second was to drag her into his arms and never let her go.

As he reached the table she stepped to the side and opened her arms for him to walk into her embrace, a wide smile playing about her lips and pleasure flashing in her eyes.

He dragged her roughly to him, burying his face in her hair and whispering, 'I missed you today.'

'I missed you too,' she murmured back.

He dragged in a deep breath, desperate to fill his senses with her soft, familiar scent—

And suddenly everything felt wrong.

His vision swam in front of him and a slow sinking sensation began to pull him down towards the floor.

That scent.

He knew it.

He *knew* it, but he didn't know why.

There was something completely wrong about it, but also completely right.

Elena and that scent went together.

But not in a good way.

Images began to cloud his mind's eye: of the two of them at university, studying in each other's rooms, laughing together. He felt flashes of happiness, then insecurity, then a cold hard rage that swelled up from somewhere deep inside him, dragging the breath from his lungs.

'Caleb? What's wrong?'

He heard Elena's voice as if it was coming to him

from a distance. Nausea welled in his gut and he pushed her away from him, needing to be free of her hold, to get away from the smell that was causing his mind to rebel against him. His head pounded as if his brain had suddenly swollen and was pressing against the walls of his skull, the pain so intense he stumbled forwards, grabbing a chair to steady himself.

He felt her hand on his shoulder but he shrugged her off, not wanting her to touch him.

Then, like a floodgate opening, it all came rushing back: the soul-crushing disappointment and the hurt and humiliation he'd endured after he'd opened himself up to loving her back then. The way he'd trusted her implicitly with his heart and she'd taken it, played with it for a while then smashed it to pieces at his feet.

He'd made a total fool of himself for her.

After leading him to believe she cared about him as much as he did her and promising to come back after the Christmas holidays free to be with him, he'd gone home to Spain for the holidays, actually feeling happy for once to be going back there so he could tell his mother about the woman he'd fallen in love with.

She'd been so pleased for him; in fact it had been the first time they'd connected on any kind of emotional level since he'd been a young boy, perhaps because he finally understood how she could love someone so much she would do whatever it took to have them—that loving someone would be worth being estranged from others for.

After what had seemed like an interminable amount of time at home he'd gone back to Cambridge, desperate to see Elena after having promised not to call her whilst she was at home, to give her the time and space to deal with breaking up with Jimmy in a gentle and kind manner, only to find she was avoiding him.

He'd thought he was being paranoid at first, that it was bad timing when he kept missing her at her college. Until he'd finally tracked her down, panic surging through his veins, and she'd been visibly reluctant to see or speak to him. The cold distant look in her eyes had sent shivers of horror through him, which only increased when she'd told him in a toneless voice how she'd decided to stay with Jimmy after all, how she felt that he, Caleb, was too wild for her, too dangerous a proposition, too unpredictable. She needed to be with someone like Jimmy because she needed stability and calm in her life.

He'd felt belittled, rejected, foolish, but most of all heartsick at losing the woman he'd felt so sure felt the same way he did.

Taking a deep, much-needed breath, he finally straightened and turned to look into Elena's beautiful, deceitful face, feeling a deep, hot rage overtake him.

It hadn't been an undeniable romantic attraction that had connected them with such intensity over these last few days: it had been hatred.

'I remember, Elena,' he said, his voice raspy and strained as he forced the words past his throat. 'I remember why we stopped being *friends*.' He spat the last word out, feeling disgusted with himself for allowing her to take him in like this.

She'd used his memory loss against him to wheedle

out what she wanted from him. And he, like a fool, had fallen for it. Fallen for her. Again.

'What are you talking about? Caleb, I don't understand. What just happened here?' She looked panicked by his pronouncement, as well she should.

He crossed his arms. 'I know exactly what's been happening over the last few days. You've been using the fallout from the accident to get close to me.'

She stared at him, her cheeks flushed with colour and her brow pinched so tightly white lines formed on her skin.

'Did you invite me here tonight to humiliate me in public? To pay me back for what happened fifteen years ago?' she whispered, blinking as if trying to hold back tears.

He pushed away a sting of misplaced concern, forcing himself to remember that she was the one in the wrong here. 'No, of course not! I only remembered it all just now. The perfume you're wearing… It triggered something.' His head gave another throb of pain and he squeezed his eyes shut until it receded.

'Caleb? Are you okay?' The worry in her voice hit him straight in the chest, winding him.

'I'm fine,' he growled, not wanting to feel the way she was making him feel with her concerned, soothing *act*. The only person she'd ever cared about was herself and he needed to remember that.

'I see you for what you really are now, Elena,' he bit out angrily.

She swallowed hard, her face blanching, and glanced around her anxiously.

He suddenly realised that the room had become awfully quiet. When he looked round he saw that all the diners near them were staring their way in morbid fascination.

'Look, shall we sit down and talk about this rationally?' Elena said with a quaver in her voice, pulling out her chair with a shaking hand and sitting on it.

After a moment of indecision he pulled out his own chair and sat down opposite her, folding his arms. He was interested to hear how she was going to try and explain her self-serving actions away.

'What do you mean, you've only just remembered what happened?' she hissed, leaning forwards and putting her hands onto the table between them. 'You said your memory had fully come back!'

He shrugged dismissively. 'No. I lied about that. I didn't want you to think I was weak.' He leant back in his chair and narrowed his eyes at her. 'I pieced a story together from what you'd said about us and...' he paused, struggling to unclench his jaw to force out the name '...Jimmy. But I remember now. I remember the way you led me on then pushed me away when you changed your mind about who would serve your needs best.'

She held up both hands towards him in a halting gesture. 'I thought you understood how sorry I was about that. How I knew it had been the worst mistake of my life. I've been trying to make amends for the way I behaved then.'

'So you could manipulate me into getting what you wanted.'

Her hands bunched into fists now. 'No, Caleb, it wasn't like that.'

'So why did you stay after I'd told you I didn't want anything more to do with you and your business? Why were you so keen to look after me at the hospital?'

'Because I care about you, Caleb!' she shot back passionately. 'And there was a misunderstanding between the hospital staff about who I was to you that I got caught up in. But I was there because I felt awful about you getting hurt.'

'Because you were responsible for it.' It all made sense now. Cold, cruel sense.

'No! At least not directly. You were crossing the road to talk to me and you didn't look properly.'

'And why was that?'

She didn't seem to be able to meet his eye. 'I guess you were distracted.'

'You mean I was angry with you for not taking no for an answer?'

She visibly swallowed. 'Yes.'

'And then you stuck around when you thought I couldn't remember what had happened.'

'I was trying to make things right between us.'

'You mean when you realised I'd forgotten all about it you thought you'd be able to get what you wanted by pretending to care about me. By charming your way into my bed!'

Her eyes widened in dismay. 'What? No—!'

'I know exactly what you've been doing, Elena— you've been playing me this whole time, hoping to seduce me into giving you what you needed when I'd already told you no,' he bit out, anger and humiliation and heartache making his voice shake.

She gaped at him in stunned surprise, her face now bleached of colour. 'No, Caleb.' Her voice came out as a ragged whisper. 'That's not what happened!'

Elena felt sick.

How could he suddenly be acting so coldly towards her after the closeness they'd shared?

Who was she kidding? She knew how, because she'd done exactly the same thing to him fifteen years ago.

She swallowed hard, her mind whirring, trying to think of some way to convince him that she'd meant well by staying here to look after him and that she genuinely cared about him, but before she could say anything else he frowned, then shook his head as if another revelation had just struck him.

'You only went to that dinner meeting with Carter with me so I'd feel compelled to say yes to your own partnership.'

Gritting her teeth, she let out a moan of frustration. 'You asked me to go with you and I wanted to help you! Not for my own benefit, but for yours!'

He was nodding now though, as if he wasn't listening to her and things were suddenly making sense in his head. 'You guided me towards asking you to help me, planting the idea about me needing someone who understood the business. You manipulated me.'

'I did not,' she said as calmly as she could manage, trying like mad to control the shake of anger and hurt in her voice. 'It was your idea and there was no way I could refuse to help and leave you alone with your head injury. And I wanted to help, Caleb. Genuinely.'

He let out a low, disdainful laugh. 'Being genuine is not one of your strong points, Elena.'

'Maybe not fifteen years ago but, I promise you, it is now.'

'They why didn't you tell me everything when we had all our heart-to-hearts? There were plenty of opportunities.'

'Because I was afraid you'd kick me to the kerb. I was worried about you—about the fact you didn't seem to have anyone else to look after you. From what I've seen, you still seem intent on pushing away anyone who gets even vaguely close to you. I don't want you to end up old and alone. You deserve more than that. You deserve to be loved. And to be happy. You're a good man; you just need to believe it.'

He snorted. 'I know my own worth, Elena.'

'Do you?'

'Yes. *I* would never have slept with someone who couldn't remember the callous way I'd treated them in the past.'

She shoved her fingers into her hair in frustration. 'You told me you'd remembered.'

'Did you really believe I'd forgive you for the way you treated me back then, just like that?' He snapped his fingers, shooting her a look of disgust.

Dropping her head into her hands now, she let out a long, low sigh. 'I guess I knew deep down that something wasn't quite right, but I really wanted to believe things were okay with us again so I pushed any misgivings I had to one side.'

When she looked up again he was staring at her as if he didn't believe a word of it, his expression dark and unyielding.

'Yes, okay, I was being naïve,' she said, frustration making her belligerent now. 'It was wrong of me to let it happen.'

'So why did you?'

His question brought her up short. 'I—'

'You could have stopped me.'

'I couldn't. I didn't want to.'

'Why not, Elena?'

'Because I wanted you, all right!' she blurted, furious with herself for losing her cool.

'You wanted my battery, you mean,' he bit out, leaning towards her.

'No!' She took a breath, trying to calm her raging emotions. 'Well, yes. Okay.' She leant forwards too, fixing him with what she hoped was an honest and open expression. 'I need your battery because I have a lot of good people relying on me to find a way to save their jobs, but sleeping with you was a totally separate thing. I wanted to do it for me. For us.'

'For *us*?'

'Yes! I've missed you over the years and I didn't realise how much until I saw you again. How unhappy I was without you.'

There was a heavy beat of silence where they stared at each other, their breathing rapid and the body language tense.

She thought she saw a flash of vulnerability in his eyes, but the next second it was gone, replaced with cool indifference. 'If you're saying that because you're worried I'm going to back out of the partnership then don't bother. I'm not that much of a monster,' he growled, reaching into his jacket and withdrawing a sheaf of papers, which he tossed onto the table in front of her. 'It's a contract I had drawn up earlier today which agrees to a partnership with your company.'

She stared at it in shock for a moment before dragging her gaze back to his.

'Caleb, thank you—'

But, before she could finish her sentence, he cut her off. 'My colleagues will be handling it from here so we won't need to have any more contact. I hope that makes you happy.'

She glared at him, her heart thumping against her chest and her jaw tight with frustration. 'Don't be ridiculous— of course it doesn't make me happy to not have any more contact with you!'

He huffed out a disdainful laugh, the expression in his eyes hauntingly distant, then without another word he went to stand up.

'Please, Caleb, stay,' she said desperately, reaching out a hand in an attempt to stall him. 'We need to talk more about this.'

'There's nothing left to say,' he stated coldly, brushing away her attempt to touch him and standing up, and before she could utter another word he turned and walked swiftly away from the table without looking back.

Elena sat there, numb with shock, battling down a

painful ache deep inside her, afraid that once she let it rise to the surface she wouldn't be able to stop the tears that would inevitably come with it.

Everything might have just gone to hell but there was no way she was going to blub in the middle of a restaurant.

Gesturing to a passing waiter, she asked him to bring the bill for the champagne that she'd ordered and that neither of them had touched. She paid with her credit card, her movements jerky with anguish, then got up shakily and brushed herself down, setting back her shoulders before walking out of there, hyper-aware of the fascinated looks she was getting from the other diners.

Dumped on Valentine's night. It didn't get much more humiliating than that.

Once outside, she walked quickly down a side alley, away from prying eyes, and leant against the wall, burying her face in her hands.

But she refused to let herself cry.

She'd known, of course, on some subconscious level that Caleb had been lying about getting his memory back—that he'd been swept up in the excitement of closing the deal with the Americans and had wanted to celebrate with her the best way he knew how. And, to her shame, she'd let him, pretending to herself she believed that he remembered her even though he'd not remotely reacted in the way she'd been expecting.

Because she'd wanted him so badly she'd ached with longing.

The truth was, she'd been utterly selfish. She *had* taken

advantage of his memory loss after the accident, not admitting it to herself at the time, but hoping—praying—it would never come back.

She'd brought all this on herself.

Just like she'd done fifteen years ago.

Caleb had trusted her implicitly then too, so much so he'd opened himself up to her—the first person he'd ever done that with after enduring such a punishing and isolated childhood—and she'd thrown his love and trust back in his face, deeming it worthless.

Then she'd hidden, like a coward, avoiding him at every turn until he'd been forced to come to her dorm room and practically break down the door to speak to her. She'd been afraid to face his disappointment in her so had put up a wall of ice to protect herself, telling him she'd made a mistake, he was too wild, too unpredictable for her, they could never be happy, not in the long run. She needed someone more stable, like Jimmy. He'd looked at her as if his world had just crashed in around him, before turning and walking away.

And that had been the last time he'd ever spoken to her. From that point on he'd acted as if she didn't exist. He'd looked through her as if she was nothing—a waste of space.

And she'd known deep down that she'd deserved it.

He'd practically gone to ground after that, skipping the lectures where she'd normally see him and never seeming to be at his dorm room when she dropped in, hoping to catch him and apologise and explain her horrible behaviour. And then he'd gone back to Spain as soon as the last lecture had finished, pushing past her when she'd tried to talk to him as if she meant nothing to him any more.

It had left an aching hole in her that had never closed over, even fifteen years later.

Because he'd been the love of her life.

It had tormented her more than she'd wanted to admit to herself over the years, chipping away at her self-respect, causing her to find fault in every man she'd dated, leaving her to wonder whether she'd ever be happy in a relationship again.

Until now.

But just when she'd thought she'd paid her dues and things were finally good between them again she'd lost him all over again.

CHAPTER TEN

CALEB MARCHED INTO his apartment, slamming the front door so hard behind him the angry sound of it reverberated around the space for a good few seconds.

How could he have let this happen? He'd known there was something strange going on but he'd blamed it on his memory loss instead of looking harder at the woman who had appeared out of nowhere like a ray of sunshine on a dark day.

Slumping onto the sofa, he winced in pain as his cracked rib reminded him that he'd been weakened by the accident in more ways than one.

But then hadn't he known, deep down, that there was more to her story than she was telling him and he'd let himself fall for her anyway?

Because he had—hard and intensely. The thought of being with her had consumed him over the last few days, just like it had when he was younger. He knew why he'd not wanted to look too closely at what was going on. It was because he'd wanted her to be genuinely interested in exploring a relationship with him—wanted it more than he'd ever wanted anything in his life.

So he'd allowed himself to trust her, to begin to care about her—no, who was he kidding, he'd fallen in love with her and she'd used that to get what she wanted from him.

Once again she'd played him for a fool.

He felt as though his heart had been ripped from his chest. All that emotion that had been building inside him from the moment he'd seen her again swelled to an almost unbearable size, closing his throat, crushing his lungs, filling his head with unbearable pain.

No doubt she was already at the airport, ready to head home, happy in the knowledge that she'd achieved her objective here: to get him to sell her his battery, no matter what she'd had to do to get it.

Anger flashed through him, propelling him off the sofa and towards his bedroom where her things were still hanging in his wardrobe and sitting on his shelves.

Well, he wanted them gone. He didn't want a trace of her left in his house now. He couldn't stand the pain of thinking about what he could have had if only she'd really wanted *him*.

Grabbing her small suitcase from where she'd stashed it in the wardrobe, he stuffed her clothes roughly into it willy-nilly, not caring how much it hurt his rib to do so—in fact, welcoming the pain it brought because it momentarily overrode the ache in his heart—then went to the bathroom and scooped all her toiletries into it too, forcing down the lid and roughly zipping it up.

Picking up the case, he strode to the front door, opened it, then tossed it into the hallway, where it bounced a couple of times before coming to rest on its side, looking battered and forlorn in the grandiose, brightly lit space.

Pushing away a rush of anguish, he slammed the door on it and strode into his kitchen, grabbing a glass tumbler out of the cupboard and splashing a good measure of whisky into it.

He knocked it back, feeling the burn in the back of his throat and registering the warmth as it hit his stomach, though deriving no pleasure from it whatsoever.

Pouring himself another large shot, he took it into the living area and slumped down onto the sofa again, staring out of the window at the dark night sky, which had become stormy with wind and rain that lashed against the glass, trying not to think about how painfully alone he was here in this big echoing apartment.

Despite the way Elena had treated him, his traitorous body still ached for her. His throat was tense from holding back the urge to rage and swear at the world, his chest tight with sorrow and frustration.

He knew, with ringing clarity now, why he'd deliberately sabotaged his engagement to his ex, Adela. He'd been afraid to trust her love for him for this very reason. His survival instinct had kicked in and he'd pushed her away before she could do it to him first.

Because he'd been afraid of something like this happening to him again.

The sad truth was he'd fallen for Adela in the first place because she'd reminded him of Elena. Adela had exhibited many of Elena's traits; she'd even looked a bit like her, but of course he knew deep down that she could never be her. That was why he'd broken off their engagement. It wouldn't have been fair to Adela to have always been second best in his heart.

Perhaps he was destined to always be alone. It would at least be easier that way. Like it had been when he was younger.

He was also acutely aware now that keeping his relationship with his mother at arm's length had had a serious effect on the way he dealt with all his close relationships to this day.

At least after her cancer was diagnosed he'd made sure to visit her more and they'd brokered a kind of unspoken peace between them. He'd never totally understood the life choices she'd made, but he'd come to finally accept them, and her. During those sad, desolate hours at the end of her life she'd made it clear to him that she'd always loved him and that she regretted the distance that had always been between them.

It had torn him up inside, the futility of it, because she was gone now and all he was left with was a sense of deep sorrow for the time he'd wasted spurning her instead of loving and accepting her for who she was.

And now he'd lost the woman he'd hoped to spend his future with too.

The woman he loved.

Knocking back the second whisky, he closed his eyes and tried to blank his mind of her—to shut out the pain and grief that made him feel as though someone had stripped him to the bone—but it was no good; he knew there was no forgetting Elena Jones.

* * *

Elena paced the streets, barely noticing the rain as it began to fall steadily from the sky, seeping into her new dress and plastering her hair to her head.

How could things have gone so wrong so quickly? She'd known before, of course, that there was a chance they might when she'd thought his memory was still missing, but for him to have lied about remembering her, then shown her how wonderful they could be together, only then to regain his memory and reject her was devastating.

Lightning flashed overhead, shocking her out of her frustrated, meandering thoughts, and she ducked under a nearby awning of a restaurant where a few other tourists had gathered, taking shelter from the storm. What was she doing? Moping around Barcelona in the rain wasn't going to solve the problem; the only way she was going to get him to listen to her was to turn up at his apartment and refuse to leave until he did.

She wasn't going to run from him again, not this time. She was going to do what she should have done all those years ago—be brave and fight for what she really wanted, no matter the consequences. She'd never be able to forgive herself if she didn't, not now she knew what she'd be missing—a positive, life-affirming partnership with the man she loved.

Seeing an available taxi driving down the street, she ran back out into the rain and hailed it, jumping into the back seat and giving the driver Caleb's address in a voice shaking with nerves and determination.

She would not give up on them. Not this time.

The journey seemed to take an age as they joined the slow-moving traffic and more and more people jumped into taxis to shelter from the rain. Elena tapped her foot anxiously, wondering what sort of reception she'd get when he opened the door and found her standing there. Would he be angry, cold, indifferent? Or, now that he'd had some time to calm down and reflect rationally on it all, would he be relieved to see her?

She hoped so.

Oh, how she hoped.

The taxi finally drew up outside his building and she shoved the fare towards the driver, telling him to keep the change in her haste to get to Caleb, and dashed across the pavement and up to the entry door to his block. Pulling out the spare key card that Caleb had lent her that morning, so she could get in and out while he was out at work, she pressed it against the pad and sighed with relief when the door lock clicked open. She wouldn't have put it past him to have the code reconfigured to keep her out.

The lift was already at ground level and it took her straight up to his apartment. Walking into the hallway, she came to a surprised stop when she saw a suitcase lying haphazardly in the middle of the floor. She frowned at the incongruity of it, wondering absentmindedly what it was doing there. And then it hit her like a fist to the gut.

It was hers.

Caleb must have packed her things and thrown them out here in case she had the gall to return for them. Well, she wasn't going to let that deter her. Marching up to his door, she hammered loudly on it, her heart thumping in her throat as she stood there listening for his heavy footsteps coming towards her. It occurred to her wildly that she wasn't exactly looking her best at the moment—a lot like a drowned rat, in fact—but she shoved the thought away, knowing this was no time for vanity.

The door swung open and she looked up into Caleb's handsome face, forcing herself not to take a step backwards as she registered the anger in his expression.

'Your things are behind you in the hall,' he said curtly, the bitterness in his voice making her stomach roll.

'I'm not here for my things; I'm here for you,' she stated baldly, keeping her gaze locked with his and her chin determinedly up.

A range of expressions passed over his face: from bemusement to resentment and finally, and most worryingly, to incredulity.

'Let me in, Caleb,' she said calmly, but with a determination that rose from her very soul.

'You can say what you need to right here,' he said, folding his arms in front of him, effectively blocking her way past him with his enormous bulk.

The coldness in his eyes shook her, but there was no way she was going to let him scare her off now. She knew that the kind, compassionate man she'd got to know again over the last few days was still in there somewhere; she just needed to get him to hear what she had to say then maybe she'd be able to draw him back out again.

'Okay, fine, if it has to be said here in your hallway then it will be.' She took a breath and set back her shoulders.

'You were right; I wasn't honest with you and I should have been from the very start, but I was afraid you'd push me away and I desperately wanted to make up for the way I treated you in the past. I was selfish and cruel then but, please believe me, I'm not that same self-absorbed girl I used to be. I'm a different person now. A better one, I hope. Surely you've seen proof of that over the last few days.'

He didn't give any indication that she was getting through to him, his posture remaining stiff and his expression impassive, so she decided just to get it all out in the hope that something she said would strike a chord with him.

'I know I told you that I decided I couldn't marry Jimmy because our relationship was staid and—boring.' She winced at how awful that sounded. What a terrible person she'd been, to them both.

Caleb still didn't say anything, his expression remaining indifferent.

She took another steadying breath, then let the words rush out. 'But the truth is, I broke up with him because I realised I'd never feel about him the way I felt about you.'

There was a flicker of something in his eyes and she held her breath for a moment, praying for a reaction, but he steadfastly refused to give her one.

Swallowing hard, she bunched her fists for courage.

'Back then I was afraid of how unpredictable you were, how you didn't fit into the way I'd envisioned my

life turning out, but mostly how I still wanted you—
desperately—despite all of that. After years of keeping
a tight control over my life, that completely rattled me.
So I stuck with Jimmy, the safe bet, the man I could
control. Because I was a coward.'

He wasn't looking at her now, but staring off into
the distance. Folding her arms, she steeled herself to
hold it together.

'I realised later on, of course, once I'd grown up a
little, that a certain amount of conflict can be good for a
relationship. I guess it gives it the edge it needs to keep
things exciting and fresh. As long as there's enough
love between a couple… I think I mistook passion for
dysfunction in my parents' marriage but they're still
together today, so it shows what I know.'

She was aware that she was dripping water onto the
floor now and that she'd begun to shiver with cold, but
she pushed aside her discomfort, feeling it was probably a fitting state for her confession.

'I think I've really been single for so long because I
stopped trusting my judgement when it comes to relationships. I was ashamed of the way I'd acted in the past
and avoided getting close to anyone again in case I made
the same mistakes. But after spending this incredible
time with you here I realised that if I want to be happy
it's time to stop being afraid of what might go wrong.'

She took a step closer to him. 'And embrace what
could go right. Because I'm so happy when I'm with
you.' Her voice broke as she took another step forwards
and saw him tense, then tighten and raise his arms like
a barrier.

'You really think I'm going to be able to trust you again?' he muttered.

'I do. Because I think you want to; it's just your pride getting in the way.'

'My *pride*? You broke your word to me and you lied; why should I believe you won't do that again?'

'Because I'm not the girl you remember, Caleb. I'm older and wiser now.' She took a deep, shaky breath. 'I was so ridiculously naïve back then, I had no idea what I really needed.' She gave him a beseeching smile, holding her breath as she waited to see whether she'd finally got through to him.

'You have to understand that you scared me at the time. You were so full of anger and bitterness I didn't know whether I could handle you. I wasn't a very strong person then.'

'I didn't need your strength, Elena. I needed your loyalty and respect.'

It felt as though his words had slapped her in the face. She knew he was right; she'd disrespected him in the worst possible way. He trusted her with the whole of his already damaged heart and she'd toyed with it for a while, then thrown it back at him, broken and beyond repair. It had been the worst thing she could have done to him; no wonder he'd turned into the hardened character she'd first met here last week.

'I don't blame you for being reluctant to trust my word after I made such a mess of things last time, but please, Caleb, *please* give me another chance.'

Her heart started to race and her body flushed hot

with trepidation as she looked up into his hooded eyes and said, 'I love you.'

He stared at her, a deep frown marring his face.

'You *love* me?' His tone was so troubled her heart went right out to him.

'Yes, and I want us to make this relationship work.'

He shook his head, the expression in his eyes a little wild as if he was fighting with himself about how to respond.

Her chest gave a little jolt of hope at the thought that perhaps she might finally be getting through to him.

Turning away from her, he began to pace up and down the hall, raking his hands through his hair and making it stand on end. He looked troubled, anxious—but *encouraged* maybe?

'I don't know, Elena. It's a lot to process. I thought I knew you—'

'You *do* know me. Everything I've told you about myself is true. Everything we've done together has been genuine and came from a place of love and respect for you.'

Still he shook his head, as if not daring to believe it.

'I understand why you're feeling this way. It has to be so confusing losing your memory like that,' she said in desperation. 'Then finding out you were missing a big chunk of important information.' She walked to him now and put her hands on his arms, gripping them hard and using the whole of her strength to stop him from pacing.

'Listen to me, Caleb Araya. I am not letting you push me away again. I know I was in the wrong fifteen years ago, but everything that's happened between us in the last week has been real. And I think you feel the same, though you're too stubborn to admit it.'

Caleb stared at this brave, fierce woman in front of him and felt the heavy weight of unhappiness lift a little from his chest.

He knew what she was saying made sense; she'd been nothing but kind and caring towards him since leaving the hospital and he was acutely aware that he was letting his fear and panic get in the way of common sense. His chest gave a sharp throb as he accepted that if it hadn't been for her courage to stand up to him and assert her steadying influence at the meeting he would have lost Carter's business. She'd done that to help him. Because she cared about him. He knew that really, deep in his heart.

In reality, it had been his fault this had all turned into such an awful mess in the blink of an eye because he'd lied about his memory coming back so they could take their relationship further; and it had definitely been him who had asked her to go with him to the meeting with Carter. He remembered the look of wary uncertainty on her face now when he'd suggested it. That, he knew without a doubt, had been absolutely genuine.

He could recognise all that now—now he'd started to see through the fog of fear and panic that had engulfed him earlier.

Looking inside himself, he knew he'd forgiven her a long time ago for what had happened between them. Really, he'd hated himself for being so weak and proud, but until now he'd been too afraid to admit it to himself because it was easier to hate someone than to admit how much you loved them. How much it tore you apart to not have that love returned.

A small defiant part of him still wanted to hang on to the animosity he'd hidden his feelings behind, to keep himself safe from any more pain and uncertainty, but he knew he couldn't do that. Not after she'd been brave enough to turn up here, dripping wet and bedraggled, to lay her heart at his feet when she could have just got on a plane with her signed contract and never had to face him again.

He wouldn't do that to her because what he wanted most in the world was a real and honest relationship with her, even if their journey together was likely to be littered with obstacles and challenges.

She made him happy.

He loved her and she loved him and when it came down to it that was all that really mattered.

Seeming to sense a softening in his attitude, she moved closer to him and tentatively raised a hand to his face. The warmth of her touch heated his skin, starting a fire in his chest which radiated out through his body until every centimetre of him ached to hold her against him again.

'Please, Caleb, please forgive me. Let me back in,' she whispered.

The crack of pain and desperation in her voice broke through the very last of his reserve and he felt the final tendrils of his anger leave him, washed away by the dizzying elation of her presence here—the place where she belonged.

Cupping her jaw in his hands, he smiled at her, drawing her closer. 'There's nothing to forgive. I've been wrong to hold what happened between us all those years ago against you, but it was easier to hate you than face what I'd become: a bitter, cold-hearted fool.'

She opened her mouth as if to disagree but he held up his hand, asking her to wait until he'd finished.

'Being with you has brought me alive again. I love being around you; the world feels like a better place when you're here.'

He frowned as he remembered the horrified look on her face in the restaurant just before he'd stormed away in angry confusion. 'When my memory came back earlier this evening I think I panicked. I suddenly had all these conflicting thoughts and feelings racing through my head, and I didn't know what was truth and what was fiction any more. My natural instinct was to push you away to protect myself. I was afraid you didn't really care about me the way I'd hoped you did and it scared the hell out of me.'

He stroked his thumbs across her cheeks, brushing away the tears that had begun to streak down her face.

'Because I love you, Elena,' he murmured, holding her gaze with his for one precious moment, seeing relief and love light up in her eyes, before bringing his mouth down to hers with a kiss that took his breath away at the utter perfection of it.

He felt her finally relax against him and he pulled her closer, wrapping his arms around her and pressing their bodies tightly together, feeling the strongest compulsion to never let her go again.

'Caleb, your rib,' she muttered against his shoulder where her face was squashed by his encircled arms.

'It's fine. Don't worry.'

'I don't want to hurt you,' she said, pulling away to look up into his face.

'You won't,' he said with conviction.

'You know, we're probably going to be one of those couples that constantly strikes sparks off each other,' she said with a hint of worry in her eyes.

'I hope so,' he said, dipping down to nuzzle her neck and feeling great satisfaction in the little shiver of enjoyment she gave. 'It will keep life exciting.'

'So we'll have to make sure our kids know how much we love each other,' she said with determination in her voice.

He drew back and raised both eyebrows. 'Kids?'

She nodded firmly. 'Yes. I want three.'

'That's brave,' he said, adding a wry lilt of humour to his voice, though deep down he knew that having children with her would make him the happiest man in the world. She'd be an incredible mother: caring, brave and compassionate, and would fight tooth and nail for her children's happiness and security, making sure they knew how loved they were, how wanted.

'I am brave now,' she said. 'I refuse to be afraid of the future any more. We'll take life as it comes, you and I, and deal with anything it throws at us together.'

'I like your style, Elena Jones,' he murmured, bending to kiss her hard and let her know just how much he meant that.

'And I like yours, Caleb Araya,' she said once she'd got her breath back.

And with that sentiment lifting his heart he took her hand in his and led her out of the cold empty hallway and into the shelter of his home.

EPILOGUE

Two years later

IT WAS UNSEASONABLY warm for London in February as Caleb strode through Green Park on his way to meet Elena by the Tube station and he loosened his tie and undid the top button of his shirt, finding relief as the gentle breeze hit his heated skin. He was taking her out for high tea at The Ritz to celebrate her recent design award for her Zipabout cars and was running a little late after a meeting in the City had gone on longer than he'd anticipated.

They'd both been astonished and delighted by the huge impact that the Zipabout cars had had on the electric car industry and Elena was already deep into the design and pre-manufacture of a new model on the back of its success. He was ridiculously proud of all she'd achieved and infinitely delighted to be able to say he'd played some small part in it.

He saw the cars everywhere he went now, both here in England, where they spent big chunks of time in order for Elena to keep in close contact with her company, and also in Spain, where they'd made a permanent home together in the Pedralbes area in the district of Les Corts, which they'd chosen for its wide avenues and green open spaces as well as the spectacular views towards Barcelona.

He hadn't needed much persuasion to move from his rather sequestered, cavernous flat in L'Eixample and into a comfortable four-bed house set within a friendly community of families and professionals, and for the first time in his life he felt truly settled where he lived. Content.

As he rounded the bend near the station his gaze alighted on a figure walking towards him, her long blonde hair glowing in the soft winter sunshine and her cheeks flushed with colour.

The most beautiful woman in the world.

His wife.

She waved when she saw him, her mouth curving into a beatific smile that both melted his heart and made his pulse race. Despite all the time they spent together now, he still hated being separated from her, rushing at the end of each day to get back home. Not a day went by when he didn't thank his lucky stars for the accident that had brought them together, even if it had been in the most dramatic and extraordinary of ways.

Blessedly, he'd been physically fine after all the bruising had finally gone down and after a few more weeks the rest of his memory had returned in full, along with a sense of regret for all the time he'd spent hanging on to the anger from his past that had kept him so isolated from the rest of the world.

But there were no regrets about his life now.

There were times, of course, when he and Elena butted heads but, instead of being afraid of the conflict they embraced it, getting any bottled-up feelings out into the open and using it as a kind of catharsis. They found as long as they kept communicating they were able to work through anything that crossed their path and Caleb made sure to tell Elena every day just how much he loved her.

Returning her smile, he glanced down in love-struck awe at her belly, which was straining against the trench coat she was wearing. In about three months' time there would be someone else for him to love with the same kind of fierce abandon too. Their child.

'Hello, beautiful,' he said as they reached each other and he drew her towards him for a kiss, savouring the feel of her mouth on his and breathing in her reassuring scent.

'How was your meeting?' she asked with a breathy laugh when he finally let her go.

'It went well, I think, though they were more impressed by the fact I'm married to you,' he said, gently brushing her hair away from her face to gaze into her eyes. 'My incredible, talented wife.'

She raised both eyebrows in an expression of wry modesty, then smiled, unable to keep a straight face. 'I couldn't have done it without you,' she murmured, sliding her hands up to cup his jaw and leaning forwards to kiss him firmly on the lips. 'So let's go and celebrate our perfect partnership.'

And with that they linked hands and walked together to their next destination, driven on by the excitement of all the new adventures they had lying ahead of them.

* * * * *

If you enjoyed this book by Christy McKellen,
look out for
A COUNTESS FOR CHRISTMAS
also by Christy McKellen

Or if you enjoyed this gorgeous Mediterranean hero,
look out for another in
HER FIRST-DATE HONEYMOON
by Katrina Cudmore

Both available as ebooks!

MEET THE FORTUNES

Fortune of the Month: Sophie Fortune Robinson

Age: 24

Vital statistics: Long brown hair, big brown eyes and a big fat trust fund.

Claim to fame: At Robinson Tech, she's in charge of hiring and firing—and is most likely to steal hearts.

Romantic prospects: She is Jerome Fortune's youngest daughter, so why shouldn't she get what—or whom—she wants?

Time is running out. Valentine's Day is coming soon, which means I've got only fourteen days to get Thom Nichols, that superhot guy in Marketing, to notice me. My sister Olivia thinks I shouldn't try so hard, but what does she know?

Luckily, I've got a secret weapon:
Mason Montgomery. He works across the hall from me in IT. It's really helpful to have a man's point of view on all this. Mason is a great guy, and I trust him completely. He's handsome and smart and loyal as a Saint Bernard, and he gives good advice to boot. With Mason's help I'm sure to land my Mr. Right. Who is Thom Nichols. *Not* Mason. Or at least, that's what I keep telling myself…

* * *

The Fortunes of Texas:
The Secret Fortunes—
A new generation of heroes and heartbreakers!

HER SWEETEST FORTUNE

BY
STELLA BAGWELL

First Published in Great Britain 2017
By Mills & Boon, an imprint of HarperCollins*Publishers*
1 London Bridge Street, London, SE1 9GF

© 2017 Harlequin Books S.A.

Special thanks and acknowledgement are given to Stella Bagwell for her contribution to the Fortunes of Texas: The Secret Fortunes continuity.

ISBN: 978-0-263-93081-8

23-0217

Our policy is to use papers that are natural, renewable and recyclable products and made from wood grown in sustainable forests. The logging and manufacturing processes conform to the legal environmental regulations of the country of origin.

Printed and bound in Spain
by CPI, Barcelona

After writing more than eighty books for Mills & Boon, **Stella Bagwell** still finds it exciting to create new stories and bring her characters to life. She loves all things Western and has been married to her own real cowboy for forty-four years. Living on the South Texas coast, she also enjoys being outdoors and helping her husband care for the horses, cats and dog that call their small ranch home. The couple has one son, who teaches high school mathematics and is also an athletic director. Stella loves hearing from readers. They can contact her at stellabagwell@gmail.com.

To Susan Litman for all her hard work on
the fabulous Fortune saga. Thank you!

Chapter One

She had to do something and fast!

For the past several hours, the words of warning had made a monotonous loop through Sophie Fortune Robinson's mind, making it virtually impossible to concentrate on the work scattered across her desk.

As assistant director of human resources at Robinson Tech, it was Sophie's responsibility to make sure two new training programs were ready to be implemented in a few short days. At the rate she was going, the task would never get finished.

Darn it! If Sophie hadn't turned a corner at just the right moment, she would've been spared the sickening sight of her dream man with another woman. Now the image of Thom Nichols stepping off the elevator with his arm wrapped around Tanya Whitmore's slender waist was stuck in Sophie's head.

The sexy grin he'd been giving the willowy blonde

had made it quite apparent he was enjoying every minute of her company. The realization had left Sophie nauseous and even more desperate. She couldn't sit back and wait for Thom Nichols to take notice of her. She had to come up with some sort of strategy to snare the man's attention.

But how did a woman go about making herself appealing to the sexiest man alive? There was hardly a female working at Robinson Tech who didn't sigh at the mere mention of Thom's name. Sophie didn't want to think of her opposition in terms of numbers: it would be too staggering. Besides, she already knew the task of snaring her man wasn't going to be easy.

But Sophie's father, the giant tech mogul Gerald Robinson, had lectured her plenty of times about setting goals and achieving them through hard work and confidence. The same could be applied in this situation. Her goal was to have Thom Nichols as her Valentine dream date.

Now, if she could just figure out how to make that happen.

"Sophie? What are you doing here at this hour?"

Since everyone in her department had left hours ago, the unexpected voice caught her by surprise, especially when she'd been sitting there with her head in the clouds.

Glancing over her shoulder, she saw Mason Montgomery shoving back the cuff of a pale blue dress shirt to study his watch. The tall, dark-haired computer programmer had probably seen her staring off into space like some lovesick teenager. The notion sent a flood of pink embarrassment to her cheeks.

Mason was far too intellectual and mature to understand a woman's crush on an attractive man. Or was he? With him working just across the hall from her, they'd often exchanged greetings and talked about work or current events, but they'd never been more than casual

friends. He was a crackerjack programmer who'd created several highly successful apps for the company. He
was also mannerly and nice-looking in a boy-next-door
kind of way. He just wasn't Thom Nichols.

"Oh, hi, Mason. I guess I've been so engrossed in my
work I didn't notice the time." Which wasn't a complete
lie, she thought. It had been hours since she'd glanced at
the clock on her desk, but only because she'd been too
busy fantasizing about her Valentine date. At least, the
man she was hoping would become her Valentine.

A frown furrowed his forehead. "Surely your father
doesn't expect you to wear yourself out. I realize he's a
stickler about deadlines, but I don't think he'd want his
daughter to collapse with fatigue."

Laughing, Sophie swiveled her chair so that she was
facing her late night visitor. "Most everyone in the building thinks Gerald Robinson is a taskmaster, but he's really just a big teddy bear with a loud growl."

His smile exposed a row of straight white teeth and
Sophie could see the expression was sincere. She liked
that about Mason Montgomery. He always seemed genuine. But Thom's dazzling smile could charm the fleas
right off a cat. How could any other man compare to that?

"Drop the *teddy* and I'll believe you."

She tossed strands of long brown hair over her shoulder before gesturing to a thick folder lying open on her
desk. "I've been going over a presentation for a new job-
training program the company will soon put in place.
Actually, there's a new program for your department
and marketing."

His brows lifting with interest, he moved inside the
cubicle and rested a hip against the side of her desk. "Oh?
Robinson Tech is going to put its programmers through
more training?"

She laughed at his wary expression. "Only the newly hired employees. Not the old veterans like you."

"Ouch!" he said with a chuckle. "I'm not so sure I like that *old* part."

Shaking her head, she gave him another smile. "I just meant you've worked here for a long time. As for your age, you couldn't be much older than me. I'm twenty-four."

"Try five years," he admitted. "I'm twenty-nine."

"Ooooh, that's terribly old," she joked, then added in a more serious tone, "Speaking of working late, I've noticed you've been burning the midnight oil here lately. You know, my father wouldn't want you collapsing from fatigue, either."

His brown eyes twinkling, he picked up a hunk of raw amethyst Sophie used for a paper weight. "We're getting a new app ready to roll in a few days. I want to make sure there are no glitches before Wes sends it on to your father for final approval. Sometimes that means losing sleep and a meal or two. But there's no need for you to worry you might have to scrape me off the floor. I've been eating my spinach."

Mason was hardly a muscle man, Sophie decided, as she studied him from beneath her lashes. But he had a trim, athletic build that implied he hit the gym on a regular basis. Although from the long hours he put in at Robinson Tech, she couldn't imagine where he found the extra time for himself.

"Mmm. I like my spinach in enchiladas," she said. "But I'd eat it raw or standing on my head if it would make me as tech savvy as you."

He shook his head. "And I wish I had your gift for communicating with people. I've seen you in action—how easy it is for you to soothe irate employees. I wouldn't have the patience to listen to their complaints, much less calm their tempers. And you can do something around here that no one else can do."

Intrigued, she leaned back in her chair and arched a brow at him. "Oh? I can't imagine what that might be."

"You can put a smile on our boss's face. I've never seen anyone but you make Gerald Robinson happy."

Her short laugh dismissed the compliment. "That's only because I'm the baby of his eight children. My siblings all complain that our father lets me get away with murder. But that's not really true. I just happen to be a positive thinker."

A doubtful grin lifted one corner of his mouth. "Positive thinker, huh? So that puts you in your father's good graces?"

She shot him a clever smile. "In a roundabout way. I happen to think if you can dream it, you can do it. And Dad likes it when people get things done."

Mason tossed the piece of lilac-colored quartz from one hand to the other and forced his gaze to remain on the rock rather than Sophie's lovely face. Not for anything did he want her to think he was staring. Even though he wanted to.

Of all the women who worked at Robinson Tech, Sophie had to be the most beautiful, he decided. Her long brown hair hung straight against her back, while her creamy skin glowed as though she was lit from within. And those brown eyes fringed with long, black lashes were like looking into a cup of hot, sweet chocolate.

She was the youngest child of the famous Fortune Robinson family. Their wealth was the sort that a simple man like Mason could only dream about. And yet none of those obstacles had stopped him from watching her from afar and wondering how it might be to actually take her on a date. If that made him a fool, then he was a big one, even by Texas standards.

"So you're a dreamer." His gaze settled on her face and suddenly he felt a hard tug deep inside him. Unfortunately, the sensation had nothing to do with him missing dinner and everything about the effervescent glow in her eyes. "Tell me, Sophie, what does a woman like you dream about?"

Her cheeks turned a darker pink. A telltale sign that when he'd walked up on her a few moments ago, she'd been thinking about a man. What else could put that sort of spaced out look on a woman's face?

She shrugged one slender shoulder and the slight movement caused Mason's gaze to dip from her face to the curve of her breasts pushing against the magenta colored top, then farther downward to where a close fitting black skirt stopped just above her knees and a pair of strappy high heels covered her small feet.

"Oh, I dream about lots of things," she said. "Like work and travel and family. But mostly I dream about—"

His eyes lifted to see a smile tilting the corners of her soft, pink lips. As Mason studied the moist curves, he felt the sudden urge to clear his throat.

"About what?" he prodded.

Her gaze dropped shyly from his. "Finding true love like some of my brother and sisters. They're married and happy and planning families of their own." She sighed. "But I need the right man for that. And I think I've found him."

The right man. Austin, Texas was full of eligible bachelors, but he couldn't imagine any of them being good enough for Sophie. So who could possibly be the right man for this pampered princess, he wondered, while attempting to swat away a stab of foolish jealousy.

Folding his arms against his chest, he hoped he appeared cool instead of moonstruck. "Does the lucky guy know he's targeted yet?"

With a nervous little laugh, she said, "Uh, not exactly. But I'm planning on letting him know soon. Very soon."

It was stupid of Mason to feel deflated, but he did. Sophie could fly to any place in the world anytime she wanted. The man who'd caught her eye could be in Paris or London, anywhere besides Austin. "Do I know this guy?"

She picked up a pencil and tapped it against a notepad. As Mason looked at her dainty hands with their perfectly manicured fingernails, he doubted she'd ever had to lift more than a pencil. But to her credit, she and her siblings contributed long hours to their father's company, even though their financial security had been set the day they'd been born.

She said, "I'm not ready to name names, but yes, you certainly know him. He's handsome and very smart. And has a great job here at Robinson Tech."

Hey, she could be describing him, Mason thought hopefully. He was smart and certain people had told him he was handsome. He also had a great job with the company.

"Sounds like a nice guy," Mason admitted.

A wistful smile put a foggy look in her brown eyes. "Oh, he's very nice. And practically oozes charisma. When my guy walks into a room all the women catch their breath and stare. And wish *he* belonged to *them*."

Dang. That definitely crossed him off the list of possibilities. Though finding a date for himself wasn't exactly as difficult as moving a mountain, Mason hardly had women swooning at his feet. He was the one with the shoulder they wanted to cry on. The one they came running to whenever some reckless rebel threw them over for a biker chick or rich cougar. Always the friend, but rarely the lover. That was good ole Mason.

"Nadine, one of my coworkers, says there are plenty of hunky men working in this building. Your guy must be one of them," he said.

A sly look crossed her face. "He's definitely suave. But he has an edge about him, too. Just enough to keep a woman guessing. Without making him too complex, that is."

Thom Nichols. Damn it! She was talking about that phony, two-timing womanizer who ate women for breakfast and spit their bones to his Doberman pinscher. But Mason could hardly express his opinion about the man to Sophie. He'd learned long ago that putting down a boyfriend was not the way to score points with a woman.

Clearing his throat, he asked, "Do you really think any man could be as perfect as you're making this one out to be?"

The long sigh she released troubled Mason greatly. Even if he didn't have a chance in a million with this woman, he'd hate to see her hurt by lothario Thom.

"Well, I think he's perfect for me," she reasoned. "And Valentine's Day will be here in a couple of weeks. By then I plan to have Mr. Right exactly where I want him."

She patted the side of her hip, but rather than envisioning Thom standing next to Sophie, Mason was visualizing himself at her side. And suddenly he was determined to make the image come true. She might be thinking of Thom as her Mr. Right, but Mason was going to do everything possible to make her see she was all wrong about the plastic marketing strategist. And that Mason was her *real* Mr. Right.

Placing the amethyst back on a neat stack of legal papers, Mason straightened away from the desk. "Well, it's getting really late and I still have a few things to do at home before the morning gets here and everything starts over."

"You should get yourself a maid," Sophie suggested. "You'd be surprised by how much she'd ease your work-load."

Mason was thinking he'd much rather have a woman to warm his bed than a maid to clean his house. Preferably one with long brown hair, killer legs and a waist that would fit right between his two hands.

Grinning, he winked at her and started out of the cubicle. "No thanks," he tossed over his shoulder. "I'll just eat more spinach."

"Have you lost your mind, Sophie? You, of all people, chasing after a man! I just don't get it."

She glared at her sister Olivia, who'd made herself comfortable in one of the matching wingchairs in the sitting area of Sophie's enormous bedroom suite. Even though Olivia had recently moved into a place of her own, she often stopped by the Robinson estate to visit. Sophie had always admired her older sister and often sought her advice on personal matters. Only moments earlier, Sophie had confided her plans to snare Thom Nichols and much to her chagrin, Olivia had immediately exploded with protests.

"No. You wouldn't understand," Sophie said, trying to keep the bite of sarcasm from her voice. "You don't have the same dreams that I do. You don't care if you ever have a man in your life."

Sighing, Olivia crossed her legs, as though talking sense to her younger sister was going to be a long, arduous endeavor. "We're not talking about me, Sophie. This is about you. You making a fool of yourself by chasing after a man."

Hadn't their own mother made a fool of herself by living with a man who'd cheated on her for years? Sophie felt like flinging the nasty question at Olivia, but bit it back instead. It wasn't her place to judge either of her parents for the artificial state of their marriage. For some reason Sophie couldn't fathom, the two remained steadfastly together. Even so, the connection between her mother and father was about as warm as a trip to Antarctica. And Sophie was determined that she would never settle for such a cold relationship with a man.

"I'm not actually going to chase him," Sophie corrected as she walked over to the double doors that opened to an enormous walk-in closet. "I'm just going to give him a little nudge—a reminder that I'm in the building and available."

Olivia snorted. "Thom Nichols believes every woman in the building is available to him. I just don't see the attraction you have for the man."

Gasping, Sophie shot a look of disbelief at her sister. "Are you joking? He has to be the sexiest man alive! Well, at least in the state of Texas!"

"We live in a mighty big state, Sophie. Just how would you describe a sexy man? Would you know one if you saw one?"

Momentarily ignoring Olivia's barbed questions, Sophie snatched several pieces of clothing from the closet and carried them over to a king-sized bed.

"Apparently you need a lesson in identifying a sexy hunk from the regular crowd," Sophie told her. "He's tall, dark haired, has a killer smile and walks with just enough swag to let a woman know he's full of confidence."

"Hmmp. You mean with just enough conceit to let us know he's struck on himself."

Sophie glanced over to see Olivia shaking her head with disgust. Her sister's cynical attitude irked her and saddened her at the same time. With gently waving hair that was a much darker brown than Sophie's and beautiful features to match, her older sister could attract any man she wanted, but so far she viewed men and marriage as something worse than a chronic disease.

"Why do you have to be so jaded?" Sophie asked. "I wish now I'd never told you about my plans to go after Thom. It's obvious you don't understand how I feel."

With a rueful sigh, Olivia pushed herself out of the chair and walked over to Sophie. "You're right, I don't understand. So why don't you tell me how you feel about Thom?"

In an effort to gauge her sister's sincerity, Sophie looked into Olivia's brown eyes that were incredibly similar to her own.

"Do you honestly want to know?" Sophie asked. "Or are you just patronizing me?"

"I honestly want to know." She reached over and plucked a black knit dress from the pile of clothing on the bed. "I need to understand why a young, beautiful woman like you feels the need to change yourself just to snag a man. If you have to be someone you're not in order to make him like you, then you're deluding yourself that it will ever work."

Deflated by Olivia's negative viewpoint, Sophie sank onto the bed. "I've had my eye on him for a long time," Sophie told her. "And the more I've watched him, the more I'm sure he was put on this earth to be my one true love."

Olivia let out a loud, mocking groan, then immediately plopped a hand over her mouth. "Sorry. I couldn't help it."

Sophie turned her misty gaze on a far corner of the room and swallowed hard. Not one of her seven legitimate siblings believed she was mature enough to take on a serious relationship with a man, much less think about marriage or a family. They all viewed her as the baby, the one offspring of Charlotte and Gerald Robinson who had been so sheltered, it would take years for her to grow up and acquire a head full of wisdom. Sometimes she even wondered how she'd gotten her job at Robinson Tech. Was it because she was well trained for the job, or because her father was the boss?

"Sure. I know. It all sounds silly to you," Sophie mumbled.

"Oh, Sophie, don't be so defensive." Easing down next to her, Olivia wrapped an arm around Sophie's shoulders. "I'm sorry. It's just that I don't think you grasp yet what love is. And I don't want you to get hurt while you're learning."

Blinking at the tears stinging her eyes, Sophie looked directly at her sister. "I'll tell you one thing. I know what love *isn't*," she said in a brittle tone. "It isn't like this sham between our parents! Furthermore, I'd stay a spinster for the rest of my life if it meant avoiding the sort of marriage our mother has endured over the years."

"Sophie!" Olivia scolded. "How can you say that? Dad has given Mother and all of us kids anything and everything we could possibly want."

"So in other words, you're saying Mother stays with Dad because of his money and this." Sophie waved her arm, indicating the spacious room with its extravagant furnishings. "This high-class lifestyle he can provide her."

Frowning, Olivia tossed the black dress back onto the bed, then looked toward the door as though she feared their mother might walk in at any moment. "That's an awful thing to say, Sophie!" she said in a hushed tone. "Mother stays with Dad because she loves him!"

"Really? How could that be when she and the whole world know that Dad has had numerous affairs? You're telling me that love can actually exist under those conditions?"

"Of course I am," Olivia insisted. "Why else would she stay if she didn't love him?"

Sophie had been asking herself that very question for some time now, and the more she did, the more she considered the idea that their mother might be hiding something from the whole family. But since that was only speculation, she was hardly going to mention her suspicions to Olivia. And she definitely wasn't going to comment about their father anymore tonight. In Olivia's eyes, Gerald Robinson could do little wrong. She'd chosen to forgive and forget about his philandering. Probably because Olivia happened to be one of their father's favorites and he doted on her even more than he did Sophie.

Instead she switched the conversation back to her dream man.

"Thom is handsome and dynamic," Sophie told her. "And I plan to make him mine by Valentine's Day."

"Exactly what does your plan entail?"

Sophie walked over to the cheval mirror and twisted her hair into a loose knot atop her head. "Don't worry, I'm not going to change who I am. I'm only going to tweak the outside a bit. Maybe some highlights in my hair or some new clothes. Some sexy knee-high boots might do the trick."

"And when you do catch his attention? Then what?"

Sophie smiled confidently at Olivia's image in the mirror. "Then he'll begin to look at all of me. Not just the outside."

With a rueful shake of her head, Olivia warned, "You are headed for disaster, my dear sister. Thom Nichols wants two things from a woman. Sex and money. He's hardly interested in finding the love of a lifetime."

Sophie's lips pressed into an angry line as she turned to face her sister. "Go ahead and be cynical and negative. Do your best to make me look foolish just because I want a man to love and for him to love me!"

Olivia threw up her hands in a gesture of surrender. "I give up. I can see this is something you're going to have to figure out for yourself. And far be it from me to ruin your quest for love."

"You'll see," Sophie countered with conviction. "By Valentine's Day I'm going to have my man."

"I hope you do get the right man—for you, that is. And I hope by Valentine's Day you'll begin to see the whole picture. Presently, this crush you have on Thom is giving you tunnel vision."

Sophie frowned with confusion. "What is that supposed to mean?"

"The only man you see in front of you is Thom. You might allow yourself to look around a bit. You might find out that Mr. Right is someone else."

Sophie scoffed. "I'm not shopping for high heels. I know what I want when I see it. I don't have to keep looking for another man. Thom is perfect for me."

A wan smile on her face, Olivia leaned forward and

kissed Sophie's cheek. "It's getting late. I'll see you to-morrow."

As Sophie watched her sister leave the bedroom, a tinge of sadness began to push her frustration aside. A few kind words of encouragement from Olivia would have been far nicer than a prediction of failure. She'd made it sound like Sophie didn't have enough sense to differentiate between a skirt chaser and a gentleman.

Sighing, Sophie sank onto the edge of the bed and plucked a family photo from the nightstand. The framed image was one of the few pictures that included all her brothers and sisters. With their busy lives taking them in all directions her whole family wasn't often together. But this particular photo had been taken at their parents' twenty-fifth wedding anniversary and everyone, including Charlotte and Gerald, looked happy. Yet that had been eleven years ago, long before anyone knew about Gerald's hidden identity or his affairs.

A year ago, her older brother, Ben, had been instrumental in uncovering the truth. Their forceful father, one of the most famous tech moguls in the world, wasn't really Gerald Robinson. He was Jerome Fortune, a member of the famous Fortune family. As if that wasn't enough of a stunner, during the investigation, Ben had found a thirty-three-year-old illegitimate son of Gerald's named Keaton Whitfield living in London.

Since that time, their newly discovered half brother had moved to Austin and started building a rapport with all his siblings. Sophie had to admit she liked Keaton and didn't begrudge his place in the family. Yet the whole revelation of her father's other life had shaken her to the core.

All at once she'd had to accept the fact that her father had never been the man she'd believed him to be. And as for her mother, who could possibly know why Charlotte had hung around for all these years? It sure as heck wasn't for love as Olivia had suggested.

Face it, Sophie, your parents are phonies and so are you! The only reason you have an important position at Robinson Tech, or anything else for that matter, is because of your name. It certainly hasn't come from your brains, or beauty, or hard work. The sooner you realize the truth, the better off you'll be.

Disgusted with the degrading voice in her head, she put the photo back and squeezed her eyes shut.

If her parents were shams, then their marriage was even more of a joke, Sophie miserably concluded. So what did that make their children? Mere symbols of a fake love? Moreover, what did it make Sophie?

Her lips pressed into a determined line, Sophie looked over at the clothes she'd tossed onto the bed. In one aspect, Olivia had been correct. The outside of her wasn't nearly as important as the inside. Yes, she wanted to look just as attractive as her sisters and all the other beautiful women of Austin. But she also wanted everyone to see she was more than just the youngest child of a famous and wealthy family. And she was hardly a fool for wanting the same genuine sort of love that her siblings Ben, Wes, Graham, Rachel and Zoe had found, she thought.

By Valentine's Day, Thom was going to see she was worthy of him. And then everything she'd ever wanted in her life was going to fall into place.

Chapter Two

"They make a nice-looking couple. The office heart-throb and the boss's daughter. Can you think of a more perfect pairing than that?"

"Yeah, about a million of them," Mason muttered under his breath.

"What did you say?"

Mason forced his gaze away from Sophie and Thom, who were sitting together at the far end of a long utility table. In the past year he could count on one hand the times he'd seen Thom taking midafternoon coffee in the second floor breakroom. Which could only mean that Sophie had gone to work on her plan and persuaded him to join her.

Mason looked over at the platinum-haired woman sitting next to him. Nadine had been working in the programming department for many years, long before Mason had ever taken a job at Robinson Tech. Divorced and somewhere in her forties, she pushed the envelope of the company's dress code, but her flamboyant appearance belied her shrewd mind. Even though Mason had graduated in the top half of his college class, he didn't possess half the knowledge about programming that Nadine held in that sassy head of hers.

"I said they're all wrong for each other. Totally wrong."

Nadine turned a frown on Mason. "You don't say? How did you come to that conclusion?"

Mason squeezed the foam cup of cold coffee so hard it nearly collapsed in his hand. "It should be obvious," he said. "Everyone in this building knows he's a player."

Nadine shrugged. "So? Maybe that doesn't bother Sophie. Besides, when I called them a couple I didn't mean it literally. Geez, Mason, lighten up. The two of them are merely having coffee together. Not discussing their marriage vows."

If Nadine had heard Sophie talking last night about snaring Mr. Right, she wouldn't be making light of the situation. Couldn't Nadine see how Sophie was leaning her head toward Thom's and smiling at him like he was the last male on earth? It was more than obvious that she was on a serious mission to catch Thom Nichols. And what was even clearer was that Mason couldn't just sit around and watch himself lose the lady of his dreams to a no-good womanizer.

"I wouldn't be so sure," Mason muttered as he studied Sophie from the corner of his eye. Today she was wearing a short black dress that resembled a sweater. The fabric outlined her petite curves while black suede boots with chunky heels fit snugly around her shapely calves. A pink-and-black printed scarf hung around her neck, as did dangling jet bead earrings. She looked more than lovely, he decided. She looked downright sexy. And the fact that it was Thom who, at the moment, was receiving her undivided attention clawed jealously at Mason.

"Why, Mason Montgomery, I do believe I hear a green streak in your voice," Nadine declared. "Are you interested in Sophie Robinson?"

"Fortune Robinson," he corrected. "Remember? The family discovered they're actually a part of Kate Fortune's bunch. You know—the famous cosmetic heiress."

Nadine nodded. "I remember about a year ago when the news came out about Gerald. But I keep forgetting about the kids tacking on the Fortune name." Pausing, she clicked her tongue. "Poor little Sophie. She's such a sweet girl. It must've been hard on her—learning all that scandalous stuff about her father."

Mason could hardly imagine how it would feel to learn your father was actually someone you never knew. His own dad was a hard working pipeline technician for a gas and oil company in San Antonio. Hadley Montgomery had always been a strong anchor for Mason and his two older brothers. Finding out he'd had a secret life would shake the very ground Mason walked on.

"I imagine Sophie and her siblings have tried to keep a stiff upper lip through all of it," Mason replied. "After all, they can't help what their father has done."

Mason suddenly heard Sophie's light laugh at the far end of the table. The happy sound cut straight through him and he wondered if he was destined to become a fool over women. It hadn't been that long ago that Melody had broken his heart by deserting him for another man. He was an idiot for thinking things could be different with Sophie. She was already so besotted with Thom Nichols it was like she was wearing blinders.

Nadine's shrewd chuckle momentarily distracted him. "Well, the revelation about Gerald most likely made all the siblings richer than they were already. Can you imagine how it must feel to have that sort of wealth? They'll never have to worry about paying a utility bill or wondering if they can afford to eat more than macaroni and cheese for supper."

Along with her crush on Thom Nichols, Sophie's wealth was one more wall standing between them. But Mason was determined to knock down those obstacles and clear the path for a chance with her.

"Sophie might be filthy rich, but she's not a snob. She works very hard."

Nadine shot him an impish smile. "How would you know? I never see you cross the hall to HR. You always have your head buried in your own work."

If Mason explained to Nadine that he often spotted Sophie working late at night, then he'd also be admitting he had a habit of staying long after quitting time, too. And Nadine might misconstrue things and get the idea that Mason put in overtime just for a chance to see Sophie alone. Which was completely untrue. Until last night, he thought sheepishly.

"For your information," Mason said matter-of-factly, "the state bird of Texas is the mockingbird and we have plenty of them flying around the building. They tell me lots of things."

"Pertaining to Sophie, I presume." Nadine picked up her smartphone and pretended to swipe. "I'm going to find the best psychiatrist in the city of Austin. Hopefully a doctor can help you with this bird disorder you've developed."

Shaking his head, Mason shoved back his chair. "My coffee is cold. I'm going back to work. Are you ready?"

Groaning, Nadine ran a hand through her wispy blonde hair and glanced around the room. "Sure, I'm ready. There's no men around here giving me the goo-goo eye anyway."

Mason smirked. "If a man was, you'd promptly tell him to go stick his head in a garbage can."

Nadine laughed. "Not if he was the *right* man."

Mr. Right. Mason was sick of hearing that term and even sicker of picturing Thom Nichols as the definition.

He rose to his feet and started to follow Nadine out of the breakroom, when behind them, Sophie suddenly called out to him.

"Here's your chance," Nadine whispered. "Better go say hello. I'll see you later."

Feeling like a nervous teenager, but trying to be cool, Mason walked to the end of the table where his dream lady and Mr. Heartthrob were chatting as though they'd been friends forever. To say this was a fast turn of events would be putting it mildly.

"Hi, Mason!" she said cheerfully. "I saw you leaving and wanted to say hello before you got away."

"Hello, Sophie. Thom." He smiled at Sophie then forced a polite glance at Thom. The other man reminded Mason of one of those handsome movie stars who always played the hero on screen, but in reality couldn't do so much as change a flat tire if a dozen lives were depending on him. "How's the coffee?"

"Great," Thom quickly answered and gestured to the small thermos sitting in front of him. "Sophie brought her own special brew from home and talked me into trying some."

Mason wanted to knock the leering smile he was giving Sophie right off the other man's face. Instead, he focused his gaze on Sophie.

"Good planning," he said sagely. "About the coffee, I mean."

Color swept across Sophie's cheeks and Mason knew she'd picked up on his subtle comment.

"I try to think of the little things. They make the work day go brighter," she said with a wide smile, then looked adoringly at Thom. "Did you know Thom is heading the marketing for your new sports app? The media blitz he's planning is bound to make it a huge seller."

Mason had rather believe the app would be a huge seller because he'd developed a good product. Not because of a slick talking salesman who could convince folks on Galveston Island to buy a set of snow chains.

Mason said, "I like to think Sports & More is a worthwhile project that deserves plenty of marketing."

"You're lucky, Mason," Thom spoke up. "Mr. Robinson made the decision to spend a bankroll on the marketing for Sports & More. You must have done something right this time. I love sports, but to be honest, I perform better on the dance floor than I do the gym floor."

In Mason's opinion, the grin Thom was giving Sophie could only be described as lecherous. Which made it even more puzzling to Mason as to why she'd want a guy like Thom in her life. But women viewed things differently than men, and clearly she was seeing something in Thom that Mason was missing. Whatever the reason for her infatuation with the man, Mason couldn't just stand passively around and watch this beautiful woman get her heart crushed.

"I'm sure you've had lots of practice doing the… hustle," Mason replied.

Sophie's brows arched upward, but she didn't make any sort of reply. Thom merely let out a cocky laugh. Mason decided he should make a quick exit before he really insulted Thom and made both of them angry.

Glancing at his watch, Mason said, "Well, my break is over. Nice to see you two."

Once he'd returned to his desk, it was only a matter of seconds before Nadine sauntered into his cubicle and propped a hip on his desk. "Okay, what happened? Did you score points with the girl?"

Frowning, he tried to focus on the computer screen in front of him, but the only thing in front of his eyes was Sophie. "I wasn't trying to score points. Which is just as well. I came close to calling Thom a creep right to his face."

Nadine groaned. "Let me give you some advice, Mason. The more you toss insults in Thom's direction, the more she's going to defend him."

He turned and glowered at her. "I know that much. It's just that whenever I'm around the guy I get the urge to vomit. And then things start coming out of my mouth before I can stop them."

"Look, my friend, if you're really interested in snagging Sophie's attention, you need to forget about Thom Nichols and start concentrating on how to make yourself more appealing to her. If you do things right, she'll start looking at you instead of him."

"You think so?"

"Trust me. You have loads to offer a woman." She patted his shoulder. "I better get to work. Wes has assigned me the job of coming up with a mother/baby app store. I can't imagine what our boss was thinking. My daughter is twenty years old now. What do I remember about having a baby?"

"Hmm. I expect it's like riding a bike. Once you learn, you never forget."

Nadine laughed, causing Mason to chuckle along with her.

"Well, a person can get rusty if he doesn't practice," he agreed. "But you can always knock off a little rust."

"And how am I supposed to do that? Have another baby?"

"Why not? Women your age are having babies all the time."

Her expression softened in a way Mason had never seen before and then she reached out and gently patted his cheek. "You are the sweetest man ever. Sophie's an idiot if she doesn't latch on to you."

Sweet. Mason didn't want to be a piece of candy. He wanted to be viewed as authoritative, masculine and tough. He wanted women, particularly Sophie, to see him as a take-charge kind of guy who could melt a heart with just one smoldering look. He wanted to be more like his brothers, Doug and Shawn. Neither one of them ever had to worry over catching a woman's attention. Their problem was trying to decide which one they wanted and on what night of the week.

But Doug was an assistant prosecutor in Bexar County, a fierce lion in the courtroom. And Shawn was a lieutenant on the San Antonio police force. They were both handsome and forceful, with jobs that women admired. Even as children, Mason had never felt as though he could compete with his stronger, older brothers. And time hadn't changed Mason's feelings. Sure, he had a great job and his physical appearance wasn't exactly homely. But compared to his brothers, he was a geek.

If he ever expected to get Sophie to notice him, then he was going to have to be more like Doug and Shawn and a whole lot less like himself, he thought grimly.

More than an hour later, Mason was working when Sophie suddenly walked into his cubicle, nearly sending him into shock. The only time she'd ever stopped by his desk was when she'd personally helped him with a health insurance issue.

But it was clear this visit of hers had nothing to do with insurance. She was grinning from ear to ear and practically dancing on her toes.

She pulled up a chair and leaned her head close to his. The soft scent of her perfume swirled around him and tugged on his already dazed senses.

"Mason, I'm sorry if I'm interrupting your work," she said in a hushed tone. "But I'm so excited I had to tell someone! And since I shared my plans with you last night— Well, it's happened!"

Totally bemused, he stared at her beaming face. "It has?"

"Yes! Already! Can you believe it? Here I was thinking I was going to have to do handsprings out in the hall to get Thom to take a second look at me and all it took was a cup of exotic coffee."

Mason had never felt so deflated in his life. "You two looked pretty chummy in the break room."

"Chummy? Mason, you're so funny." Laughing lightly, she gave his knee a gentle squeeze. "He's asked me out on a date! A real date! Tonight! Isn't it incredible?"

Mason felt like handing her the letter opener on his desk and telling her to stab him right in the gut. The act would have been more merciful than the news she was giving him.

He looked into her brown eyes and wondered if they would ever shine for him the way they were shining at this moment.

"A date, huh? That was fast work."

"You're telling me! I only started my plan today. I never expected to have results this quick." Her expression suddenly sobering, she glanced around the large room to make sure no one was listening. "Mason, you're a really honest guy. Tell me, do you think Thom might've asked me out just because—well, because I'm Gerald Robinson's daughter?"

Hell yes! Mason wanted to shout the words at her. But he held them back. One thing he was certain of, Sophie was a soft, gentle person. It would hurt her deeply if she thought her dream man might be using her for his own gain. Mason couldn't do that to her. Not right now. He couldn't bring himself to shatter the deliriously happy look on her face.

The more you insult Thom Nichols, the more Sophie will defend him. At this moment, Nadine's words couldn't have been more right.

Unable to keep looking her in the eye, Mason's gaze drifted to the computer screen. But for all he could see, the words might as well have been written in a foreign language. "Oh, Sophie, I wouldn't worry about that. Thom already has a good position in the company. He hardly needs you to help him get in your father's good graces."

"I guess that's true enough," she said quietly. "I shouldn't have ever let the idea cross my mind. It's just a date. Not a marriage proposal."

Thank God, Mason thought. If that ever happened, he'd have to speak up.

"That's true. And anyway, you're an intelligent woman. You'd know right off if a man was trying to use you."

Her eyes grew soft. And then suddenly without any warning at all, she leaned forward and pressed a kiss to his cheek.

"Thank you, Mason. You're wonderful!"

To his utter amazement, she pressed another kiss

to same spot she'd already branded with her lips, then jumped to her feet.

"Stop by my desk tomorrow and I'll let you know how things go," she told him, then with a wiggle of her fingers she hurried away.

Mason lifted fingertips to the spot she'd kissed not once, but twice. The skin was still tingling as though she'd stuck a naked electric wire to his cheek. If a simple kiss to the side of his face had caused this much reaction, the feel of her lips against his would probably have him dancing like a drunk idiot atop his desk.

Darting a glance toward Nadine's desk, he realized the woman must have seen the whole interchange between him and Sophie. She was smiling broadly and giving him a thumbs up. The encouraging signal had Mason stifling a loud groan. Nadine didn't know Sophie had merely stopped by to announce her date with Thom. And at the moment, Mason felt too sick to set his coworker straight.

Later that evening at the Robinson estate, Sophie was hurrying to her bedroom when her mother called out to her.

"Sophie? Why are you running through the house like a child?"

Laughing, Sophie stopped in her tracks and waited until her mother caught up to her.

"Probably because I feel like a happy kid tonight. Don't you ever feel that way, Mother? Like kicking up your heels and doing pirouettes?"

"I like to think I'm in good physical condition for my age," Charlotte told her daughter, "but I'm not exactly ready for ballet leaps and spins."

For a woman in her midseventies, Sophie's mother still looked youthful. Of course, it helped that she could afford to get routine facials and have her own personal trainer, along with a chef who designed meals to keep her weight down and her skin and hair glowing.

Smiling brightly, Sophie said, "I refuse to believe that, Mother. I happen to think you could dance all night."

Charlotte pursed her lips with disapproval. "Those occasions are long over for me, Sophie."

Sophie frowned. "That's nonsense. Dad doesn't think in those terms. He still does plenty of fun things."

"Fun," Charlotte repeated in a mocking tone. "Your father views the whole world as his playground. That will never change."

It was a rare occasion that Charlotte made any sort of comment about her husband. More often than not, she went about her business as though Gerald didn't exist.

Looping her arm through her mother's, Sophie urged her down the hallway to her bedroom. "Come sit and help me pick out something nice to wear," she told Charlotte. "I have a date tonight and I want to look extra special."

"Who is this special date?" her mother asked, taking a seat in one of the wingback chairs. "Do I know the young man?"

"I doubt it," Sophie called from inside the closet. "He works for the company—in marketing. His name is Thom Nichols."

"Nichols," Charlotte repeated thoughtfully. "Is he related to Drew Nichols, who owns Austin Capital Bank and Trust?"

"I have no idea," Sophie answered as she stepped out with clothes tossed over her arm.

Charlotte gasped with dismay. "You have no idea? You're going out with the man and you don't know any more than that about him?"

The branches of a family tree were very important to

Charlotte. So was public perception. Which made Sophie wonder how her mother had stood so stanchly by her husband when the news of his London love child had hit the rumor mill in Austin.

"Oh, Mother, I hardly need to know the size of Thom's wallet before I go on a date with him."

Her spine ramrod straight, Charlotte scooted to the edge of the chair. "I am not talking about money. As a Robinson you have a social standing to uphold and—"

"A Fortune Robinson," Sophie interrupted dourly. "Surely you haven't forgotten I have an extra name now. But then, I suppose as a Fortune, I have an equally important reputation to uphold."

Her hands clasped tightly together in her lap, Charlotte said stiffly, "The added name is a fact I don't care to ponder on."

"That's perfectly understandable," Sophie said gently. She walked over and sank onto the dressing bench facing her mother. "Ever since Keaton has come into the family I've been wondering about you, Mother."

A shutter fell across Charlotte's face, making her features unreadable. "There's no reason for you to be wondering about me. I'm fine. And I'll remain fine."

Not wanting to add to her mother's suffering, Sophie chose her next words carefully.

"Actually, I've watched the way you've conducted yourself through this whole scandal, Mother, and I've been amazed. I couldn't have been nearly as strong and steadfast as you've been."

The rigidness of Charlotte's face eased a fraction as her glance returned to Sophie. "It's not been a picnic for me by any means. But I understand your father completely. Actually, I understand him better than anyone," she said. "And sometimes a wife just has to put on a brave face and look the other way."

The other way? Sophie was incredulous, but she carefully hid the reaction from her mother. Charlotte had grown up in a past era, where women had different roles in life. Especially when it came to men and marriage.

"Maybe so, Mother. And I know a person is supposed to be forgiving. But I happen to think you deserve better from Dad. For the life of me, I can't imagine why you stay married to him."

Her mother shot her a stern look of warning. "Your father and I have a complicated relationship. It's also unbreakable. I can assure you of that."

Unbreakable because her mother refused to let go of a cold marriage? Or maybe it was her father who kept his wife bound to his side for purposes other than love?

"Anything can break, Mother, with enough pressure."

"Gerald has provided me, you and everyone in his family with a wonderful life. Not one of you children has a thing to complain about. So don't."

The firm tone of Charlotte's voice told Sophie not to push the issue, so she would honor her mother's wishes and let the subject drop. But that didn't mean Sophie would stop speculating and wondering if there could be more to her mother's loyal devotion to her cheating husband.

Smiling, she focused on her upcoming date instead, standing and holding up a pale pink mini dress with black accents. "What do you think about this for dinner and a movie?"

"Dinner and a movie? You're calling that a special date?"

Sophie's laugh tinkled through the bedroom. "It's the man that's making it special. Not where we're going."

Clasping the dress to her, Sophie waltzed over the plush carpet, while her mother eyed her with speculation.

"Sophie, you always were an impulsive, dreamy child. I'd hoped that by the time you graduated college you'd be more realistic and settled. But it's clear you're still flittering around like a butterfly, believing life is nothing more than a rose garden. One of these days you're going to have to face the real world."

Pausing in front of Charlotte's chair, Sophie fought hard not to roll her eyes. If it wasn't so sad, her mother's comment would be laughable. Did she think pretending to have a loving, caring husband wasn't delusional?

"I crammed four years of college into three and I've held down a demanding job ever since," she said stiffly. "I'd call that very real, Mother."

Charlotte's features softened somewhat. "Oh, Sophie darling, there's no sense in you getting all defensive. I only meant—well, you're a romantic soul. You believe life is full of hearts and flowers and kisses. And I suppose there's nothing wrong with that—in small doses. But you also need to be firmly grounded."

When Sophie came home sporting an engagement ring, then her mother would see her butterfly daughter was perfectly capable of landing safely on her feet.

Determined not to let anything spoil her evening ahead, Sophie dropped a kiss on her mother's smooth cheek. "Don't worry, Mother. I promise not to let Thom sweep me off my feet tonight."

But I'm sure as heck going to try to sweep him off his.

Chapter Three

Several hours later, a bored Sophie stared at the theater screen while fighting back a yawn. She'd never been into action movies and this one, with its ridiculous, computerized explosions and car chases, was hardly enough to hold her attention.

When Thom had asked her what movie she'd like to see tonight, Sophie had generously insisted he choose, with hopes he'd view her as easy to please. She'd hardly expected him to take her to see *Road Devils: The Final Battle*. So far there hadn't been one meaningful exchange of dialogue. But that hadn't seemed to bother Thom; he appeared to be enthralled with the story. For the past hour and a half, he'd rarely glanced in her direction.

So much for taking pains with her hair and makeup, she thought wryly, as she sipped her diet soda and darted a glance over at Thom. At the moment, he was munching on butter-drenched popcorn, his gaze fixated on the gun battle on the screen. Even though he'd not been all that attentive, she had to admit he looked devilishly handsome tonight in close-fitting brown trousers and a black shirt. But was gazing at a good-looking face all she wanted?

The question had barely had time to roll through her mind when suddenly, for no unexplainable reason, Mason popped into her thoughts. Would he have brought her to this sort of juvenile flick?

Are you going crazy, Sophie? You've been bragging to everyone how you're going to snag Thom. Now you're finally out with him and you start thinking about Mason Montgomery! He's just a friend at work. He's not the man of your dreams!

The scolding voice in her head was correct. This was hardly the time for her thoughts to be straying to Mason. Yet this was the second time in the past few hours that a vision of the other man had appeared to her.

Earlier, when she and Thom had been sitting in a restaurant eating a simple meal of fish and French fries, a dish she'd learned was Thom's favorite, the image of Mason cutting into a rare steak and sipping red wine had popped into her mind. It was ridiculous! She had no idea whether Mason liked to eat such a masculine meal. Besides, Thom was the he-man of the two. Wasn't he?

"Wow, that was a great ending, don't you think?"

Ending? Sophie glanced around to see the credits were rolling on the screen and people were already filing toward the exits.

"Oh. Yes, for sure. It was very exciting," she said, hoping he wouldn't guess she'd mentally blanked out the last hour of the movie.

He tossed his empty soda cup into the popcorn tub and dropped the whole thing to the floor for the janitors to clean up.

"Ready?" he asked.

She nodded, while telling herself his untidiness was hardly anything to be concerned about. He was probably very orderly at his own place. Besides, it wasn't like she had to clean up after him.

Are you even ready to see this guy's apartment, Sophie? And what would you do if he tried to seduce you into his bed?

Frowning at the silly questions that continued to pop into her head, she nodded at him and reached for her coat. After he'd helped her into the garment, the two of them left the theater. Once they were outside, Sophie dropped her soda cup into a nearby trashcan.

As they walked across the parking lot to his car, Thom glanced at his watch. "It's getting rather late. I think we should call it a night. We both have to be at work early in the morning."

So much for worrying about going to his apartment, she thought. He couldn't even manage a stop off at a coffee house.

Sophie tried not to show her disappointment. After all, this was their first date. Just one of many, she hoped. She shouldn't be expecting him to behave as though he was reluctant to tear himself away from her company.

"Fine. I can always use the extra time to shampoo my hair and shave my legs—again."

He tossed her a puzzled look. "What?"

She chuckled and then realizing he was clueless, she shrugged. "Oh, nothing. Just a girl thing."

"You're a good sport, Sophie. I like that about you."

At least there was something about her he liked, Sophie decided. Although she would've preferred to hear him say how competent she was at her job. The way that Mason had complimented her.

Mason. Mason. Why did the man keep lurking at the edge of her mind?

Thankfully, Thom put his arm around her waist and as they walked the remaining distance to the car, she was able to push the ridiculous question from her mind.

When they reached the sleek, little sports car, he politely helped her into the bucket seat. No sensible economy car for this guy, Sophie decided. Apparently he wanted his mode of transportation to match his image. Cool and sexy.

She'd been sitting only inches away from the man for the past few hours. By now she should be feeling the itch to get closer. Instead, she was wondering about the other women he'd dated. No doubt most of them had been eager to get their hands on him. Shouldn't she be wanting to scoot closer and snuggle her cheek against his shoulder? Was she just not getting herself in the right frame of mind?

Minutes later, Sophie was still mulling over the troublesome ideas when they approached the iron security gates connecting the high stone walls surrounding the Robinson Estate.

After Sophie keyed in a code to allow them entry, Thom drove down a long drive lined with live oak trees. In the summer months, the multi-winged mansion was shaded by more live oaks, along with several massive pecan trees. Presently, winter had bared the branches of the pecan trees.

Normally, when Sophie went on a date, she met the guy at a chosen spot downtown. It saved him the inconvenience of driving to the estate and dealing with security. It also took away the intimidation factor. A few of her past dates had taken one look at her home and never asked her out again. But Thom was far more self-assured than that and she'd wanted this whole evening to feel like a special beginning.

After parking in the wide circular drive illuminated by solar footlights, Thom helped her from the car and walked her to the door. The arm at the back of her waist felt strong and sturdy, but she wasn't getting any warm or cuddly vibes from the contact. Maybe that was because she was still a little miffed at being brought home early as though she had a curfew.

"This is some serious digs, Sophie," he said as he eyed the elaborate entrance to the only home she'd ever known. "Bet the inside is even fancier than the outside."

The subtle hint brought Sophie up short. Did he want her to invite him in for a drink—with her father?

Hating herself for thinking such unseemly things about this man, she forced a smile on her face. "It's nice and comfortable," she said simply. "I'd invite you in, but like you said, it's getting late and I wouldn't want to disturb my parents. You understand, of course."

He smiled back and Sophie was relieved that he didn't appear to be offended. This was Thom. Her Thom. She wanted things between them to start off well. Even so, she had no intentions of being a pushover.

"Sure. Maybe next time," he suggested.

Tilting her head back, she studied his perfectly carved features. "Would you like there to be a next time?" she asked.

He shrugged. "Why not? I'm willing if you are."

His response wasn't exactly what she'd been hoping for, but this was just the beginning of things, she assured herself.

Lowering her lashes, she said demurely, "Yes. I'm willing."

"Great."

The simple word was said offhandedly as he shoved back the sleeve of his jacket to check his watch. Again. If time was more important to him than she was, she thought bleakly, she was doing something very wrong.

"Well, it's rather cold out here," she said. "Maybe we'd better say good-night."

Sophie turned toward the door, but before she could key in the entry code, his arm snaked around her waist and drew her toward him.

"I can't let you go in without a proper good-night," he said with practiced ease.

Finally! The word was zipping through Sophie's mind as she planted her hands on his chest and tilted her head slightly back. At last! Her dream man was going to kiss her!

Her heart tripping with anticipation, she waited for his kiss. But shockingly, when his lips met hers, her initial instinct was to push him away and step back. Somehow, she managed to catch herself before the crazy reaction ruined everything. Then, forcing herself to lean into him, she attempted to put real feeling into the kiss.

His lips moved expertly over hers with just enough pressure to convey that he was interested. The feeling was pleasant enough for Sophie, but there was no passion igniting inside her. No sweet singing birds sounding in her ears. No trembling in her knees. Even after he lifted his head, she was still anxiously waiting, expecting some last-minute explosion.

Smiling smugly, certain the dazed look on her face was a result of dreamy desire, he patted the top of her head. "Good night, Sophie. See you tomorrow."

"Yes. Good night."

As Sophie watched him walk back to his car, she was

struck by the stunning realization that something was very wrong with her.

Thom Nichols, the man of her dreams, had just kissed her and she hadn't felt a thing.

The next evening Mason was still at his desk, deep in work, when Nadine stopped by his cubicle.

"Hey, guy, haven't you looked at the clock? It's quitting time."

He glanced around to see Nadine was already buttoned up in a fake fur coat that resembled a cheetah. In spite of her smile, she looked drained.

"I'll be going soon," he told her. "I have a few more things I want to finish. How's the mother/baby app going?"

Groaning, she rolled her head one way and then the other. "I'm losing my mind. That's how it's going. Wanna help?"

Mason chuckled. "I have plenty of work waiting on me. Besides, I know nothing about mothers and babies."

Nadine grinned suggestively. "This would be a good opportunity for you to learn."

"Hah! It'll be years before I have a child. If ever," he said flatly.

"Aw, come on, Mason. I can see deep down you were made to be a family man. Don't disappointment me."

Mason shot her a glum look and Nadine promptly stepped into the cubicle as though she'd forgotten she was on her way out of the building.

"It's been months since Christa threw you over for that high-rolling real estate agent. If you're still pining over her, let me assure you, she's not worthy to wipe the sweat off your brow, much less be your wife."

Mason gave her a weary smile. "Thanks for the compliment. But forget about Christa. Believe me, I have."

"Really? Then tell me why you've been going around all day like you've lost your dog?"

"I don't have a dog."

"Don't evade the question. Something…" Her red lips formed an O as she shot him a shrewd glance. "It's about Sophie, isn't it? You were very unhappy at seeing her with Thom in the breakroom yesterday. What's happened? You think you've lost your chance with her or something?"

Mason tossed his pen onto the desk, where it promptly rolled to the back and fell between the wall and the kickboard. A sign of just how his luck was going, he thought dismally. "She went out on a date with him last night."

Nadine's brows arched upward. "Really? How would you know that?"

"Yesterday, when you saw her here at my desk, she was telling me that Thom had asked her out. She was jumping up and down with excitement." He shook his head while trying to ignore the heavy feeling of dejection settling in the pit of his stomach. "She has her heart set on having a big Valentine's date with Thom. And knowing Sophie's determination, she'll probably get it."

"Poor girl. She's letting that pretty face of Thom's blind her. I expect it won't take long for the blinders to fall off and then she'll start looking for a man with real substance. And we know where she can find one of those," Nadine added with a sage grin.

"Do we?"

Before Nadine could answer, Dexter Johnson, another programmer, stopped by Mason's cubicle.

"Oh. You two are still here. Are we supposed to be

staying over for a meeting or something? I didn't get a memo about it."

In his midthirties, Dexter had black hair that waved in a giant bush about his pale face. A wide smile exposed a set of longer than normal eyeteeth, prompting the nickname Vamp. And though it was done with affectionate teasing, Mason didn't approve of his colleagues' humor. When it came to computers, though, Dexter was practically a genius. Along with that, he was a nice, unpretentious guy.

"Don't worry, Dexter. There's no meeting. Nadine and I are just having a little visit."

"Oh, well, I'll let you two get on with it."

Before he could move on, Mason said, "You don't have to go. Pull up a chair and join us."

Even though Dexter was clearly warmed by the invitation, he quickly shook his head. "No thanks. I need to get home. They're predicting sleet tonight. Not good walking weather. And I'm too chintzy to catch a cab."

Nadine wrapped her arm around Dexter's slender shoulders. "Forget about walking, or the cab. You can ride with me. Your apartment is right on my way."

Dexter's thin face brightened. "Are you sure? I don't want to be a bother."

"No bother at all. I'm happy to have the company. So if you're ready, let's go." She urged Dexter away from the cubicle, while tossing a smile over her shoulder at Mason. "Get your swagger on, Mason. Your time is coming. Good night."

Mason waved, then turned back to his computer.

Swagger? Him? He was hardly the guy who roared in on a motorcycle wearing black leather chaps and a slick pompadour. How was Mason supposed to get swagger when everybody saw him as the boy next door with the kind face and comfortable shoulder?

For the next two hours, Mason tried to dive into his work and forget about Sophie's date with Thom. But each time he thought he'd cleared his mind, her pestering image came right back to him.

Sophie had told him to stop by her desk today and she'd give him a report on her date. But regardless of how much he wanted a chance to talk with her, he was hardly keen on hearing about Thom Nichols sweeping her off to some magical spot and kissing her until she fainted with delight.

No. Mason didn't need to hear any of that. But when he finally shut down his computer and walked out into the corridor to leave, he spotted a light still burning in human resources and knew it had to be Sophie. No one else put in the long hours that she did.

With his jacket slung over his shoulder, he stood near the elevator doors, trying to decide whether to go speak to her, when the light suddenly went dark and Sophie stepped into the corridor.

Spotting him immediately, she waved. "Mason! I didn't know you were still here."

His heart tripping at a ridiculous rate, he watched her stride quickly toward him, while thinking she looked as fresh as if it was eight thirty in the morning and she'd just arrived, instead of nearly three hours past quitting time.

"Hi, Sophie. I just now saw the light and wondered if it was you," he confessed.

Her lower lip thrust forward in a playful pout. "And you weren't going to stop by and see me? Shame on you. I expected to see you today."

So she could brag about her date with Thom, he thought sickly. "Well, I've been very busy today. I'm still doing last-minute tests on the sports app. And then there's a new project."

"You're so incredibly smart, Mason. I doubt you ever worry about the work you produce. In fact, I've heard Wes bragging on you before. You're one of his favorites," she added, then gave him a coy wink. "But don't let him know I told you so."

At least there was one Fortune Robinson who appreciated him, Mason thought dryly.

"I wouldn't think of repeating that little tidbit," he assured her.

For some reason he felt compelled at the moment to grab the bull by the horn, as the saying went. Raking a hand through his hair, he asked her, "Uh, seeing as how you're leaving, too, would you like to grab a cup of coffee?"

For one split second she appeared surprised by his invitation and then a bright smile lifted the corners of her lips. "Sure. I'd love a cup."

Feeling as though the floor beneath his feet had just turned to air, he reached for the coat she was carrying. "Better let me help you with this," he said. "I hear there's bad weather coming tonight."

Standing behind her, he held the coat so that she could slip her arms into it and Mason was immediately struck by her petite stature and the grace with which she moved. As always, she smelled like a cloud of sunny flowers and he longed to drop his face to the crown of her hair and draw in the subtle scent.

"Thanks," she told him as she buttoned the coat and wrapped a dark purple scarf around her neck. "I hate being cold. I'll be happy when three-digit temperatures get here."

He chuckled. "Don't worry. Summer will be here before you can say the rat ran over the cheese barrel."

She shot him a quizzical look. "'The rat ran over the cheese barrel.' Where did you get that phrase?"

He grinned. "I made it up."

She laughed then, and looped her arm through his. "You're so funny, Mason. Thank you for making me laugh."

Funny. How was he supposed to get any kind of serious swagger going when Sophie viewed him as some sort of standup comedian?

He didn't know, but he had to get his new and improved Mason going soon or Thom Nichols was going to snare this sweet Fortune on his arm.

Chapter Four

Bernie's was five doors down from the Robinson Tech offices in an old building that had once been a pharmacy with a soda fountain. Down through the years, the medicinal side of the business had fallen by the wayside and the remaining space turned into a casual diner that catered to nearby office workers.

Sophie had always adored the place because of its homey, nostalgic feel and simple food that could be eaten with your fingers. Something their mother had never allowed her and her siblings to do while growing up on the Robinson estate.

"Where would you like to sit? The counter or a table?" Mason asked as they entered the eating establishment.

Sophie glanced from the Formica and chrome tables to the long wooden counter with red stools.

"Hmm. Let's sit at the counter. I'm still a kid at heart. I like to swivel around. Don't you?"

"Merry-go-rounds make me nauseous and bar stools make me even more drunk," he joked.

She laughed. "I think that's a result of the drink sitting in front of you rather than the swiveling bar stool."

He grinned. "You might be right."

He reached for her hand and as he led her around a group of tables to reach the counter, Sophie couldn't help thinking how nice his hand felt against hers and how completely natural it was to be in his company. With Mason she didn't have to worry about how she looked or the things she said. She didn't have to work at impressing him. He liked her as she was and that was the reason she'd been so happy to see him a few minutes ago in the corridor outside her office. Talking with Mason always made her feel better.

After taking seats at one end of the counter, they removed their coats and draped them across their laps. Then a barrel-chested man wearing a white apron came over to take their orders.

"Good evening, Miss Sophie," he greeted her with a toothy grin. "How are you tonight?"

"I'm fine, Leo. Thank you for asking. And you?"

"I'm cold," he complained as he rubbed a hand over his bald head. "I want the sun to come out. The birds to sing. The bluebonnets to bloom."

"From your lips to God's ears, Leo," she said. "I'm cold, too. So give me a cup of the strongest, hottest coffee you have. And do you have something good for dessert this evening?"

"Bread pudding with raisins and rum sauce."

"I'll take a dish." She looked over at Mason to see he was arching a brow at her. "What? Is something wrong?"

"I didn't know women ate rich desserts. I mean, women that look like you."

Leo chortled and Sophie found herself blushing. She'd not ever thought about Mason looking at her figure in any form or fashion. But she needed to remember he was a man and a very nice looking one to boot. Something she'd not really noticed until recently.

"Well, I make sure I work off the calories. Every little bite of something sweet is worth the pain to me."

Clearing his throat, he looked at Leo. "Give me what she's getting."

Leo glanced curiously from Mason to Sophie before he ambled off. "Coming right up."

Sophie cleared her throat. "I suppose you want to hear about my date with Thom."

Behind the bar, a small radio was tuned to a blues station, while above their heads a flat screen TV was silently broadcasting an NBA game. Mason appeared to have his attention focused on the basketball game, but Sophie got the feeling that he was waiting intently for her to continue.

"That's right," he said off-handedly, "you and Thom did have a date last night. I'd almost forgotten."

Had he really forgotten or was he just teasing, Sophie wondered. With Mason it was hard to tell. Frankly, Sophie was relieved he wasn't making a big issue of asking her about the date. Not after the way it had bombed so miserably.

"Well, you do have more to think about than me," she said, while wishing Leo would hurry up with their order. She needed to do something with her hands. For some strange reason she kept wanting to reach over and rest one on Mason's arm or knee. What was the matter with her anyway? It wasn't like her to touch any man. Even Thom. A point that had been all too evident last night.

He turned his head and Sophie found herself looking into his brown eyes. They were very dark with a few lighter flecks radiating out from the pupils and at the moment they appeared to be zeroing in on her lips. Which gave her the ridiculous urge to flick her tongue out and lick away the tingling sensation.

"So how was your date? Have a good time?" he asked.

The need to clear her throat hit her once again, but Sophie resisted. Not for anything did she want Mason to think she was hemming and hawing about her date with Thom. Especially one that she'd announced to him with such fanfare.

"It was nice," she said simply.

"Nice? I figured you were going to tell me it was spectacular, stupendous, and a bunch of other S words."

How about *silly* or *slow*, Sophie thought, then quickly scolded herself for such negative notions. Maybe her date hadn't been half of what she'd wanted or expected from Thom. That didn't mean he was wrong for her. She truly believed he was her Mr. Right. After they spent more time together, she was certain their relationship would start to gel perfectly.

The bright smile she forced on her lips was hardly genuine, but she couldn't let Mason guess that her date with Thom had been about as exciting as watching an inchworm cross a sidewalk.

"It was a start," she said. "By the time Valentine's Day rolls around, I'm sure things will be getting—uh, heated."

A wan smile slanted his lips before he turned his attention back to the game. Sophie was glad she could use the diversion to change the subject completely.

"Are you a big sports fan?"

"I'm not a fanatic by any means. But I enjoy basketball and baseball." He inclined his head toward the small screen. "The San Antonio Spurs are playing at home tonight and I'm wondering if either of my brothers are at the game. Both of them have season tickets. Sometimes I drive down and go with them."

She looked at him with interest. "Oh. You have brothers?"

He nodded. "They both live in San Antonio. One is a lieutenant on the city police force. The other is an assistant district attorney for Bexar County."

"Mmm. That's impressive. You must be very proud of them."

He shrugged. "Yeah. They're both a bit older than me. So I've pretty much spent my whole life trying to be as successful as they are. But I doubt I'll ever make it."

Leo arrived then with their coffee and dessert. As she stirred half and half into her cup, she studied his strong profile.

"Now why would you say something like that about yourself?" she asked him. "Don't you consider working for Robinson Tech as being successful?"

"Since I'm working for your father, I plead the fifth," he said, his voice full of wry humor.

"No. Seriously, Mason. You're a brain. Everyone says so. And the new sports app you've created has great potential. Otherwise, Dad would never be investing money in a media blitz."

He sampled the pudding before he replied, "Yes, I can create things to use on our computers and smartphones. But that isn't like my brother Shawn facing bullets on the streets. Or Doug arguing in court to make sure a dangerous criminal is put behind bars. They both work to make our lives safer. What I do is—well, it's for entertainment. What my brothers do is meaningful."

Strange how very much she could relate to this man.

For as long as she could remember, she'd always considered herself the inferior one of the family. The youngest sibling that didn't quite stack up to the others. It was an awful feeling and she hated to think that Mason ever suffered in such a way.

"So what? Everyone needs a little entertainment and fun in our lives," she told him. "If we were all rocket scientists or doctors it would be a pretty boring world, wouldn't it?"

"You don't have to placate me, Sophie. I can live with my lot in life."

She laughed softly as she dug into the bowl of bread pudding. "Coming from you, that's ridiculous. Now, me, I have a reason to feel lacking. All of my siblings are attractive and highly successful. Take Wes, for instance. He's the vice president of research and development. He's a creative whiz and now has a beautiful wife who adores him. I'm in human resources because I'm good at resolving arguments. And my love life is—well, not exactly there yet."

"Wes and Vivian seem like the perfect match. Just like the app they promoted during Valentine's Day last year. My Perfect Match is still making the company tons of money." His cup paused halfway to his lips as he glanced at her thoughtfully. "What do you think about that concept of dating, anyway? That a couple should get together because their views and likes are the same?"

"I'm not sure I believe in it. I mean, where's the passion? Take you, for instance. How you kiss would be a heck of a lot more important to me than how you vote at the ballot box."

He sputtered, then coughed. "I'm afraid I'm not that experienced in either of those departments. I—well, I do both things. I'm just not sure if I'm doing them right."

"Oh, Mason. You're so—"

"I know," he interrupted, "I'm so funny."

This time she couldn't stop the urge to reach over and give his knee a gentle squeeze. "I mean that in the nicest possible way, Mason."

He smiled at her and for a split second, Sophie thought she spotted a warm gleam in his eyes. But just as quickly she dismissed the idea. Mason wouldn't be thinking of her in that way. They were friends. Nothing more.

"Yes, I know you do."

She pulled her hand away from his knee and gave herself a mental shake. "So tell me what you think about My Perfect Match. You have to agree it brought my brother and Vivian together."

He chuckled. "It brought them together in a round-about way. Not because the computer matched them up. As for me, I believe a person needs to let nature take its course. My dad says it was love at first sight for him when he first saw Mom. That was at a junior high prom. He asked her to dance, even though he didn't know how. Fortunately she overlooked that minor problem and they've been together ever since."

"Since junior high? What about the love at first sight—is it still going?"

"Strong as ever," he answered. "Which only proves that opposites do attract. Mom likes pop music and Dad prefers country. Mom loves Italian food, while Dad wants meat and potatoes. They both agree to go to the coast to relax, which means Mom wants to lie on the beach, while Dad fishes. But they complement each other in lots of ways and respect each other's opinion. Something that has kept them in love all these years."

Sophie couldn't imagine how it would be to have parents that were actually in love and wanted to spend time together. "I guess it must be obvious to you and your brothers that your parents love each other," she said, unaware of the wistful note in her voice.

"If you're asking whether we ever catch them kissing in the kitchen, then yes. That happens quite often. Why? Doesn't that ever happen in your house?"

The only time Sophie saw her mother in the kitchen was to give the cook instructions. As for her father, he never entered that part of the house and usually took his meals in his bedroom or study with a stack of work at his elbow. As for kissing his wife, she couldn't remember ever seeing it happen. Which made Sophie wonder how the two of them ever got close enough to create eight children. There must have been a spark at some point, she reasoned. But somewhere along the way, the sparks had been doused with ice.

She said, "Not exactly. My parents have been married for thirty-six years. A record these days, I suppose. But they mostly go their separate ways. And follow different interests."

"Hmm. Well, I'm sure your father is a very busy man," he replied tactfully.

Busy could hardly describe her father's life. He was always on the go, jetting around the world for one reason or another. Whenever he was home, he usually had a phone to his ear or was dashing off to a meeting or work.

Sophie couldn't count the times she'd wished she'd been born into a regular family. With a father who held a common job and considered time spent with his children far more important than earning money. And more importantly, a father who would never dream of cheating on the wife he loved.

But she couldn't express any of this to Mason. It would

reflect badly to start pouring out her family problems to a Robinson Tech employee. Besides that, it would be downright embarrassing. Mason was a nice guy from a loving, close-knit family. He wouldn't understand what it was like to have a father who'd faked his own death and kept a woman in every port.

Sipping her coffee, she tried to push away the sadness that had suddenly crept over her. "Do your parents still work or are they retired?"

He chuckled. "Retired? They're both in their late fifties, but I doubt either of them will ever retire unless health issues force them to. Dad is a pipeline technician for a gas and oil company based in San Antonio and Mom is a high school English teacher. And before you ask, yes, she still corrects our grammar."

Sophie laughed softly. "I'm sure she never had to correct you."

He chuckled. "Oh, no. I ain't never used bad grammar."

She dipped into the pudding and realized with a start that she was very near the bottom of the bowl. She'd been so engrossed in Mason's conversation she hadn't even noticed.

"Are your brothers married?"

"No. Doug came close once, but things didn't pan out for him." He shrugged a shoulder. "Both my brothers are too busy playing the field to settle down. But I expect they will someday."

And what about you, Mason? Are you longing to find someone to love as much as I am?

Strange that those questions would be going through her mind, Sophie thought. And stranger still that she was thinking what a great husband Mason would make for some lucky woman. He was a good-looking guy with a manner that was a nice mixture of gentle and strong. He was a hard worker, polite and trustworthy.

He just wasn't Thom.

Okay. Nice. A start. As Mason and Sophie walked back to the parking garage of Robinson Tech, he happily repeated Sophie's lukewarm date description to himself. All day he'd been expecting to hear Sophie gush about her date with Thom. He'd been dreading seeing the dreamy look in her eye and knowing that Thom had put it there. Instead, she'd barely mentioned the date and the look in her eyes had been cold sober instead of a lovey-dovey haze. Which could only mean that Sophie's evening with Thom had been lackluster.

Maybe Mason had a chance with Sophie after all.

The celebration going on in his mind must have caused him to miss her next words, because suddenly he became aware of her calling his name.

"Mason? Hello? Have you gone into a trance?"

Giving himself a hard, mental shake, he looked at her. "I'm sorry, Sophie. I was thinking about—uh—work. Were you saying something?"

Laughing lightly, she looped her arm through his and the affectionate gesture made Mason want to forget that they were walking down a city sidewalk. At the moment, the street was mostly quiet, the concrete walkway covered with shadows. He could pull her into his arms and kiss her soundly on the lips before anyone noticed. Except her. And for all he knew, she might just slap his face.

She said, "I was asking if you had anything special planned for Valentine's Day. I'll bet you have some lovely woman hidden somewhere that none of us knows about."

The woman was hidden, all right, Mason thought drolly. She was so hidden he couldn't find her. Unless he looked at the one who was momentarily hanging on to his arm. But she had her heart set on another man.

He called himself ten kinds of fool for wanting this woman. She was so out of his league they might as well be living on separate ends of the galaxy. And yet he couldn't stop this yearning inside him.

"Uh—no. No special plans. I'm not sure the woman I have in mind would agree to go out with me anyway."

"Oh, Mason, I can't believe that. I'll bet she's just dying for you to ask her out. Why don't you try it? No one should spend Valentine's Day alone."

He choked, then sputtered as he attempted to clear his throat. "It would certainly surprise her."

As Dexter had predicted, the temperature was growing much colder and a fine mist of ice particles was beginning to gather on his jacket. That must be the reason Sophie had hugged herself closer to his side, he decided. She was cold.

"Then I say go for it. That's what I plan to do with Thom. Just give it my best shot and pray that all turns out like it should." She glanced thoughtfully over at him. "If I remember right, I used to see you with a cute blond. I think she worked in marketing."

Yeah, all the promiscuous people work in the marketing department, he wanted to tell her. Instead he said, "Yes. That was Christa Dobbins. She's gone now. She left Robinson Tech and moved in with a high roller."

"A gambler?" Sophie asked incredulously.

"No. I meant high roller as in money. The man is some sort of hot shot real estate agent."

"Oh, so she got dollar signs in her eyes. I'm sorry things didn't work out for you."

At the time, Mason had been sorry, too. He'd believed Christa was the woman he wanted to spend the rest of his life with. But now in hindsight, he was relieved he'd not gone so far as to give her an engagement ring. Given Christa's roaming eye, she would've made a horrible wife.

"No need to be sorry. We weren't *that* serious." At least, Christa hadn't been, Mason thought dourly. As for him, he'd been a sap for a while, but hopefully he'd learned from the broken heart.

By now they had reached the parking garage and as they stepped inside, Sophie pointed to the elevator. "I'm parked on the second floor. What about you?"

"Second floor, too."

"Great," she said, still clinging to his arm. "You can walk with me the rest of the way. I hate being here alone at night."

Concerned, he looked down at her. She always seemed like such a tigress that he couldn't imagine her being afraid of anything. "Are you afraid someone might jump you?"

"Well, I'm not overly concerned. It's just that…well, I'm a Fortune Robinson. And sometimes bad people have bad things on their minds—especially when it comes to money. Dad has always advised us kids to be alert and smart when we're out alone."

"Hmm. I see. I guess money can cause problems."

Feeling more protective than he could ever remember, Mason curled his arm around her shoulders. "You don't have to worry about that tonight. Not with me."

The grateful smile she gave him made Mason feel like he could jump over the moon.

"Thanks, Mason," she said, then gestured toward a small red sports car parked near a stairwell. "That's mine."

Mason walked her to her vehicle then waited patiently

for her to dig out her keys. Once she had them in hand, she pressed a button and the engine sprang to life, along with the headlights.

So much for the problems of being rich, he thought. He doubted the heater in his well-used car would warm up before he reached his apartment.

And you think you have a chance with this woman? You have definitely slipped a cog, Mason. She's accustomed to luxury. You deal in the essentials. Get real. Or get ready for a giant disappointment.

"Well, I should be getting home," she said. "Thanks for the coffee and dessert, Mason. And I really enjoyed our chat."

"I enjoyed it, too." Far, far too much, he thought. "Uh, maybe we can do it again sometime."

"Oh, for sure," she happily agreed.

His brows lifted skeptically. "You don't think Thom might be jealous if he heard about it—us having coffee, I mean?"

Her laugh echoed through the parking garage and Mason inwardly cringed. He supposed it was ludicrous to think a sex symbol like Thom Nichols would ever be jealous of him.

"Of course not. You and I are friends. And anyway," she added coyly, "as much as I want Thom to be my Valentine, I'd never let him pick and choose my friends."

Friends. Mason supposed that was better than nothing. At least, it had gotten him a little coffee date with her. Now if he could just figure out how to get her to make the leap from friends to lovers.

"That's good—that you don't intend to let him take away your independence," he told her. "A woman needs to hang on to a certain amount of self-reliance."

A wan smile lifted one corner of her pretty pink lips. "I wish my mother could hear you say that."

Her unexpected comment had him casting her a puzzled look. "Really? Why is that?"

She shrugged, then shook her head. "Nothing important. She's just a bit old-fashioned about things. That's all. Good night, Mason."

Before he could stop himself, he bent his head and pressed a soft kiss to her cheek. "Just a little goodbye between friends," he murmured.

Something flashed in her eyes and then with her hands anchored on his forearms, she rose on her toes and planted a kiss to the middle of his chin.

"Yes. Just between friends," she said gently, then quickly opened the car door and slid inside.

Mason stepped out of the way and the next thing he knew the taillights of Sophie's car were disappearing out the exit and he was staring after them like a little lost puppy.

Get a grip, Mason. She's only a woman. The world is full of them.

Yes, but none of them looked or sounded or smelled like Sophie Fortune Robinson, he argued with the sarcastic voice going off in his head.

But right now Sophie wanted Thom. Or at least, she believed she did. A detail that Mason had to change before Thom turned on that phony charm of his and managed to get his foot in the door of the Fortune Robinson mansion and stepped right into Sophie's heart.

Chapter Five

The next afternoon, Dennis Noland, the director of human resources, made a rare stop by Sophie's cubicle. The tall, thin man with graying black hair looked unusually harried as he pulled up a chair.

"This is a nice surprise," Sophie told him. "Although from the looks of you, I'm not so sure you have good news."

The man batted a dismissive hand through the air. "It's nothing about work. My wife has been sick and our daughter is having marital problems. Lanna is six months pregnant and wants to move in with us. Sophie, we still have a twelve-year-old son at home. I don't want her problems spilling onto him." He raked a hand through his rumpled hair, then shook his head. "Sorry. I didn't mean to walk in here and start pouring out my personal problems. Hell, I'm supposed to be an expert at dealing with this sort of stuff."

From the moment Sophie had been promoted to Dennis's assistant director, he'd been like a papa bear watching over his cub. He'd always given her enough rein to build her confidence, yet was never far away if she had any doubts. If Dennis had ever believed she'd gotten the position because of her father, he'd never implied or even hinted that was the case, and she was grateful to him for that.

Reaching over, she gave his arm a reassuring pat. "Forget it, Dennis. You can pour it out to me anytime you feel the need. And as for dealing with people, employees are far different than family members. You'll figure out how to handle your daughter's problem in the best possible way."

He blew out a long breath. "Thanks, Sophie. I hope I can live up to your faith in me. But that's enough about family matters. I stopped by to see if you've finished with the details on the training program for the marketing department. Since it's supposed to go into effect next week, I'd like to give the employees time to look over everything."

Thank goodness she'd been working overtime every night, Sophie thought. Otherwise, she wouldn't have been close to finishing this bloated project.

"It'll be ready in the next hour," she told him. "I'll have Reece print and bind enough copies for the entire department. In the meantime, you go get some coffee. Better yet, call your wife. That should make you feel better."

Nodding, he rose to his feet. "Talking with Aileen always makes things look brighter." He gave her a wan smile. "How did you know that? You're not married."

Not yet, Sophie thought, but if she could steer fate in the right direction, she might be married in the near future. Then everyone would see her as Mrs. Thom Nichols, a smart, mature woman, who was desirable enough to win the most eligible bachelor in Robinson Tech.

"Just a guess," she said sagely.

"Well, I'm sure you've watched your parents and learned that a man and wife need each other to lean on." He mustered a grin. "So I'm going to go do a little leaning for a few minutes. If you need me, you know where to find me."

As Sophie watched him walk off, she realized neither Dennis nor anyone would ever guess the truth about her parents. In public they put up enough of a front to make it appear as though they were a normal, loving couple. But she knew if Gerald needed to talk to someone to help brighten his mood, calling Charlotte would never cross his mind.

Just one more reason Sophie was going to make sure that she married a man who loved her utterly and completely and that she loved him just as much. She wouldn't settle for anything less.

Unbidden, a picture formed in her mind. A memory, really. She suddenly saw Mason and the way he'd looked at her just before he'd pressed a kiss to her cheek. At that very moment, she'd felt a reckless impulse to throw herself against him and lift her mouth to his. If she hadn't jumped in her car and abruptly driven away, she might have succumbed to the crazy urge.

Dear Lord, something strange was going on with her mind! Mason wasn't the man in her future plans. He wasn't the guy she'd been gazing at for weeks and imagining herself walking down a petal-strewn aisle to meet at the marriage altar.

Why was Mason's image pestering her now with his half-cocked smiles and warm brown eyes? Why did she keep remembering the fondness in his voice as he talked of his family? And why did touching him feel so comfortable and right?

Because Mason is a friend, Sophie. And friends make us feel cozy and happy and relaxed. And most of all, a friend makes us feel loved.

Loved. Yes, strange or not, Mason did make her feel loved.

But she didn't want a friend. She wanted a companion, a lover, a husband.

She wanted Thom. Didn't she?

Later that afternoon, Sophie stood in the marketing department, when Olivia suddenly walked up behind her and said in a hushed tone, "Mr. Sexy is giving you the eye. I think he's getting impatient because you've not spoken to him yet. Just look at him leaning against the wall. He thinks he's cooler than a grape Popsicle on a hundred degree day with a line of women just waiting to take a bite of him. Really, Sophie, what do you see in the guy?"

"Every female in this room—other than you, that is— would give their eyeteeth to get their hands on him."

"He's nothing more than eye candy," Olivia argued.

"He's a brilliant marketing strategist. I've even heard Dad say that much."

"Oh, he's definitely smart," Olivia agreed. "In the slyest possible way. All I can say is be careful."

Sophie gave her sister a confident smile. "Don't worry. When it comes to Thom, I know exactly what I'm doing. What are you doing here in marketing anyway?"

"Checking on some media matters. What about you?"

"Spreading word about a training program soon to go into effect."

With a little wave, Olivia said, "Better go do your spreading. But if I were you I'd make Thom wait until last. Let him know you're not easy."

Darting her sister an annoyed glance, Sophie made her way to Thom's cubicle. She could feel every female eye watching the two of them. The idea that they might be jealous of her was a heady thought. And yet in other ways it made her uncomfortable. If Thom was that much of a prized possession, how did she expect to hang on to him?

She couldn't let herself worry about such things now. She had to concentrate on snagging him first.

"Hello, Sophie. I was about to think you were going to ignore me."

Smiling coyly, she shook back her hair, making her long silver earrings jingle against her neck. "Not at all. I was working my way to you."

He held up the folder she'd instructed Reece to pass out a little more than an hour ago. "I see the old man thinks we need more training."

A frown pulled her brows together. "Excuse me? Old man?"

"Yeah. Your father. He's the boss of this place, isn't he?"

Not liking the sarcastic tone in his voice, she started to walk away, then decided that would hardly be conducive in creating a meaningful relationship with this man.

"If you're referring to the new training program, then no. It wasn't Dad's idea. It was Ben's. Why? Do you have a problem with it?"

He must have sensed her displeasure because he suddenly cleared his throat and straightened to his full height. "No. No trouble. I can't see how anyone expects us to get our work done if we have to stop and attend training classes. Is there really that much new stuff going on in marketing that we don't already know?"

She got the feeling Thom had to check himself to keep from saying "I" instead of "we." Well, she did like for a man to feel confident about himself; however, she couldn't stand a know-it-all. She hoped she didn't learn Thom was the latter.

"Digital technology has opened up a whole new world of connecting with the consumer. Robinson Tech needs to remain on the leading edge of that connection."

He reached out and touched a finger to her cheek and Sophie had to fight to stop herself from stepping back from the contact.

"Sorry, Sophie. I suppose if my family owned the company like yours does, I'd be defending its strategies, too. But let's forget about work," he said suddenly. "What are you doing Sunday night?"

Eating bread pudding with Mason. Now that would be a nice thing to be doing.

Mentally shoving aside that image, she gave Thom her best smile and tried to feel excited. "What did you have in mind?"

He stepped closer and bent his face next to her ear. "Some special time together," he said with a purr. "I'll pick you up at seven."

Even though he seemed to be taking her for granted, she decided not to make an issue of his approach. What did it matter how he asked her out? Another date with Thom was exactly what she'd been hoping for.

"Sounds good," she said, deliberately stepping back to put a respectable distance between them. "Should I dress up? Or will it be casual?"

"Casual. Definitely. I have tickets to a wrestling match at the U of A. It's going to be a blast."

She pressed her lips together to keep them from gaping open. Was he serious? "Collegiate wrestling?"

His eyes gleaming, he shook his head. "No. That's too tame. This is the pro stuff that gets wild and entertaining. Believe me, I had to fork over a small fortune to a scalper for the tickets. The event has been sold out for weeks."

She couldn't say no now. Not after she'd already agreed to the date. Yet she was already imagining herself sitting for hours, watching hulking, sweaty men straining to throw each other to the floor. She wasn't sure she could endure it.

"Sounds interesting," she said with fake enthusiasm.

His cocky smile grew deeper. "I felt sure you'd like the idea. We'll drink beer and yell our guts out. I can't wait."

Neither could Sophie. She was already wishing the whole evening was over.

"I'll bring some throat lozenges so I won't lose my voice."

"That's my girl," he said with a patronizing wink. "You know, this thing with you and me is working out fine. We're compatible. Just like My Perfect Match."

That's because they were destined for each other, Sophie thought, and if she had to sacrifice a little to get the man she wanted, then she could endure most anything. Even overgrown men dressed in tights.

Later that day, Mason had just stepped out of the men's room on the top floor of the building when he spotted Sophie emerging from the elevator. Pleasure shot through him as she gave him a little wave and started walking in his direction.

"Mason, how nice to run into you," she said. "What are you doing all the way up here?"

She was wearing a close-fitting skirt today that

stopped just short of her knees. The fabric was a geometric print of greens and blues. A crisp blue shirt was tucked inside while a wide leather belt cinched in her tiny waist. She looked professional yet very sexy and he wondered just how much Thom had taken notice of her since their date together. The man had his pick of women, but even he was probably surprised at having the boss's daughter interested in him. And no doubt pleased to be given the chance to step into such a famous and wealthy family.

"Believe it or not, I've just had a brief meeting with your father. He actually wanted to commend me on creating the Sports & More app."

Her face brightened. "That's wonderful, Mason. Dad doesn't often do that sort of thing. You should feel honored."

"Actually, I'm feeling relieved. I was quaking when I walked into his office. He's not the sort of man you have a simple chat with."

She chuckled. "No. Dad can be formidable at times. But he recognizes good work when he sees it."

"So what are you doing up here on the top tier?" he asked.

"I'm on my way to speak with Ben. I'm getting loads of grumbling from the marketing department about the new training program. I thought my brother should be forewarned."

"Oh. Then I should let you be on your way."

She glanced at her watch, which had a fashionably large face circled by rhinestones. What was he thinking? Sophie had probably never worn a rhinestone in her life. No, those sparklers were most likely diamonds.

"Ben isn't expecting me for another five minutes,"

she said, then asked, "So did you take my advice and ask that special woman of yours on a Valentine's date?"

The question whacked him between the eyes and for a moment he was too dazed to answer.

Put on your swagger, Mason. She needs to believe women are throwing themselves at you whether they are or not.

As he fumbled for the right words, he straightened the knot of his red and blue tie. This morning when he'd dressed for work, he'd thought the neckwear had given him that sharp businessman look. But the way Sophie was studying him now, he was beginning to wonder if he appeared to be coming down with smallpox.

"Oh, yes, the date. Well, I'm trying to decide which one I want to give hearts and flowers. Most women place a serious romantic significance on Valentine's Day and I want to make sure I'm sending the right signals to the right woman."

"I understand. You don't want to hurt her by giving her false hope and perhaps cause her to believe you're about to present her with a ring. That's so thoughtful of you."

Mason felt like the biggest liar that had ever walked the earth, even though he wasn't actually fibbing about anything. He did want to send the right signals to the right woman. Sophie just didn't realize that *she* was the woman. Yet giving her, or any woman, a ring was something he'd not considered.

When Christa had thrown him over for the rich real estate guy, his self-esteem had fallen flatter than a punctured tire. Even now, after months had passed, he still had to remind himself that everyone made mistakes and he'd made a big one in trusting the flirty blonde with his heart.

"Is that what you're thinking?" he asked. "That Thom might give you an engagement ring for Valentine's Day?"

A blush instantly transformed her cheeks to a deep pink, while a sly smile tilted the corners of her lips. "Well, it's a little early for those kinds of thoughts. But things are definitely moving in the right direction. He's asked me on another date for tomorrow night. So he must like something about me," she added with a bat of her eyelashes.

Yeah. He likes your money and everything your daddy can do for him. Aloud, Mason said, "I'm sure he finds you enchanting, Sophie."

Her brown eyes turned soft and warm as she suddenly stepped forward and rested a hand on his forearm. The simple touch caused Mason's heart to leap into high gear and even though they were standing in the middle of the corridor and a few steps away from her brother's office, he wanted to take her into his arms and taste her lips.

"You're so sweet, Mason. The woman you choose for your Valentine's date is going to be very lucky."

He breathed in deeply, then wished he hadn't as her sweet scent filled his head. He'd be smelling her for the rest of the day and into the night. "Thank you, Sophie. And I hope you enjoy your date tomorrow night."

"I do, too." Smiling cheerfully, she turned and entered her brother's office. "Wish me luck!" she called over her shoulder.

The only thing Mason wished was for the blinders to fall off Sophie's eyes, so that she'd look right past Thom…and straight at him.

"How about wishing you happiness?" he suggested.

"That's even better!"

With a little wave she disappeared behind the glass

door, leaving Mason standing there trying to gather his thoughts.

It was already the fourth day of the month. That meant Mason only had ten days left to turn Sophie's head. So far Thom appeared to have missed the mark in the romance department; otherwise, she would've been waltzing around Robinson Tech on a dreamy cloud these past couple of days. Mason could only pray her date with Thom tomorrow night was a complete flop.

This was supposed to be a blast?

For the past hour and a half Sophie had been asking herself that very question while hundreds of spectators around her screamed and clapped and yelled things like: Break his arms! Kick him! Finish him off! And to make matters worse, Thom was one of the loudest.

As though the deafening roar of the rowdy crowd and the sight of men and women wrestlers trying to break their opponent's bones wasn't enough to deal with, a fanatical female fan seated behind Sophie had lurched forward and spilled a glass of cold beer down her back. The woman had been very apologetic and had tried to help Sophie sop up the mess with a handful of tissues, but the effort had done little.

Sophie had never been so relieved in her life when the wild event finally ended and she and Thom headed across the jammed parking lot to his car.

"Oh, man, that was the greatest! When Rocco tore off Meteor's mask I thought the arena was going to erupt!"

"It did," Sophie said flatly. "I'm still wet."

Grinning, Thom reached over and curled his arm around her shoulders. "Sophie, honey, I'm so proud of you for the way you handled that little accident. No cursing or catfight. Just first-class all the way."

Had he honestly dated women who'd resorted to that, she wondered. Oh, God, this just wasn't working. Thom was turning out to be nothing like she'd expected.

"You know, you're the first girl I've found that actually likes the things I do. That's why I asked you out again. We seem to click. Don't you think?"

Sophie had felt a click, all right. Like a light switch being flipped to the off position.

"So what do you do when your dates have different interests than you?"

"Oh, that's it for me. I drop them. I mean, why waste precious time and effort on something that isn't going to work?"

Why indeed, Sophie thought, but kept the retort to herself. The guy was clueless, not to mention self-absorbed. "So you never think about doing something the woman enjoys?"

"Not really. If I have to make myself miserable just to make her happy, then things aren't going to work anyway. It's just like the My Perfect Match app that Wes and Vivian promoted last Valentine's Day. A man and woman have to like the same things to make a relationship last."

She wanted to remind Thom that her brother and Vivian had learned a crucial lesson while they promoted the dating app. They both discovered that it took passion, respect, sacrifice and genuine love to hold a couple together. Did Thom ever think in those serious terms, or was he all about making himself happy? At this very moment she had the sinking feeling that Thom was all about Thom.

"But we don't have to worry about that," Thom followed up on Sophie's silence. "Looks like we enjoy the very same things. Lucky, huh?"

Luck had nothing to do with it. Sophie had put her

flirt on and made it obvious to Thom that she was interested in him. Luck hadn't made her join the endless numbers of women at Robinson Tech who gazed at this man from afar and fell under the spell of his good looks and flashy smile.

She'd heard through the office grapevine that he'd gone through several girlfriends. Yet Sophie hadn't allowed the talk to scare her off her mission. After all, gossip was rarely accurate, she'd reasoned. But now, she was beginning to think the talk about Thom sifting through a stack of women might be true.

"Yes," she finally forced herself to say. "It's fortunate when two people click."

His arm squeezed her shoulders and drew her closer to his side. Two weeks ago when Thom was only her dream man, the gesture would have sent her flying to the moon. Now, she actually wanted to put some distance between them. Like ten or fifteen miles for starters.

Oh, God, how had her thinking gotten so messed up? What was she doing with this narcissistic man?

"After all the food I consumed during the match, I couldn't eat another bite. But I'll take you by a burger place or something if you're hungry."

How thoughtful that he'd go to so much trouble for her, Sophie thought wryly. During the wild event, Thom had eaten two hotdogs and a giant serving of nachos. She'd sipped on a diet soda. Along the way, she'd lost her appetite for him and any kind of food.

"Oh, no. I couldn't eat a bite," she swiftly declined, then added, "Actually, after all that excitement, I think I'm ready to go home. Monday mornings are always rough in my department. I'd like to get plenty of rest tonight."

For a moment, her suggestion to end the evening appeared to have taken him aback, but then he smiled and gestured toward his car which now was only a short distance away.

"Sure. I need to run an errand before I go home anyway."

To buy another mirror so you can sit around and admire yourself, Sophie wanted to ask. Then quickly shamed herself. What was the matter with her anyway? This was only her second date with Thom. She was simply annoyed because she'd had to sit through more than two hours of a raucous sporting event, instead of being treated to a quiet romantic evening with just the two of them.

The drive to the Robinson estate took nearly twenty minutes and most of that had passed without much conversation. Not that talking would have meant that much to him anyway. As soon as Thom had helped her into the car and started the engine, he'd tuned the radio to a satellite sports station and cranked up the volume. By the time he pulled up in front of the house, Sophie had heard all she'd wanted to hear about multimillion-dollar athletes and their legal troubles.

As soon as he cut the engine, Sophie grabbed her shoulder bag and reached for the door handle. "Thanks for the evening, Thom. It was…nice."

Shifting toward her, he said, "It's still rather early, Sophie. Are you sure you wouldn't like to invite me in for a cup of coffee or something?"

She noticed his deep voice had taken on a purring sound that should have caused goosebumps to rush over her skin. Any normal red-blooded woman would be leaning toward him, inviting him to kiss her. Instead, she wanted to stick her head out the window and gulp in several breaths of clean air.

Moments of silence passed as she floundered for some sort of excuse, then finally she said, "Tonight really isn't a good night. My mother—"

"I'd love to meet your mother," he quickly countered before she had a chance to finish. "With a daughter like you, she'd have to be a very lovely woman."

"That's nice of you, Thom."

Grinning, he leaned closer until his face was only inches from hers. "I know when I'm looking at a good thing."

If that was supposed to be a compliment, she wasn't impressed. "Well, my mother goes to bed early. She wouldn't appreciate us waking her at this late hour."

"Hmm. I'm sure with a house this size, we could find a spot far away from her room. She'd never even know we were around."

"I don't—"

Before she could finish, he'd planted his lips over hers and Sophie had little choice but to respond with as much fervor as she could muster. But the intimate contact left her as cold as the temperature outside the car and she had to force herself to go through the motions.

She must be frigid! The frantic thought raced through her mind as Thom finally eased away from her and rested his hands on the steering wheel. How could she kiss this man and feel nothing? Except the need to escape. Oh, Lord, if Olivia ever learned of this, she'd be gloating. She'd never quit saying I told you so.

The desperate thought had Sophie impulsively reaching for his hand as she tried to salvage what little was left of their evening. This had to be her fault. She wasn't trying enough. There had to be a sexy part of her just waiting to burst into flames. She had to find it and fast or Thom was going to lose all interest.

"Thank you for tonight, Thom."

"Are you sure you really want me to leave?" He squeezed her hand and urged her ever so slightly toward him. "I could still use a drink."

"Next time, I promise. I'll see you tomorrow at work," she said in a rushed voice. "Good night."

Before he had the chance to make any more moves, she practically leaped from the car and without a backward glance, hurried straight to the house.

By the time she was standing inside the foyer, she heard Thom's sports car drive away. The sound left her with a feeling of immense relief, coupled with a sense of utter disappointment. A few days ago, she'd been dreaming all sorts of beautiful images of Thom taking her into his arms and kissing her until she was drunk with desire. She'd pictured him sliding an engagement ring on her finger. A ring she could flash to her family and friends to give them proof that she was wanted by one of the most eligible bachelors in Austin. Winning Thom would be proof she was worthy of a man's love.

Had she been totally wrong about him? Even about herself?

Tears suddenly burned the backs of her eyes and as she closed the lids and waited for the sting to subside, Mason's face suddenly appeared in her mind.

Mason seemed to understand all the things Sophie was thinking, feeling, even hoping. She had no doubt that if he was standing in front of her now, she could rest her cheek against his chest and he would do everything in his power to comfort her.

Mason. Was he the reason she couldn't feel anything when Thom touched her? Had Mason gotten into her subconscious and started controlling her thoughts? Or had she unwittingly invited him to walk straight into her heart?

Either way, she had to get a grip on herself and her mixed emotions. Otherwise, her plans for her future with Thom were going to evaporate long before Valentine's Day ever arrived.

With a heavy sigh, she walked through the quiet house. Apparently her father was out of town again or buried in his study, strategizing on making his next million. The thought had her glancing in the direction of her mother's bedroom.

A lonely strip of light told Sophie her mother had already retired to her private sanctuary to read or watch TV. She wouldn't be pillowing her cheek on her husband's shoulder or cuddling close to the warmth of his body. There would be no good-night kiss or talk of a tomorrow together.

The sad realization was not a new one for Sophie, but tonight it struck her even more deeply. She'd never thought she'd inherited her mother's traits. Everyone said she had the fighting spirit of her father. But after tonight and that tepid kiss with Thom, she could only wonder if she was going to end up like her mother. Too cold to let herself really love anyone.

Chapter Six

The next morning, as soon as Sophie walked into the HR department, Dennis met her with a new project, one that would keep her busy for the next few weeks. Which was just fine with her. She needed something to take her mind off the disappointment she was feeling over her lack of chemistry with Thom.

A few minutes ago, Olivia had stopped by her desk on the pretense of asking questions about the new training program, but Sophie knew her sister really wanted to know about her date last night. It had taken all of Sophie's willpower not to break down and admit to Olivia that she feared she'd made a mistake in going after Thom. But the memory of her sister's know-it-all prediction of failure had given Sophie the strength to keep her real feelings to herself. No doubt Olivia would gloat in the future. But for now, Sophie wasn't ready to throw in the towel. Who knew? Thom's behavior might get better. Or Sophie might find some way to melt the frigid ice inside her.

"Break time, Sophie. Better make the most of it before Dennis throws another stack of work on your desk."

Sophie looked up to see Faye, a middle-aged woman who worked in a nearby cubicle. Married with four children, Faye always had a cheerful smile, no matter what was going on at work or home, and Sophie admired her for being such a positive person.

"Oh, I hadn't noticed the time. A cup of coffee would be nice. If I can unglue myself from this chair."

Chuckling, Faye walked on toward the exit. "I'll try not to drain the pot dry before you get there."

After putting her computer into safe mode, Sophie made her way to the nearest ladies' room. As she walked, she noticed the bright winter sun streaming through the windows at the far end of the corridor and the sight lifted her otherwise dreary spirits. The day was beautiful. She was determined to forget about her problems and enjoy every second of it.

Inside the ladies' room, she smiled a greeting to some coworkers before making her way to a vacant stall.

Moments later, she was adjusting her clothing and hoping the last of the pastries hadn't been taken from the break room, when she suddenly caught the sound of women's voices beyond the stall door. Although they were speaking in hushed tones, she could hear them clearly.

"Who does she think she is, anyway? Princess Sophie Fortune Robinson?" one woman said in a sarcastic tone.

Another female voice replied, "I don't know, but I can tell you one thing for sure. The only reason Thom Nichols would ever give her a second look is because of her daddy. Everyone knows Thom wants to move into an executive office. What easier way to do it than date the boss's daughter?"

They were talking about her! But why? She'd never used her family position to climb over any Robinson Tech employee. She always tried to be kind and helpful to everyone. And what they were saying about Thom…

"Exactly," the first woman added. "I mean, she's really not very pretty. And those clothes she wears—"

The woman followed up with a groan and Sophie glanced down at the skirt and blouse she'd dressed in this morning. She'd thought the shirred purple skirt was chic, along with the pale pink blouse tucked in at the waist.

"Well, her clothes obviously cost a fortune, but someone ought to tell her how to wear them," the second woman replied.

"She's a spoiled daddy's girl. That's the only reason Sophie got her job and everyone in this company knows it. You'd think Thom would have better taste."

"Hah. Money always makes up for beauty and class."

And both of you have neither, Sophie wanted to shout at the women.

Blinking back tears, she waited in the stall until she was certain the two women had left before she finally found the courage to emerge. As she washed her hands and dried her eyes, she told herself there would always be women who hated her simply for who she was. And yet their words had cut deep.

Was Thom dating her just because of her father? Just because he had his eye on an executive position?

Fighting back tears, but quickly losing the battle, she rushed from the ladies' room and headed back to her desk. No way could she go to the break room now. Everyone, including those two nasty mouthed women, would see her tears and the gossip would start all over again. Only this time they'd be laughing behind her back.

Quickly striding down the corridor, she kept her head down and tried to wipe away the tears that continued to stream down her cheeks.

"Sophie!"

Suddenly two male hands caught her shoulders and she looked up through a watery wall to see she'd very nearly run smack into Mason.

"Oh, Mason!" His name came out with a mixture of anguish and relief, and before she realized what she was doing, she grabbed the front of his shirt with both hands. "I'm so glad it's you."

"Sophie, what's wrong? Something has upset you."

She blinked and did her best to smile. Not for anything could she repeat what she'd heard in the ladies' room to this man.

"I—I'm just having a bit of a rough morning. I'll be okay."

Sophie was crying! The sight of her tears shook Mason far more than he would've ever expected and before he could think about what he was doing, he slipped his arm around her shoulders and urged her toward a nearby alcove where a pair of dark green couches was flanked by tall fig trees and surrounded by a row of arched windows.

"Come with me and let's sit for a minute," he told her. "You can't return to your desk in this shape."

He helped her onto one of the couches, then took a seat next to her. She promptly produced a tissue from a tiny pocket on her skirt and dabbed her cheeks. Even though her brown eyes were red and watery they were still the most beautiful eyes he'd ever gazed into, Mason decided.

"I'm so sorry that you're seeing me like this, Mason.

This isn't me. I can't even remember the last time I got weepy."

Now that Mason thought about it, he couldn't remember a time he'd seen Sophie without a dazzling smile on her face. She was always happy and upbeat. So what had caused all the tears, he wondered. Thom?

"Did you have a run-in with an employee?"

She shook her head and Mason felt a small measure of relief.

"No. I'm just doubting myself a little. Sometimes a woman has days when she feels…less than beautiful. I guess this is one of mine."

Reaching for her hand, he pressed it between his. "Sophie, listen to me. You don't have any reason to doubt yourself as a woman or as the assistant HR director. You're beautiful and capable. Don't let anyone tell you differently. Okay?"

Her somber gaze slowly surveyed his face and Mason suddenly felt a connection between them that he'd never felt before. It was warm and strong and deep enough to make his heart beat with hope.

"You're right. I shouldn't allow anyone or anything to stop me from feeling positive about myself."

"That's the spirit." He tucked his forefinger beneath her chin. "Now let's see that gorgeous smile of yours."

Her cherry colored lips automatically curved into a smile, but the expression didn't light her eyes and that worried him.

"That's better," he said, "but you still don't look completely happy to me."

Shaking her head, she glanced away, then bit down on her bottom lip. "Mason, do you think—well—that Thom is really interested in me?"

Thom! The wolf in designer clothing! Mason would

like to punch him in the jaw and warn him to stay as far away from Sophie as he could possibly get. But Thom appeared to be what Sophie wanted and it certainly wouldn't score any points with her to beat the jerk to a pulp.

"What makes you think Thom might not be interested? He's dated you twice now. By the way, how did last night go?"

With her stare glued to the window, it was impossible to see what was going on behind her eyes. But Mason got the impression she wasn't ready to talk about any of it. Whether that was because the date had been good or bad, he could only guess.

"Oh, it was…enlightening. Thom seems to think we're perfect for each other. He believes if we registered with My Perfect Match, the computer would put us together instantly."

Sure. Perfect for Thom, Mason thought. He ventured to ask, "Is that what you think? That you're perfectly matched?"

She shrugged and the indifferent response surprised Mason. It also sent his spirits on another soaring leap. She wasn't singing Thom's praises. She wasn't prattling on about having a fabulous time in his company. According to her less than enthusiastic reaction, something wasn't working out quite right with the two of them, Mason decided. Which meant he still had a chance to win her over.

"I've always thought he would be perfect for me. But I'm realizing now that I need to get to know him better. People are always different outside of work. But then, you probably see that same thing with the women you date."

Oh, yes, his women. He scoffed inwardly. He hadn't

dated since his fiasco with Christa, but that was a fact he was going to keep to himself. For now, at least.

"Yes, sometimes people can turn into real monsters when they're not under the scrutiny of a boss. Actually, once I leave Robinson Tech in the evenings I grow fangs and wolf hair."

She looked at him and giggled and the sound made him smile. More than anything he wanted Sophie to be happy.

"Mason, you're so funny."

"It's good to hear you laugh," he told her.

She squeezed his fingers and Mason wished they were in a private place where the rest of the world couldn't intervene. He wanted so very much to pull her into his arms and tuck her head beneath his chin, to show her how much he wanted her. But would he ever have that chance? And even if he did, how would she react? She seemed to like him. But liking was nothing like wanting. Or loving.

"You always make me feel better," she said softly.

His thumb stroked the back of her soft hand. "Sophie, if anyone ever hurts you—if you ever need me—I'm right across the hall. All you have to do is come to me for help. You know that, don't you?"

Smiling now, she leaned close and pressed a kiss to his cheek. The touch of her lips, the scent of her skin and hair whirled his senses to a drunken daze.

"Yes, I know," she whispered. "Thank you, Mason."

She rose to her feet and Mason was forced to release her hand.

"I'd better get back to my desk," she said. "Dennis just handed me a new project this morning."

Rising from the couch, he took hold of her arm. "Come on, I'll walk you back."

At the door of the HR department, Mason stood with his hand still wrapped around Sophie's arm and even though it was time for him to let go, he was reluctant to end the sweet contact.

"So will you be working late tonight? Or do you have another hot date with Thom?"

She glanced up and down the busy corridor as though she expected the suave snake charmer to appear at any moment. Did she think Thom might actually be jealous of him? The notion made him want to puff out his chest.

"What makes you think it was hot?" she asked guardedly.

"Hmm. Well, isn't Thom in the running for sexiest man alive?"

"I don't know about that," she replied and then her gaze landed back on his face and she smiled brightly. "Uh, I'm pretty sure I'll be working late tonight. What about you?"

He nodded as he anticipated spending a few private minutes with her. "Definitely. Mr. Robinson—your father—and Wes have given me the task of producing a health app to go along with the Sports & More app. And they both want the finished product on their desks as quickly as possible."

She smiled again and this time her eyes sparkled. Mason wanted to shout hallelujah at the sight of her lifting mood.

"Congratulations," she said. "Obviously you're doing all the right things. Maybe you'll have a chance to tell me more about the new project tonight."

This had to be his lucky day, Mason decided, as a ridiculous thrill rushed through him. He'd climbed out of bed this morning feeling as though winter was never going to end. Now, just hearing Sophie suggest she'd see him tonight made it feel like daffodils and green grass were just around the corner.

"Sure. We'll have another coffee or something."

Nodding, she started through the door. "That would be great. See you later."

Mason was walking down the hall, whistling happily under his breath, when he noticed Thom approaching him from the break room. Judging by the smirk on his face, the other man wasn't exactly in a friendly mood.

"Hey, Montgomery, having trouble with your job?"

Mason arched a brow at him. "No. Are you?"

Thom inclined his head toward the human resources department. "That's where an employee goes when he feels…slighted."

Mason had never liked Thom Nichols and the feeling had only intensified since Sophie had told him her plan of trying to snare the man for her Valentine's date.

"I couldn't be happier about where my career is headed. And my private life," Mason said coolly.

"Same here," Thom quipped. "Dating the boss's daughter certainly has its merits. Before long I might be moving to an office on the top floor. Maybe right next to old man Robinson himself."

Only in your dreams, Mason thought. "She has a name. Why don't you use it?"

Thom rolled his eyes. "Montgomery, you always were a polite sap. If you'd loosen up and quit the stuffed-shirt act, you might get somewhere with the women. In fact, Christa might still be around."

It was all Mason could do to keep from ramming his fist into Thom's gut. But Mason wouldn't give him the satisfaction of knowing he'd gotten under his skin.

"Christa is none of your business."

A phony smile exposed Thom's white teeth. Mason figured he'd spent thousands to make them perfect.

"Just like Sophie is none of yours."

So that's what this little chat was all about, Mason concluded. Thom had spotted him and Sophie talking. Well, well. Who would've thought Mr. Sexy could ever doubt his ability to keep a woman interested?

"Sophie is a friend," Mason said flatly. "And I don't want to see her hurt."

Thom's nostrils flared as he unnecessarily straightened the knot of his tie. "I have no intentions of hurting Sophie. So don't give her a second thought."

Like hell, Mason muttered to himself. To Thom, he said, "I hope you don't try to tell Sophie who she should be thinking about. Women aren't too keen on that sort of domination."

Thom shot him an incredulous look, then after a moment, burst out in sarcastic laughter. "You? Giving me advice on handling a woman? That's hilarious, Montgomery." Then he abruptly walked away.

Mason stared after him, thinking he'd rather be struck by lightning than to let Thom get his greedy hooks into Sophie's soft heart.

Later that evening, well after most everyone had left, Sophie continued to work at her desk. She told herself she wasn't going to cross the hall and seek out Mason. No, if he wanted to have coffee with her, then she'd wait until he showed up to ask her. And if he didn't, she'd go home and forget about him.

Which was exactly what she should do. After all, Thom was the man she was after. He was the man who should be inviting her to the coffee shop. Not Mason.

But the only time Thom had mentioned coffee was when they'd been sitting in front of the Robinson doorstep.

Olivia would warn her that Thom was using her to wiggle his way into the bosom of the family. Although Olivia was so jaded she would naturally think in those terms, Sophie was beginning to realize her sister might be right. The more Sophie thought about Thom's behavior, the more she was realizing his feelings for her were far from sincere. She didn't want to believe she was dumb enough to have developed a crush on that sort of man, but it appeared as though she had.

Eventually, her rambling thoughts got the better of her and she grabbed her handbag and headed to Mason's cubicle.

Mason was the only person left in his department and as she neared his desk, she paused to take a longer look at the man who'd always been so kind to her. At the moment, his head was bent over a stack of papers, causing a lock of his dark hair to flop away from his forehead. His brows were pulled together in deep concentration as he shrugged one shoulder and then the other in an effort to ease the stiffness.

She must have unconsciously made a move or taken a step, because he suddenly turned toward her. As soon as he spotted her, he stood and smiled.

"How long have you been there? You should've yelled at me."

She entered his cubicle. "You were in deep thought. I didn't want to disturb you."

"You could never disturb me."

He pulled up an extra chair and gestured for her to sit. "Make yourself comfortable, Sophie, while I clean up. Have you finished work for the evening?"

"Yes. My mind refused to focus any longer so I gave up and decided to see if you were faring any better."

Sophie sank into the chair and all of a sudden a strange awareness came over her. For no reason at all, she noticed the room was quiet and practically dark. And Mason was sitting only inches away from her. He smelled like piney woods and fresh rain, and she noticed the dark hair inching over the back of his collar had a rich, shiny texture. Beneath his mustard-colored shirt, the muscles of his back and shoulders rippled ever so slightly as he moved. What would it be like to touch all that masculine strength? How would his lips taste? How would his hands feel against her skin?

The thoughts stirred the feminine parts of her and stung her cheeks with unexpected warmth. What was she doing thinking such erotic things about this man? He was her friend, not her lover!

"I've accomplished enough for one day." He stuffed the stack of papers in his desk, then swiveled his chair toward hers. "There. That's out of the way. Are you ready to head to Bernie's?"

As she crossed her legs and smoothed the hem of her skirt, she noticed his eyes traveling down the length of her calf which was covered with the soft brown leather of her dress boot. It was the first time she'd ever seen him looking at her in such a physical way and it only added more fire to her heated thoughts.

"I—uh—well, I thought we might talk a minute before we leave." She nervously licked her lips as her gaze dropped to her lap. "Unless you're in a hurry."

"No hurry. I don't have anything waiting for me at home. Do you?"

Home. Not since she and her brothers and sisters had been children and the house had held the sound of voices and laughter had she thought of the Robinson estate as home. The place she lived in now was little more than rooms that provided luxurious shelter.

"Not at all." She lifted her gaze back to his face and as their eyes met, her heart gave an odd little jerk. "Uh, do you live alone? I mean, you don't share the place with a friend?"

He shook his head as his eyes remained locked on hers. "I have an apartment on the north side of town. And the only one I ever shared it with was a dog, but he's not there anymore."

"Please don't tell me something happened to him."

A faint grin cocked the corner of his lips and Sophie felt a breath rush out of her.

"Andy is just fine. He lives with my oldest brother down in San Antonio. I didn't feel right about leaving him alone in the apartment day after day with no place outside to run and play. With my brother, he has a fenced-in backyard and another dog to be his buddy. I hated giving him up, but I wanted him to be happy."

"You did the right thing," she said softly. "We all need companionship."

He cleared his throat, then absently rubbed a hand against his chest. Sophie wondered what he would think if she moved his hand aside and placed hers there. How would it feel to slip her fingers between the pieces of fabric and touch his warm skin?

Shocked by the naughty thought, she tried to focus on Thom and Valentine's Day and all the hopes she'd had for the two of them, but at this very moment, none of that seemed to hold any importance. Had she lost her mind?

Clasping her hands together and resting them on her knee, she forced her gaze to move from Mason and on to something else. Beyond his left arm, she spotted a framed photo on his desk and she peered at it closely, trying to discern if Mason was one of the three men in the picture.

"Is that some of your family in the photo?"

"That's me and my brothers. We'd been fishing that day down at Corpus."

Curious now, she left her chair to pick up the frame. The three men with windblown hair and sunburned faces were smiling and laughing. Mason was only wearing a pair of swimming trunks and Sophie was mesmerized by the chiseled abs and long, muscular limbs.

"You three look like you were having lots of fun."

"We always have fun when we're together."

Sophie wished she could say the same about her own family. Most of the time they were discussing their father's philandering and whether any more of his illegitimate children were going to show up.

"You're so lucky, Mason. More than you could possibly know."

She leaned over to replace the photo on his desk. At the same moment, his chair swiveled toward hers. When the arm made contact with her thigh, the bump knocked her off balance and she teetered toward him.

"Oh!"

She managed to drop the photo onto the desktop without breaking it, but lost her footing in the process. Instinctively she grabbed his shoulder for support and then suddenly she found herself draped across his lap, her face only inches away from him.

"Sophie."

He whispered her name and the sound caressed her like a ray of hot sun on a cold day.

"Mason, I—"

She didn't have a chance to say more. Somehow, someway, their lips had made contact and her senses were rocketing upward with such a force, she couldn't think or breathe.

The taste of his lips was like a rich dessert. The more she consumed, the more she wanted.

Oh, my. Oh, my. This was a kiss. This was paradise! Now that she'd found it, she didn't want to leave. She wanted to let herself be carried away on the shiny stars exploding behind her eyelids, sending shards of tingling heat throughout her body.

But eventually Mason eased his mouth from hers and reality came rushing in like a gust of cold wind.

Scrambling from his lap, she turned her back and quickly straightened her clothing. Behind her, Mason rose to his feet.

"Sophie, I—" His words broke off as his hands settled over her shoulders. "I can't explain what just happened. I hope you're not angry with me."

Angry? A choir of voices were still rejoicing in her head. She'd never been so happy in her life. She wasn't a chunk of ice! She could feel and want and burn with need just like any normal woman.

But what did this mean? And what could Mason possibly be thinking of her now? That she was a promiscuous two-timer? Oh, Lord, she was making a mess of everything.

Passing a hand over her heated face, she said, "How could I be angry, Mason? You didn't ask me to fall in your lap."

She suddenly realized she was trembling all over and she wondered if their kiss had affected him as deeply as it had her.

"I didn't mean to bump you with my chair. But I—I'm not going to apologize for kissing you. It was nice. Very nice."

The sound of his hushed voice so close made her shiver and for a split second she considered giving in to the wild impulse and throwing herself straight at him. But Mason wasn't the man of her plans! She had to remember Thom and resist the crazy urges that were trying to take control of her senses.

"It was nice for me, too. I—I didn't know that friends could kiss that way. But it's done. So let's forget it and move on." She turned to face him and her heart made a silly leap at the look on his handsome face. There was something very mysterious and sober in his brown eyes. Something she'd very much like to unravel. "Okay?"

He gently touched her cheek and the tender gesture melted Sophie like candy in the hand of a child.

"Whatever you want, Sophie."

She couldn't make any sort of reply to that. She was too busy fighting the urge to kiss him again.

Thankfully, he attempted to break the awkward tension swirling around them. "Let me help you with your coat and we'll walk down to Bernie's. I don't know about you, but I could eat a big bowl of dessert right now."

Trying to ignore the electricity that seemed to be arcing between them, Sophie forced out a light laugh and reached for her faux fur jacket. "I could eat two bowls!"

She handed him the garment and as he held it open for her, she felt a rush of silly tears. Mason made her feel all the right things. But she'd never thought of him as her Mr. Right. Did that make her immature or just down right stupid? And what was she going to do about Thom?

Behind her, Mason switched off the desk lamp and planted a hand against the small of her back.

"Ready?" he asked.

"Sure. All ready."

Her hands trembling, she reached for her handbag. Thankfully, he'd never guess just how ready she was to let herself make love to him.

The young redhead was known to be a partygirl. Maybe it was all a show to make... There seemed to be... matter how he tried to didn't even... redeem the... and the... fortunes.

Chapter Seven

Sophie absently rolled a pen between her palms as she sat on the corner of her sister's desk. In fifteen minutes she was going to meet with a local magazine writer, Ariana Lamonte, and Sophie wasn't looking forward to the interview. She supposed there were plenty of people who were interested to read what it was like to be part of the Fortune family. But Sophie couldn't explain what it had been like to go through the name change and learn her father had been living a life of deceit for many years. She'd not totally digested it all yet, so how could she tell anyone what it felt like to become a Fortune?

"I'm not keen on meeting with the woman, Olivia. She didn't exactly put a nice slant on her blog about Keaton. I cringe to think what she might write about me."

Olivia shot Sophie a droll look. "She didn't say anything unflattering about our new half brother."

"Maybe you didn't think so, but I'm sure it made him

and Francesca very uncomfortable. Surely you've not forgotten she implied Keaton was a ladies' man—like our father."

Sophie followed Olivia's gaze across the work area to where Thom was chatting with a female programmer. The young redhead was known to be a party girl. Maybe she had her own plans to make Thom her Valentine date. Strange how that notion didn't even make a bleep on the radar of Sophie's feelings.

A few minutes ago, when Sophie had entered the research and development department her first glance had been toward Mason's desk, but to her disappointment, his cubicle had been empty. And then she'd spotted Thom by the water cooler. She'd simply given him a casual wave and continued straight to Olivia's cubicle. No doubt he was probably wondering why she'd not made a point to talk with him. To be honest, she wasn't quite sure why she'd avoided him. Other than the fact that it would be terribly uncomfortable to make conversation with Thom while her mind was preoccupied with Mason's red-hot kiss. Ever since last night, the reckless moments she'd spent in his lap had been looping over and over in her mind, making it impossible to think of little else.

"And like our company lothario," Olivia suggested with a smile.

Sophie let out a frustrated sigh. "Do you have to be so tacky? Thom might like women, but he's hardly a lothario. Unlike our father, he doesn't have illegitimate children popping up here and there."

"Give him time," Olivia retorted.

Was that how people really viewed Thom, Sophie wondered. Or was her jaded sister simply trying to put Sophie off the idea of making him her guy?

"Really, Olivia," Sophie scolded. "We were talking

about Ariana Lamonte and the blog she wrote about Keaton. Not about Thom."

Leaning back in the desk chair, Olivia crossed her arms and gave Sophie a rational look. "Like father, like son. With all that's come out about our family recently, I'm sure most everyone in Austin is thinking about Keaton and Dad in those terms. Which is totally unfair to Keaton. He's not a playboy. But Ms. Lamonte sort of slanted things in that direction. Even so, we can't avoid the media, Sophie. To try to hide from it would only make matters worse. Besides, what could the woman possibly write about you that would be unflattering? You've never done anything wrong or bad or—"

"Interesting?" Sophie finished wryly.

"You're the one who used that word," Olivia pointed out. "Not me. I was only going to say you've not done anything a person could criticize."

"Well, I'll try not to say anything that might reflect badly on our family."

"Easier said than done," Olivia told her. "I'm sure Ms. Lamonte will try to trip you up or put words in your mouth."

Sophie rose and smoothed down her figure-hugging sweater dress. She'd chosen it today because she'd wanted to look sexy and fashionable for the interview. Or so she'd told herself. Deep down, she'd hoped Mason would glance her way and see her as a woman instead of a friend.

"Gee, thanks, Olivia," she said with sarcasm. "That gives me a wealth of confidence."

Olivia laughed. "Let me know how the interview goes."

Sophie sighed. "We'll know the answer to that when Ms. Lamonte's article comes out in *Weird Life Magazine*. See you later, sis."

She left Olivia's cubicle, but before she reached the exit, Thom intercepted her and from the way his brow was arched, she got the impression he was a little confused by her behavior. He wasn't the only one. Sophie was confused by it, too.

"What's up? I thought you'd want to talk with me before you left."

Sophie glanced at her watch while hoping her cheeks didn't appear as pink as they felt. "I'd planned to. But I have a meeting in five minutes."

"Business?" he questioned.

The suspicious note she heard in his voice made no sense. Thom had no reason to be doubtful or jealous. He was the golden boy of Robinson Tech. He could have his pick of women. As for her, she was quite sure he'd not developed any deep feelings for her. Not yet, at least. Perhaps the gossipers in the ladies' room had been right about Thom, she thought. Perhaps he was viewing Sophie as a step ladder to the top of her father's company and he didn't want anything to prevent his climb.

"Uh, yes, the meeting is business related."

She smiled at him even though she wasn't feeling it, but the gesture must have pleased him, because his features softened and he moved a step closer.

"So when are we going to get together again? Tonight?"

Was it only a few days ago that she'd wanted to turn handsprings because Thom had asked her out on date? How could her feelings about him have changed in such a short time?

"Oh, it's nice of you to ask, Thom. But I have a family engagement tonight. I'll get back with you later. Right now I've got to run."

She hurried out the door, leaving him staring after her.

* * *

When Sophie entered the conference room a few doors down from Wes's office, she found Ariana Lamonte standing at a window, staring out at the Austin skyline.

"Ms. Lamonte?"

The tall, shapely woman with long dark hair turned and walked briskly toward Sophie. As she moved, a long printed skirt in orange and green swirled around a pair of brown suede boots. At the same time, the fringe on her leather jacket swayed with a life of its own. Ariana Lamonte rocked the chic bohemian look, right down to the long beaded earrings.

"Yes, I'm Ariana." She offered her hand. "And you're Sophie Fortune?"

"Sophie Fortune Robinson," she corrected. "I was a Robinson for twenty-three years. I'm not yet ready to let go of the name."

Ariana studied her thoughtfully. "And the Fortune name still feels a little strange, I'm sure."

"Exactly. Shall we sit? There should be fresh coffee over on the serving table if you'd care for any."

"No, thank you." She took a seat near the end of the table. "But please go ahead without me."

Sophie eased into the chair across from her and tried to make herself comfortable. "I'm not very good at this sort of thing—interviews about myself, that is."

"If you'd rather I didn't record our conversation I'm perfectly fine with taking notes," she suggested.

Maybe the woman wasn't only about getting a scoop on the Fortune family, Sophie thought. Or it could be Ariana Lamonte was playing nice to get Sophie in a re-laxed enough mood to spill her guts. The notion spurred Sophie's guard to an even higher level.

"I would rather you not have a recorder, Ms. Lamonte."

"Certainly. And please, call me Ariana."

The woman dug a small notepad and pen from her bag and placed it on the table. Sophie crossed her legs and began to slice the air with the toe of her high heel.

"You're very lovely, Ariana. To be honest, I was expecting an older lady with gray hair and wrinkles."

She laughed. "Plenty of people tell me a writer is supposed to be old enough to write from experience. But I don't intend to wait around for old age to set in before making my mark in the business."

"Neither do I," Sophie replied and suddenly she was thinking about Mason and how much that one little kiss had changed her. Just a tiny taste of real passion was all it had taken to reverse her course of action.

Although she hadn't yet figured out how she was going to do that without snubbing Thom and making herself look like a fool in the process.

For the next few minutes, Ariana questioned Sophie about her job, how she'd come to the decision to work for her father's company and how she'd felt when it was discovered that Gerald Robinson was actually Jerome Fortune.

"It's impossible to for me to explain how I felt at that time, Ariana. I'm still trying to digest the revelation." She studied the perfect oval of her pink nails rather than meet the scrutiny of the other woman's gaze. "It's very difficult to accept the fact that the father I knew growing up is someone else. There's that secret part of him that's a stranger to me. And that hurts—more than you can imagine."

Sophie could have gone on to say that unraveling the truth of her father's life had shaken every aspect of hers. At times she felt like a fraud, a person with a phony name who'd lived twenty-four years of lies. So many secrets still swirled around her parents. And though she reminded herself that she was her own person, she couldn't shake the fact that her family was bound together by lies rather than love. But she wasn't about to express those feelings to Ariana Lamonte or anyone. They were simply too deep and disturbing.

"I can only imagine," Ariana said, then hastily scribbled something on the page. "I'm also curious as to how Charlotte—your mother—is handling this whole situation with Keaton Fortune Whitfield becoming a part of the family."

There was so much Sophie could say about her mother. On the other hand, she didn't want Charlotte's problems broadcasted in a magazine article. Her mother had already endured enough embarrassment over the fact that her husband was a repeated adulterer.

"With Mother it's impossible to gauge what she's really feeling."

"Are you saying she hides her feelings from the family? Her children in particular?"

"I think she hides her feelings from everyone. I suppose you could describe my mother as a loner. Although she has a countless number of friends, I don't really believe she shares her private thoughts with any of them. But then, she's from an older generation. Her views on a husband-and-wife relationship are far different than yours or mine."

Ariana leveled a curious look at her. "How do you mean?"

Sophie shrugged. "Well, where Dad is concerned my mother has an overabundance of patience."

Ariana's brows arched upward. "Explain that for me."

"It's just that she…well, seems to look the other way

with my father. I could never be as understanding as she is."

"Hmm. I believe there are times when private things go on with our parents that children never discover about them. In this case, I'm wondering if your mother has a reason of her own for not kicking up a fuss about her husband's naughty behavior. Did that notion ever cross your mind?"

Sophie studied the young woman's thoughtful expression and decided she could trust her to a certain point. "More than once," she admitted.

Ariana leaned eagerly forward. "Would you be interested in finding out what's behind your mother's—shall we call it—her blind eye to her husband's womanizing?"

Sophie's lips unconsciously pressed together. If it hadn't been for Rachel's bit of snooping into their father's documents, no one in the Robinson family might ever have learned about Gerald actually being Jerome Fortune, about the nasty way his family had treated him, or how he'd faked his own death just to get away from them. But as much as Sophie would like answers about her mother, she wasn't sure she would feel right playing detective.

"I'm interested," Sophie told her. "But I'm not the person who can give you the keys to Mother's past, or the motives for her behavior. She refuses to discuss Dad and their marriage with me."

A smile crossed Ariana's face. "Sometimes you can pick up clues without even trying. If you keep your eyes and ears open I have a feeling you'll learn far more than you ever imagined."

Sophie wasn't exactly sure what the writer was hinting at, but after the recent events within her family, she doubted there was much left to shock her.

"Are you insinuating that you know something about my mother that I don't?"

The smile on Ariana's face turned suggestive. "Not exactly. But I do believe she has a story of her own. And any writer worth a grain of salt is interested in telling a good story."

And any loving daughter would want to keep the awful truth about her parents safely hidden away. Or would she? Was hiding the truth the best way to deal with a problem?

Sophie didn't know what to think anymore. Not about her parents, herself, or her misguided plans to snare her dream man.

Much later that evening, Mason rubbed his tired eyes and switched off his desk lamp. For the past several hours he'd been working non-stop on the health app. The new project was a chance to show Wes and Gerald Robinson what he could do.

However, after last night and that wild kiss he'd shared with Sophie, he'd not been able to focus for more than five minutes at a time on his work or, for that matter, anything else. All his mind wanted to dwell on was how soft and sweet her lips had tasted and how eagerly she'd kissed him back. She'd wanted him. He'd felt her desire as much as he'd felt his own. But what did it mean? What could it mean when her heart had seemed so set on Thom Nichols?

Last night, while they'd sat in Bernie's drinking coffee and eating Italian cream cake, both had avoided mentioning the kiss or anything remotely connected to it. But Mason had felt the awkward tension between them and understood the intimate act had changed everything

Groaning at the memory, Mason grabbed his jacket and left his cubicle. One glance at the dark entrance to the HR department told him Sophie wasn't working late tonight. The realization caused his spirits to plummet and he wondered if she'd gone out on another date with Thom.

Why not, Mason? That kiss doesn't make you her one and only. So don't go thinking you're something special to her. The two of you are friends. Not lovers. She wants Thom Nichols. She believes she can drag that little Bantam rooster away from all his hens. She's too blinded by his charm to see how much you adore her.

Maybe she was looking past him right now, Mason mentally retorted to the mocking voice in his head, but he still had time. Valentine's Day was a week away. By then he was going to come up with a plan of his own. Mason couldn't allow the woman of *his* dreams to spend the special night of love with anyone but him.

Down in the parking garage, he got in his car, but instead of starting the engine, pulled out his phone. Moments later, his oldest brother's voice sounded in his ear.

"Hey, Mason, what's going on in Austin?"

Mason leaned his head back and massaged his aching eyes. "Not much. Are you busy?"

Doug chuckled. "Just going through a stack of depositions. The usual thing."

"Sorry. That was a stupid question, wasn't it? I won't keep you long. I only wanted to see how everyone was doing." Finding Sophie had already left the building had unexpectedly filled Mason with thoughts of his family. Even though it was only eighty miles down to San Antonio, there were times Mason felt like he was a world away from his brothers and parents. "Mom and Dad okay?"

"Busy as ever. Dad's job sent him to New Mexico for

a week, but he's back now. And Mom has been trying to set up Valentine's dates for Shawn and me. You know her, she desperately wants grandchildren. Why don't you give her some?"

A wife and babies. At one time Mason had believed he'd be the first of the Montgomery brothers to settle down and start a family. But after Christa had walked out, he'd begun to doubt whether he was cut out for love and marriage.

Groaning, Mason said, "I'm not in the mood to talk about Valentine's Day."

"What's wrong? Don't tell me you're having romance trouble again. After that stomping Christa gave you, I thought you'd sworn off dating."

"I did—I have. Except I—"

"You've met someone and she's turned your head. So what's wrong? She won't give you the time of day?"

Sophie had given him far more than Mason had expected. But he wanted more and he wouldn't be satisfied until she looked at him with stars in her eyes and love in her heart.

"She—uh—likes me enough. But—"

"You want to be more than friends," Doug finished Mason's thoughts.

"You got it. But I'm beginning to think I'm being a big fool—again," Mason said as he glanced around the nearly empty parking garage.

"Why? Don't tell me you've fallen for another flirty blonde with mush between her ears."

Wincing, Mason asked with sarcasm, "Why do I call you? To be reminded of my mistakes?"

Doug chuckled. "We all make mistakes, Mason. And you call me because you want advice from an expert."

Mason sputtered. "On women? I realize you have

them lined up on your doorstep, but I'm not ready to call you an expert on the subject."

There was a moment of silence and then Doug said, "Seriously, Mason, are you troubled about something?"

"Troubled. Confused. Dazed. Yeah, I guess I'm a little of all those things. This woman is really out of my league, Doug. Truthfully, I have no business even thinking about her, much less looking her way. She comes from a wealthy family. Extremely wealthy."

"Money doesn't make a man, Mason."

"This is about more than a bank account. Her father owns Robinson Tech."

This time Doug's silence stretched to a point where Mason was beginning to think the cell signal had dropped.

"Doug? Are you still there?"

"I'm here. I was just thinking that when my little brother picks a woman, he *really* picks one."

"I admit it's crazy. She could never be serious about a guy like me. But—"

"Listen, Mason," Doug interrupted. "This woman could walk the face of the earth and never find a better guy than you."

Mason sat up straight. "You've never said anything like that to me before."

"I haven't? Well, I should have. You've always followed your heart. That's why you're Mom's favorite."

In spite of his doubts, Mason grinned. "You don't have to lay it on that thick, brother."

"Who's laying it on? So when are you coming down to see us? If I can get some of these trials out of the way, we'll go to Padre and do a little fishing."

Mason chuckled. "By the time I get my new project

finished and you get the court docket wiped clean it will be the middle of summer."

"Great. Let's mark the calendar. In the meantime, Mason, you keep asking yourself if that girl is good enough for you. Not the other way around. Okay?"

"I hear you. Thanks, Doug."

The two men exchanged goodbyes and Mason ended the connection and started the car. As he backed out of the parking slot, he noticed two cars parked together in the row behind him. One of them was Thom Nichols's sports car. The white economy car parked next to it belonged to a redhead who worked in R&D.

If Thom's car was still here that meant he most likely wasn't with Sophie. However, Mason had never seen him working overtime. Did that mean he was out with the redhead? The idea caused Mason's jaw to clamp tight. Sophie definitely needed to know about the seedy side of her dream man. But he wasn't going to be the one to tell her. He could only hope that Sophie would learn the truth for herself. Before Thom had a chance to break her heart.

Sophie was sitting in the family room, scanning a stack of work she'd brought home, when she heard footsteps on the Italian tile and looked up to see her mother walking toward her.

Glancing at the tall grandfather clock to the left of an oil painting that Charlotte had paid thousands for at a European auction, Sophie noticed it was only a few minutes past ten.

"Hello, Mother. I thought you'd gone to the theatre. Is the play over this early?"

The older woman dropped her jeweled handbag onto an antique loveseat and slowly eased off her brocade jacket. "I couldn't sit to the end. The whole thing was too boring. But to give the actors credit, no one could have made that dialogue believable. The only saving grace was that the cost of the ticket goes to one of my favorite charities."

That was one positive thing about her mother, Sophie thought. If there was a cause Charlotte felt deeply about, she would generously contribute both her time and money to help it flourish.

"I'm sorry you didn't enjoy it," Sophie told her. "What about your friend Alice? Did she stay to watch the end?"

"No. We left together. Her husband hasn't been feeling well, so she wanted to get home early to check on him."

She wondered if her mother would have done the same.

Charlotte eased into an armchair angled to Sophie's. "I'm glad I caught you," she said. "Olivia informed me that you talked with that magazine writer today. What's her name? Lamonte?"

Sophie nodded. "Ariana Lamonte. She's writing about what it means to become a Fortune."

"Hmmp. Surely the woman could find something more worthwhile to focus on besides the Fortune family."

Sophie frowned at the bitterness in her mother's voice. "Are you forgetting that I am one of those Fortunes? That all your children are now Fortunes?"

"It's a fact I try not to dwell on," she said bluntly, then smoothing a hand over her long, black skirt, she gave Sophie a sidelong glance. "What did you and Ms. Lamonte discuss during your interview?"

What would her mother think if she told her that Ariana Lamonte was more than curious about her behavior? "Just the routine things. Mainly she wanted to hear how I felt about getting a half brother that none of the family knew existed. She also wanted to know what it was like for me to learn how my father had chosen to fake his own death rather than live as Jerome Fortune."

"Sophie! I don't like you speaking about your father in that sarcastic tone."

Sighing, Sophie looked away from her mother's stern face. Drama and secrets seemed to always surround her family. Why couldn't she have been born to regular parents like Mason's? No doubt he'd been conceived in love. Whereas, Sophie could only imagine Charlotte getting pregnant by doing her wifely duty and little more.

"I apologize, Mother. I'm trying to understand what motivated Dad to take on a different identity. But apart from that deceit, some of the things he's done are very… well, disappointing."

"He's your father and he loves you," she said as though that made up for everything.

But did her father, whom she now had to think of as Jerome Fortune, really love her? Or had the affection he'd shown her over the years only been a part of his deception? Oh, Lord, she didn't know what was real or pretense anymore. Not with her parents or with Thom.

"If you say so."

Charlotte's lips tightened, but she didn't issue any more scolding words. Instead, she settled back in her chair and asked, "I'm sure the subject of your mother came up in the interview. What did Ms. Lamonte ask about me?"

Are you asking because you have something to hide?

The question darted through Sophie's mind as she studied her mother's regal features. "I think Ms. Lamonte is like everyone else in this city," Sophie said. "She's wondering how you're dealing with all this scandal about Dad."

"And what did you tell her?"

Sophie frowned. Her mother seemed overly curious about the interview. What could possibly concern her about a simple magazine article? Over the years the Robinsons had dealt with all sorts of bad publicity. Granted, nothing as bad as the recent tabloids, though.

"Don't fret, Mother. I told her how you were standing faithfully behind your husband. And that we're all unified as a family. I'm not so sure she understands your attitude. Frankly, neither do I. But that's another matter entirely, isn't it?"

"Entirely." Clearing her throat, she rose to her feet. "Be advised, Sophie, not to say any more than necessary to this woman. After reading her feature about Keaton I have a feeling she doesn't have any regard for a person's private life."

Not wanting to cause her mother any more distress, Sophie planted a swift kiss on her cheek. "Don't concern yourself about it, Mother. I measured my words carefully. Besides, we're a strong bunch. We can weather any kind of media storm."

In an unusual display of affection, Charlotte patted her cheek. "You're right. I'll say good-night now. I've had a busy day."

As she turned to go, Sophie asked, "When is Dad going to be home? I haven't seen him the past few evenings."

"He called from LA earlier this afternoon. He'll be staying on another day or two. Business, of course."

Of course, Sophie thought sadly. And as she watched her mother leave the family room, Sophie was more determined than ever to make her life different.

She wasn't going to make the same mistake of wasting away in a cold marriage. She was going to marry a man she loved, who would love her in return. A man who would take her into his arms and wrap her in warmth and passion and fill her heart with happiness.

A man exactly like…Mason.

Chapter Eight

The next morning, Sophie marched into Dennis's office, dropped a bound folder on his desk and pounded it with her forefinger, while her boss watched on with mild amusement.

"Is something wrong?" he asked.

Folding her arms against her breasts, Sophie stared at him. "Wrong? Have you read this thing?"

"Not yet. All I know is that Ben decided the company needed to save money by changing insurance carriers." He pointed to the folder. "And this is what we have now."

"This is a crock of you-know-what. It's outrageous. As soon as the employees see all the medical procedures being dropped from their coverage, they're going to riot. Ben must have been out of his mind when he decided to go with this provider."

"Health insurance is in turmoil these days and I think there was a lot of lobbying going on by this company to get Robinson Tech's business," Dennis told her. "And your brother was in a cut-and-save mood."

Sophie snorted. "You know, when a flood of employees show up here to protest, I'm going to send them straight upstairs to Ben's office. He'll be in a different mood then."

Dennis shook his head. "Give your brother a break. He's just become a new father. He has a lot on his mind."

Sophie's expression suddenly softened. "Yes, little Lacey is adorable. I've never seen my big brother so enamored with anyone or anything. He behaves as though he's the first man to ever have a daughter."

"It is a special event when a child comes into your life. You'll learn when it happens to you, Sophie."

Becoming a mother was never going to happen to her unless she connected with the right man. And right now she was trying to decide how she could extricate herself from this mess she'd made with Thom. Perhaps she should just write *FOOL* across her forehead in big letters, take her lumps, and get it over with. But Valentine's Day was less than a week away and she'd gotten a text from Thom this morning hinting that he was already making big plans for the evening.

More wrestling or monster action movies? The mere thought of it made her sick.

"Okay, Dennis, I'll send notices out to all our employees about the change in insurance. Just get ready to hear plenty of howling."

She picked up the folder and left her boss's office. As she walked back to her desk, she spotted Mason. This morning he was wearing black slacks and a plum colored dress shirt that emphasized the faint bronze mix in his brown hair. As she watched him move toward her, she was amazed that it had taken her so long to really see what an attractive man he was. If she'd not been so busy developing such a thoughtless crush on Thom, she might have taken more notice of Mason. And never gotten herself into the embarrassing situation she was in now.

She walked over to meet him. "Good morning, Mason," she greeted with a wide smile. "I hope you're not here in my department to complain."

He grinned. "Me, complain? Never. It's my break time. If you can leave your desk, I thought we might have a cup of coffee together."

Fifteen minutes with Mason would do her a world of good. "That sounds wonderful. Let me just put this away." She held up the folder.

As he followed her into her cubicle Sophie was acutely aware of him standing a few steps behind her. The faint scent of his masculine cologne teased her nostrils while waves of heat seemed to be radiating from his body. That kiss of his had done something to her, she thought. Since then, whenever he got close, her nerves seemed to send up radar that picked up every little nuance about the man.

"What's this?" he asked. "I didn't know you were a hockey fan."

"I'm not." Sophie turned to see him staring at a ticket lying on the corner of her desk. Apparently someone had left it there while she'd been in Dennis's office.

"Someone apparently thinks you are."

"Let me see." She picked up the ticket and found a small note stuck to the back. It read: *We can catch a commuter flight and be in Dallas in time for the game. I'm looking forward to a fabulous evening with you. Thom.*

Sophie wanted to look up at the ceiling and let out a loud groan. Instead, she glanced at Mason and tried to hide her frustration. "Thom wants to take me to Dallas to see the Stars play tonight."

"Hmm. Rather a long drive to be making on a weeknight. You'd have to leave work early this afternoon to make it in time."

The faint note of disapproval she heard in Mason's voice made her wonder if he might actually be jealous of Thom. But that sort of thinking was farfetched. Even if he had planted that hot kiss on her lips, Mason thought of himself as Sophie's friend. Nothing more.

"He expects to catch a commuter flight," Sophie said, as her mind whirled in search of more than one reasonable excuse to put the man off.

Mason grunted. "His salary must be measurably larger than mine to spend that sort of money on a sporting event."

"Thom loves sports," she said dully. "Of all kinds."

"No doubt," he said dryly.

Sophie looked at him. "What does that mean?"

He shook his head. "Nothing. Just that most men do—love all kinds of sports."

Looping her arm through his, Sophie urged him out of the cubicle. "Well, I seriously doubt Thom's salary is a dime more than yours. His position with the company is not more important than yours. As for this hockey game, I can't go."

"You can't?"

He sounded surprised and Sophie figured he was probably wondering why she would turn down any date with Thom. If she told Mason he was part of the reason, he'd probably think she was joking. And after the big deal she'd made about Thom being the fantasy man of Robinson Tech, she couldn't blame him. Or even worse, he might get the impression that she was, as her mother had implied, a butterfly fluttering from one man to the next, incapable of making a choice.

"Uh—no. It's—well, this evening is not a good time.

I have—other things to do." *Like dream about you,* she wanted to say, but didn't.

He slanted her a sly grin. "You can always use the weather as an excuse. There are snow or ice warnings for tonight."

"Oh! Thank you, Mason!"

"For what? Giving you a bad weather forecast?"

She felt a blush slowly creeping over her cheeks. "Well, I don't necessarily like icy weather. But Thom— Sometimes it's hard to make him understand I'm not at his beck and call any given time of the week."

They entered the break room and she was relieved to see that Thom wasn't anywhere in sight. In fact, the room was empty.

"Maybe you should just be honest with him, Sophie. Tell him that you don't like hockey and you'd rather not go."

His suggestion caused her eyes to roll. "What a novel idea. Brutal honesty. You wouldn't like it if a woman told you she didn't like the plans you made for the two of you."

He shrugged. "Maybe. But I wouldn't mind changing my plans to something we'd both enjoy."

"Really? You'd do that?"

"Sure. If the woman was that important to me." He guided her over to a chair and helped her into it. "You sit. I'll get our coffee. Cream and sugar, right?"

"Yes, thank you."

While Mason gathered the drinks, Sophie realized he remembered things about her that Thom had never taken the time to notice. He gave her encouraging words at just the right time and made her laugh when her spirits desperately needed a lift. He inherently seemed to know what she was thinking and feeling. And Sophie was quickly beginning to see just what a rare thing that was to find in a man.

"Here you go." He placed the cup in front of her, then sat to her left. "A boost for the midmorning blues."

Her expression wry, she glanced over at him. "What makes you think I have the midmorning blues?"

"Just a guess. Your shoulders aren't quite as squared as they usually are."

For the most part, she could see that he was teasing, but the remark had her straightening her back anyway.

"I've been so busy I've hardly had time to look up. What about you?"

"This health app is turning out to be much harder than I anticipated. There are so many products out there already. I want this to be fresh and new. Something that will grab the public's attention. I just haven't come up with the right ideas yet. Basically I want to tie sports with health and make the couch potatoes realize that being fit can also be fun. That's been done, too. But hopefully I can put a different slant on it."

She looked at him and the appreciation he saw in her brown eyes made him want to do handsprings. He'd had people praise his work before. Even Gerald Robinson himself. But having Sophie's admiration lifted his ego to another level.

"You will. I have every faith in you. So do Wes and my dad. Or the two of them would've never assigned you the task."

He watched her sip the coffee, while wishing he had the right to lean over and whisper loving words in her ear, to kiss her and call her his own. Perhaps that was crazy thinking on his part, but he couldn't stop himself. Doug had pointed out that money didn't make a person and Mason believed he was right. Even if Sophie was barely scraping by on a pitiful income, he would still be infatuated with her effervescent personality, the caring and warmth that radiated from her eyes.

Mason forced his thoughts back to the conversation. "Pleasing those two men puts me in a pressure cooker," he joked.

Her lips tilted into a soft smile and Mason inwardly groaned. She had to figure out how wrong Thom was for her, he thought desperately. Otherwise, Mason's heart was going to be broken. Along with Sophie's. Because there was no doubt in his mind that Thom was a user and Sophie was just soft enough and vulnerable enough to let him.

"Wes doesn't always put what's on his mind into words, and that makes some people view him as a cold stuffed shirt. But he's really fair minded. Dad is tough and expects everyone around him to be the same. But like I said before, there's a softer side to him if you take the time to look."

To have a father like Gerald Robinson was something Mason wouldn't wish on his worst enemy. He'd noticed that Sophie didn't talk that much about her family, but whenever she did, he got the impression they weren't exactly like the warm, fun-loving groups depicted on a 1950s sitcom. And given the scandals that had recently surrounded the Robinsons, he could certainly see why their family ties might be strained.

"When I left the building last night you were already gone," he told her. "I was going to see how your interview with Ariana Lamonte went. I could tell you were dreading it."

She was carefully clutching her cup and as Mason studied her dainty fingers, he tried to block out the image of Thom sliding an engagement ring onto her left hand.

"It wasn't anything like I expected. She was much younger than I thought she would be. And clever. She certainly knows how to make a person talk. We chatted mostly about Robinson Tech and what made me decide to work for my father. And of course, she wanted to know my feelings about becoming a Fortune." She sighed and shook back her long brown hair. "The woman should know that discovering your father—that you're not really who you thought you were all these years—well, it's something that can't be described in words. It's like the ground has tilted beneath my feet and still hasn't righted itself."

This was the most she'd ever mentioned to Mason about the scandal that had rocked Austin and the business world beyond. The fact that she would share this much with him made him feel special. It also made him want to comfort and reassure her.

Reaching over, he curled his fingers around her slender forearm. "Sophie, no one is accountable for the choices a relative makes. No matter how right or wrong those choices might be."

She turned a rueful expression on him. "You're right, Mason. It's just that when you learn someone you love hasn't been entirely truthful with you—it hurts. A lot."

He gently squeezed her arm. "You can't let it drag you down, Sophie."

"I don't intend to let it," she said with conviction, then glanced at the clock. "I'd better get back to my desk."

"Yeah, I've got to get back to work, too," he said.

Moments later, while they were walking side by side down the busy corridor, Mason dared to ask, "So what do you plan to do about the hockey game?"

She slanted him a look from beneath her dark lashes.

"I'm going to give him a weather forecast. He surely can't think I've stirred up a weather storm just to avoid a date."

Mason felt like letting out a loud whoop and making several triumphant fist pumps. Instead he tried to appear as cool as Agent 007 ordering a shaken martini. "He'd never think it in a million years."

At the door of the human resources department, Mason was trying to think up some sort of excuse to see her later tonight, when she suddenly turned and swept him with a demure look.

"Valentine's Day is less than a week away," she said. "Do you have your special date lined up yet?"

He cleared his throat and for one reckless second considered the idea of asking her flat out to be his Valentine's date. But she'd already made it clear she wanted to be with Thom on that special night. And Mason wasn't good with rejection.

"Uh—no. Not yet. I'm still considering."

She frowned at him. "Mason! If you don't quit dragging your feet you're going to end up spending Valentine's alone. And no one should have to be alone on such a special night of love."

"You're right. I'm going to get my act together and show my lady love just how much I adore her."

"Now you're talking," she said, then with a little wave, disappeared through the door.

His mind still on Sophie, he didn't notice Thom until he'd crossed the corridor to his own department. By then, the other man was walking straight toward him and from the tight look on his face, he didn't appear all that happy. Had he seen Mason and Sophie together?

"Hello, Nichols. You need to see someone in R&D?"

"Not exactly. I'm on my way out of the building. For a business luncheon across town."

That was the way with the marketing personnel, Mason thought. They seemed to always get added perks. Especially Thom.

"Better take a coat. Bad weather is moving in," he warned.

"Thanks for the advice, but I don't like coats. Never wear one."

Tough guy. Sure, Mason thought drily. If the truth was known, the man probably wore flannel pajamas and slept under an electric blanket.

"Suit yourself," Mason said, then started to leave.

Thom moved just enough to one side to block Mason's path.

With a smug grin, he said, "I thought you might like to know that Sophie and I are getting on great. In fact, I have a huge evening planned for Valentine's night. The woman loves sports, but this time I've decided to surprise her and blitz her with an evening of pure romance."

Mason suddenly felt ill. The hockey game hadn't impressed her, but the romance would. What in hell was he going to do to stop this from happening? He had to come up with something. He couldn't just sit around and hope that Sophie would get over this crush she had on Thom. He had to come up with a plan to ambush Sophie's heart before Thom could ever get his hands on her.

His mind already preoccupied with options, he muttered, "Sophie will be thrilled, I'm sure."

The grin on Thom's face deepened. "Dinner at the Riverside restaurant, dancing, flowers—the works."

At least he'd not mentioned a ring, Mason thought. But that would be coming soon, no doubt. If he was right, Thom would never let Sophie slip away. Not if he believed she'd be a boost to his bank account and career.

Mason glanced thoughtfully toward the entrance to

Sophie's department. She clearly didn't want to go on a date with Thom tonight. Whether that was because she disliked hockey or something else, Mason wasn't sure. But either way, the idea gave him a glimmer of hope.

Mason said, "Sounds look you've put a lot of thought into this Valentine evening for Sophie."

"I've put more than a thought into it. I've already invested a small fortune in it. If this doesn't make her swoon at my feet, then she'd have to be colder than a block of ice."

Ice. Before the day was over, Mason prayed the stuff would fall from the sky in bucket loads. He didn't want Sophie going anywhere for any reason with this man.

"Uh, speaking of ice," he said casually, "did you know Austin is under a winter storm warning for sleet this evening?"

Thom looked stunned before muttering several curse words. "Are you kidding me?"

"I checked the weather site on my computer less than an hour ago. Isn't it weird? We rarely ever have brutal weather like that. The weather gods must have it out for us."

A tight grimace pulled his features. "Or me," he muttered. "Excuse me, Montgomery. I need to go."

"Have a nice lunch," Mason called to the man's retreating back, then whistling under his breath, he headed back to work.

Later that afternoon, Sophie had just finished speaking with Thom and was on her way out of marketing, when she heard a low hissing noise to her right.

Glancing over, she was surprised to see Olivia trying to draw her attention. Knowing she very well couldn't avoid her sister, Sophie walked over to her.

"What's up?" she asked.

"I'm on my way back to programming," Olivia replied. "Let's step out in the corridor."

Sophie followed her sister into the hall where they found a quiet alcove.

Olivia said, "I just saw you talking with Thom. He looked none too happy. Have you already called it quits with him?"

Sophie frowned. "What are you doing? Did you follow me here just to keep a watchful eye on me?"

Olivia shot her a droll look. "No. I had to confer with someone about advertising. But I should be following you, since you seem to have lost all common sense."

Hoping the mix of emotions churning inside her didn't show on her face, Sophie said, "I hate to disappoint you, but I can still think for myself. As for Thom, he's not exactly your business but I'll tell you anyway. He had this big evening planned to fly to Dallas tonight. I told him I couldn't make it. I explained that Dad would have a fit if I boarded a small plane with the threat of an ice storm looming."

"And Thom didn't take it well, I see. Hmm. Sorry, sis, I take everything back. He's the one lacking common sense. Not you."

Sophie smiled at her. "Thanks. I can use my brain once in a while."

As Olivia folded her arms against her chest Sophie thought how beautiful her sister looked in the lapis blue dress she was wearing and the way her dark hair waved so perfectly around her face. Olivia was always so poised and sure of herself. She would never get herself into an awkward situation with a man like Sophie had. Olivia was too smart for that. A fact which only made Sophie feel even more foolish.

Olivia asked, "What's the deal anyway? Is flying to Dallas a bit much for the middle of the week?"

Sophie shrugged while wondering how much she could say to her sister without revealing the fact that she was quickly and decisively coming to the conclusion that Thom was a jerk. "Actually, I was thinking the same thing." Leaning closer to Olivia, she lowered her voice. "When I first told you my plans to get Thom to be my Valentine's date—"

"It was more than getting him as your date, Sophie," Olivia interrupted. "The way you were talking, he was the man who was going to slip a wedding ring on your finger."

Perhaps all that gushing she'd done about Thom to her sister had been a bit overboard. Funny, but most of what she'd said, she couldn't even remember now. But at the time Sophie had truly believed she'd been mapping out her very future. Which only proved how quickly life could alter course.

"Okay, so maybe I was letting my dreams get a little out of hand. I'm walking on earth now. And I've been doing plenty of thinking these past few days."

"About Thom?" Olivia prodded with a tad of sarcasm. "Or something more important?"

"About Thom and…other things." Her expression turned sober as she looked at her sister. "Olivia, do you ever wonder about people? The ones who are supposed to be our friends? The ones who are supposed to love us? Sometimes I ask myself if they're close to me simply because I'm me or because my name is Fortune Robinson."

Olivia swatted a dismissive hand through the air. "That's just a part of who we are. Sure, there will always be people who want to use us. But you don't have to be rich to be used, you know. Even a poor woman can be taken advantage of by a man. That is what you're thinking about, isn't it? That Thom or some man might pretend he loves you just so he can get at your wealth?"

Now was hardly the time or place to be getting into such a conversation with her sister. But she couldn't stop herself.

She nodded glumly. "There are times I wonder if I can trust anyone. I mean, we don't even know if our parents are being honest with us."

Olivia frowned. "Our parents," she repeated blankly. "Everyone knows Dad has carried secrets, but you said 'parents.' Mom doesn't have Dad's deceptive ways."

"Do you know that for certain?"

Olivia was shooting her a disgusted look when Olivia's cell phone rang.

Sophie used the interruption to give her sister a departing wave, then scurried toward the elevator. She'd already said more to her sister than she should have.

Chapter Nine

Four days later, Sophie was sitting at her desk, wondering how she could finish the day when a smiling Mason suddenly strolled in carrying a foam container.

"What is that?" she asked, gesturing to the object in his hand. "It smells like food."

He pulled up the extra chair she kept in her cubicle and sat a short distance away from her.

"It's a snack. Just for you. I've been to Bernie's."

Excited now, she grabbed the container. "Bread pudding! Oh, you darling man!"

He pulled a plastic spoon from the pocket on his shirt and handed it to her.

"I stopped by to see if you wanted to have lunch, but your neighbor told me you were in a meeting with Dennis."

Nodding, Sophie quickly dug into the rich sweet. "Mmm. That's right. I haven't even had a chance to eat lunch. We've been bombarded over this health insurance thing. I think Dennis and I have convinced Ben if he sticks with this new plan his employees are going to flee like rats on a sinking ship."

Mason grunted with faint amusement. "I have no intentions of running out of the building. If I did that, how would I ever see your smiling face?"

He was so sweet and funny and endearing. And special. How had she worked near him for so long without noticing him? Why had she let Thom's sexy grin and confident attitude turn her head when she should have been looking at a man she could trust?

She playfully wrinkled her nose at him. "I would never allow you to quit Robinson Tech. I'd be lonely without you. And hungry," she added teasingly.

He glanced at a heart shaped box of candy lying on the far end of her desk. "Looks like you've already been given something to eat. Pecan pralines."

She tried not to grimace. "Thom sent me the chocolates this morning. But I can't eat them. I had already told him that I can't eat nuts—especially pecans, but he seems to have forgotten." Or never bothered to pay attention to her in the first place, she thought drearily. Since she'd turned down the Dallas date, Thom had started leaving little gifts on her desk, along with silly little notes that sounded as phony as a three dollar bill. Like she was the only woman he'd ever fallen for, or wanted so much. Who was the man trying to fool?

Who do you think, Sophie? You're the one who thought Thom was a prince on a white horse. You're the one who flirted your way into his life without ever really taking a good, hard look at him. You thought because every other woman in the building wanted him, he had to be Mr. Wonderful. Now he's a nuisance. One that you don't know how to get rid of without making yourself look like an idiot.

"I'm sure Thom will make up for the candy on your Valentine date."

It wasn't only the chocolate that had her mentally shaking her head. Last Friday she'd found a beautifully wrapped package on her desk only to find the contents was a woolen scarf that had looked like something a lumberjack in the far north would wear. The day before that, she'd found a DVD of pro wrestling matches in the seat of her desk chair, along with a note that had read: *In memory of our special night together.*

There had been a time when Sophie would have cherished anything Thom might have given her. Even the most garish gift would've been appreciated if he'd given it with genuine sincerity. But these past few days she'd begun to doubt Thom's motives, not to mention his integrity.

Sophie took another mouthful of pudding. Why couldn't Thom have given her something as thoughtful as her favorite dessert?

Because Thom doesn't know you like Mason does. Because Thom will never know much about anyone, except himself.

"It really doesn't matter," she said honestly. Nothing about Thom seemed to matter to her anymore.

"I'm sure you know he has big plans for your date tomorrow night. You must be very excited about that."

Frowning with confusion, she looked at him. "Big plans? How would you know?"

"He made a point of telling me. A 'blitz of romance' is the way he described it to me."

She could hardly keep her mouth from falling open. "He told you that?"

He nodded and for a split second Sophie thought she saw a flash in his eyes that looked something like disapproval. Or had it been jealousy? The notion gave her a glimmer of hope. If there was a slight chance that Mason could see her as more than a friend, she had to grab it and hold on for dear life.

He said, "I suppose I shouldn't have mentioned it. He probably wants to surprise you."

Any sort of romance from Thom Nichols would be more than a surprise, it would be a stunner. As far as she was concerned, the man had the romance of a rock.

"It would be a surprise all right," she muttered.

She could feel his eyes studying her closely and she glanced up to see confusion on his face.

Before she could say more, he asked, "What's wrong?"

Everything, Sophie wanted to say. But she couldn't pour her heart out to Mason now. Especially here at work where coworkers might overhear. The gossip mill would spin so fast it would probably catch fire.

"Nothing is wrong," she said, trying her best to sound casual. "I'm just a little tired, that's all. Dealing with this insurance change has been a giant headache."

"Hmm. You normally thrive on challenges. And I've never seen you tired." His eyes narrowed with concern. "I hope you're not coming down with the flu. That would be awful to finally get your Valentine date and then not be able to enjoy yourself."

Sick? Mason was partly right. She was definitely heartsick over her misjudgment of Thom, she thought grimly. "I feel fine, Mason. Really."

She swallowed the last bite of pudding and tossed the container into the trash.

"I'm glad to hear it," he said. "I just thought—"

She glanced around to see him shaking his head with

doubt and for one wild second Sophie wanted to leap from the chair and throw herself into his arms. Mason could make everything right. He could fix the troubled thoughts in her mind and the hollow ache in her heart. But he didn't know that. He might not even want to know it.

"I keep remembering back to the night when you first talked about Thom and your hopes to get him for your Valentine date. You were so excited about the prospect. And now that you've accomplished your goal, I figured you'd be dancing around the building in anticipation of tomorrow. Instead you look about as perky as a wet hen."

She wrinkled her nose at him. "I'm not a farm girl. What does a wet hen look like?"

"Droopy. Instead of clucking and running around the chicken yard strutting her stuff, she's standing at the edge of the flock trying to shake the water off her feathers. In your case, you look like you're trying to shake off a flood of tears."

His assessment, corny as it sounded, was so accurate it was eerie. Instead of dancing, she was brooding. And though she was a girl who rarely ever shed a tear, these past few days there'd been several times she'd had to fight them off.

It shouldn't surprise her that Mason could read her so well. He seemed to pick up on her feelings, even when she was trying to hide them.

She straightened her shoulders and leveled him the most confident look she could muster. "I'm sure I need to freshen my lipstick. But I don't believe I look anywhere near shedding a tear. As for me dancing around the department, Dennis is a very lenient boss, but he might not appreciate the merriment."

A faint smile twisted his lips and Sophie couldn't help but look at them and relive the kiss they'd shared. Tomorrow night he'd surely be kissing his Valentine sweetheart. Each time she'd asked him about his date, he'd skirted the answer. Sophie didn't have a clue as to who he might be dating, but she knew one thing: She fervently wished it was her.

"I'm glad I don't need to drag out my handkerchief and wipe your cheeks." He glanced at the digital clock on her desk. "I've been here too long. I need to get back to work."

He started out of her cubicle. Before Sophie realized what she was doing, she practically leaped out of her chair and blocked his path.

"Mason, before you go, I—" Not knowing how to express her feelings in words, she rose on the tips of her toes and kissed his cheek.

His brow arched in question and she said, "That's for the pudding. And for helping me shake the water off my feathers."

She expected her comment to gain a smile from him, but she couldn't find a speck of amusement on his face. Instead, he gently patted her cheek.

"If I don't see you before tomorrow evening, good luck with your plans. Thom is a lucky man."

As she stood there watching him go and wishing she had the right to run after him, her cell phone jangled with a text message.

Crossing to her desk, she picked up the phone and read the message. The sender was Olivia.

We're waiting on you in the conference room. Have you forgotten?

Oh, Lord, the moment Mason had shown up with the pudding, she'd forgotten all about the family meeting.

Hurrying now, Sophie dashed off a note to anyone

who might come looking for her, then grabbed her handbag and left the cubicle.

The last thing she needed today was to listen to Ben talk about digging up more of their father's indiscretions. But Sophie was a Fortune Robinson and she, along with the rest of her siblings, needed to help hold their fractured family together.

Moments later, she stepped into the conference room and felt every eye on her as she sat at the long table where her four brothers, Ben, Wes, Graham, and Kieran sat waiting, along with her three sisters, Rachel, Olivia and Zoe.

"Hi, everyone! I'm sorry," she apologized, her voice breathless from rushing. "I got busy and forgot the time."

"Don't worry about it, Sophie. Five minutes isn't going to kill us," Graham, the cowboy of the bunch, spoke up.

"That's right," Rachel replied. "Since I don't get over to Austin that often, it's given me a little extra time to visit with everyone."

After her older sister had married Matteo Mendoza and settled down in Horseback Hollow, the family didn't see her nearly as often. Sophie missed her sister, but on the other hand, she was very glad that Rachel had found true love and happiness.

Sophie took a seat next to Olivia and glanced around the group. "Have I missed anything?"

Wes said dryly, "Not unless you count hearing Ben describe his baby daughter's burps as big news."

Ben leveled a sardonic look at his twin brother. "Just wait, Wes. Your time is coming. When you and Vivian have a daughter, she'll be the smartest most beautiful child on earth."

Wes chuckled. "Viv wants twins. I can only hope they're boys."

A few teasing shots were passed back and forth between the siblings until Ben decided to get down to business.

"I'm sure all of you have been wondering what I've called this meeting about," he said.

"I think we all pretty much assume you have more news about Dad," Wes said, then added dully, "As if we haven't already had enough."

Ben glanced around the table at each of his siblings and Sophie's stomach clenched in a tight knot. Wes was right. The family had already been forced to accept so many discoveries about their father. She wasn't sure she could bear any more surprises, but from the look on Ben's face, she feared she was about to get one.

Ben continued, "As you all know, Keaton and I have been doing more digging into Dad's—uh, past connections and—"

"Don't you mean transgressions?" Wes interrupted.

Frowning at his twin brother, Ben said, "Call them whatever you like. But the truth is we've discovered we have a half sister and she's living right here in Austin."

Sophie felt as if someone had slapped her across the face. She wasn't just stunned. She was sick to her stomach.

"Ben, you must be joking," Graham spoke up. "How could we have a half sister living right under our noses and not know it?"

Glancing around the table, Sophie noticed that all her siblings, except Olivia, appeared to be shocked.

"This is hardly a joke," Ben retorted.

"Who is she? Do we know her?"

The questions came from Zoe who'd been so instrumental in persuading their father to admit he was actually a Fortune by birth.

Ben answered, "Chloe Elliott. Her mother is Janet Reynolds."

Rachel gasped. "The woman who lived down the street from us? You can't mean her! That's indecent!"

"Indecent or not, it's the truth," Ben assured her. "Keaton and I have covered every angle concerning Mrs. Reynolds and her daughter. Chloe is definitely our sister."

"Illegitimate half sister," Sophie couldn't stop herself from pointing out. "Dear God, when is this going to stop?"

Wes's expression turned grim. "I have a feeling this is just the beginning."

From the very start, Wes had been against digging into the mystery of their father's birthright. He'd believed opening a can of worms would hurt everyone in the family more than help. Sophie could now see just how right her brother had been.

Ben said, "The way I see it if we have more brothers and sisters out there somewhere, then we need to know it."

Ben could think in those terms, but not everyone else in the family had to side with him, Sophie thought.

Glancing to her left she could see that Rachel had gone pale. To her right Olivia appeared maddeningly indifferent and, if anything, Zoe looked sad. As for Sophie she was so angry and disgusted it was all she could do to keep from scraping back her chair and running from the room.

It was one thing for their father to have had a discreet affair in London years ago, far away from his family here in Austin. But this affair with Mrs. Reynolds had been carried out right under their noses! It was embarrassing and sickening!

From down the table, Kieran asked, "Does Mother know about this yet?"

"I've given her the news," Ben stated. "She looked

grim, but for the most part she took it pretty calmly. I tried to encourage her to talk about the situation, but she hardly said a word. So I decided not to press her."

The nauseous feeling in the pit of Sophie's stomach turned to a cold, lead weight.

No one understands your father like I do.

Only days ago Sophie had tried to talk with her mother about her marriage. Charlotte's calm acceptance of her husband's infidelity had both infuriated and puzzled Sophie. But hearing about a second illegitimate child might change her mother's attitude. Would this finally push her to file for divorce?

"Of course Mother didn't say much," Wes muttered. "She was too crushed."

Ben nodded. "Facing the truth isn't easy."

No, it was more like hell. Sophie could attest to that. These past few days she'd had to accept the truth about Thom. She'd had to take a long look at herself and the bad judgment she'd used in thinking he was the perfect man for her. The man she wanted to spend the rest of her life with. Yes, the truth was painful.

"We all need to rally around Mother," Graham said. "She needs to know her children love and support her."

After Graham expressed his thoughts, everyone at the table began talking at once. Except for Olivia. She appeared totally unaffected by the news.

Infuriated by her sister's attitude, Sophie asked, "What is it with you, anyway? How can you sit there so calmly? Saying nothing?"

Olivia shrugged. "What is there to say? We've known for some time now that Dad has been unfaithful throughout his marriage. I'm sure Chloe isn't going to be the last one to show up with a connection to our family name."

Unfortunately, Sophie believed her sister was right.

And if more of their father's *other* children started showing up, just exactly what would their mother do?

Even though her parents lived pretty much separate lives, the notion that her mother might actually divorce him shook Sophie deeply. Perhaps because she was the baby of the family, and the last symbol of them ever being connected in a loving manner. Or maybe it was the fact that Chloe Elliott appeared to be so close to her own age; it made her feel even more deceived.

"I'll never trust another man in my life!" Sophie muttered angrily.

Olivia showed more surprise over Sophie's bitter remark than she had over the news about their father hooking up with Mrs. Reynolds. "What about Thom?"

Her jaw set, Sophie snatched up the handbag she'd placed beneath her chair. "Thom who?" she asked sarcastically.

"Sophie! Get a grip," Olivia said. "You can't let this get to you."

"I can't keep sitting here listening to any more of this, either. You can fill me in later!"

Before Olivia or anyone else at the table could stop her, Sophie rushed from the room, hoping she could get back to her desk before she burst into tears.

The next morning Sophie stared glumly at her image in the cheval mirror. The cream and black patterned dress she was wearing looked okay, but it hardly screamed romance. It was Valentine's Day, the day she'd been so eagerly looking forward to. Under any other circumstances, she would've taken great pains in choosing her outfit, especially knowing full well that many of the women at Robinson Tech would be dressed in something red or pink and as romantic as one could get and still be appropriate for office wear.

But after yesterday and Ben's announcement about Chloe Elliott, Sophie was in no mood for Valentine's Day or a special night on the town. The father she'd known and loved had turned out to be a habitual cheater. And Thom's sexy veneer had turned out to be just that. A coating on the surface with nothing substantial underneath.

On the very day she should be feeling on top of the world, Sophie felt like the dregs of a nasty drink. And the day was only going to get worse, she realized. Once she arrived at work, she was going straight to Thom and call off their date. Then she was going to have to sit at her desk for the remainder of the day and wonder about the lucky lady who would be dancing with Mason tonight. Kissing Mason.

Nadine stared suspiciously at the single pink rose Mason sat on her desk.

"What is this? It's not my birthday, thank God. Forty-six is quite old enough," she told him.

Mason gave her a cheeky smile. "Surely forty-six is not so old that you forgot today is Valentine's Day. Got a date for tonight?"

The platinum blonde picked up the rose and drew it to her nose. "No. What about you?"

"I doubt it. Unless by some miracle things change between now and then."

Nadine continued to hold the rose and Mason could see she'd been touched by his little gift. Too bad he couldn't present Sophie with a rose and make her forget all about that damned Thom Nichols.

Nadine frowned. "Are you still thinking about the boss's daughter?"

"I've never stopped thinking about her. But it looks like she'll be on a big romantic date with Thom. The creep. I'd really like to hogtie him, put him in a dark closet somewhere, and not let him out until tomorrow."

Nadine laughed. "Forget about Thom. Why don't you go to Sophie and persuade her that you're the man, not Thom?"

"Because it won't work. I've tried to make her notice me. But it hasn't seemed to help." He'd even kissed Sophie. And though she'd seemed receptive, she'd certainly not talked about dropping Thom.

"Then you need to use a different tactic. Knowing you, you've probably been too nice. Give her a little alpha-male treatment. Show her you can take the bull by the horns."

"This isn't a rodeo, Nadine."

"No, but this is Texas and we Texas women like our men tough."

"Tough. Gotcha." Mason curled his arm and made a muscle. "How's that?"

Laughing, Nadine left her chair and planted a kiss on his cheek. "Thanks for the rose, sweetie. Now get out of here. Go get your little black book and find yourself another date for tonight. Any woman that would actually want to go out with Thom Nichols isn't worth having."

Mason was back at his desk, trying to get his mind focused on work when he was summoned to a meeting with the director of marketing. Marketing was the last department he wanted to visit today. The thought of seeing Thom's gloating face put a bitter taste in his mouth, but there was nothing Mason could do about it. Except hope that Thom was gone to another part of the building.

* * *

"Sophie! Over here! Do you have a minute?"

Sophie paused in the middle of the marketing department to see Elsa, one of Robinson Tech's longtime employees, hurrying toward her. Thin and prematurely gray, the woman always had a weary look about her, but today she appeared completely stressed.

"Is anything wrong, Elsa?"

"Not exactly. I'm just extremely worried, that's all. I've been wanting to talk with you about the health insurance changes."

You and about a hundred others, Sophie thought dismally. "I realize it's a jarring change, Elsa. It has been for most all the employees. Was there something specific that concerned you about the policy?"

She nodded. "My thirteen-year-old son. A part of his face was accidentally burned a few months ago. He's healed now. But once school is out this summer the doctor wants to do another surgery to reduce the scarring. Under this new policy the procedure will be considered cosmetic, which means they won't pay. Sophie, this isn't just a vanity case! My son is disfigured and—"

Sophie reached out and took a firm hold on the woman's shoulder. "You don't have to say more, Elsa. I understand completely. And I want you to quit worrying about this. The new policy won't take effect for a couple of months, so there's still time for the surgery. I intend to talk to my brother about this whole situation. Ben will make the right decisions, I'm sure."

A measure of relief came over the woman's face. "Thank you, Sophie. You've already made me feel better."

Sophie gave her a few more encouraging words, then walked to Thom's desk. When she didn't find him there, she was about to look elsewhere, when he suddenly stepped up behind her.

"Are you here to see me, Ms. Fortune?"

As much as she disliked him leaving the Robinson off her name, she tried to put on a pleasant expression as she turned to face him.

"Yes, actually, you're the man I'm here to see. Elsa sidelined me."

"Yes, I noticed," he said with an impatient roll of his eyes. "She's always whining about something. I honestly wish the woman worked on a different floor."

She could hardly believe his unfeeling attitude. "I wouldn't be saying anything bad about Elsa. She's a good woman and a hard worker."

He must have detected the sharp edge to her voice because his brows lifted briefly in surprise and then he said, "Surely you're not up here to discuss another employee with me."

"No." She glanced around her. People were coming and going; a small group was gathered at the water cooler. It was hardly the perfect spot to cancel a date. "Is there somewhere around here that's more private?"

A leering grin suddenly spread across his face. "By all means."

Taking her by the arm, he led her to a small room that was used for private meetings.

Once they stepped inside and he shut the door, he planted a swift kiss on her cheek. It was the first time he'd ever displayed any sort of affection toward her during working hours and she wondered why she was suddenly seeing a different side to him. Had he been picking up on her discontent?

Feeling worse than awkward, she attempted a pleasant smile. "Do you have a minute? Or am I interrupting your morning?"

"I'm waiting on a few of my coworkers to join me. We're working on an advertising idea to promote Robinson Tech's newest tablet. If things go as planned I may have to fly to California to negotiate the details of a new TV ad."

Too bad he wasn't leaving today, Sophie thought. It would have spared her this uncomfortable task.

"Sounds like you're on an upward climb."

He slicked a hand along the side of his hair. "One of these days your father will realize this company can't exist without me."

If he'd made the statement in a teasing context, she would've laughed. But he wasn't teasing and his arrogance suddenly made her task far easier.

"Well, Dad has a good business eye," she said. "He instinctively knows when an employee is a true asset to the company."

He glanced over her shoulder, as though he was more interested in who was about to walk through the door than what she had to say.

"Er—so, was there some reason you needed to talk with me?"

She let out a weary breath. Ever since the family meeting yesterday, Sophie had felt as though someone had stomped on her. Now as she moved about the Robinson Tech building, she found herself looking at the employees close to her age and wondering if any of them might be a secret offspring of her father. She couldn't imagine anything being more embarrassing.

"Actually, I wanted to tell you that I'm not up to going out tonight. I'm not feeling very well. In fact, I almost didn't come to work this morning."

Which was partly true, Sophie thought. She was mentally and physically sick. Her spirits were squashed so flat, she could hardly think of putting in a productive day of work. Much less going on a date with this man.

Thom stared at her in shock. "Sophie! Are you trying to be funny? If so, I don't find any of this a bit humorous."

"Look, Thom, I do not feel like joking. Or going out on a date. I'm sorry. You'll just have to give me a rain check."

Clearly outraged, he said, "I've already spent a ton of money for this date! I'll have to cancel reservations and that's going to cost me, too! How can you do this to me at the last minute? Today is Valentine's Day! I thought you wanted to make a big hoopla about the day. Damn it, Sophie, I just don't get you!"

No. He never would *get* her, Sophie thought dismally. That was the whole problem. His lame gifts and phony-sounding messages proved that. "I'm sorry, Thom. Really. I'm just not feeling up to a big night."

His angry gaze swept up and down the length of her. "You look perfectly fine to me. You're well enough to work today. But not well enough for a date with me?"

Sophie had to bite down on her tongue to stop herself from telling him to go jump in the deepest lake he could find. "I'm sorry you don't believe me, Thom. Like I said, you'll have to give me a rain check."

"Sophie—"

Not sticking around to hear more, Sophie turned on her heel and left the room.

She was almost to the elevator when a hand grabbed her shoulder and she whirled around to see it belonged to her sister, Olivia.

"Sophie, what in the world is wrong? You look sick."

"Too bad someone else can't see that," she muttered, then shook her head at the look of confusion on Olivia's face. "Sorry, sis, I'm not having a good morning, that's all."

Olivia's eyes narrowed as she glanced in the general direction of Thom's desk. "Oh. Having trouble with your boyfriend?"

Thom wasn't her boyfriend. He was a jerk, Sophie thought dismally. And she'd been worse than stupid for wanting to date him in the first place.

"I am trying to forget about men. Completely!"

Olivia was stunned. "Today? This is the day for love and romance! This holiday was tailor-made for a woman like you!"

She shot her sister a cynical stare. "You mean for a woman looking at the world through rose-colored lenses? Or a butterfly flitting around without enough sense to see that men are always thinking about themselves and never to be trusted? Believe me, Olivia, I can do without this day just fine!"

Angry tears threatened to spill onto her cheeks and Olivia quickly pulled her into an empty office, away from any prying eyes that might be looking their way.

"Sophie, this isn't like you at all," she said in a hushed tone. "You've got to get a grip on yourself. Are you still upset over the news about Dad? About him and Mrs. Reynolds?"

Once she'd left the family meeting yesterday, Sophie had avoided speaking with any of her siblings and when she'd gotten home her mother had been nowhere in sight. Which had been a relief. Discussing such a painful issue with her was the last thing she'd wanted to do.

"Upset? Is that how you'd describe it? I'm crushed, Olivia. Totally crushed that our father had no more respect for his family than to consort with our neighbor! Now Chloe Elliott will no doubt want to worm her way into the family. Well, as far as I'm concerned, she's not one of us and never will be!"

"Sophie! You might as well start toughening up that soft skin of yours right now! Dad is no angel. We've all known that for some time now. And you shouldn't allow his behavior to dictate how you feel about men and love and marriage."

Marriage! Dear God, the thought of spending one night of married life with Thom was enough to put her into a straightjacket.

Swallowing hard, she sniffed and straightened her shoulders. "Don't worry about me, sis. I can see very clearly now. Dad's thoughtless behavior toward Mother and his children proves to me that true love is far more than a handsome face or bulging bank account."

"I don't know what's going on in that pretty head of yours, but you need to clear it." Olivia gave her a brief hug. "I have to get back to work. Now put a smile on your face and have a happy Valentine's Day."

Oh, sure, Sophie thought, as she headed toward the elevator. She'd called off her date with Thom and would be spending the night alone. It wasn't the sort of Valentine's evening she'd envisioned two weeks ago. But so much had happened since, there was nothing she could do about it now.

A part of her wanted to run to Mason and throw herself into his arms. She wanted to pour her heart out to him and hear his strong voice assure her that everything would soon be better. But Mason had his own life. No doubt he was looking forward to a night out with his lady love. Today was not the time to burden him with her father's shortcomings, or her busted dreams about

Thom. She was going to have to deal with her misery on her own.

But as she passed the entrance to his department, it took every bit of willpower she possessed to walk on and forget about Mason and the comfort of his arms.

Chapter Ten

At the end of the work day, Sophie was the last person to turn off her computer and pull on her coat. She'd purposely stayed behind as her coworkers had left for their dates. Most every female in her department had gotten flowers or candy delivered to their desks. The only thing Sophie had gotten was more complaints concerning the insurance changes.

What are you whining about, Sophie? Thom has been sending you all kinds of gifts. You never appreciated any of them. And if you hadn't feigned sickness and called off your date, you would've probably gotten roses or candy. You're getting just what you deserve.

The accusing voice in her head left a bitter taste in her mouth. She tried to ignore both as she buttoned her coat. She might be down for the evening, she thought as she made her way out of the building and to the parking garage, but by tomorrow she would pull herself together and put on a brave face. If anything, she wanted to show Mason she was a strong woman. Not a whiner.

Darkness had settled over the city more than an hour ago. The dim lights illuminating the garage showed only a handful of vehicles left on this level. Which was hardly surprising. Everyone had been in a hurry to go off on a night of romance.

She had no idea what, if anything, her parents were doing. With the news breaking about Mrs. Reynolds and Chloe, she figured her father had most likely found an out-of-town business meeting to attend.

Trying to shove away the melancholy cloak wrapping itself around her, Sophie hurried to her car. The sooner she got home, the sooner she could sink herself into a hot bubble bath with a glass of wine. By then she might forget she'd wasted all this time pursuing Thom, when Mason was the man she should have set her eyes on.

She was unlocking the door, when she suddenly stopped in her tracks and stared at the cuddly red teddy bear propped against the windshield.

Who could have left the precious stuffed toy? Oh, please, not Thom, she thought. She couldn't bear to deal with him again.

A note was stuffed under one of the bear's arms and Sophie quickly retrieved it.

No one should spend Valentine's Day alone.

Clutching the bear to her breast, she glanced around to see if there was anyone who could tell her who'd left the stuffed animal. And then she spotted a man standing next to a nearby car.

Was that Mason?

Her heart tripping over itself, she took a hesitant step forward. Across the expanse of concrete, the man emerged from the shadows and joyous relief flooded through her.

"So you found Mr. Bear?" Mason asked, a sheepish grin on his face.

Hope spurted through her. She didn't exactly comprehend how or why Mason was standing there in front of her. But at the moment, it didn't matter. The sight of his handsome face sent her spirits soaring.

"You're the one who left this adorable little guy on my car?" she asked.

Nodding, he said, "I thought you might be needing someone to hug about now."

The urge to laugh and cry hit her at the same time, creating a hard lump in her throat. She tried to swallow it away, and her voice came out sounding like a husky whisper.

"I thought—uh—shouldn't you be leaving soon?" she asked in confusion. "Your date must be waiting for you."

He shrugged as a guilty expression crossed his handsome face. "To be honest, I don't have a date, Sophie. I never cared much for going out on Valentine's Day. Everyone has such high expectations—like they're going on a romantic fantasy. Then the reality of the evening sets in and all those hopes fall flat. It's deflating."

Strange how only moments ago the parking garage had felt freezing and spooky, but with Mason standing close to her, she was as warm as if she was standing on the beach of a tropical island.

"Before—well, before things happened I always loved this day," she admitted. "Valentine's Day is a time when a woman can get mushy and flirty and no one will laugh at you for being a romantic. And there's hardly a woman alive who doesn't dream of finding her prince. But today…"

"What about today?" he gently urged.

She glanced down at the bear's fuzzy red ears. "It's not been a good day. I came to work dreading it and I stayed late hoping no one would see I was going home alone. Especially after the way I crowed to you about Thom and how I was going to make Mr. Perfect all mine."

"I don't understand, Sophie. I thought you had your Mr. Perfect right where you wanted him. The big Valentine's date—everything just as you'd planned."

Her head swung back and forth as she lifted her troubled gaze up to his brown eyes. "It was too perfect, Mason. And nothing like I thought it would be. Everything about it—from the very start—was absolutely wrong. *I* was wrong for imagining Thom was the man for me."

He let out a long breath and Sophie had to wonder what he was thinking about her now. That she was fickle and couldn't be trusted? She could hardly blame him. One minute she'd been purring about Thom and next minute she'd given him the boot. The whole thing made her look worse than shallow.

"I confess, Sophie, I was in the marketing department this morning and I overheard you telling Thom you weren't feeling well. Are you feeling better now?"

So that was how he'd known she wasn't going with Thom tonight, Sophie concluded. Sometime after that, he must have purchased the bear with the intention of waiting until she showed up at her car. What did it mean?

"I have a confession, too, Mason. I wasn't really sick. Not physically sick, that is. Emotionally—well, that's a different matter."

His eyes continued to study her face and it suddenly dawned on Sophie that Mason had given her the benefit of the doubt about being sick, whereas Thom had brushed her off and practically accused her of lying. The two men were as different as night and day. And it had become crystal clear to her as to who was the better man.

He stepped closer and her heart nearly stopped as he smoothed a finger along her cheekbone. "Sophie, it would make me happy to see a smile on your face."

She must truly be standing on a hot beach, she decided, because her heart was melting right into the palm of his hand.

"You don't think I'm awful for cancelling the date with Thom?"

His gaze delved deep into hers. "Sophie—"

Suddenly anything else he might have planned to say went unspoken. Instead, he lowered his head and kissed her.

The sweet contact instinctively caused her eyes to close, her lips to part. The feel of Mason's mouth upon hers sent a shower of hot sensations pouring through her body, prompting her to move closer, to savor even more of the masculine taste of him.

Wild and reckless and oh, so good. That was Mason's kiss and not for anything did she want it to stop. It didn't matter that they were standing in a cold, parking garage or that any passerby could see them. Touching Mason, kissing him, being close to him was taking away all the doubt and misery in her heart. This man was all she wanted or needed.

By the time he finally lifted his head, Sophie was completely dazed and realized she probably looked it.

"Umm—that was quite a Valentine's Day kiss."

He grinned and tugged on one of the bear's ears. "To go with little red here."

She smiled impishly up at him. "Thank you for the bear. And the kiss."

His hand kneaded her shoulder and Sophie felt the heat of his fingers all the way through the heavy coat.

He asked, "Would you like to go out for dinner?"

Not about to play coy, Sophie punched the button to relock her car, then looped her arm through his. "I'm hardly dressed for a night on the town, but I would love to go out to dinner."

"You look perfect to me. Let's go see if we can find a restaurant that isn't booked solid."

Fifteen minutes later, Mason tossed his phone onto the console between the bucket seats and groaned with frustration. "Everything is booked up. I can't find one nice restaurant in Austin with available seating. Looks like we're going to have to settle for fast food. What about pizza?"

Laughing, she fastened her seatbelt. "Sounds wonderful to me. Let's go."

Grateful that she was being so understanding, he said, "There's a pizza joint not far from my place. The food is delicious and the service fast. How does that sound?"

"I'm in your hands."

As Mason drove through the city traffic, he kept glancing over at Sophie and wondering how his luck had managed to change in the matter of one short day.

If he hadn't overheard Sophie cancelling her date with Thom this morning, he would've never known she'd be spending the evening alone and he'd have missed the opportunity to spend this special evening with her. Now, somehow, he had to make the most of it.

A few minutes later, as the two of them sat in the pizza parlor waiting on their order, a group of rowdy kids romped through the tables and yelled across the room.

The chaotic atmosphere was hardly the sort of evening he wanted to give Sophie.

"I'm sorry about this, Sophie. This is not the romantic dinner I'd envisioned."

She reached across the table and squeezed his hand. "Don't fret about it. Just spending the evening with you is enough for me. But maybe we should get the pizza to go and find someplace quieter to eat."

Was being with him really enough for her, Mason wondered. These past few days he'd sensed that all was not well between Sophie and Thom. Still, that didn't mean that she'd suddenly fallen head over heels for Mason. He needed to put the brakes on his runaway feelings. He couldn't let his hopes get out of control just because she'd kissed him like she'd never wanted it to end.

"I could take you home," he offered.

She shook her head. "I still live with my parents. And I have no idea if either of them is home."

He nodded, his mind whirling with possibilities, none of which seemed appropriate. Finally he asked, "What about going to my place? It's only about five minutes away. It's nothing fancy, but it would definitely be quieter than this."

She laughed as a plastic fork went whizzing by his head, while Mason glared at the pair of adults who seemed oblivious to the children's unruly behavior.

"That sounds nice, Mason. I'd like to go to your place."

Minutes later, Mason showed her into a charming, second-floor apartment with a small balcony that looked out at the river.

While he switched on a pair of table lamps and lowered the overhead lighting, she gazed curiously around the living area. "This is so homey and comfortable, Mason. I love it."

He chuckled. "I don't expect it's anything like your home. But I try to keep it tidy and make the most of the space I have." He inclined his head toward a short hall-way to his left. "If you'd care to freshen up before we eat, the bathroom is that way."

"Thanks. I would like that. I actually think some food hit the back of my head while we were waiting in the pizza parlor," she said with a laugh.

"Take your time. I'll get our dinner ready. Where would you like to eat? At the table or the couch? You choose."

She glanced at the dark green leather couch with a long coffee table sitting in front of it. "Oh, then I choose the couch. If you don't mind it would feel great to kick off my heels and get comfortable."

Mind? Mason didn't know how many times he'd dreamed of having her on that couch. The fact that she wanted to get comfortable was making his fantasy re-ally come true.

"Then the couch it will be," he told her.

While she was gone, Mason placed the pizza box on the coffee table, then fetched napkins and paper plates, and just in case she didn't want to use her fingers, added two forks.

When she reappeared a few moments later, he saw she'd freshened her pink lipstick and brushed her brown hair to a sleek curtain against her back. She looked like a walking dream and he could only hope he didn't wake up and find he was actually alone.

"Have a seat and I'll get some sodas. Or if you'd prefer I have beer." He started toward the kitchen, then tossed teasingly over his shoulder, "Sorry, I'd offer you champagne, but I'm all out. I didn't know I was going to be entertaining a beautiful woman tonight."

She called across the room to him, "We don't need champagne to make a Valentine's toast. Soda will do just fine."

"Sophie, did anyone ever tell you—"

"That I'm a good sport? Oh, please, Mason, whatever you do, don't say that to me."

He emerged from the kitchen carrying two chilled cans of cola. As he took a seat next to her, he said, "I wasn't going to say that. I was going to say that I've never seen you behave like a spoiled little rich girl."

She wrinkled her nose at him. "And hopefully you never will. If I ever do act like that I hope someone will bop me over the head. Don't get me wrong, I'll be the first to admit that I've been spoiled. But that doesn't mean I always need to have everything perfect. I want to be able to appreciate the simple joys of life, Mason. Otherwise, I'd be missing out on the things that are the most worthwhile."

He smiled at her. "Like pizza for Valentine's dinner?"

"Exactly," she answered. "I can't think of anything I'd rather be eating tonight or any other place I'd rather be than here with you."

He handed her one of the sodas, then opened the pizza box.

After serving her a slice, he helped himself and settled back against the couch. She was already eating with gusto and the fact that she appeared to be enjoying herself surprised him somewhat. Partly because she was a Fortune Robinson and could buy the finest gourmet food, even an entire restaurant if she chose to. And partly because he'd never really gotten the hang of how to entertain a woman. At least, not a woman like Sophie.

He said, "I think you actually meant that."

"Mmm. This is delicious and well worth the wait," she said of the pizza. Then she turned to face him. "And why wouldn't I mean it? You didn't twist my arm to get me here."

"I know. But you had such high hopes for tonight. This wasn't the sort of date you envisioned, I'm sure."

"I'm certain Thom had made reservations at one of the ritziest places in town. He might even have given me flowers and taken me dancing. Only because he felt obliged to do those things for me. Not because he actually wanted to." She shook her head. "Believe me, Mason. That's not the sort of date I wanted. I want things to be genuine. And with Thom—I'm not sure that he cares about anyone's feelings. Except his own."

He momentarily forgot about the pizza he'd lifted halfway to his mouth. "When did you come to this conclusion? I thought— well, for the last few days he was giving you gifts and planning this night and you didn't say anything. I thought you were still gaga over the man."

Her face tinged with color, she lowered the plate to her lap and slanted him a rueful glance. "In a way, Mason, I suppose I'm just as phony as Thom. I've been pretending all this time. I didn't want anyone to guess that after our first date I realized he and I would never be the real thing. It was just too embarrassing. My sister Olivia had tried to warn me and I wouldn't listen to her advice. You see, where men are concerned, she has a cynical streak, so I thought she was just being negative. Now I'm going to have to listen to her say I told you so. Not to mention the gossip that will go on at Robinson Tech once the news gets out that I called it quits with Thom. After everyone could see I was chasing after him."

"Sophie, you're being too hard on yourself. You didn't

chase after Thom. You merely made him notice you. Which, if the truth was known, he'd already done. You just made it easy for him to ask you on a date."

She smiled at him and Mason wondered why she was the only woman who'd ever made him feel so vulnerable and weak, yet so oddly happy. It didn't make sense. But was love supposed to make sense?

Whoa, Mason, you're getting way ahead of yourself. You don't love Sophie. You're enamored with her, for sure. And you'd like to take her in your arms and kiss her until the two of you end up in the bedroom. But that isn't love. And, besides, this woman is going to move on to a bigger and better man than you.

"You're being way too kind, Mason. But thank you for listening. And for trying to make me look not so much of a fool."

Her comment broke through the warning voice in his head and he glanced over to see her eyes had suddenly clouded with doubts and sadness. In all the time he'd known Sophie, he'd never seen her as she'd been these past few days. It was like her confidence and sassiness had flown out the window. If Thom had caused this abrupt change in her, then he'd like to choke him until he turned blue in the face.

"Sophie, you can tell me if this is none of my business. But is this all about Thom? Or has something else been bothering you?"

Instead of looking at him, she stared at her plate. "I do have other things on my mind, Mason. But I'd really rather not talk about them now. Maybe later." She looked at him, her eyes pleading. "Tonight I just want us to enjoy this time together. Okay?"

Although Mason would've liked for her to open up to him and share her problems, he wasn't about to push his luck. But eventually, if he got his wish, she might want to talk about all the things she'd buried in her heart.

He scooted close enough to wrap his fingers around her forearm. "It's perfectly okay, Sophie. So let's dig in and finish this pizza before it gets cold."

With a look of relief, she began to eat and Mason purposely changed the direction of their conversation to a safer topic. Eventually they began to talk about their college days and the sticky situations they'd gotten into both in class and on campus. Which had them both laughing.

Finally she placed her empty plate on the coffee table, then kicked off her heels and drew her legs up beneath her. She was wearing black lacy tights and Mason could hardly keep his eyes off the shapely calves, slim ankles and dainty feet. Beneath the black stockings there would be smooth creamy skin that would be soft and warm beneath his hand. The need to touch her was growing with each passing minute.

Rising restlessly to his feet, he said, "Uh—I could turn on the TV, or put some music on the stereo?"

"Some music might be nice. If you have something that's not too intrusive."

"I have plenty of elevator music—the kind we listen to all day at work. How does that sound?"

"It sounds like you're trying to pull my leg."

He laughed and her soft chuckle joined in.

"Okay. I'm teasing. I'd really like to take a shotgun to the speaker over my desk."

"I know. If we didn't have to listen to that morbid music, we all might be more productive." She looked at him with raised brows. "We're not at work, so what are you going to play for me?"

He walked over to the stereo and began to dig through a stack of CDs until he found the one he thought she might enjoy. "Something soft and romantic," he said. "For Valentine's night."

Soon the sexy R&B music floated quietly out of the speakers, and he walked back over to the couch.

Holding his hand out to her, he asked, "Would you care to dance, my lady?"

"I would love to," she murmured.

Placing her hand in his, she uncurled herself from the couch and stepped into his arms. His first instinct was to wrap his arm around her and crush her warm body to his. But she viewed him as a friend and a gentleman she could trust. He needed to keep a respectable distance between them, he reminded himself.

Earlier this evening in the parking garage, she wasn't kissing you like a friend, Mason. She was kissing you like a lover. Now isn't the time to hold back. Show her exactly how much you want her.

He was trying to ignore the prodding voice in his head when she said, "The music is nice. You have good taste, Mason."

"I'm glad you like it," he murmured as he dared to rest his cheek against her silky hair. "But you probably should've put your heels back on. I'm not that good a dancer. I might step on your toes."

"I'm not worried. Besides, dancing barefoot with you feels…very good. Why would I want to stop and put on my shoes?"

As she spoke, he could feel her drawing closer until the tips of her breasts were brushing against his chest, her hips swaying rhythmically against him. The intimate contact filled him with sizzling sensations and before he realized what he was doing, both his arms had wrapped around her, his hands linked at the small of her back.

"We still have time to go to a club—to dance and celebrate. All you have to do is say the word."

"We're dancing and celebrating right now. And honestly, I don't want to be crammed in a crowd." She looked up at him, then brushed a finger against a spot on his chin. "You have a speck of cheese. Right there."

"I'm messy. Thanks." He looked down at her and his gaze focused on the plump, pink curves of her lips. "And you have a tiny dot of sauce at the corner of your mouth."

"I do?" She paused long enough to lick both corners. "Did I get it?"

The only thing she'd managed to do was make his insides clench with longing. He struggled to keep from groaning out loud. "No. It's still there. Let me."

He wiped the speck of sauce away, but his gaze remained frozen on her lips. Had there been some sort of potion in the soda or pizza? He seemed to have forgotten how to breathe and the temperature in the apartment felt as though it had zoomed up to ninety degrees or higher.

"Sophie, either I'm getting sick or being this close to you is doing something strange to me."

Her hands were suddenly on the middle of his chest, sliding slowly upward toward his collar bone. Mason swallowed and tried to keep his head from reeling.

"It's doing something to me, too. But I don't think it's strange, Mason. I think it's natural and nice and nothing to run from."

Run. Yes, that's what he should do. Run to the balcony or out on the stairs. Anywhere he could breathe and clear his head of this drunken desire that was taking control of him. But he didn't want to move away from her. At least, not until he could taste her lips again.

"I'm glad you think so. Because I—"

The remainder of his words stuck in his throat and,

no matter how he tried, he couldn't cough them up or swallow them down.

Her eyes were glowing and her lips tilted in a provocative smile. "Because you want to kiss me?"

The softly spoken invitation was more than Mason could resist. Without a second thought, he drew her in the tight circle of his arms and, with a hungry growl, took her lips with his.

A flash fire roared through him and as his hands roamed her back and her soft curves melted into his body, he recognized this feeling was not just a man wanting a woman. He was holding something precious in his arms. He wanted to cherish and protect everything she was giving him, not take advantage of her vulnerable emotions by asking her for more.

The thoughts in his head continued to wage a war with the very real needs flowing through his body. But eventually common sense won the fight and he gently eased his lips from hers and set her away from him.

"I—I'm sorry, Sophie. This is getting out of hand."

She stared at him, her eyes full of confusion, her swollen lips parted with surprise. He could see words practically forming on her tongue, but they were never released. Instead, she turned her back to him and walked to the opposite side of the room.

As Mason studied her slumped shoulders, he felt sick with loss. Moreover, he felt like a coward. This was his chance to show Sophie exactly how he felt about her. If he let this moment slip away, he might never be given another.

With that desperate thought pushing at his back, Mason took a fateful step in her direction. Then another. And another. Until his hands were on her shoulders, urging her back to him.

Chapter Eleven

Fighting a wall of stinging tears, Sophie tried to pull herself together and give Mason an understanding smile. But try as she might, her lips refused to do little more than wobble into a half-hearted grin.

"I'm sorry, too, Mason," she said hoarsely. "Maybe you should just drive me home."

"Sophie, I—"

"You don't have to explain, Mason," she gently interrupted. "I understand completely. You've always thought of me as a friend. And that's the way you want things to remain between us—just friends. I can accept that."

An incredulous expression swept over his face and then he shook his head. "You don't understand, Sophie! For ages—from the very beginning I met you—I've wanted us to be more than friends! But with all that's been going on in your life—I'm trying to do the right thing and give you more time. To think about you and me. I don't want to rush you and make a mess of everything."

Relief and joy swirled inside her until she felt as though her bare feet weren't even touching the hardwood floor.

"You're not rushing, Mason. And sometimes a little mess is a good thing. A whole lot better than perfect."

For one anxious second, she thought he was going to argue the point, but then his eyelids suddenly lowered and his lips found their way back to hers.

This time there was no restraint on his part, or hers. She felt no barriers standing between them or had thoughts of escape dashing through her whirling head. The only thing on her mind now was getting closer to the man she wanted.

Wrapping her arms around his neck, Sophie let every guard down, every vulnerable spot inside her show as she lost herself in the magic of his kiss. And almost instantly, she was transported to a place where nothing mattered but the masculine taste of his lips and the achingly wonderful warmth pouring through her.

Over and over he took her mouth in a succession of deep, scorching kisses that stole her breath and had her hands clinging to his shoulders to support her shaky legs.

Finally, he tore his mouth from hers and spoke between long, ragged breaths. "This—isn't—enough, Sophie. I want you. All of you."

Cradling his face between her palms, she whispered up to him, "Oh, yes, Mason. I want that, too. Very much."

His hands pushed into her hair until his fingers were tilting her face up to his searching gaze. "Are you sure, Sophie? Just because it's Valentine's Day doesn't mean—"

"I don't care if it's the Fourth of July or Friday the 13th," she whispered with conviction. "I'd want you just as much."

His gaze searched her face one last time and then he reached for her hand and led her out of the room. As Sophie followed him, her heart was pounding so hard the noise in her ears was drowning out the soft music playing on the stereo. This morning she'd been miserable and all day she'd told herself she wanted nothing more to do with any man. That all of them were nothing more than low, slithering snakes.

But that hadn't included Mason. No, he was the only man on earth that made her feel safe and wanted. And yes, a teeny bit loved. Thinking like that perhaps made her an even bigger fool than she'd made of herself these past two weeks. But tonight Sophie wasn't going to let herself dwell on all the things she'd rather forget. She was with Mason and for now the world felt right.

At the end of the hall they turned left and the next thing Sophie knew they were standing in his bedroom.

Mason clicked on a bedside lamp, shedding a pool of light across a bed with tumbled navy blue bedcovers and pillows stacked against a brass headboard.

"Sorry, Sophie," he voiced the husky apology. "The bed isn't made, but the sheets are clean."

She laughed softly as she curled her arms around his waist and hugged him. "Who cares about bedcovers? We're just going to mess them up anyway."

His hands slid down her back until they were cupping her rounded bottom and drawing her hips toward his. "Sophie, why did it take so long for this to happen? Why didn't we figure this out sooner? I think I've wanted you forever."

Desire was already simmering deep within her. It was impossible to imagine how it was going to feel once their bodies were united. The mere thought of it was sending shivers of anticipation through her.

"I thought you only wanted me as your friend—someone to talk to. I didn't know." She stroked the pads of her fingers along the strong line of his jaw. He felt so strong and warm. And with each breath she drew in, the male scent of his skin and hair filled her head like a strong drink of wine.

His head dipped alongside hers until his nose was nuzzling her neck. "Yes, we're friends. And we talk as friends. But tonight we've done enough talking. Don't you think?"

Her fingers reached for the buttons on his shirt. "I think we can figure out plenty of other things to keep us occupied," she whispered.

He planted another long, breathtaking kiss on her lips, but once the erotic contact ended they began shedding their clothing, each assisting the other with zippers and buttons, until finally Sophie was stripped down to a lacy pink bra and panties and Mason a pair of dark printed boxers.

Sophie's hungry gaze barely had time to scan his hard, muscled chest and arms and slip to his corded abs, before he picked her up and laid her on the bed.

With a breathless laugh, she reached for his hand and tugged him beside her. They turned toward each other, until the front of her body was pressed against his.

To feel his bare skin rubbing against hers was as erotic as the touch of his fingers sliding down her breastbone until they reached one plump little breast. His fingers teased the nipple, until the offending barrier of her bra became a frustration.

He quickly removed the scrap of fabric and tossed it to the floor with the rest of their clothing, then turned his attention back to her breasts and the budded nipples just waiting for his touch. He didn't disappoint as he bent his head and suckled first one and then the other.

White hot fire shot straight to the core of her, causing her lower body to involuntarily arch toward his.

Moaning, she thrust her fingers into his hair and held his head fast against her. Too soon the exquisite pleasure turned into needy pain and she tugged on his hair to signal her need for relief.

He lifted his head and in that split second when their eyes met, Sophie felt a connection so deep and real that tears stung the backs of her eyes. This was the special thing she'd been searching for. And now that she'd found it, she had to hold tight and cherish every second of passion that Mason was giving her.

"Oh, Mason, I want you," she whispered. "So much that it's scary."

Groaning, he brought his lips back to hers. "That's the way it's supposed to be. Wild and scary and special."

As the last word was spoken against her lips, Sophie circled her arms around his neck and opened her mouth to his. In a matter of seconds he was kissing her with a need so deep it rocked her senses. And when his tongue slipped inside, she eagerly responded, reveling in the taste of him, while wanting more and more.

Somewhere in the back of her spinning mind, she recognized his hands were tracing her heated skin, exploring the hills and valleys, pausing at her breasts and belly, before finally moving downward to the juncture between her thighs.

He quickly stripped away her panties and when his fingers found her most intimate spot, she moaned with need, her hips arching toward the pleasure he was bestowing.

Incredible. No one had ever touched her like this, she

thought wildly. No one had ever turned her whole being into one aching flame. It was carrying her away and the helpless feeling had her frantically grabbing his shoulders and crying out.

"It's okay, Sophie," he whispered in a voice rough with passion. "Just ride it out. Let yourself feel everything."

The sound of his masculine voice urging her onward was all it took for Sophie to surrender to everything he was giving. And all at once she was spinning out of control, her body writhing against his hand, her cries of pleasure like music to his ears.

Before the quaking aftermaths subsided, his mouth was back on hers, his tongue thrusting deep as it searched the ribbed roof and the sharp edges of her teeth. After the explosion that had just gone off inside her, she'd not expected to feel more. But she'd been wrong. Hot passion was throbbing inside her once again, driving her hands to move over the hard muscles of his torso, her legs to wrap invitingly around his.

Eventually, he tore his mouth away from hers and by then they were both gulping for air and Sophie wondered if he was just as dazed as she was by the urgent need that had suddenly and completely combusted between them.

"Sophie, I think you want this as much as I do, but what's going on with us—it's happened so fast. If you're uncertain, tell me. Because when this is over I don't want you to look at me with hate or regret."

Her throat was so tight with raw emotions she could barely force her words out. "Yes, Mason! Yes, I want this. I want you. There will be no regret. Not now. Not ever."

He pressed his lips gently to hers, then eased away to open a drawer on the nightstand. "I'll get some protection."

Even though Sophie could count on one hand the

times she'd had intimate relations with a man in the past five years, she did take the Pill. But she didn't bother explaining this to Mason. She wanted him to feel safe and protected.

Moments later, he returned to her and as he positioned himself over her, Sophie shivered with a need that went far beyond the physical. She wasn't just giving her body to this man. She was trusting her heart to him.

As he hovered over her, his hands gently cradled her face and the tender touch overwhelmed her with sweet emotions, the sort she'd dreamed about.

"You're my Valentine, Sophie. My sweetest Valentine." His head shook back and forth as though he was trying to wake himself from a dream. "I didn't know we were going to be making love. I never thought this would happen. But now that we are— Oh, Sophie, I'm shaking."

Linking her hands at the back of his neck, she drew him down to her and whispered against his lips. "I'm shaking, too. But it will be special. So special."

"Yes. Oh, yes."

She opened her legs to him and then slowly, gently, he entered her warm, welcoming body.

The intimate connection was even more incredible than she expected and for long moments, she could scarcely breathe. But then he began to move and suddenly hot vibrations were radiating through her body, filling her with a need so reckless and wild she couldn't contain it.

Before long, she was matching the rhythm of his movements, straining to give him everything he was giving her. Over and over their bodies crashed together in mindless ecstasy.

Sophie lost all awareness of time and place. All she knew was Mason's hot body pushing her, driving her to a place she'd never been before. Her heart was racing, pounding in her ears like a frantic drumbeat, while her breaths had turned into little more than raspy gulps.

This white hot passion was everything and more than she'd been searching for, but never found until tonight. Until she'd stepped into Mason's arms. This couldn't be a one-time thing. No, this fire between them had to be the kind that never died. Never turned cold.

Just as the desperate thoughts rolled through her mind, she could feel his strokes growing faster and faster. The speed tugged her along and before she realized just how far she'd climbed, she was standing on the edge of a star, where moon dust was showering over her, and her heart was overflowing with warm, precious love.

"Sophie, Sophie."

As she floated through the starlight, she heard him call her name, but she couldn't utter a word. All she could do was cling to him and wait for her whirling senses to return to her body.

Long moments passed before she slowly became aware of Mason's torso draped over hers, his damp cheek resting upon her shoulder. She could feel his heart thudding rapidly against her breast, his warm breath fanning her arm.

She threaded her fingers through his damp hair, loving the way the waves felt against her skin.

"I'm heavy. I need to move." He rolled to one side and reached for a pillow. After he'd stuffed it beneath her head, he lay beside her and she shifted so that her face was aligned with his.

"I never expected my Valentine's evening to be like this." She reached over and slid her hand down his muscled arm. "Thank you, Mason, for not wanting me to be alone."

He smiled. "I'm the selfish one, Sophie. I wanted you to be with me tonight. So I'm thanking you for being here—next to me." He cupped her face with his hand. "You're so beautiful, Sophie. Inside and out. Have I ever told you that?"

Her heart swelling with emotions, she caught his hand and drew it to her lips. "Not exactly," she murmured. "But the lighting is bad in here. You might change your mind tomorrow."

Chuckling, he drew her tight against him and buried his face in the damp curve of her neck. "Are you trying to be as funny as me?"

"I'm trying to be real."

He eased his head back and Sophie could see the humor in his eyes had disappeared.

"Sophie, please, don't ever doubt me. Maybe it sounds like I'm just mouthing words that I think you want to hear. But I'm not. Eventually, you're going to see that I'm being honest with you."

Curling an arm around his waist, she pressed her cheek against his chest and closed her eyes. "You're a good man, Mason. And if it seems like I'm being mistrustful, well, I—I'm having trouble hanging on to my trust in anyone. I'm having trouble keeping my faith about anything—especially love and marriage."

"Sophie," he gently scolded. "That's not like you. Has Thom done something unforgivable? I know you said you'd rather not talk about it. But maybe talking about it now would help."

His fingers were making gentle, soothing circles upon her back and the sound of his steady heartbeat beneath her ears was lulling her into a safe cocoon. One that she never wanted to leave.

"It's not Thom. Yes, he was a big disappointment.

That's not exactly right, either. I'm very disappointed in myself for being so stupid about him. No, this is something else. It's—" She tilted her head back so that she could see his face. "It's about my family, Mason. Things are so—I'm so mixed up. I don't know what to think anymore. Yesterday we had a family meeting—just us siblings. And Ben has discovered that we have a half sister we never knew existed. An offspring of one of my father's numerous affairs. This young woman lives right here in Austin. Actually, her mother was our neighbor! Oh, Mason, can you imagine your father having an affair with your neighbor? And having a child from it? I don't know what to believe anymore. Who to trust."

His hand smoothed the tangled hair from her brow. "Honestly, Sophie, I can't imagine any of it. My dad has always been rock solid for his family. To learn otherwise would really shake me. You've already had to deal with his fake identity. That should be enough. And then the half brother from London. I thought surely that would be the end of things."

She bit her bottom lip as tears threatened to slip from her eyes. "I shouldn't be telling you any of this. My father's your boss. But I—oh, Mason, you're the only one I can really talk to about this. My sisters—well, Olivia, is just plain indifferent. I can't understand where she's coming from. And Zoe, she's always been in Dad's camp. Then there's Rachel. She's the one who sort of unearthed all of this about Dad in the first place. I think she's been pretty shaken by it all, too. But she's married and lives in Horseback Hollow now. She's not always around for me to commiserate with."

He continued to stroke her hair and the strong rhythmic feel of his fingers helped to ease her troubled mind.

"As far as I'm concerned, you don't have to worry,

Sophie. What you tell me in private will stay private. But I'm curious about one thing. What does your mother say about all this? Do you think your parents might get a divorce? Is that what's troubling you?"

His questions pulled a long groan from Sophie's throat. "I'm clueless about my parents, Mason. When Mother found out about Keaton it was like she just turned the other cheek. Not long ago I tried to talk with her about it, but she doesn't want to discuss it. Maybe she doesn't want to go through a messy divorce and split up millions of dollars of assets. Or maybe she still loves Dad in spite of everything. I just don't know. But if more illegitimate children start to appear, I can't fathom her just turning a blind eye to the awful truth. Oh, Mason, don't you see? My family isn't real to me anymore. Everything is fake and cloaked in secrecy."

He wrapped his arms around her and pulled her tight against him. "Sophie, there's nothing fake about you. You're one of the most real people I've ever known. You can't let any of this drag you down or make you doubt yourself."

All of a sudden she wanted to tell him how very much she adored him. She wanted him to understand how making love to him had been so perfect and right. But this was the first time they'd been together as a real couple. She didn't want to spoil things by going too fast.

"Being here with you is the most real thing that's ever happened to me, Mason," she murmured. "Is it too late to say Happy Valentine's Day?"

"It's not a bit too late. The night is just starting."

It was the wee hours of the morning when Mason drove Sophie back to the parking garage to pick up her car. Although he'd wanted her to stay overnight at his place, she'd reasoned that it wouldn't be smart for the other Robinson Tech employees to see them arriving at work together. At least, not yet. Not until everyone could see that Sophie was no longer dating Thom. She hardly needed to add more gossip about her family to what was already going around the office.

Mason had been none too happy about Sophie's desire to keep their relationship a secret. But he'd understood her reasons and had finally promised to go along with her wishes. The fact that he was willing to do that for her made her love him even more.

Love. Had she already fallen in love with Mason? One session of hot, mind-blowing sex shouldn't make her heart fall in love.

No, it was more than sex that was making her heart want to sing with joy, she thought. Making love to Mason had been perfect. More perfect than she could've ever imagined. But the truth was, she'd been falling in love with him for some time now. She'd just been too blind to see it.

She was walking through the house on the way to her bedroom, thinking about Mason and how her life had taken an abrupt change, when she spotted a dim light filtering from the partially opened doorway of her father's study.

Even though Gerald Robinson was a workaholic, she'd never seen him in his study at nearly four in the morning. Or was that her father burning the midnight oil? As far as she knew, he was still out of town.

With the red bear Mason had given her clutched beneath one arm, Sophie silently tiptoed to the door. She peered in and stared in complete confusion. Her mother was sitting at the desk, carefully studying papers scattered in front of her. Her mother never involved herself in

Robinson Tech business. Nor in the household accounts; a private secretary took care of them. So what was she doing? Digging into her husband's secret transactions? Or perhaps it was love letters?

A part of Sophie wanted to barge into the room and demand answers. She wanted to scream at her mother that she was sick of the lies and secrets. But that wouldn't be a particularly smart move. Knowing Charlotte, she would simply dismiss Sophie's confrontation as childish and order her out of the study. No, if Sophie wanted to discover the truth, she'd have to be far more patient and subtle about going after it.

Sophie, there's nothing fake about you. You're one of the most real people I've ever known.

Mason's words suddenly returned to her and Sophie glanced down at the bear she was clutching tightly to her breast. For Mason's sake, for her own sake, she couldn't hide from the truth about her family. Nor could she hide from these newborn feelings in her heart.

Her faith in her family had been shattered, but she had to trust Mason. She had to believe that their relationship would grow into something strong and unbreakable. She had to keep telling herself that her life, her marriage was going to be real and filled with love. She was not going to be a cold woman sitting alone at her husband's desk at four in the morning.

Chapter Twelve

Three days later on Friday morning, Mason got a call from his brother, Doug. Because it was unusual for him to be phoning him at work, Mason answered rather than let it go to his voice mail.

"Don't worry, I'm still able to tell time," Doug joked. "It's ten in the morning and we're both busy, so I'll just keep you a minute. I wanted to see if you'd like to drive down and go to the Spurs game tonight. Shawn's going, too. They're playing the Grizzlies, so it should be good."

Normally, Mason wouldn't hesitate. Basketball and his brothers' company would make for a great evening, even with the eighty mile drive down to San Antonio. But it wouldn't be worth missing a chance to be with Sophie.

"Sounds good, Doug. But I think I'm going to be busy tonight."

"You think? You mean you don't know yet? Don't tell me you're working late. I'm the one who's supposed to be chained to my desk. I shouldn't keep the scales of justice waiting and all that. But if I can put off a case, then you can put off an app."

Mason settled back in his chair. "It's not work. It's a woman."

There was pause, then Doug said, "If that's the case, then I can hardly blame you."

Since the night of Valentine's Day, Mason and Sophie had been together every night at his apartment. Normally, that much time with any woman, including Christa, would have cooled his ardor. But with Sophie the time together had only kindled his desire. If possible, the sex between them had grown even hotter. And as good as that was, Mason couldn't help but feel uneasy.

Tonight he wanted to take her out to a nice dinner, but he doubted she would agree to such a date. She'd be afraid the two of them would be seen together, he thought grimly. He could understand her wanting to keep their relationship a secret, up to a point. But the more he dwelt on the problem, the more he recalled how she'd seemed quite proud to be seen sitting with Thom in the break room. But Thom Nichols was Mr. Dreamboat, the marketing strategist. Being seen with him had been different than Mason, the computer geek.

"Mason? Are you still there? Can you hear me?"

Mason wiped a hand over his face. "Sorry, Doug. I was thinking."

"Is that what you call it?"

His brother's wry question caused Mason to groan. "Doug, do you remember me telling you a few days back about a woman? The wealthy one?"

"Vaguely," he teased, then added in a more serious tone, "Yes, I remember. The boss's daughter. Don't tell me she's the one who'd make you turn down a night of basketball."

"That's what I'm saying."

Doug whistled. "Damn, brother, you're playing with fire."

"Yeah. I'm standing close to the flames all right. But she's worth it."

"Worth losing your job?"

These past years his work at Robinson Tech had been the most important achievements he'd made in his life. The thought of putting his job in jeopardy was unnerving, but not nearly as much as losing Sophie.

"If it came to that," he said bluntly.

"Wow! Mason, you sound like you've fallen hard for this woman."

Had he fallen in love with Sophie? The question sent uncertainty drifting through him like a cold, dark fog. Sophie was so out of his league it was ridiculous. She could have most any man she set her eyes on, a man far wealthier and accomplished than Thom Nichols or anyone working for Robinson Tech.

"It's too early for that kind of thinking."

Doug responded with an amused grunt. "What about all those people who fall in love at first sight? Or believe they do."

Mason grimaced. "It doesn't last."

"Hmm. It takes work to make a relationship last, Mason. That's why you don't see me in one. I'm too lazy."

"Hah! Why not just admit that you're about as flexible as an iron rod? You really should be aiming for a judge position, my brother. You always did want to rule everybody."

Doug laughed, but the happy sound quickly sobered. "Mason, being flexible and giving is good. I just hope you don't end up doing all the bending and sacrificing. Okay?"

Mason let out a long breath. "I hear you."

The two talked for another minute before both agreed they needed to get back to work.

Mason scrubbed his face with both hands and tried to refocus his attention on work, but his conversation with Doug continued to prod at him.

Where Sophie was concerned was he doing all the bending? True, they'd not been together as a couple long enough to really weigh the situation. But so far, Mason was the one who'd given in and gone along with her request to keep their relationship hidden. When would it be time for her to start giving in and showing her family and friends that she cared about him? Would she ever want them to know?

That afternoon, as soon as Sophie found a stopping point in her work, she made a beeline to Mason's desk, only to find it empty.

"Mason and Nadine left on break a few minutes ago."

Sophie turned to see a young woman with short black hair and a calculating smile. Sophie recognized her voice. She was one of the gossiping women from the bathroom. Although she'd not gotten a look at the two gossipmongers that morning, she hadn't forgotten their pompous tone.

"Oh. I see. Well, I needed to speak with him about a work matter."

The smile on the woman's face grew even cattier and Sophie could only wonder what she'd ever done to deserve this kind of treatment. Being born a Fortune? Was that enough cause to be despised?

"Work. Yes. Maybe you should go upstairs and see Thom. I'm sure he'd love to talk about work."

Sophie would've thoroughly enjoyed telling this woman to keep her warped tongue to herself and to mind her own business. But in the long run, lowering herself to such a demeaning level wouldn't help her. No more than it would help this woman improve her behavior.

"Thanks," Sophie told her sweetly. "You've been more than helpful."

The woman lifted her nose, then turned on her heel and walked off. Sophie's teeth ground together as she turned back to Mason's desk and began to search for a scrap of paper to write a note.

"Hey, beautiful! Are you on a secret mission?"

The voice caused her to jump and she whirled around to see Mason entering the cubicle.

"Mason! I was writing you a note. Don't you keep a pencil and paper around here?"

"I rarely use the things," he said wittily. "We have these new gadgets now called cell phones that actually send text messages."

She shot him a sardonic look. "Smarty. Sometimes a handwritten note is nicer."

"Nicer," he repeated in a voice somewhere between a growl and a whisper. "Finding you here is the highlight of my day."

As he moved toward her, a sexy glow lit his brown eyes and, even though Sophie was a bit miffed with him, she couldn't stop a wide smile from spreading across her face.

"Nadine and I have been in the breakroom."

"Yes, I know. A little mockingbird told me."

"What?"

She shook her head, then glanced around to make sure

Miss Nosey had left the area. "Nothing. Did you forget that I told you I'd be by to talk about tonight?"

"No. I didn't forget. But you didn't say exactly when. If you knew I was in the breakroom, why didn't you come down there to see me?"

She shot him an impatient look. "Mason! You know why," she muttered in a hushed tone. "People are already starting to talk about us. I don't want to add fuel to the fire."

"How do you know they're starting to talk? Have you been eavesdropping?"

Shaking her head, she let out a long breath. "I just had a nasty visitor drop by here. She suggested that I go upstairs and talk to Thom instead of you."

He glanced around him as though the gossiper might still be lurking nearby. "Are you serious? Who was it?"

"I don't know her name. I think she works in marketing. Which probably means that Thom and the whole marketing department know about us now."

He frowned. "So what if they do? It's none of their business. This need you have to hide everything doesn't make sense, Sophie. Before, when we were just friends, you never worried about us being seen together."

"That's because—" She broke off as red heat swept up her face. "Well, it's different now. We can't be close together and keep our hands off each other. You know that!"

Grinning now, he stepped close enough to wrap his hand around her upper arm. "I'll tell you what I know. Right now I'd like to kiss you and carry you off to the broom closet."

The idea of being locked in any closet with Mason was enough to make her whole body tingle. But rather than admit it, she arched an innocent brow at him. "Broom closet?"

His head dipped close enough to whisper in her ear. "It's dark and we could lock the door."

Even though his rough, masculine voice sent shivers of desire over her skin, she forced herself to step away from him. "I hate to tell you this, but the janitors have keys. They can unlock the broom closets anytime they please."

He feigned a look of disappointment. "Our luck and one of them would come along and want a push broom right when things were getting...delicious."

She shot him a sexy, sidelong glance. "I need to get back to my desk. Are we still on for tonight? I can be at your place by seven."

He cleared his throat. "Yes, we're still on. But I thought I'd take you out to dinner tonight. To Pedro's. I know how much you like Tex-Mex and he dishes up some of the best in Austin."

Pedro's was a quaint little café situated in the old part of town. It still had a real screen door on the front entrance and scrubbed plank floors. The round tables were just large enough to hold two plates, two drinks and a candle in between and the scents coming from the kitchen were enough to make a person's mouth water. To be there with Mason would make the place even more special.

"I would love to go to Pedro's, Mason. Really, I would. But I—I just don't think it would be wise—yet. What if some of our friends or family saw us?"

"That's right, what if? Would the sky actually fall in, Sophie? This is getting ridiculous, don't you think? You're a grown woman. You should be able to date whomever you choose without worrying about what people are going to say."

Sophie looked away and swallowed the lump of pain in her throat. Although it had only been a few days since they'd started seeing each other, already Mason was getting weary of the subterfuge. And she could hardly blame him. It wasn't his fault that things had played out so swiftly and unexpectedly. Nor was it his fault that she'd made a fool of herself over Thom Nichols.

"I understand you're not exactly happy about this secrecy, Mason. But I'm not asking you to do it forever. I don't want people saying I dumped Thom for you. Or that you got me on the rebound."

His hand gently tugged her arm, prompting her to look at him.

"Sophie, no matter how much time passes, people are always going to talk. Especially because of who you are. You're a Fortune Robinson. Everything you do is under a microscope. That isn't going to change."

"I realize that. But, oh, Mason, I admit I'm responsible for this…situation. If I hadn't been so stupid about Thom none of this would be happening. I just don't want to look like a two-timer or schemer! Especially after the things that have come out about Dad. Everyone is going to think our family is not to be trusted!"

His expression softened. "Sophie, I understand you've been having a rough time of it lately with your family. I just want—well, I just want us to be together. Out in the open. Like a real couple."

"And we will be, Mason. I promise. Just give it a little longer. In the meantime, I'd still like to be with you tonight. Am I invited to your place or not?"

Slowly, the tension on his face began to ease and then he chuckled under his breath. "Just try to stay away and I'll come after you."

* * *

Late that evening, Mason was getting ready to shut down his computer for the day when from the corner of his eye, he saw someone enter his cubicle.

He was more than surprised to see Thom sauntering up to his desk.

"What's wrong? Lost your way? Wes's office is down the corridor," Mason said with a heavy dose of sarcasm. He'd never liked the man in the first place and the feeling had only intensified. "You wouldn't be down here to see anyone but the boss, would you?"

One corner of Thom's mouth lifted in a sneer that assured Mason there was no love lost between them.

"Actually, I'm on my way out. I never did feel the need to work late just to try to impress anyone."

Anyone as in Sophie? Or anyone like Gerald Robinson? The questions rolled through Mason's thoughts as he studied the man that many women in the building had dubbed Mr. Dreamy. As far as Mason was concerned Thom Nichols was a walking nightmare.

Mason cast Thom a smug smile. "I'm not working late this evening. I happen to have a date. And I don't want to be late," he added pointedly.

The sneer on Thom's lips grew more twisted. "With Sophie, no doubt."

"I didn't say anything about Sophie."

Thom folded his arms against his chest. "Of course you didn't. The rest of the building is saying it for you."

So Sophie was right. The gossip had already started. Mason didn't care what anyone said, especially this pompous jerk. But he didn't want Sophie hurt. Not for any reason.

"Is there some reason for your visit, Nichols? If not, I'm out of here."

"No reason. I just thought I'd stop by and give you a bit of friendly advice."

"I don't remember asking you for any."

Thom shrugged and Mason thought how the guy was exactly like the taunting bully on the school playground. A fist to his mouth would definitely shut him up. But in the end Gerald Robinson would probably fire both of them. Especially because the fight revolved around his youngest daughter.

"Well, a man needs to know his limitations. I certainly learned that lesson the hard way. Think about it, Montgomery. I barely managed to hold on to Sophie for a few days and then her interest in me went south. What makes you think you can do better? The woman is a rich butterfly. She's never going to stay in one place long." With a short, mocking laugh, he started out of the cubicle. "All I can say is good luck. You're going to need it."

Biting back several choice curse words, Mason jerked on his jacket and flipped off the light. On his way out, he very nearly knocked Nadine off her feet.

Snatching a steadying hand on her shoulder, he quickly apologized, "Nadine, I'm sorry. Did I hurt you?"

She answered his question with a scoffing laugh. "It takes more than a little bump to knock this woman off her feet. Now, a kiss might do it. If only you were fifteen years older you'd be the perfect man for me."

Laughing with her, he gave her a little hug. "Ready to go? I'll walk with you to your car."

"I'll be ready as soon as I get my purse. Right now, I want to know what Mr. Phony was doing here. And yes, I'm being nosey. But I just happened to glance over here a minute ago and it looked like you had murder on your mind. Do I need to start saving money for your bail bond?"

Mason let out a weary sigh. "Thom thought he should come by and give me fair warning. Sophie will dump me just like she dumped him—swiftly and painfully."

Nadine scowled at him. "Don't listen to the man. He's obviously jealous."

"And he could be very right," Mason mumbled. "Think about it, Nadine. I'm just a regular Joe. I can't give Sophie what she's used to having."

Nadine patted his cheek. "You can give her the very thing her daddy can't buy her. Love. So there. Think about that while I fetch my purse."

Love. Yes, Sophie talked about love. About how very much she wanted her marriage to be full of warmth and love instead of the cold arrangement between her parents. But she'd never so much as hinted that she was falling in love with Mason. She'd never brought up their relationship in a long term context. She was living day to day, enjoying their time together. But that wasn't enough for Mason. Not nearly enough. And deep down, he was afraid Thom was right. Neither of them were good enough for Sophie Fortune Robinson.

By Sunday morning, the weather had turned spring-like and after much persuasion, Mason was able to talk Sophie into driving down to San Antonio to spend a day on the Riverwalk. With the sun shining brightly and the birds chattering in the trees, the day couldn't have been more beautiful. And having Sophie stroll alongside him made it even more heavenly.

Sophie had called on her inner cowgirl and donned a blue chambray shirt with a pink skirt and a pair of fancy cowboy boots. Her hair was pulled up in a high ponytail and the casual style made her look very young and very adorable. Mason found himself looking at her instead of the Riverwalk.

"Do your parents live downtown?" she asked, as the two of them meandered along the narrow river's edge.

"No. They live on the west side, in the same little stucco house they lived in when we boys were born. If you offered them a mansion right on the river, they'd just laugh and say they're happy where they are."

She looked at him with a faintly wistful expression and Mason wondered if she'd been expecting him to take her to meet his family today. Since she was still on this quest to keep their relationship a secret, he figured she would hardly want to announce it to his family. And to be honest, he wasn't yet ready to take Sophie to meet his parents. For a long time now, the Montgomerys had wanted to see their sons settle down and start producing grandbabies. Mason didn't want his parents, especially his mother, getting the idea that he and Sophie were getting serious about each other. Not when there was the very real possibility that in the next few weeks she'd be giving him the cold shoulder.

"Sophie, you didn't think you were here to meet my family, did you?"

The awkward question caused her cheeks to turn pink and she swiftly diverted her gaze to a passing tourist boat. "No. I don't expect that sort of… commitment from you. Meeting your parents would be a serious step. And you and I—well, we're just getting started with this dating thing."

She looked at him through lowered lashes and gave him a wobbly smile. Mason took her by the arm and led her over to a park bench which was partially shaded by a live oak.

Once they were seated, he took her hand and folded it between his. "Sophie, are you getting tired of me?"

"Tired? That's a silly question, Mason. We've been together every night since our Valentine's date. Why would you think such a thing?"

Not about to reveal the doubts he'd been feeling, he simply shrugged. "I don't know. You just seem a little withdrawn. Especially when we started talking about my parents."

Sighing, she said, "I'm not hurt about that, Mason. It just made me think of my parents and all that's going on with them. I wish to heck Ben would just leave it all alone! At least, that's what I think some of the time. Other times, I believe he's doing the right thing. If we have other siblings out there, we should probably know about them." She looked at him, her brown eyes swirling with dark shadows. "But then I think about Mother and what must be going through her mind. It's all so hard to deal with, Mason. And now something else has come up."

He cast her a questioning glance. "Oh. What now?"

"This coming Thursday night, we've all been invited to the Fortune Ranch for a family dinner. Kate Fortune wants to get to know the Fortune Robinsons better. Which I suppose is a nice thing. But I'm not sure I'm ready to mix and mingle with that side of the family. After all, they treated Dad so badly he faked his own death to get away from them. If that isn't an awkward setting, then I don't know what is."

Mason shook his head. "But that happened years ago. From what you've told me, Kate is trying her best to make amends for the brutal way your father was treated by his parents. You shouldn't feel awkward. If anything you should feel grateful that she's being so welcoming."

"Yes, I suppose so. And she's kindly encouraged each

of us to bring along a guest. But I—I'm planning on going alone. I just want to get the whole evening over with."

In spite of the warm sun filtering through the tree limbs, Mason felt chilled. She could have invited him to the family dinner, but she was going alone. That proved just how much she thought Mason would fit into her highbrow family.

What are you carrying on about, Mason? You're less than twenty minutes away from your parents' house and you have no intention of taking Sophie to meet them. Is that because you don't think she'd fit in? Because you think she's too good to ever be a Montgomery?

Yes! He wanted to scream the word at the accusing voice in his head. Sophie was too good for him. That was the whole crux of the matter. And the sooner he realized it, the better off they'd both be.

The gentle pressure of her fingers on his claimed his attention. She was studying him with a faint frown and Mason only hoped she couldn't read his thoughts.

"Mason, a few minutes ago you were asking me if something was wrong, but I'm thinking it's you who has a problem. You seem preoccupied. Has something happened to upset you?"

Only that you've made it clear that your family and I don't mix.

Giving her his best smile, he said, "Not at all. It's a warm, gorgeous day. I have a beautiful woman to enjoy it with. What could possibly be wrong?"

Leaning forward, she kissed his cheek and in that moment, Mason realized his heart was lying right in the palm of her hand. No matter how hopeless it all seemed, he had to stick it out to the bitter end.

"You don't want fried chicken for lunch. That's it, isn't it?" she teased.

He grunted with amusement. "Fried chicken? Who said anything about that?"

She snuggled closer and Mason's gaze focused on her soft lips. If the two of them weren't sitting on a public bench, he'd kiss her until his mind was blank of worries. Until nothing mattered except making love to her.

She said, "I did. It's my favorite meal. Do you think we could find any around here?"

On this perfect Sunday the heiress wanted fried chicken. Maybe there was still hope for a future with her, he thought wryly. Could it be that deep down she was just a regular girl looking for a regular guy? For today he was going to let himself believe just that.

"This is the best news I've heard since my daughter and her husband decided to call off the divorce." Dennis grinned happily at Sophie, who was standing in front of his desk. "And this is all your doing, Sophie. I'm proud of you."

Any other time Sophie would've felt like dancing around her boss's office. But not today. The satisfaction she felt over her worthy accomplishment was dimmed by the reality that she'd be going to the Fortune Ranch tonight instead of spending it making love to Mason.

"I really didn't do anything special, Dennis. Once I pointed out all the gaps in the new insurance coverage, Ben was in agreement to come up with an improved plan. That's why he's a sharp businessman. He realizes happy employees are much more productive."

"Well, I only hope that your family and everyone in this building can see what a conscientious person you are. How hard you work for everyone's benefit, not just your own."

Yes, Dennis would praise her. As for her family, she wasn't sure any of them took that much notice of her work or what she hoped to do with her life. Her mother considered her flighty and Olivia thought she was foolish. No telling what the others were thinking, especially now that gossip about her ditching Thom and picking up Mason was circulating around the building.

"Thanks, Dennis. Coming from you that means a lot."

He started to say something else when the phone on his desk rang. "Excuse me, Sophie. I'd better get this. It's a call I've been waiting on."

Once she left Dennis's office, she spotted Olivia waving an arm to catch her attention.

The two women met near the alcove where Mason had comforted her the day she'd overheard the nasty talk in the restroom. He'd made her feel special and given her the extra strength she'd needed to keep her chin up. Had she been falling in love with him then? Or had the love she felt for him as a friend suddenly blossomed like a seed in springtime? She didn't know. She only knew that her feelings for Mason were growing so big they were scaring her.

"What's up?" Sophie asked her sister.

"I wanted to see what you're wearing to the dinner party tonight. I went out on my lunch hour today and bought a new gown. I hope it'll be okay."

Sophie shrugged. "I haven't thought about it. I'm sure I can find something in my closet to impress the Fortunes."

Olivia rolled her eyes. "Sophie, we are the Fortunes, too."

"How could I forget?" Sophie asked sardonically. "We're getting new Fortune relatives every day."

Olivia regarded her skeptically. "Is that what's eating at you? You're afraid Ben is going to use the setting tonight to announce another one of Dad's illegitimate children? Forget it. He wouldn't do anything that crass. Not in front of Mother."

Sophie hoped not.

Sighing, she said, "I really don't want to go to this party tonight."

Olivia frowned at her. "Why? It will be fun to go to the Fortune Ranch. Maybe Kate will give us some of her fabulous cosmetics. Especially her famous Youth Serum. And it will give you an opportunity to show Mason our side of the family. You have invited him, haven't you?"

Olivia's question caught her by complete surprise. "No. I haven't invited him. I'm going alone."

Olivia's big brown eyes grew even wider. "Alone! But why? I understand that things ended rather quickly with Thom and developed even faster with Mason, but that's nothing to be embarrassed about. I'm just happy that you came to your senses and latched on to a nice man. And tonight would give you a chance to show Mother and Dad that you're serious about Mason. You are, aren't you?"

Sophie's mind was suddenly whirling. Not only with thoughts of Mason, but also about Olivia, and how her sister appeared to know so much about Sophie's personal life. She hadn't told anyone in her family about Mason yet. She'd been waiting for the right time. And waiting, too, for Mason to show some sign that he wanted their relationship to be the permanent kind. But so far he hadn't mentioned anything about love, much less forever.

"How did you know about Mason?"

Olivia rolled her eyes. "Sophie, I'm not blind. I've seen the two of you at Bernie's with your heads together.

And Mother tells me you've been staying out late every night. It's not hard to put two and two together."

Sophie felt her cheeks turning red. "Mother has noticed me being gone? That's surprising. She hasn't mentioned it to me. I wonder why she said something about it to you."

Olivia shrugged. "Who knows? She probably thinks you'll get defensive and clam up."

The same way that she did? The suspicious thought raced through Sophie's mind, but she kept it to herself. Just as she'd kept to herself the image of Charlotte sitting at Gerald's desk in the wee hours of the morning.

"Maybe so," Sophie murmured. "And considering everything, she does have a lot on her mind."

"That's putting it mildly," Olivia said. "Well, I need to get back to my desk. I'll see you tonight. Since you're not taking Mason, are you riding out to the ranch with Mother and Dad?"

Cooped up for miles in the frozen atmosphere of her parents' car would be more than Sophie could endure for one evening. "No. I'll be taking my car. Why don't you ride with me?"

"Thanks, Sophie. I'll come out early. We'll get ready together and make it a real sister night." Olivia dropped a swift kiss on her cheek, then walked away.

Tonight would give you a chance to show Mother and Dad that you're serious about Mason.

Olivia's words continued to nag at Sophie and by the time she passed the entrance to R&D, she was very nearly ready to walk straight to his desk and beg him to go with her to the Fortune bash.

But then she remembered how forward she'd been with Thom and how quickly it had all blown up in her face. No, she wasn't going to press Mason into attending the family outing with her. If he ever decided he was ready to take that serious step, she wanted him to do it on his own. Not because she was pushing and prodding him toward a proposal of marriage.

But would he ever want to take such a step with her?

Her throat aching with raw emotions, she hurried down the corridor and wondered why love had to surround itself with so much pain and worry.

Love? Is that the reason she felt so melancholy? Because she was finally and truly in love?

She was going to have to answer that question and soon. Because something was telling her that Mason was about to demand the truth of her feelings. About him and her, and what she wanted for the future.

Chapter Thirteen

Her petite curves draped with an organza gown of pale peach, and her long hair twisted into an elaborate chignon, Sophie glanced over the rim of her cocktail glass at the guests gathered in the grand room of the Fortune Ranch house.

The men were all dressed in dark, elegant suits, while the women wore long, bejeweled gowns, the cost of which would've fed a family of four for months.

"I used to think our home was elaborate, but this place is unbelievable." Olivia shook her head with awe. "Makes me wonder how long it took Kate to put her stamp on the place. I doubt it looked like this when it was the Silver Spur Ranch. Look at those drapes. There's enough material there to open a fabric store. And every room seems to have a bar. I suppose Kate wants to make sure she keeps her guests relaxed."

The place was more than elaborate, Sophie agreed.

It was like stepping into a fairy tale where everything was too beautiful and lavish to be real. Wide archways on three sides of the room made the area appear even more spacious. Instead of artificial lighting, the middle of the incredibly tall ceiling was lit by the stars shining through an enormous skylight. To the right, several feet away from Sophie and Olivia was a marble fireplace with an elevated hearth. Presently, mesquite logs crackled and simmered, throwing off enough heat to make the room comfortable for the women with bared shoulders.

"Well, I'll say one thing, everything is done tastefully. The western accents are just enough to let a person know they're in Texas. But not enough to be ostentatious."

A young male server paused in front of the two women. Sophie chose a canapé made with gulf shrimp and cream cheese. Olivia placed her empty cocktail glass on the man's tray and picked up a fresh one.

Maybe that was what she needed, Sophie thought ruefully. A bit of alcohol to numb the raw edges of her nerves. But she'd never much cared for the stuff. Besides, a cocktail wasn't going to make her forget about her parents' sham of a marriage, or the real idea that Mason only wanted her for a lover.

"Mother looks especially nice tonight," Olivia commented as she sipped her drink. "That pale blue dress flatters her."

"She'd look even better if she would smile," Sophie said dully. "But in her situation I suppose she's forgotten how."

Olivia slanted her a disappointed look. "Sophie, what in the world is coming over you? I'm the cynical one. Not you. Where's that cheerful attitude of yours?"

Sophie let out a long sigh. "You're right. I'm going to go mix and mingle and try to lift my spirits."

For the next hour, she moved around the crowd, greeting other family members, including her new stepbrother, Keaton Fortune Whitfield. Eventually she found herself face-to-face with Kate Fortune and her husband, Sterling Foster. Expecting the woman to be austere, Sophie was pleasantly surprised when Kate greeted her with sincere warmth.

By the time their short chat had ended, Sophie had to admit that Kate Fortune was an incredible woman. At ninety-one she looked years younger. Her slim figure remained straight and spry and her skin as dewy and fresh as a first rose in spring. No doubt a result of using her famous Youth Serum cream.

However, Kate's appearance was only a part of her dynamic presence. She had a razor-sharp mind, especially concerning business. The billionaire matriarch obviously had the knack to accurately gauge the needs of the consumer and to come up with the perfect product.

Yet as impressed as she was with Kate Fortune, it was her husband that touched Sophie in an emotional way. The suave, elderly gentleman was clearly very much in love with his wife. Each time he looked at her or lightly touched her hand, it was like he was touching an angel.

Was it crazy for Sophie to want that same thing for herself?

Sophie was standing at the back of the room, mulling over the question as she watched her mother and father interact with the other guests. So far tonight, the only time she'd seen them together was when they'd first arrived.

That sad fact shouldn't be bothering Sophie so much. It wasn't like her parents had been all lovey-dovey and then, all at once, everything had gone cold. But since she and Mason had become intimate, Sophie had started to look at everything differently. And she was seeing more and more how love, and nothing else, mattered in this world.

"It's a nice party, don't you think?"

The soft, feminine voice had Sophie turning to see a petite woman with wavy blonde hair that barely touched her shoulders. Her dress was a romantic floral with a delicate ruffle edging the neckline.

Until this moment, Sophie hadn't spotted this pretty young woman in the crowd of guests. And though she didn't immediately recognize her, something about her face seemed vaguely familiar.

Sophie said, "Yes. Ms. Fortune and her husband have certainly gone all out."

The woman, who appeared to be around Sophie's age, moved closer and thrust out her hand in greeting. "I don't think we've met before. I'm Chloe Elliott. And you are?"

Even though the woman was smiling warmly, the only thing Sophie could feel was icy shock. This was her father's illegitimate daughter! What was she doing here? Why did she think she could come here and mingle with Sophie and her brothers and sisters as though she were one of them?

Ignoring her outstretched hand, Sophie's expression turned as cold as the sick feeling inside her. "I'm Sophie Fortune Robinson. And don't ever think of calling me sister! Because you're not my sister! And you never will be!"

Chloe Elliott appeared totally stunned, but not nearly as much as Sophie. Horrified by the words that had come out of her mouth, she hurried across the enormous room and snatched up a glass from a tray full of drinks.

Not bothering to determine what the amber tinged

drink might be, she took a giant swig and instantly choked on the fire sliding down her throat.

"Sophie! Are you all right?"

Glancing up, Sophie saw her mother frowning at her with a mixture of concern and admonition.

Careful to keep her voice hushed, Sophie answered, "No! I am not all right! I really want to leave!"

Thankfully, Charlotte didn't ask her why. Instead, she took a firm hold on Sophie's shoulder. "Leaving is out of the question. You're not going to embarrass yourself or your family. There are times, Sophie, when we women have to be strong and plaster a happy smile on our faces. This is one of those times. So don't disappoint me—or your father."

Sophie looked at her in amazement, while fighting the urge to laugh hysterically. Disappoint her father? Hadn't Charlotte already noticed her husband's illegitimate daughter walking among the guests? Didn't she care?

After downing a second, more careful sip of her drink, Sophie said, "All right, Mother. I'll pretend—for tonight. But don't expect me to keep pretending. I simply can't be like you."

By the next afternoon, Mason was more than smarting over Sophie's decision to go to the Fortune party without him. It wasn't that he was all that keen to rub elbows with wealthy society. To be honest, he would have probably felt uncomfortable during the whole affair. No, his feelings went deeper than that. Sophie had dismissed him as though he was the last person she would consider good enough to mix and mingle with her family.

All last night, he'd sat in his apartment alone, brooding and calling himself all sorts of a fool. It was plain he was headed down a dead-end path with Sophie. The two of them came from entirely different worlds. Just the thought of asking her to marry him, to live with him in a home he provided her, was laughable. And in the end, that was most likely what he'd get from her. A laugh. The sort of home he could give Sophie would never measure up. The sort of life he could afford to give her would always fall short. It would never work. No matter how much he dreamed and hoped and tried.

"Hey, handsome. Ready for a coffee break?"

The sound of Sophie's sweet voice shot right through his churning thoughts as she walked into his cubicle.

A red knit dress clung to her perfect little curves while her long hair was swept behind her ear on one side. She looked good enough to eat and it was all Mason could do to keep from pulling her into his arms.

Steeling himself against her charming smile, he raised his brows with faint surprise. "A coffee break? Aren't you worried that someone will see us talking, or God forbid, touching one another?"

His sarcasm clearly stunned her. Well, it had stunned Mason, too. He didn't want to be mean. Nor did he want to hurt her. But he was tired of giving in to her without getting any sort of reassurances that their relationship meant more to her than jumping into bed together.

Her smile faded as she walked over and leaned a hip against the edge of his desk.

"Actually, I'm not worried. I don't give a damn about gossipers anymore."

"Really? You couldn't prove it by me."

She frowned at him in confusion. "Mason, what's wrong?"

You're breaking my heart and you don't even know it. That's what's wrong.

The words were silently screaming inside him as he turned the chair so that he was facing his computer screen instead of her.

"Nothing. I'm way behind on my work."

A long stretch of silence passed till she asked, "What about tonight? Maybe we could go to Pedro's."

A few days ago, he'd have felt like she'd handed him the moon. Now her offer felt like too little, too late.

"Sorry. I've promised my brothers to go with them to a Spurs game. So I'm going to San Antonio tonight. I won't be home."

She let out a groan of disgust. "Basketball," she muttered. "I've never been so sick of hearing about sports events in my entire life!"

Anger had him whirling the chair so that he was facing her once again. "And I'm sick of hearing how hard it is for you to be a Fortune!"

She stared at him in disbelief. "Did I hear you right?"

"Every word," he said coolly. "You act as though no one else has family issues. No one else has been betrayed or lied to or hurt. Well, grow up and open your eyes, Sophie. You're just one of many."

Tears flooded her eyes and for one second Mason weakened to the point where he almost reached for her. He almost asked her to forgive him for being such a heartless bastard. But deep down, his pride and every ounce of common sense urged him to hold his ground.

She stepped away from the desk and Mason could see her hands had balled into tight fists at her sides. "If that's what you think of me, then I'm glad I found it out now. I wouldn't want to keep torturing you with my monotonous problems."

Swallowing the ball of pain in his throat, he said, "It

was fun for a while, Sophie. But I've been thinking and I believe it's time we broke things off. For both our sakes."

Sniffing, she tossed her hair back over her shoulder. "Are you doing this because of last night? Because I didn't invite you to the Fortune dinner party?"

"No," he said and realized he truly meant it. This wasn't just about a party. This was about the fundamental differences in their lives. One day soon she would realize they were wrong for each other and move on to a man who would really be her Mr. Perfect. As for him, he expected he would spend the rest of his life trying to forget her. "I'm doing this to save us both a lot of heartache. Now if you don't mind, I'm busy. I need to get back to work."

She gave him one last look, then turned and walked stiffly out of the cubicle. The moment she was out of sight, Mason slumped forward in his chair and dropped his head in his hands.

Minutes later he was still sitting that way when Nadine poked her head into his work space. "Ready for some coffee, honey?"

He lifted his head and by then Nadine must have realized something was amiss. She hurried over to him.

"Mason, you look like hell! What's wrong? What's happened?"

Pushing himself to his feet, he shook his head. "Nothing's happened, Nadine. Except that I've just given up the most important thing in my life."

Nadine's lips pressed to a thin line of disgust. "Don't tell me. Ms. Fortune just gave you the shaft."

"No," he said, barely able to speak around the bitter gall rising in his throat. "I'm the one who called it quits."

Nadine shook her head. "You! But, Mason, why? I don't understand. You were crazy about the woman!"

"That's exactly why, Nadine. I want her to be happy. Not just for now. But for the rest of her life. And I'm not the man who can keep her happy."

"Oh, Mason, you're letting talk around the office get to you. You've let Thom get to you."

Mason slung his arm around Nadine's shoulders and urged her out of the cubicle. "Right now you're getting to me, Nadine. So let's go have some coffee. And all I want to hear from you is something about getting your roots done or work on your mother/baby app."

With a mirthless laugh, she wrapped an arm across his back. "Oh, hell, if I were only a few years younger."

For the next three days Sophie's feelings alternated between anger, sadness, and confusion. Anger, not just at Mason for suddenly picking a fight and ending things, but at her family and the whole world for being so messed up and wrong. Confused because she still didn't exactly understand what had come over Mason so abruptly, and sadness for the utter loss of something she'd believed had been strong and true.

Sophie had never been one to sit around and cry and mope over what could have been. She'd always been the sort to look toward the future and fight on. But losing Mason had hurt her so deeply that the world around her was like a strange and scary place. She was afraid to take any sort of step. Afraid that whatever direction she took, it would be wrong.

For the past few nights she'd sat in her bedroom and stared at the little red bear Mason had given her on Valentine's Day. The little bear had reflected all her hopes and dreams. It symbolized everything she'd ever wanted in her life. A man to love her, a marriage that was genuine, a life that would be filled with happiness and children.

Money couldn't buy her those things. And, in Mason's case, she feared her wealth had actually worked against her.

Oh, Lord, he'd been wrong, she thought sadly. Mason had no idea just how hard it was to be a Fortune. To be so insanely rich that a regular guy was too afraid to come near her. And the others were simply cons after her money. He didn't know how it felt to go home to a palatial estate where there was no love or laughter.

Somehow her brothers, Ben and Wes and Graham, and her sisters Rachel and Zoe had found their soulmates. And for a few short beautiful days Sophie had believed she'd found hers. Now, she was beginning to think that men were nothing but selfish creeps. She was trying to convince herself that she'd be better off if she marked love completely off her future plans.

Glancing to the far edge of her desk, she groaned at the sight of the latest little gift Thom had dropped on her work space. A small picture of himself inside a gaudy gilded frame. Could the man get any more narcissistic? And why did he think just because she was no longer seeing Mason that she'd be willing to date him again? It was insane.

The office gossip machine must have been working overtime to spread the news about her bust up with Mason. One day hadn't passed before she'd found a flower on her desk. A card with nothing but Thom's name had been attached. Sophie had tossed the card in the trash and given the flower to Dennis's secretary.

Yesterday, a text message from Thom had popped up on her phone, suggesting the two of them meet for drinks. She'd promptly blocked his number. Now today, the photo had arrived, but rather than toss it, she'd decided she was going to return it personally, along with firm instructions to leave her alone.

"Great! You're back at your desk. I stopped by earlier, but you weren't here."

The sound of Thom's voice made her want to scream with frustration. Instead, she swiveled her chair and asked bluntly, "Do you have a problem you need to discuss? A human resource problem?"

A smug smile crossed his face. "I do have a problem. You won't say yes to another date with me. But I intend to change your mind. We can start over, Sophie. And this time you'll see I'm serious."

He was serious all right, Sophie thought. Seriously self-absorbed.

Leaning back in her chair, she leveled a sharp look at him. "Doesn't it bother you that I've been seeing Mason?"

He shrugged and his indifference amazed her. "Why should it? He's out of your life now. A fact that I knew would happen sooner rather than later."

The man's insolence was beyond measure and though Sophie was trying to hold on to her temper, her stomach was simmering with anger and resentment.

"I'm sure," she practically sneered. "The last time I looked, I didn't see a crystal ball on your desk."

He let out a short laugh. "I hardly needed a crystal ball to tell me your little hookup with Mason wasn't going to work. The man isn't nearly good enough for a woman of your class. I pointed out that very thing to him a few days ago. And I'm sure you're relieved he took my advice. Apparently he saw the light and was smart enough to save himself a lot of awkward embarrassment by letting you dump him later."

Her mouth fell open as her tangled thoughts tried to unravel enough for her to see the whole picture.

"Are you saying that you told Mason he wasn't good enough for me?"

Grinning, he moved closer and Sophie immediately jumped to her feet and stepped back.

"Why not? It's the truth. Better that you both face facts now, rather than later. Long, pointless affairs can often get messy at the end. You both saved yourself from an ugly situation."

Furious, Sophie picked up the photo and practically threw it at him. "You're not half the man that Mason is, Thom Nichols! You never will be!"

"Really? If he's so wonderful, then why did you break up with him?"

She hadn't broken up with him, she thought miserably. Mason had broken up with her. He'd suddenly picked a fight, as though he'd deliberately wanted to push her into ending their relationship. But why? And why hadn't she stood her ground and fought to keep everything they'd built together?

Because she'd been terrified. Afraid to trust. Afraid to open her heart and admit to Mason how very much she loved him. Could the same thing have been going through his mind, she wondered frantically. Could he have been having those same doubts and fears? She had to know! She couldn't just let the best thing she'd ever had slip through her fingers without putting up a fight to hold on to him.

"Take that ridiculous picture and get out of my work space!" she said to Thom in a low, gritty voice. "Before I call security and have them throw you out!"

He lifted his nose as though he couldn't believe she could utter such a threat, much less go through with it.

"Oh, Sophie. You wouldn't do that in a million years."

"Try me," she challenged. "And you'll see I'm no longer that starry-eyed young woman who looked blindly past your faults."

His face hardened like a piece of granite. "You're going to be sorry about this, Sophie. One of these days you're going to be begging me to notice you."

Thom's parting words were laughable. But Sophie didn't laugh, even though she was silently rejoicing. Because in his own conceited way, Thom had just opened her eyes and given her hope.

Turning back to her desk, she reached for the phone. She was going to put a plan in motion and pray it worked.

"Mason, you look drained. I honestly don't think you should work anymore this evening," Nadine advised as the two walked back to the office after having burgers at Bernie's. "Your health app won't get finished if you fall over from exhaustion."

"I'm not going to fall over from exhaustion." A broken heart, maybe, Mason thought ruefully. And that was something that bed rest wouldn't fix. Unless Sophie was lying in the bed with him. And that wasn't going to happen. Not after the way he treated her.

"How do you know?" Nadine asked. "I've heard of people falling into comas from extreme fatigue."

He looked over at his friend and gave her the best smile his wounded spirits could generate. "I appreciate your concern. But even if I went home right now, I wouldn't rest. I don't think I've slept three hours in the past three nights."

"And whose fault is that?" she shot back at him. "I just don't get you, Mason. You go gaga over a woman and then deliberately break up with her. Because you want her to be happy. Well, do you think you've made her happy? I don't. I saw her this afternoon at Olivia's desk. She looked horrible—like you."

"Sophie came into research and development?" he asked with surprise. "I didn't see her."

"No. You were too busy staring at your computer screen while trying to make everyone believe you weren't somewhere in outer space."

It was just as well that Mason hadn't been aware that Sophie was close by. Each time he'd caught a glimpse of her, it had felt like someone was stabbing him with a double-edged knife.

Since their breakup, he'd felt like Austin had suddenly moved within the Arctic Circle and the days had all turned dark. Without Sophie in his life nothing felt right or good. And he'd been asking himself over and over if he'd been an utter fool to let her go.

Maybe she hadn't said anything about love. And maybe she had wanted to keep their relationship a secret. But all of that could've changed if he'd been willing to give them a chance. And now? Well, he'd said some awful things to her. Things that had cut him just to speak them aloud. How could he ever expect her to give him another chance?

"Uh, Mason, beam me up, would you? I've lost my friend and maybe I'll find him out there somewhere in a galaxy far, far away."

Nadine's sardonic voice suddenly got through his deep thoughts and he slanted her a wry glance, then glanced around to see they had reached the Robinson Tech parking garage. The same spot where everything had started between him and Sophie. If only he could turn back time.

"Sorry, Nadine. I was thinking."

"Obviously. Do you think you can make it back into

the building without me? Or do I need to guide you to your desk?"

Leaning down, he planted a swift kiss on her cheek. "Thanks. But I think I can find my way back. See you in the morning."

Nadine wished him a good night then slipped into her car. Mason watched her drive safely away before he headed inside the building.

Since the work day had ended hours ago, the corridor was eerily quiet. As he approached the entrance to Sophie's department, he noticed there were no lights coming from that area.

And what if there was, Mason? Would you finally gather enough courage to face her? To beg her to give you another chance?

Tormented by the voice in his head, he wiped a hand over his face and trudged on. A part of him wished Nadine was right and he would fall into a temporary coma. At least then, he'd get a reprieve from the agony of losing her.

He was thinking about all the things he wished he'd done differently and how good it would feel to pull her into his arms and kiss her, when he walked into his cubicle and stopped in his tracks.

Seconds ticked away as Mason stared in stunned fascination at a little stuffed bear sitting in his chair. The animal's shaggy golden brown hair resembled that of a grizzly. An educated grizzly, no doubt, since his paws were resting on the computer keyboard.

His heart racing madly, Mason stepped forward and discovered a note attached to the bear's leather collar.

No one should have to spend February 27th alone.

He was staring at the note, trying to tamp down the ridiculous hope that was rushing to every cell in his body, when Sophie's voice sounded behind him.

"You've been gone so long I was afraid you'd left for home."

He slowly turned to face her and his heart began to beat so hard he thought his breastbone would surely crack down the middle.

"Sophie! What are you doing here?"

Like a beautiful dream, she glided toward him.

"Waiting for you," she answered quietly.

"I don't understand." His voice closed around his words making it sound as coarse as gravel. "The bear—are you trying to say—"

She reached for his hands and as Mason wrapped his fingers tightly around hers, his gaze was riveted on the emotions flickering in her eyes. The feelings he saw in the brown depths were so soft and tender and pleading, they smacked him right in the middle of his chest.

"Mason, I don't know what happened with us. Or why you—"

Shaking his head, he interrupted her before she could say more.

"Sophie, listen to me. I've been a damned fool. These past few days I've been wanting to come to you—to try to explain—to beg you to forgive me. I was a bastard, a jerk, and all kinds of a fool for saying those things to you. But I—"

All at once her forefinger was pressed against his lips. "You had a right to say those things. I've been an idiot, Mason. More than that, I've been a big coward. I was afraid to show everyone how much I cared about you. Most of all I was afraid to show you—to tell you how very much I love you. Everything was so good with us I kept thinking it couldn't last. My parents' marriage is nothing about love, and Thom—he doesn't fathom the word. When you and I started getting close—well, the closer we got the more afraid I was to believe you could ever truly love me."

Relief washed through him, leaving his insides trembling with weakness. "Sophie, if you've been an idiot, then I've been an even bigger one. I kept thinking there was no way you could ever love a man like me. That's why I went off on you like I did. Because I believed you were going to eventually drop me anyway. That you'd move on to some man more fitting to a woman of your status."

A tentative smile tilted her lips. "Fitting? Oh, Mason, you should know by now that you fit me perfectly."

Slipping his arms around her waist, he pulled her toward him until she was pressed tightly to him. Then burying his face in the crook of her neck, he murmured in her ear, "I love you, Sophie. I should've told you that from the very start. But I was afraid you'd think I was a sap. I was even more afraid to believe I could ever have a future with you."

She eased her head back and the love he saw on her face swelled his chest until he could scarcely breathe.

"Do you want a future with me, Mason?"

"Only for the rest of our lives. Is that too long?"

Joy spread her lips into a radiant smile. "Forever isn't nearly long enough, but I'll take it."

He kissed her then and in a matter of a few seconds, desire began to sweep them both away.

Finally, he lifted his head and said in a voice rough with desire, "Let's go home—to my place. If you can call that home?"

Her arms tightened around him. "My home is going to be wherever you are, Mason. Now and always."

* * *

Early the next morning, Sophie carried a steaming mug of coffee into the bedroom and with her free hand reached down and touched Mason's bare shoulder.

Groaning, he lifted his head and opened his eyes to see her standing at the side of the bed. His navy blue robe swallowed her small curves and her face was bare of makeup, but she didn't feel self-conscious about letting Mason see her this way. During the past twelve hours she'd learned that Mason loved her for the person she was inside, not for her looks, or name, or bank account. And that fact made her so deliriously happy she was certain she was walking on air instead of a hardwood floor.

"Sophie, honey, what are you doing up already?" he asked with a sleepy smile. "And you made coffee, too?"

Laughing softly, she said, "I know it's hard to believe, but I can do one or two things in the kitchen."

He quickly propped a pillow against the headboard. Once he'd scooted up to a sitting position and settled back against the pillow, he took the coffee from her.

She watched him take a sip, then his brow arched with surprise. "Mmm. This is delicious. What did you do to it?"

She cut him a saucy glance. "I put in water and coffee grounds and turned the switch to ON."

Chuckling, he took another sip, then set the mug on the nightstand and reached for her. Sophie let out a happy squeal as he pulled her down onto his lap.

"Good morning, beautiful," he whispered against her lips.

She kissed him deeply, then eased back to look at him. With his dark hair rumpled and a shadow of a beard covering his face, he looked incredibly handsome and terribly sexy. Yet to know that he loved her—not because she was a Fortune, but because she was simply Sophie— filled her heart with a joy that was almost impossible to contain.

"Good morning, my darling. How does it feel to wake up to a woman and a cup of coffee?"

His eyes narrowed to a provocative slant. "I think this is going to be pretty darn easy to get used to. Uh—what do you think your family is going to say when I slip an engagement ring on your finger?"

She held up her left hand and imagined a ring sparkling back at her. "When is that going to happen?" she asked coyly.

"Today. That is, if I can find a stone that suits you and one that I can afford."

Shaking her head, she cradled his face with her hands. "Mason, I don't care if it's a tiny chip of a diamond or a plastic ring out of a toy machine. As long as it means that you love me. And as for my family, I'm sure my siblings will be very happy for me. As for my parents, they're in no position to give me advice about marriage."

His expression turning sober, he threaded his fingers through her long hair. "Sophie, the other day—when I said all those awful things about you being a Fortune—I was wrong. And I'm sorry. I said them out of frustration."

"It doesn't matter now, honey. Really, it doesn't."

"Yes, Sophie, it does matter. I want you to know that I do understand that being a Fortune can't be easy for you. In fact, I can see how hard it is for you to deal with your father's infidelity and illegitimate children."

"I feel like I've gone through an earthquake and I'm still searching for solid ground," Sophie admitted. "But in a way it's helped me see exactly what's most important in life. Wealth, social position, gossip and reputations, none of that means anything compared to having someone to love and share your life with. That's all I want for us, Mason."

She glanced away from him and let out a rueful sigh and Mason quickly touched a hand to her cheek.

"You're not still worried, are you? About us?"

Smiling wanly, she turned her gaze back to his. "No. But now that we're so happy and I feel so blessed, I'm beginning to see how wrong I've been about Chloe Elliott. She was at the Fortune dinner party the other night and I'm ashamed to admit I said some very nasty things to her. I was so outraged to see her there acting like family. But now—well, I've come to realize she can't help the circumstances of her birth any more than I can. I'm going to do my best to make amends with her as soon as I can."

He patted her cheek. "That's my sweet Sophie. The one I love."

A while later, after they'd eaten a quick breakfast of toast and jam, Mason headed to the shower, but Sophie wasn't in a hurry to leave the little breakfast table. Instead, she picked up her cell phone and scrolled through her contact list until she reached the name Ariana Lamonte.

The woman answered on the third ring and as Sophie responded, she turned her gaze toward the bright morning sunlight streaming through the kitchen window. Today was a new beginning to the rest of her life, she thought. From now on things could only get better.

"Ariana, this is Sophie Fortune Robinson. I hope I'm not calling too early."

"Not in the least," Ariana replied. "I'm already at my desk. Is there something I can do for you?"

Sophie took a deep breath. "As a matter of fact, there is. I'm ready to help you find out my mother's real story."

"I'm so pleased you've decided to go after the truth, Sophie. So when will you be free to meet?"

A few minutes later, Sophie had scheduled a meeting with Ariana and ended the phone call just as she felt Mason's hands settle gently on her shoulders.

Already dressed in black slacks and a pale blue dress shirt with a tie tossed around his neck, he'd clearly overheard the end of her conversation with Ariana and couldn't keep the concern from his voice. "What if you find something unpleasant about your mom? Will you be able to handle more bad news about your family?"

Their gazes met and the love she saw in his brown eyes filled her with courage and strength. "As long as you love me, Mason, I can face anything."

Bending his head, he kissed her thoroughly, then whispered against her lips, "And I'm going to love you for a long, long time. Like forever. So hurry and get ready. We have some engagement ring shopping to do."

"I'll be ready in a flash," she promised.

Ready to start their new life together.

* * * * *

*Look for the next installment of the new
Mills & Boon Cherish continuity*

THE FORTUNES OF TEXAS:
THE SECRET FORTUNES

*Young widow Chloe Elliott falls for an ex-soldier-
turned-ranch-hand with PTSD—but will her discovery
that she's linked to the famous Fortune family destroy
their chance for a future together?*

*Don't miss
FORTUNE'S SECOND-CHANCE COWBOY
by*
USA TODAY *bestselling author Marie Ferrarella*

*On sale March 2017, wherever Mills & Boon
books and ebooks are sold.*

MILLS & BOON®

Cherish™

EXPERIENCE THE ULTIMATE RUSH OF FALLING IN LOVE

A sneak peek at next month's titles...

In stores from 9th February 2017:

- **Proposal for the Wedding Planner** – Sophie Pembroke *and* **Fortune's Second-Chance Cowboy** – Marie Ferrarella
- **Return of Her Italian Duke** – Rebecca Winters *and* **The Marine Makes His Match** – Victoria Pade

In stores from 23rd February 2017:

- **The Millionaire's Royal Rescue** – Jennifer Faye *and* **Just a Little Bit Married** – Teresa Southwick
- **A Bride for the Brooding Boss** – Bella Bucannon *and* **Kiss Me, Sheriff!** – Wendy Warren

---

Just can't wait?
Buy our books online before they hit the shops!
www.millsandboon.co.uk

Also available as eBooks.

MILLS & BOON®

EXCLUSIVE EXTRACT

Pastry chef Gemma Rizzo never expected
to see Vincenzo Gagliardi again. And now
he's not just the duke who left her
broken-hearted… he's her boss!

Read on for a sneak preview of
RETURN OF HER ITALIAN DUKE

Since he'd returned to Italy, thoughts of Gemma had
come back full force. At times he'd been so preoccupied,
the guys were probably ready to give up on him. To
think that after all this time and searching for her, she
was right here. Bracing himself, he took the few steps
necessary to reach Takis's office.

With the door ajar he could see a polished-looking
woman in a blue-and-white suit with dark honey-blond
hair falling to her shoulders. She stood near the desk
with her head bowed, so he couldn't yet see her profile.

Vincenzo swallowed hard to realize Gemma was no
longer the teenager with short hair he used to spot when
she came bounding up the stone steps of the *castello*
from school wearing her uniform. She'd grown into a
curvaceous woman.

"Gemma." He said her name, but it came out gravelly.

A sharp intake of breath reverberated in the office.
She wheeled around. Those unforgettable brilliant green
eyes with the darker green rims fastened on him. A

stillness seemed to surround her. She grabbed hold of the desk.

"Vincenzo—I—I think I must be hallucinating."

"I'm in the same condition." His gaze fell on the lips he'd kissed that unforgettable night. Their shape hadn't changed, nor the lovely mold of her facial features.

She appeared to have trouble catching her breath. "What's going on? I don't understand."

"Please sit down and I'll tell you."

He could see she was trembling. When she didn't do his bidding, he said, "I have a better idea. Let's go for a ride in my car. It's parked out front. We'll drive to the lake at the back of the estate, where no one will bother us. Maybe by the time we reach it, your shock will have worn off enough to talk to me."

Hectic color spilled into her cheeks. "Surely you're joking. After ten years of silence, you suddenly show up here this morning, honestly thinking I would go anywhere with you?"

Don't miss
RETURN OF HER ITALIAN DUKE
by Rebecca Winters

Available March 2017
www.millsandboon.co.uk

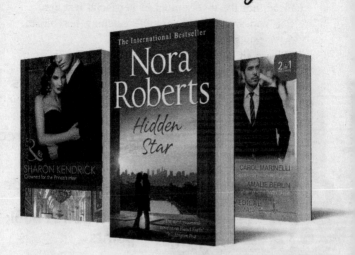

Join Britain's BIGGEST Romance Book Club

50% OFF your first parcel

- **EXCLUSIVE offers** every month
- **FREE delivery direct** to your door
- **NEVER MISS a title**
- **EARN Bonus Book points**

Call Customer Services
0844 844 1358*

or visit
millsandboon.co.uk/subscription

* This call will cost you 7 pence per minute plus your phone company's price per minute access charge.

BKCB3